Unbridled

Unbridled

MARK DANIEL

Ticknor & Fields

New York • 1990

First American Edition 1990

Copyright © 1989 by Mark Daniel

ALL RIGHTS RESERVED

For information about permission to reproduce selections
from this book, write to Permissions, Ticknor & Fields,
215 Park Avenue South, New York, New York 10003.

Library of Congress Cataloging-in-Publication Data
Daniel, Mark.
Unbridled / by Mark Daniel. – 1st American ed.
p.   cm.
ISBN 0-89919-922-4
I. Title.
PR6054.A469U5   1990   89-20210
823'.914 – dc20.   CIP

Printed in the United States of America

D 10 9 8 7 6 5 4 3 2 1

This book was previously published in the United Kingdom
by Barrie & Jenkins Ltd., with the title *Under Orders*.
Lines from "My Funny Valentine" by Lorenz Hart and
Richard Rodgers © 1954 Chappell & Co. All Rights Reserved.
Used By Permission.

For
Nick Robinson
who unwittingly got this on me,
and
Toby Eady
who fostered the brute.

ACKNOWLEDGMENTS

My thanks to Peter, Mac and Charlie Nelson for all their help, to Bobby Beasley for many a long night of wittering, and to Chris Dawes for the gift of his stunning photographs; to Victoria Legge for a dirty story, to my father for correcting errors, to Joanna Sarstedt for a deal of hard work, to my wife Ann for sacrificing her drawing-room, and to Gerard Noel for being a loyal and indulgent foul-weather friend.

Open the gates of the city and you must lock up your homes and your hearts. So saith Bob.

We keep the gates closed now, even if we cannot exactly keep them locked. We do not invite visitors, but neither do we throw them out on the rare occasions when they invite themselves.

I have to venture out sometimes too. I have to go to market to buy and sell stock. I even have to keep in touch with a few breeders and dealers if I am to sell my young 'chasers. As for Bob, he gets sudden urges to head down to Sean's Bar some nights. He needs laughter and approbation. I am not much of an audience for him.

The cast list of our lives is scarcely glamorous. It comprises my brother Bob, me, nineteen Hereford-Friesian cross cattle and a dear, bent old mare named Kiloran Bay who won six of the eleven races in which I rode her. She is in foal to High Rise. This will be her fifth foal. The last one, a hermaphrodite, was spontaneously aborted. There was no holiday last year.

I also have her three-year-old son who will be sold at Fairyhouse later this year and two other potential 'chasers which stay with me to be reared and schooled before going into training.

Margaret, a plump blonde from the village, helps with the cows. Bob is responsible for the upkeep of the house. You will not, in consequence, find it featured in *House and Garden*. The little lean-to sunporch is filled with newspapers and shrivelled brown paper, pot-plants, headcollars, skullcaps and dirty boots.

In on the right, the dark sitting-room is filled with coal bags and more newspapers. The furniture is scuffed and scored, the covers threadbare. A few silver challenge plates and china trophies remain on my desk and on the Wellington. An oil painting of me on Ice Nine hangs above the sideboard. The cigarette boxes, ashtrays, bronzes and Waterford glass have all gone. I sold some to buy stock or feed. Bob sold some without asking me.

Aside from these few relics, all that remains of the old days are the photographs. Photographs of me jumping, falling, being led in on winners and presented with trophies; photographs of Coco Collins, Fred Winter, Jack Clayton, Bobby Beasley, Stan Mellor;

photographs of Conor, of Joanna, of Claire.

When they were colouring in the Emerald Isle, they forgot this bit. We are a couple of miles north of Kilkenny. The grass is grey and crisscrossed with black herringbones by my ancient tractor's tyres. The bulging walls of the house are grey. The one street village just half a mile away is charcoal, black and, just for a little variety, dried blood red. On a grey day you feel as though you are swimming underwater.

Sometimes Bob sorts himself out and has a blitz. He hoovers, piles up the newspapers, polishes the furniture and makes a decent meal. He always hated mess. Then he sits nervously twining his long fingers until I walk in and express appreciation of his efforts.

'Dunno what you're talking about,' he jumps up and paces back and forth, flapping away my words. 'My part of the bargain, isn't it? My part of the deal. Do I go round saying, "This looks great," when you've mucked out a loose-box or something?'

We get by. That's all. We stay alive. And there's always the thought that Kiloran Bay might throw a champion before she's done. Nowadays, I need no more than that dream.

Just occasionally, however, something happens to remind me that once there was another life, that once things other than milk quotas and mastitis mattered to me. The ghosts step out of the shadows to question, to accuse.

Jimmy Knight conjured them yesterday.

It was somewhere round two o'clock. The rain was falling so hard on the tack-room roof that I did not even hear the car arrive. I was stuffing the last of the haynets when suddenly the draught lifted my hair and a high-pitched, husky voice said, 'Good to see you hard at work, mate.'

I jumped. When I spun around, alarm must have been clearly visible in my expression, for Jimmy Knight chuckled with satisfaction. He stood in a consciously masculine pose, legs set wide, hips thrust forward. He wore sparkling jodhpur boots, spotless jeans and a yellow blouson which made helicopter noises in the breeze.

Jimmy Knight has a thick neck, a square face and very short, silky hair, the colour of mushroom soup. I do not like him and he knows it. He does not care.

He is a very successful, very stylish, very hard, very crooked jockey. He rides with a single-mindedness often flattered as 'will to win' or even 'professionalism'. He is ruthless with horses and with other riders, impervious to the hopes and dreams of owners. If there is money to be made by winning a race, he will stop at nothing to

10

win it. If there is money to be made by losing it, he will lose it and to hell with his connections. I raced against him many times in the last two or three years of my racing career. He made me feel old.

I mustered a smile from somewhere. 'Jimmy!' I held out a hand. 'What are you doing in these parts, for the Lord's sake?'

'Come over for a weekend with my lady friend,' he shrugged. 'Out there in the motor waiting. Come over on the Rosslare ferry, thought, "who can I knock up and do for a drink on my way?" You know? Then I remembered you was out in these parts. Thought I'd look you up, catch up on the news.'

'You should have called,' I said. I think I made it sound like, 'If I'd known you were coming, I'd have baked a cake'. I meant, 'You should have called'.

'Nah,' he grinned, ' 's all right. Spur of the moment, you know. Got a bottle in the car, if you're short. Thought we could have a jar.'

'Yeah, well, I'm rushed off my feet,' I said mildly, 'but hold on a minute or two, I'll just hang this up and I'll be with you.'

My teeth were gritted as I turned back to the haynet.

'Where there's muck, there's brass, eh, mate?' Jimmy twanged. 'You must be bleedin' loaded.'

'Would that I were.' I picked up the full net and turned sideways to pass through the door without touching him. I squelched back to the furthest loose-box in the corner of the yard, pulled open the bottom door and pushed Kelly gently back. 'Hello, boy,' I murmured. He scratched his forehead on my arm and damn near knocked me over.

I have invested a lot in Kelly. It might just prove to have been worth it. He is a good-looking colt with plenty of bone on him, a nice head and a lot of scope. If the wind is favourable, he should fetch a fair price.

'Who's this nag, then?' The lights came on. That was a pain. That one light, so carelessly switched on by Jimmy, started up the generator four hours early.

'He's called Riptide,' I answered briskly, though in fact he had no name registered. 'Deep Run, Kiloran Bay.'

'Still got old Kill-or-Cure, have you?' He ran his hand absently down Kelly's legs. A horseman's reflex, that's all. 'Thought she'd've been Whiskas years ago.'

'She's seventeen,' I sighed.

'Is she now? Well, well. Now, for Christ's sake, Georgie, can we go inside out of this lot and have a drink?'

'Not inside,' I said quickly. 'Let's go down the village. I need some lunch. Won't have time to cook anything. Sorry, Jimmy, but

I've only got time for a quick scoopeen, then I must be back for the cows and ... you know.'

'What's the matter, Georgie?' he taunted, playing playful, 'afraid that I'll report back to the lads that you're sharing your bunk with a pig or something? My girl's been looking forward to seeing where the great jockey lives.'

'Yeah, well, too bad.' I switched off the light and shouldered past him. ''Nother time maybe.'

I bolted the door and scurried across the yard. The gun-metal blue BMW on the drive looked as though it were auditioning for an advert. For a split second, a crab clutched at my Adam's apple as I saw the long, straight dark hair of the girl in the passenger seat, then she turned to face us. She waggled her fingers at us and mimed shivering.

'OK, Jimmy,' I called above the wind, 'no room for me in that glass slipper! You go on ahead. Can't miss it. Sean's, it's called, bar and funeral parlour! I'll follow on in the van.'

'Right, mate, see you there!'

I retreated to the porch. The BMW jerked across the pitted drive. The girl in the passenger seat waved over her shoulder. The car bounced onto the road, cleared its throat, and roared.

I walked wearily into the sunporch and threw my sodden Barbour onto a Lloyd Loom chair then pushed open the sitting-room door and peered in. 'Bob?'

The curtains were drawn. Almost the only light came from the television which flickered in the corner. The commentator droned, 'He's aiming to put a lot of side on this if he's to land up on or close to the baulk cushion ...' Snooker balls clicked and burbled. I stumbled over a pile of magazines then bumped into the end of the sofa and hushed myself.

Bob lay curled on the sofa. A felt-tip pen hung from between the fingers of his dangling hand. He had rolled over onto an open loose-leaf folder. Three or four leaves lay scattered on the carpet. I picked them up. There was writing on the sheet beneath the television. I read it in the smoky flush of light:

> You,
> You matter to me,
> Though you darn near drive me wild the way
> You chatter to me
> As a lentil to a vegan
> As a statue to a pagan
> As a Thatcher to a Reagan,

You matter to me . . .

It's part of an old song which, in fact, he wrote for my daughter Joanna – eight, nine years ago. It's not significant that Bob was re-writing this particular ditty. He borrows a lot from himself these days, as though to rewrite the words is to retrieve the youth in which they were conceived, the genius which conceived them. Rifling through the snapshots for a holiday.

I listened for a moment to his deep, steady breathing, then reached down to the foot of the sofa for the rug. I spread it over him. For a moment I placed the palm of my hand on his forehead. 'See you, Bob,' I said softly, 'back soon.'

'And here he is!' Jimmy Knight swung round, extended his arm and shouted like a club MC, 'Ex-champion jock Georgie Blane! Georgie, this is Daphne. Daphne, Georgie, one of the boldest that ever sat a slippery saddle, eh, Georgie?'

'Hi.' I shook Daphne's hand.

She simpered and leaned back against Jimmy. In clinging dark blue jersey, she was dressed neither for the weather nor for Sean's. 'Hi,' she squeaked like a water-pump, 'Jimmy's told me so much about you. I used to watch you when I was at school.'

'Sean,' I turned to the big grizzled man behind the bar, 'have you met Jimmy Knight?'

'I have not, Georgie, but I thought as the face was familiar. You're on my Schweppes calendar over there as I recall.'

'And this is Daphne.'

'Daphne.'

'So, what'll it be?'

'No, no, Georgie,' Jimmy slapped my offer down, 'no. I'm paying round here. Still in work. Looks as if you should be hanging on to every penny you can get. Mine's a Guinness, please, Sean. Daphne, gin for you? Gin and tonic, please, mate, and Georgie?'

'Tomato juice, please.'

'Tomato juice?' Jimmy yelped. He staggered back in mock amaze-ment, 'Ah, come on, Georgie. I'm not buying that muck. Have a real drink.'

'Just tomato juice, please.'

'Look, mate, I know you're retired and all that, but surely that doesn't mean you've retired from ordinary manhood too. Let me

13

get you a man's drink. I mean, this is your old friend and comrade Jimmy here! I can't buy bleeding tomato juice!'

'Fine. I'll buy it myself, Jimmy,' I said wearily. He knew damned well that I was off the sauce and he knew the reasons why, but he had to play the game. It made him feel like a big man. I'd been through all this so many times before, and with bigger and better men than Jimmy Knight. Myself, for one.

Sean winked at me as he handed me the drink. 'Have it on me, Georgie.'

'Right, now,' I straightened with a smile, 'so what's the news?'

'Nothing much,' Jimmy shrugged, "cept what you read in the 'papers. I s'pose you can still get your hands on a racing page?'

'Sometimes. See you're doing all right.'

'Yeah. Well. Never enough, is it? Your mate Oliver Parker got done on some tax rap. Hear about that? Got off, though.'

'Pity. No friend of mine.'

'Oh, no? This guy, Daphne,' he spoke conspiratorially through his teeth. 'This guy had some faintly iffy dealings once upon a time with a certain Mr Parker. You remember Parker, don't you?'

She frowned. 'No.'

'Yes you do! Met him at Chepstow. Tall, creepy guy. Face all twisted up. Mumbles.'

'No.'

'You must do.'

'No, Jimmy.'

Jimmy rolled his eyes heavenward and sighed. 'I don't know,' he said, 'I really don't. Oh, yeah, and your old mate Polly Waller. You know she hopped the perch, don't you?'

'Yeah. I flew over for the memorial service.'

'Georgie had this thing going with a filthy rich old bird, big owner, may've heard of her. Leedy Wollah, no less.'

"Sright,' I nodded. 'She was good to me.'

'Ooh, I'll bet,' Daphne laughed and wriggled.

'And what about you, Georgie?' Jimmy swaggered. 'Shit-shovelling showing a profit, is it?'

'Keeping me alive, thanks, Jimmy. And safe. It's a good life. I've had my fill of chasing my own tail.'

'And a lot of other tails, from all I've heard.'

'Yeah, that too. Sean, have you got anything left in the way of lunch for us? Sandwich, something? Shergarburger, sausage ...?'

It went on for an hour.

14

I do not know why Jimmy Knight so urgently needed to prove himself a better man than I. He, after all, was still doing the job that I yearned to do. He was still in the money. Perhaps it was because I have a place in the history books while he feared – probably justifiably – that he never would. Perhaps his Daphne was more exacting than she seemed and he had to impress her. Perhaps too the sight of me struggling for a living acted on him like a *memento mori*. One day soon he too would be a weren't-you-the-man, with other concerns on waking than the next race and the next, and the next ...

His aggression grew with each drink and each equable answer that I gave. At the risk of sounding complacent, your man was proving just why he would never be my match as a rider. He was all explosive energy. I have learned to wait and to waste no effort. I just smiled and ate my dry chicken sandwiches and prayed that he would remember an urgent appointment. In Sweden.

'Of course, in Georgie's day, when I first started, things were different,' he was saying, 'I mean, there was less dough in the game for starters. Whole thing was a lot more amateur. Good fun, but. I mean, look at the speed records. Being broken every day, right?'

I rose to that one. 'I saw a creature called Arkle,' I reminded him, 'I rode against Harlequin.'

'There you go!' he chortled. 'You guys. Always harking back. I'll probably be the same when I hang up my boots, God save us. No age in history can ever be as good as your own. Fact is, the *general* standard – I'm not talking about your odd freaks now – the general standard is infinitely higher. Lot tougher staying at the top these days, you must admit that, Georgie.'

'Yeah. Probably right, Jimmy,' I stood and frowned at my watch. 'Still, I've been hanging about too long. My old dears'll be pining for me. Better be going. Give my regards to the weighing-room, will you, Jimmy?'

'Er, Georgie ...' Sean's soft voice behind me.

I turned, questioning. Sean raised his eyebrows as though he wore bifocals. He nodded towards the door. Even as I understood, the latch clicked upward and Bob walked in.

He swung round the door and into a conveniently placed chair in one smooth movement. His hair flopped over his face and touched his lips, which twitched downward in a shy little smile. He frowned and his head rotated slowly as though he were watching the flight of a dying bluebottle. I walked quickly over to him. 'Hi, Bob,' I said, 'I was just on my way.'

15

'Right,' he nodded. 'I'll come with you. Just wanted to get a bottle for 'sevening.'

'Sure. I'll do that. Sean, got a bottle of whiskey?'

'Sure, Georgie. Won't be a minute.'

'Who's your friend, Georgie?' Jimmy's voice came from so close behind me that I felt the warm puffs of his breath on the back of my neck.

'Oh, Jimmy. Yup. This is my brother Bobby.'

'Oh, right, right! I remember. Singer or something, aren't you? I remember. Jimmy Knight.' He held out his hand.

Bob looked at it for a moment, very seriously, then reached up to take it. When he released it, his own hand fell back like that of a dead man. 'Should've told me,' he mumbled, then took a deep breath. Suddenly he sat up straight and spoke clearly. He smiled broadly. 'You should have told me you had friends here, G. Jimmy Knight. Sure, I remember you. You used to ride that ratty little chestnut thing – what was it called? I kept backing the sod and Georgie kept beating you into second. Oh, shit, forget my own name next ...'

'No Secret,' I supplied quickly.

'That's the one. That's the one. No Secret. Remember it. No ... Ratty little beast. Chestnut.'

'Jesus Christ,' Jimmy Knight sighed.

'Right,' I took the bottle from Sean with a nod of thanks. 'Come on, Bob. Let's be on our way.'

He pulled himself up on the back of the chair. It did not work first time, but he made it at the second attempt and stood rocking and studying his feet.

'Well,' said Jimmy, barely attempting to conceal his delight, 'nice to see you're doing all right. I'll be passing by this way quite a bit. I'll drop in again.'

'Don't bother, Jimmy.' I opened the door and bustled Bobby through.

''S'no bother,' he was suddenly bullish. His hands swung loosely at his sides.

'Just don't bother,' I said grimly.

Red spots appeared in his cheeks. 'Well, bloody hell. Thanks a lot, Georgie, I mean, really, thanks a bleeding ton. Bit of charity. Think we'll drop in, give the old bastard a bit of a cheering up, and this is what we get for it, eh? Well, stuff you, Georgie Blane.' His words caught up with one another and rolled over me as I crossed the little car park and helped Bob into the passenger seat. 'How are the mighty fallen, eh, Georgie? How are the bleeding mighty fallen.

16

Cocky as all hell you used to be, and now look at you, both of you. Back in the bleeding bog where you belong, eh? Well, don't come looking for any charity from me, I can tell you, I'd ...'

I slammed the door and turned the ignition key as fast as I could. He was still talking as I turned onto the road and, trembling slightly, steered us homeward.

The bag had been opened and shaken.

The spirits were walking abroad.

Let me have a minute or two. Just a taste, first, of the glory glory days when I was immortal. Please, before the clouds draw in – it won't take long.

Oh, and oh, just look at me then. Crystal chandeliers coruscate – 'glitter' just will not do – coruscate above my head. The girl that I love sits at my side. People whom I have admired since childhood nod or wave to me as they stroll between the tables. Multi-millionaires stop to slap my shoulder and to say, 'Good luck, Georgie,' or, 'How's it going, Georgie?'

It's going great thanks. I'm twenty-two and hopeful and well pleased with myself. And mildly terrified.

We're in Liverpool's Adelphi Hotel on the eve of the Grand National, so all of us are mildly terrified or, at the least, apprehensive. Even those of us who aren't drinking spend a lot of time in the loo.

The trainers have worked towards this day. The owners have invested dreams and shekels. And we, the jockeys, know that tomorrow we must ride four and a half muddy miles and jump thirty of the world's biggest, most dangerous obstacles.

Or, still worse, less.

The waiters, of course, could not care less about the race. They are interested only in mushrooms. They concentrate very hard on the form and the texture of mushrooms. And *petits pois* of course, and watercress. Horses and the gossip of horsemen are downright tawdry by comparison.

They linger at our table only because our vegetables are particularly interesting. Why, they haven't the faintest clue who we are. So that tall, thin man with white hair and bright blue eyes is called Captain Collins, is he? And he's a distinguished trainer of racehorses? There's a thing. One would have taken him for a gentleman. And the elderly lady with the bubbly ash-blonde hair and the flashing fingers owns a runner in the Grand National? Well, and I never did. And the other chap, the one with the bull chest and the dark hair? Georgie Blane, the jockey? What is this hotel coming to?

With much bowing, they at last move off. Louella Heaton-Gordon bubbles like boiling custard. 'Honest, I'd no more than set my foot on the foyer carpet – literally! I'd not so much as seen my room when he comes sidling up to me like he was selling mucky postcards or something. You know? "Psst. Mrs Heaton-Gordon. A word in your ear." – that sort of thing . . .'

Mrs Heaton-Gordon is the jubilant widow of a Manchester businessman. He died all of a sudden, leaving her a solid, well-invested fortune and two bad racehorses. She discovered sex and champagne, packed the two nags off to the knackers and reinvested her funds in Nassau casinos and twenty-two horses, almost all of them good.

Secret State, whom I'm to ride tomorrow, is one of the best. He has only one problem. He likes to lie down on the job.

'. . . "thirty thousand," he said. I mean, thirty thousand for Secret State! Well, I mean, love, we paid eighteen for him, didn't we, Coco, and that was two years ago.' She stabs her tournedos and licks her thick red lips as the rosy blood runs. 'Thirty grand! I ask you. I'd've spat if my mouth hadn't dried.'

'Yes,' Coco Collins smiles. 'Yes, he's worth more than that. And if,' he sips champagne with dry lips, 'if he gets round tomorrow, win or lose, he'll be worth a great deal more. He'll have learned the most valuable lesson in his life. It's gonna be a bumpy ride, Georgie.'

'Mmm,' I nod. 'Sure. But I'll tell you this. If we do get round, we'll be there or thereabouts. It's just that big "if".'

Coco leans back.

It's a funny thing. I must have eaten a hundred meals with the man, and he is renowned for his love of good food, yet I can never remember him in the act of eating. He always seems to be leaning back and savouring his wine or exhaling Sullivan and Powell Turkish cigarette smoke through his nostrils while those bright, amused blue eyes scan the room. His hair is like lychee flesh in the flush of light from the chandeliers. His long face is deeply lined and deeply tanned.

I won the Cheltenham Gold Cup for him last month, and now he has offered me a retainer for next season. For a newly arrived tenderfoot kid to turn down a Collins retainer would be to make the funniest new Irish joke for years.

'What I still don't understand,' Mrs Heaton-Gordon whines, 'is why you insist on going for the National, seeing as he's a sloppy jumper.' She leans forward. She folds fat fingers like a child psychologist.

She knows the answer of course. Coco must have explained it to her ten times, but she needs reassurance. I could do with a bit of reassurance too, but she is the paymistress. 'The thing is, you see,' I butt in, 'these here are the biggest fences in the world. He can jump them all right, but he's always been an idle old bugger. So he looks at these great big fences and he says, "Blimey O'Reilly, this is serious!" and he starts to pay a bit of attention. Maybe he hits one or two of them. As long as he stands up, he'll treat the rest with due circumspection, because Aintree fences are built thick and solid. They hit you hard and they hurt.'

'He's right, Louella,' Coco twangs. 'That's why so many horses fall at the first. It's a piddling little fence, but I've come a cropper there; so has Georgie. First because there's a high-speed cavalry charge up to it, and second because the fence is unexpectedly solid compared with anything else they've ever encountered.'

'I'm still afraid, Coco,' she nods to the waiter as he removes her plate, 'so many horses get injured or killed ...'

'So do jockeys, Louella, and no more here than elsewhere.' Coco waves away the remains of his steak. 'But that's the nature of the game, isn't it? We're looking for excellence here. Not just speed, but intelligence, guts, stamina and sheer streetwise racing ability which, even with human athletes, is not the same thing as speed. Imagine if we made the National safer, hmm? We'd always be dissatisfied, always wondering whether this horse really was the best, whether perhaps we might achieve something more. We just have to have this ultimate test. It's like God. Didn't exist, have to invent it. We have the comparatives, so the superlative must exist. You know?'

'But what if poor Sammy ...?' She shakes her head as though to dislodge the thought. 'Sammy' is the animal's stable name.

'Don't worry.' Coco places long brown fingers over her thick white ones, 'Most horses love to jump the National course. Look at the loose horses. If Georgie dismounts tomorrow, I guarantee that Sammy will keep on running and jumping. He loves to compete.'

'But Becher's; those horrible drops.'

'Drops on the landing-side are a help,' I tell her. It is only half-true. It certainly isn't true of vertiginous drops like that at Becher's, but I am growing impatient with her harping on about things which I am trying hard to forget. 'They give your lad a chance to straighten his legs before he lands. And listen, Mrs Heaton-Gordon. If Sammy breaks his neck tomorrow, he'll do it painlessly, doing the thing he loves best. If he gets round, he'll have become one of the best 'chasers in the world.'

'Right,' Coco nods. 'The only person who might not come so well out of it is Georgie,' he smiles happily. 'Still, he's like the horse. He loves the game too.'

'Poppycock.' I turn my glass slowly between finger and thumb, examining the oily shadows on the tablecloth. 'I hate it, actually, but I couldn't stand to stop it and that's the sum of it. If Claire here said, "I won't marry you unless you hang up your boots," I'd have to say "Goodbye, doll." '

'And you don't mind, Claire, love?'

'Not as long as he falls on his head,' Claire's soft voice seems to come from another world. 'No, actually, I don't mind. I mean, he was a jockey before I met him, so that was part of him, part of the man I so idiotically said "yes" to.' She quickly lays a hand on mine, though whether in affection or to stop me twiddling the glass, I do not know.

'But you have to give up one day, Georgie,' Mrs Heaton-Gordon persists.

'Yeah, sure, and one day I have to die an' all. It's just that usually you get tired, so that when the right time comes you accept death gratefully. You're glad of the chance to sleep. It's stopping before I'm ready that would bug me.'

'Lunacy,' pronounces Louella Heaton-Gordon.

'Yeah, well, maybe. There are worse forms, eh, Cap'n Collins?'

'There are worse forms,' Coco nods. 'Oh, yes. And we do recover, Louella. Most of us, any road. God save those who never do.'

'Amen.' Claire's hand tightens over mine.

'Amen,' I echo absently, then think.

Things start to warm up. First someone with a startling gift for animal impressions instigates a panic-stricken search amongst the waiters with his high-pitched yapping and growling. Then a Northern trainer's wife gets the idea that the girl sitting opposite is making eyes at her husband, so she grabs this girl's left earring and pulls hard. There is a lot of shrieking at that, a lot of blood. It is all very exciting.

Then a journalist's secretary called Shelagh, a fair little floozie if ever I knew one, decides to prove that she is one of the lads. By revealing her evidently female body. She is down to the knickers and bra stage before she is restrained by a gabbling maitre d'. Now she sits in her crisp white underwear, sprawled like a grandee with her legs wide apart. Peonies bloom in her cheeks. Her eyes glitter with compulsive, angry sensuality. She raises her glass to her lips. Red wine trickles down her chin. She looks down, sees the spreading stains on her bra, the glistening flesh of her breasts, decides that she likes it and slowly pours the rest of the glass's contents down her cleavage.

The men about her do not notice. They drink and laugh and shout about horses.

In another corner, someone has started up a raucous rendition of *When Irish Eyes are Smiling*. From here on in, you can gauge that party's sobriety by the extent of republicanism manifest in their songs. *The Mountains of Mourne* is just a one bottle song: *The Wearing of the Green* represents a quart of John Powers' best; *My Old Fenian Gun* is at best drooled, at worst backed by contrapuntal vomiting in the bass line. Which may explain why we never won a war. We can't really get angry until we're too incapacitated to do anything about it. 'All their wars were merry, and all their songs were sad.' Hey ho.

Elsewhere, excited rumours spread. Black Mischief, last year's second and this year's top weight, has been sold during the course of the evening, it is said, to an American tobacco farmer named Mackendrick. Elena Graham, event-riding daughter of a Lambourn trainer, has been stroking the thighs of both Maurizio and Adele dei Francesci throughout dinner and has now staggered to bed with both of them. Corin Stanton (amateur rider, third class) is snorting coke with his chums in the loo. The world, in short, has changed not a jot. All is as it always was. A few people have come a little nearer to death. That is all.

The earlier burble of chat now nears the sea with its crashing waves and the occasional squawks of seabirds. Movement between the tables is general. A large dark woman with Polynesian looks lurches over to us and places her glittering gold shoes on the table before imperiously berating Coco. 'Y're meant to be my trainer ...' Various fresh-faced young bucks surround Claire and in adenoidal tones discuss what Gerard did at the Heythrop point to point, how Miranda was well mounted at Badminton and why Cynthia had to leave the von Hamburg-zu-Essen-und-Change-at-Frankfurts' ball.

I am faintly jealous, as ever, partly because I don't know these people and never will and partly, I suppose, because the young men, like Claire, are taller than I. If I didn't know that they regard me with some respect, if only because they are pleased to be acquainted with a jockey, and that I have four races to ride on the morrow, I might have got drunk.

Perhaps not. It isn't a problem just now.

Claire just nods and laughs and responds according to the ancient formulae for such things, but amidst these swirling red, purple and white faces, these rough or reedy voices, she seems clear and cool, light and still, like a single marble column amidst the debris caused by a bomb.

Claire, I should explain, is a mermaid. Her eyes are cool, her voice is warm. She has long dark hair which shifts like fine seaweed.

Her love mystifies me. Although I am privileged to receive it, I cannot understand it. I feel sometimes that she, or the gods, are somehow joking at my expense and I know, delightfully, that it cannot last. She will return one day, like the seal-woman of legend, to her own. I could never follow her to her world, though she could for a while live in mine.

Always, it seems, even when we make love, there is something of her that I cannot reach – something dignified, assured and mysterious. I think that perhaps that is why I shall always love her. I can have other women – not that I ever have, if truth be told – but I can never have Claire, never wholly hold her.

No. It's not just that which makes me think of her as a creature of the sea. It's something about her manner, her appearance.

I find it difficult to explain.

We are all pushed in, of course, at the beginning, and told to sink or swim. Some of us flounder and protest and struggle near the surface all our lives and take several others with us when at last we drown. Some – like me, I think – swim calmly and well enough for a while in this unfamiliar environment but must return frequently to the air above for deep draughts of pre-natal, post-mortem oblivion.

A few, a happy few, buoyed by faith in the author of it all, are blithe and serene. They know they belong. They are in control because they have yielded control. The vagaries of currents and tides don't worry them. They go with them and know that all is well. These are creatures of the water. You can see it somehow in their wide, scrutinising eyes, their loose-limbed nakedness even when they are clothed.

I met her during a race at Plumpton. We were both crouched over our mounts' necks in the back straight, a distance or more ahead of our rivals. The people standing on either side of the course heard the tattoo of the horses' hooves. We heard only the regular high-school backseat sound of the saddles, the Cheyne-Stokes inhalation and exhalation of each stride. She wore a fetching little

22

knitwear number of pale blue and yellow, a jaunty primrose silk cap and tight white breeches which cupped and hugged and stroked her every contour and made me want to start one length behind her and finish one length behind her. Fortunately, the pig that I was privileged to ride had other ideas. He jumped upsides.

'Hi,' I grunted.

Her head turned for a fraction of a second. I caught a glimpse of pale grey eyes behind mud-spattered goggles. Pale pink lips twitched into a half smile over bright teeth. 'Hi.'

Then we were on top of the next plain fence. We took it together. The birch crackled beneath us. Horses and humans puffed out air.

'He's going nice,' I shouted as we regained our steady gallop. 'Yours?'

'My mother's. You're Georgie Blane, aren't you?'

'I am. And you are Claire Sleaford. Nice to meet you.'

'Don't think we'd better shake hands,' she panted. 'The stewards might get ideas.'

'They might at that. Keep it till after the contest. Big bastard open ditch here, and we're going down steep. Ground's cut up on the rails side, so pull out now and sit square . . .' I broke off to make sure that my own horse had his approach right. One, two, three and 'Hup!' I yelled.

Again for a moment all that I could hear was the small arms fire of the birch-twigs and the groaning of saddles, the grunts as our horses landed side by side. Her chap pecked on landing, but she kept a good sedate middle seat and a nice long rein. I checked my horse so that she could catch up.

She wiped her eyes with her sleeve. 'You going to win, then?'

'Nah. You are, aren't you?'

'I've got a chance on form. Only problem's the jockey. Comes to a finish between us, I'm stuffed. I've seen you.'

'I've seen you too. You're OK.'

She flashed me a grateful big grin as we rounded the turn.

'Right,' I said, 'we've got to start looking keen and serious now. Meet me outside the weighing-room after the last?'

She said nothing. Just looked amused, sat down, clicked her tongue and urged her horse on. I set off in pursuit.

Maybe I was concentrating too hard on those breeches. Maybe I wanted to show off by putting in a huge, stylish jump. Maybe I was just thumb in bum, mind in neutral. It has been known. Not only did I not see the red light, I rode at it with all the verve and relish of Nolan at the Russian guns.

It's a cardinal rule, learned at mummy's knee. Never, but never must you be half a length behind another horse as it takes off. Horses are companionable that way. When one jumps, the others all think it would be fun too.

This time, it was she who called 'Hup!' Both horses heard her. Both horses jumped. Hers flew over; mine, a stride further off, rammed the fence amidships.

He ploughed through it all right, but our relationship had long since irretrievably broken down. I was projected forward, arse over tit. I had time to curse and to see the quick white glimmer of her teeth as she turned and gathered up the reins. Then the ground hit me and I damned near bit my tongue off.

'God, he looked funny,' Claire recalls happily. It's a story that both of us have told a hundred times. At first, each told it from his or her own point of view. Gradually it became an amalgam. Like a liturgy, it is the body of the tale, the very form of the words, which gives us pleasure and makes us feel close. 'There he sat, spitting out teeth and grass and shaking his head as all the others jumped by him, and he looked so daft and pathetic that I just had to pick him up from First Aid. He'd broken his collarbone again. And then I drove him home to Mummy and Daddy because they were just next door anyway and the next day was a Sunday, and he ate us out of house and home and just sort of stuck around.'

'So you literally fell for her, Georgie,' Mrs Heaton-Gordon meets her cue like a good 'un.

We laugh in the right place too.

Yes, it is different. It is always different. We all whistle and swear a lot, pretending that this is just another race. We don't fool anyone, least of all ourselves.

For starters, there are so many more of us than for normal races. Usually I know all the faces and half-naked bodies in the changing-room. We professionals who are lucky enough to ride regularly know every deep-drawn, wind-grazed line on our fellows' faces, every scar and physical idiosyncrasy on their bodies.

Then there are the less fortunate pros, on their way up or down or on an endless nightmare plateau, who get anything from five to ten rides a week. They too are familiar. The best of the amateurs also know the language, the rituals, the codes of the weighing-room.

These basically constitute the band of brothers. But on National day, although they are all here, there are many outsiders in amongst them – rich, nervous young men with thin, undamaged bodies and fair faces, American grandfathers with sagging tits who always wanted to do this and can't, just at the moment, remember why; the odd American pro too, and a couple of central European amateurs. The changing-room is no longer our own on National day.

And of course, our apprehensiveness puts Acapulco gold edges on our perceptions. It is not really fear of death or injury which causes our arses to twitch. I am in truth no more frightened of the Aintree fences than of any others. I like to jump big, well-made fences, and a fatal – or, still worse, debilitating – accident can as well occur at a piddling plain fence at Devon and Exeter as at Becher's or the Chair.

It's partly, I suppose, the awareness that we are more likely to fall here than in any other race, partly the knowledge that several millions of people will be watching us as we do so. Principally, however, I think that it is that every last one of us is in with a chance, however small, of attaining a victory which will for better or for worse transform his life. That is what makes the stomach contract like a giant mollusc gulping and turns the nipples to candy kisses.

I have ridden in just two Nationals to date. In the first, I was deposited at the first. My depositor was not out of the race. He went on, alone, to bring down the favourite at the Chair and to chip a couple of Jack Carlton's vertebrae. My second ride was better. I got round on a first-class, intelligent veteran called Flashpoint. He showed me the way and struggled in sixth.

And this time, for the first time, I am in with a squeak. Secret State might be a sloppy jumper, but he stays forever, has heart aplenty and has shown a good turn of foot over hurdles.

'Keep well behind us, would you, mate?' Robin Nuttall grins down at me where I sit on the bench. He wears nothing but thermal long-johns and a towel slung round his neck.

'Nah,' I tell him, 'I reckon as I'll show you a pretty pair of heels.'

'Don't bother, mate. We'll be getting the aerial view before Becher's. One sniff of an obstacle and that pig rolls over. I'd cut my losses and dismount at the first.'

'Yeah, well,' I shrug, 'we'll see. I reckon as we might just win this one.'

'You're joking!' he waffles through his green and gold sweater. His tousled head emerges. Not a pretty sight, but an amiable one. 'Hear that, lads? Supermick here reckons he's gonna take this.'

There's a chorus of good-natured jeers. Even the valets join in. From my left, however, comes a sound like burning pine-needles.

It's far from good-natured. 'Bog fuckin' bastard. Jumped-up little fucker, do you, just you wait.'

'Absolutely, Bernie. Quite so,' Robin Nuttall bows. 'Couldn't have put it better meself. You tell him. Quite right.'

Bernie Coates' scarred white body is slumped beside me in baggy Y-fronts. He scowls, which makes precious little difference to his face. Having demonstrated his habitual eloquence and goodwill to all men, it seems, he has nothing more to say.

Crooks are two a penny in flat-racing. Until the government shows some sense and abolishes bookmakers, there will always be too much money available for the venal rider who gets left at the start or comes too late. In 'chasing, however, where there is less cash involved and where most of the boys are farmers' sons and in it 'for the crack', race-fixing is much rarer. All right, so only a fool backs an odds-on favourite in a small novice hurdle, but, in general, jumping races are run straight.

Bernie Coates is the exception rather than the rule. Once, he was stable jockey to one of the best Middleham yards and won some good races. Now, it seems, he has decided that there are better ways of making money than by winning. It is he who approaches young jockeys with promises of backhanders and disciplines them if they refuse to comply.

Already he lives in his particular hell. His face is thin and deeply lined. His mouth opens at one side only to let clogged obscenities dribble down his chin. Bernie is commendably uncritical. He hates just about everybody except, perhaps, his wife and his daughter whom he keeps far from the evils of the racecourse. For all that once he had barged me all over the course at Sandown, snarling 'Fuckin' do gooder Irish bastard' and such, I could not bring myself to hate him back. He obviously once had dreams. He could not otherwise have extended his uncritical hatred so evidently to himself.

I even manage to wish him good luck as, ten minutes later, I hand my saddle to Captain Collins and Bernie takes my place on the Clerk's scales. Bernie mutters something inaudible which nonetheless pollutes the atmosphere like a quiet fart.

The earlier mizzle has passed by the time we troop back out onto the course. It's good weather for hard riding. The going is officially 'good to soft', which in Irish means 'perfect'. The sky is one large pigeon breast. The breeze is just cold enough to make people say 'brrr', but they make no steam as they do so. I stop occasionally to sign autographs on my way through the enormous crowd to the paddock.

Captain Collins, Mrs Heaton-Gordon and a tall sinister looking Maltese in a camelhair coat await me. The Maltese, Mrs Heaton-Gordon explains in her best bargain-basement Barbie doll manner, is a 'dear friend'.

The crowd all about us makes that very special sort of noise that is kept for big occasions, the high-pitched tense buzzing of a high voltage cable, at once noisy and somehow hushed.

We stand slightly uncomfortably, watching Secret State going round. He always was a good mover. He 'uses himself' as he walks, which means that his tail swings a lot. He looks very calm and very well. We don't talk much. There's not much to say. We agree that I will jump off near the centre of the track. I always do at Aintree. And that's that. No one has a strategy for the National. You get round if you can, worry about each fence as you come to it, win if you can.

Occasionally Mrs Heaton-Gordon says useful things like, 'Oh, God, I am nervous,' and the nails of her right hand scrabble slowly at the veins on the back of her left. Sometimes she looks around at her fellow-owners. 'Would you look at that 'at!' she reverts to broad Lancashire, or, 'Get me, eh? Standin' 'ere in the same boat as the Queen Mum. Isn't she wonderful?' She speaks too fast, trying to banish the silence which blows between us like a wind. We're all grateful when at last the order comes for jockeys to mount.

And as soon as I sit in the saddle, I know that I've got a fight on my hands.

He doesn't play up or anything. He just lets me know by a certain telepathy, a certain tell-tale muscular tension, that the excitement of the day has got to him and that he is going to beat every other animal in the race if it kills him. And that is exactly what I am worried about. If he goes at it like that, we'll be down at the first.

You've got to hunt the National. Eddy Harty told me that, and he was dead right. You can't race over these fences. You have to steady your mount and pretend to enjoy a good hunt, avoid trouble, enjoy the scenery. Secret State is in no mood to be steadied. I have a quarter of a mile before the first fence in which to sort him out.

So soon as the tapes go up, most of the lads will set off on the collar in order to get up front and clear of fallers and loose horses. A quarter of a mile is a hell of a long stretch in which to build up speed. Secret State is going to want to be up there with them. If I fight him too hard, he'll no longer have his mind on the job. If I give him his head, he'll hit that first fence at nigh on forty miles an hour and discover too late that these are not hurdles.

I soothe him a lot at the start. I tell him that he's a great lad and that there is nothing to worry about. I try to send telepathic pictures of the race as I see it. If he gets the message, he screws it up unread and throws it in the bin. He sees a much more attractive picture: Secret State at the head of the pack, Champion the Wonderhorse flying over the plains, pursued by awe-struck inferiors. He doesn't seem to care that I have no desire to fly. Anywhere, much.

The usual panic-stricken chorus of profanities and appeals to the starter begins. On an impulse, I lengthen the leathers by two holes. If we are going hunting, we'll ride hunting-style, and anyhow, I need every extra ounce of grip, every extra inch of communicative flesh in contact with his. I sit up very straight and cross the reins right beneath my groin. Very elegant, very nineteenth-century. Robin Nuttall rides up alongside me. 'Posing for a print, are we, Georgie?'

'Yeah.' I smile. 'The High-Mettled Racer Shortly Before its Demise.'

'If I didn't know better, I'd say you were windy.'

'You'd be dead right.'

'Don't blame you,' he laughs.

'You going in for the cavalry charge with the kids?'

'Nah. Thought I'd stay at the back and see who gets shot.'

'Me too,' I shudder. 'Mind if I stick to your tail for a while?'

'Sure. It'll be cold when you're gone.'

We move forward slowly, right in the centre of the track. Someone whose voice I vaguely recognise calls, 'No, sir, please, sir! Oh, hell, sir!' The tapes snap up. The distant crowd makes a noise like a scratchy old seventy-eight record. We're away.

It is like a dream, so total is my absorption from the off. I hear no sounds, see no crowds, no cameras. I concentrate to the exclusion of all else on keeping the rhythm right and on anticipating and avoiding all dangers.

The cinema convention of slow motion makes sense at such times. You have so much time in which to do what must be done. I do not know whether it is the commonplace consequence of large doses of adrenalin or whether it demands some peculiar innate quality. I know only that this trance of absolute concentration has visited me often on great occasions when I have needed it most. I have looked for it in vain. It comes when it chooses. Identity vanishes; memories, prejudices, associations, all go. Every part of me – conscious, unconscious, body, soul, call them what you will – is co-ordinated for the attainment of one end.

I live for that feeling.

Secret State, for one, can't resist it. He springs off like a kangaroo, but I draw him gently back, tuck him in behind the chestnut 'quarters of Robin's mount and bend his neck a bit, just to get him balanced and show him who's boss. The others thunder on ahead. I pay no attention. They can do what they will. Mine is a watching and waiting brief. This horse and I are going to get round. That is all that matters.

Perhaps I put a little extra pressure on the reins to collect him before the first. Perhaps he just happens to put himself absolutely right for it. In that state, you do not so much do things to others as work with them. Either way, he meets the fence and takes it perfectly. Beneath me three or four jockeys lie huddled, clutching their heads for fear of flashing, fatal hooves.

The next four fences are easy too. Now, Becher's.

The problem with Becher's is not so much the two and a half foot drop on the landing side as the brook itself. You take the fence too slowly or too steeply, you nose-dive into the brook or find yourself scrabbling impossibly for a foothold on its bank. You have to stand off, get a clear run and take it flat and fast. A racing-dive, not a swallow-dive.

Galloping up to Becher's, you can see only the kicking heels of the leaders then the bobbing caps of the survivors ahead. Two of the pairs of heels have no corresponding caps. That means fallers. I just have to pray that they've run on straight rather than crashing or veering to left or right beneath the fence.

I kick on.

Secret State's belly scrapes through the top of the fence with a noise like Velcro. The great drop looks deeper than I remember. It always does. Two horses and four jockeys lie sprawled on the turf. Just ahead of me and to my left, a grey gets his forefeet caught up and plunges straight down into the brook. There's a loud crunch and a grunt as the wind is punched from its already dead body. The jockey yelps. One second later, those stiff white legs will swing over and any horse still where we are will have his feet knocked out from under him, but we're back on *terra firma* and I'm breathlessly picking up the reins and urging on, on.

Secret State is shaken, but he's got the message. I detect a new bloody-mindedness in him.

At the next, a glimpse of tumbling green and gold and a cry tells me that Robin is down. At the Canal Turn, my horse jumps like an old Aintree hand and gains two lengths or more. At the Chair, a loose dun swerves right across our path and Secret State actually swings sideways in mid-air in order to avoid it with no more than a couple of centimetres to spare. Then, miraculously, we're hacking out into open country again.

The second circuit is safer than the first. The chaff – the bad jumpers, the windy riders – have gone. Now all that you have to battle with is the fences. And fatigue.

Seventeen, eighteen, nineteen, twenty, a bad peck at twenty-one, then Becher's again. We're eighth now, perhaps ten, eleven lengths behind the leader and still going sweet. Beside me, Bernie Coates is too preoccupied to notice, still less to abuse me. His sooty jaw juts forward and works as though he were chewing gum, though I know that he takes his teeth out before a race. His coch-y-bondu eyebrows mesh. His horse, a big, dark brown veteran which I have ridden twice, is going as well as mine. This is one race which even Bernie doesn't choose to lose. He clicks twice with his tongue. I let him go. He's a length and a half up on us as he takes off for the one after Becher's. That's half a length too much. He's too close.

His brave old horse somehow smashes through the top of the fence, dragging its legs and a lot of evergreen after it. Secret State stumbles slightly on landing. Bernie is just two feet away. His horse is almost stationary. Bernie clings onto its drooping neck for dear life, but he's toppling.

'Hey up!' I reach out and grab the waistband of his breeches. I heave. His emaciated frame rises easily. I leave him to recover his balance and set off again in pursuit of the leaders.

It is not, as the Sunday papers will claim, 'a gallant, old-fashioned act of sportsmanship', nor is it a Christian act of benevolence. Bernie's a jockey. That's all. I don't like him, but he's one of us.

Two tired horses come down at Valentine's, which just leaves Black Mischief and Tommy O'Brien, Trasimene and Lord Rupert Blackadder, Mountgrace and Ivor Jenkins and Dronero and Justin Greene ahead of us as we cross the Melling Road for the last time. We can take Dronero. Justin's already hard at work. Mountgrace too is no better than a plodder. The other two, however, though carrying bigger weights than Secret State, are strong, class horses. I beat Trasimene into a second place in the Cheltenham Gold Cup.

We pass Dronero at the second last where Secret State puts in a big one. We catch Mountgrace on the run-up to the last. We're just four lengths behind the two leaders as we take the final fence.

I don't know what happens now. I know that the yells of the crowd make the stands ring. I know that I'm trying to blink away mud and sweat and maybe tears. I can't spare a hand to wipe them away. Every aching muscle thrusts Secret State forward.

Rupert Blackadder roars, 'Come back, you bastard!' at my left shoulder. I ride through a blizzard of sensation. The crowd's cheers and jeers meld into a constant throbbing thunder.

I see Black Mischief somewhere in all this, and realise, in a moment of elation, that he is reeling and that Tommy is working flat out with stick and hands and heels. I'm not aware of passing them. I'm not even aware of passing the post. The video shows me crying and standing up and waving, so presumably I knew at the time that we had done it.

We've won the Grand National by half a length.

Rupert catches up with us as we slow to a hack canter. He slaps my shoulder and pants, 'Sod you, Blane! Can't you leave us any bloody thing to win?' Someone in the crowd calls raucously, 'Good on you, Georgie!' I pull Sammy up and hug his neck, just hiding for a moment from the colours and the noise in the darkness, the familiar smell of horse-sweat, the familiar rough touch of the mane. 'Thank you,' I whisper. 'Thank you, thank you, thank you ...'

An unfamiliar Liverpool voice throbs, 'Well done, kid.' I blink up at the round red face of a mounted policeman. He grasps my reins. 'Come on, Georgie.'

I sit up and wipe my eyes on my sleeve. Doris, the girl who does Sammy, is sobbing like a child. She kisses the horse's nose, then my knee. As we near the winner's enclosure, Captain Collins steps forward with a trace of a smile to pat Sammy's neck. 'Good work, Sammy,' he murmurs, then, over his shoulder, 'Well done, Georgie. How's it feel?'

I grin stupidly, sniff and say, 'Um.'

The cheer as we enter the Enclosure makes Sammy plant his forefeet and refuse to go on until I reassure him. Cameras purr and click. I dismount and unbuckle the girths with a shaking hand. Mrs Heaton-Gordon jumps up and down like a little girl. She squeezes my hand. 'I want you to have the stake money, Georgie,' she beams. 'Oh, thank you. Thank you, Coco. Thank you, you beautiful, wonderful, marvellous Sammy.'

I wish that Bob could have been here. I know that he is working in London, but nonetheless I look quickly around the crowd for that familiar lanky form. Claire leans on the rails. She blows me a kiss as I turn to walk back into the weighing-room.

Everybody loves me.

Everybody, that is, save Bernie Coates, who has limped in sixth. I shall not bother to repeat precisely what he calls me, but a genetic engineer would have been well pleased with himself had he created such a mongrel in embryo. He would have destroyed it at birth, however, on the grounds that it a) suffered from a large number of contagious diseases, b) was priapically and indiscriminately concupiscent and c) smelled filthy.

Bernie Coates hates everyone but I, it is clear, am now marked down for a specially intense distillation of his odium. You don't help people like Bernie and get away with it.

The video of my television interview five minutes later embarrasses me deeply. I shall close my eyes, take a deep breath and transcribe it verbatim. At least you cannot see me, with red spots on my forehead and abundant glossy hair hanging over my collar. My eyes are red with crying, my voice is very tremulous, very Irish.

INTERVIEWER: 'Well, Georgie, a magnificent victory. I imagine you're still pretty much out of breath after that amazing finish, hm?'

BASHFUL YOUNG JOCKEY: (Mumbles)

INTERVIEWER: 'I think we all are! That really must be one of the closest, one of the hardest fought National finishes in years. When did you first think you could win?'

BYJ: 'Well, um. I knew we were in with a chance if he jumped OK, you know? I mean, he hasn't always been the most reliable of jumpers, and ...' (large gulped breath). 'But he jumped beautiful today. Gave me a hell of a, a really good ride. Almost as if he'd been keeping it in reserve for today, you know?'

INTERVIEWER: 'Yes, ha ha, yes, absolutely. He hardly seemed to make a mistake. Well, many congratulations, and what a season it's been for you, Georgie; top of the championship table, the Gold Cup and now the National.'

BYJ: (Fetchingly) 'Yes. I've been very lucky.'

INTERVIEWER: 'And – what some of our viewers may not know, you're engaged to be married

	to another splendid jockey – not the sort of thing you can say to most people, eh?' (chuckles dementedly). 'No, but you're engaged to the lovely Claire Sleaford, of course.'
BYJ:	'Yes. Um, yes. I'd just like to say how grateful I am to everyone who's been so good to me since I came to England – Captain Collins and all the other riders, and Claire and … I mean, this is the greatest game in the world and I'm just incredibly lucky to be given the chance and …' (BYJ finds something sharp in his eye. His voice quavers.)
INTERVIEWER:	'Yes, well, I think we'd all agree with that. And what are the plans for Secret State now?'
BYJ:	(Catches sight of something in the middle distance. He blinks a lot, then smiles a broad, innocent smile.) 'I – I think you'd better ask Captain Collins about that, Julian. I don't know um.'
INTERVIEWER:	'Well, now, if you'd just talk us through it, Georgie, from the start …'
INTERVIEWER:	'… well, thank you very much and again many congratulations.'
BYJ:	'Mumble.'
INTERVIEWER:	'A happy man there. Winning Grand National jockey, Georgie Blane …'

Before he has said 'Blane', I've darted out of shot and am hugging the tall man with twinkling eyes and a big hooked nose who has strolled up through the surrounding crowd. My big little brother, Bobby Blane.

'Oh, Jaysus, man, but you're a wonder!' Bob's voice throbs like a pulse in my ear. He has not shaved. His cheek is as rough against mine as the Donegal tweed of his collar. He squeezes me until he squeaks. 'I just couldn't miss it. Couldn't sleep last night. Got up with the milklark and booked myself on a flight. I'd've killed you,

you hadn't won, 'cos it took my last penny. I just had to see it.'

'Oh, shit, but I'm glad you did.' I step back and look up at him. The passing well-wishers and the bustling, bovine crowds that watch us seem suddenly alien. To be alone with Bob would be like stripping off and taking a private hot bath after a day in the city, but I cannot lock these people out. They irritate me.

'I've got just ten minutes,' Bob announces, 'then I've got to get a taxi back to the airport.' He puts his arm around my shoulders and we wander back towards the weighing-room steps. 'Well, my old son, how's it feel to be on top of the world?'

'Mildly incredible.' I shake my head.

'Not to me. I always knew you'd do it one day. Had my doubts about that beast, though. Only put a hundred on.'

'Each way?'

'Yep.'

'Well, that's nigh on two grand. Not bad for an afternoon's work. They're giving me the stake money.'

'Christ, man, you're rolling in the stuff! You'll be getting sponsorship an' all; cars, things. And here, by the rood, is the betrothed of the National winning jockey! Greeting and hail to thee, Emer, daughter of Forgall Monach, wife of the best man in Erin. Erin's kings and princes contend for thee in jealous rivalry. As the sun surpasseth the stars of heaven, so far dost thou outshine the women of the whole world in form and shape and lineage, in youth and beauty and elegance, in good name and wisdom and address.'

'Hi, Bobby,' says Claire. She kisses me.

'Can you cope with these vertiginous heights?' Bob rattles on. 'The adulation, the hoards of filthy lucre, the covetous glances of all women?'

'I'll do my best,' she smiles faintly. She holds out her cheek for a kiss. 'I didn't know you'd be here, Bobby.'

'Sure and was my own flesh and blood to go to death or glory without me to cheer him on? I flew up. Arrived with minutes to spare. Don't think I'll need the 'plane for the return journey. I'll just click my ruby slippers, grab Toto and murmur, "Secret State". Isn't your man a marvel?'

'He'll do.' She casts me a quick, affectionate glance.

'So when shall I see you both?' Bob speaks very loudly, very fast. 'We must celebrate. I'll buy you dinner. No, you can buy me dinner. You're stinking now.'

'Let's try for Wednesday, Bob. I'm not racing Thursday. Tomorrow and Monday are going to be all bunting and photocalls. Wednesday all right for you, darling?'

'I'm not sure, Georgie,' she says coolly, 'I'll let you know.'

Bob glances at his watch. 'Well,' he slaps my upper arm, 'I've got to be going. Georgie, I'm so damned proud of you. Really. I'm going to be crowing all the way home. Let's meet at Jules' Bar, either way, Wednesday. At – what? Seven?'

'Seven's fine, Bob.' I take Claire's hand.

He looks rapidly from me to Claire and back again. 'Right. Great. That's fine. I'll see if Laura's free. And I'll hope to see you too, doll. Do your best, right? Oh, Jays, but that was worth it, G. Best day of my life. OK. I'm off. See you soon. Both of you.'

He turns and walks away. His head is held high. His hands in his trouser pockets make the skirt of his big tweed coat flare behind him. He knows no one in the crowd through which he walks, yet he turns and nods with a broad smile to someone on his right. No one turns towards him. I'm suddenly aware of his loneliness. I'd like to reach out, to call him back. But I would not know what to say, and Claire's hand holds mine tightly.

Bob waves once, without turning, and vanishes into the crowd.

I love that man.

'I love you,' I mouth to Claire.

She lies smiling happily on the plump pink pillows. Telegrams are piled high on the bedside table. Flowers line the walls, and already we've sent many more down to Clatterbridge hospital. Her left hand holds a glass of *rosé* Cristal. Her right, beneath the sheet, moves gently between her legs.

'I love you,' she gives a little low giggle. 'Come on. Put that cigarette out and come here.'

So I take one last drag, put the champagne bottle on the carpet and untie the belt of my dressing-gown.

And as I look down on her tea-coloured eyes flecked with conspiratorial lust, as I gaze up through the cascade of dark hair at her black eyes glinting wickedly in the rock-pool shadows, as she sweeps her nipples lightly over my stomach, my chest, my lips, never quite allowing me to close my lips about them, and then, as I close my eyes and surrender to the inexorable force of the tide, I marvel.

I've done nothing to deserve it, yet I have it all. I'm hopeful, but what the hell is there yet to hope for?

I sleep and wake, and it's fourteen years later. And I have my answer.

Sparrowfart. Someone kisses me. Someone strokes my flank. A soft voice with a little quaver in it says, 'Darling ...? Georgie ...?' Wet lips cover mine. Then a tongue flicks the corner of my mouth and leaves a snail's trail down my chin, my throat. The hand moves round, tickling, stroking, gently pulling. Crisp, hot hair rasps on my thigh. The tongue crackles.

They're using my temples, meanwhile, for muffled drums. A Formula One funeral with quarterhorse blackers. I feel, frankly, lousy, but it's time that I aroused myself, if that's the *mot juste*.

I still find it difficult to get up in the mornings, even after all these years, they'll quote me in tomorrow's Sunday Times Magazine feature, A Life in the Day. *Sometimes, when I'm schooling or racing up in Yorkshire or something, I just drag myself quietly out of bed and leave Claire* ('his wife of thirteen years, former debutante and jockette Claire Burton, daughter of Lord Sleaford') *asleep. Sometimes the kids* ('Joanna, thirteen, and Conor, eleven') *come bouncing in at six – usually on a day off when I'm planning on a lie-in. Beats the alarm clock any day. There's no getting back to sleep with them around ...*

I prise my eyes open and lick talcum dry lips. Her mouth is wide open in a sort of gleeful silent scream. She licks her lips too, squeaks and readjusts her body so she's lying on top of me, tit to tit. Golden hair and golden skin obscure my vision as she waffles at my collarbone. Her hand keeps working. Then I'm looking into wide grey eyes.

I can't remember her name – Sonia? Tania? Something like that. 'Come on, darling,' croaks a devil somewhere below her ribs, and then that Pentecostal tongue's at work again, lighting a flickering fuse over my throat, my chest. There's a quick cool draught as the sheet is flung back. Her nipples are hard and cold as press-studs. They tickle my thighs now. Her mouth opens with a noise like cellophane. I reach down, grab a thick handful of golden hair. Sonia/Tania says 'Mmmm'. And all I can think of to say is, 'Oh, damnation take it!'

I have to blink a bit, partly because the whole room seems to be filled with salt water. Cold lemon light full of bobbing dust sprays into the room past white, white blinds. There are two empty champagne bottles on the shiny white dressing-table top. The candlewick bedspread is white, the fox-fur over the chair back is white. They told me at school that white isn't a colour. For a nonentity, it's bloody offensive. Most nonentities are, come to think of it.

In the huge mirror above the dressing-table, I can see the crouching golden girl. It's a good sort of sight, and I watch in a nice, detached sort of way. I'm detached, but then I'm not in charge of my body. I've had time enough to learn that as I've lain on stretchers and hospital beds, commanding broken legs, arms, wrists and collarbones not to hurt. They pay little attention to me, whoever *I* may be as distinct from them. It's just the same with the male member. *I* feel like a salted slug. He's got *rigor mortis*.

It was ever thus. Take him to an orgy and he'll slouch all night in a corner. Smuggle him suitably dressed into a grandmother's tea party and all of a sudden he'll perk up and want to be let out to play. Cathedrals, too. Got a thing about cathedrals, he has. I've explored them all – Wells, Ely, Belfast, Durham, York Minster, Paddy's wigwam – the lot of them – crouched and short-stepping like Max Wall with the bends.

Hangovers are funny things too. I have them almost every day of the week, every week of the year, yet each seems somehow different and unfamiliar. Morning after morning, I clutch my head and moan and swear that I've got a terminal disease. Maybe I'm brighter than I know.

So, anyhow, this girl – I still can't remember her name – climbs up my body again and inhales with a hiss as she straddles me. A few minutes later, she's moaning like a grieving Arab and her hips are no longer moving just up and down but backwards and forwards like she's riding a hands and heels finish. Those lips slip in saliva all over my face and her breath tickles my tonsils. She sits up and her heavy golden breasts swing just inches from my nose. I get the idea at last. I grab them, growl and roll her over. The whole world rolls over with her. Then I'm driving into her, self-absorbed as much as she, trying to pummel away the insensitivity in my body.

She squeals and shudders and twice her whole body jackknifes around mine and she digs her nails into my shoulders, but it's only ten minutes later, when she's on her hands and knees and we're both slippery with sweat and she's panting and moaning and dribbling snot and I can see myself in the mirror slurping and slapping in and out of her – it's only then that body and soul – well, no: let's leave soul out of it, shall we? – body and brain, then. All right. Only then do squalid reality and ecstatically filthy fantasy coincide and I hit the jackpot. Lot of pumping, lot of grunting, lot of flashing lights. Tokens only, though. Nothing I can take away with me.

So we collapse like dolls in the ottoman and through damp and tangled hair she says, 'Jee*sus!*' which makes me feel a bit better,

37

'though I'm aware that it's the better part of a gallon of non-vintage Clicquot which turned me briefly into Superman and anyhow, she's not in bed with me because of my beautiful battered thirty-five-year-old body, still less because of my beautiful atrophied mind. She's here because she and her boss want information. They want winners. So, with a keen sense of irony, they pick on me.

Now hold hard. She's not a tart, this Sonia/Tania. Not strictly speaking. She enjoys this line of work. She likes the champagne and the furs and the famous people she gets to meet. She probably likes the sex too. Her boss is a very sharp small-time bookie and big-time gambler, name of Monty Alvin. Monty likes jockeys. He buys us lots of champagne, which he, like most racing people, refers to as 'wine'. He invites us to stay at this des. gents' res. just outside Marlborough. He offers girls like other people say, 'peanuts?' at a party. His girls are lovely, skilful, attentive – addictive. All the joys of love and none of the responsibilities. And all that Monty asks in exchange for this imperial *largesse* is a little straightforward chat about his guests' work, like, 'How's this horse been going and what coups are planned and should I lay off this or that in the National?' It's not exactly crooked. Even jockeys enjoy freedom of speech, just like any other subject. Only problem is, that information is not mine to give away. It's lent to me on trust by my paymasters.

I shudder as I withdraw from her and roll over on my back. I told them about today's runners, I know. That's not too serious. Everyone already knows about Yellow Jersey. He'll start odds on. And Gothic Rose is just an each-way chance at the weights. So what did I give them to warrant this sort of treatment?

Paulinus.

Of course. Paulinus in the Dartington Hurdle. We only ran the trial yesterday, and already I've contrived to knock the ante-post odds by fifteen points or more. 'Great,' I sigh, 'just bloody great!'

Sonia/Tania thinks I'm murmuring compliments. She makes a noise like Frankenstein's front door and nestles closer. She flings an arm around my neck. I push it back. 'Yeah, well, time I was goin', doll,' I tell her. I swing my legs from the bed. For a moment I feel like a flea on a long-playing record.

'Oh, God!' I groan. That's my regular contribution to the dawn chorus – a solid bass counterpoint to the tasteless and cheery chirping of the sparrows. 'Oh, Jesus God Almighty!' Prayer or profanation? God knows.

The watch on the bedside table says twenty past six. I take a deep breath and switch on automatic pilot. It's a familiar, well practised routine: shit, shave, shower and shog.

I'm just stealing round the door when she sits up and strokes her left tit. 'Now, I will see you again, won't I, Georgie?' she purrs. 'Soon?'

'Sure,' I nod. 'Sure, I'll be back soon. Happy Christmas, love.'

I wish that I were just being polite. There was a Greek philosopher, and all his pupils were tutting and swooning when they saw him on his way into the cathouse, but he said, 'The sin lies not in the going in, but in the not-coming-out.' He was right, too. Every time I walk away from a scene like this, I console myself with that thought. It's only a bit of a lark. I can take it or leave it ... Just as I've given up drinking and smoking a thousand times at this hour of the morning. Only trouble is, I'm a totally different man in the evening, after a day of winning, a day of losing.

Horses I can manage, but I have the same problems as anyone else, comes to riding tigers.

Monty Alvin started life as a barrowboy or something. Now he's not only got money, he's also acquired taste. Downstairs in the hall, I nod at a couple of foreshortened Tiepolo angels. There's a Turner watercolour too, four Gaudier animal drawings, a few Morandis and a very stark early ikon on a velvet-draped lectern. Funny thing, that. Punters adorn their walls with Page 3 girls and Schweppes calendars, bookies with the abridged version of Kenneth Clark's *Civilisation*. Punters, furthermore, are aware of this. And keep on punting. Explain – with diagrams where necessary.

I bump into a bare-breasted marble girl who's preparing to drop-kick her amphora. I say 'Sorry'. She sneers. There's a simple Yale lock on the door. It's not that Monty's trusting, exactly. It's just that, if he were to find a Gaudier or two missing when he gets up in the morning, I would find a couple of kneecaps, testicles and other useful appendages missing when I got home tonight. That is what they call security.

It's a bright and glassy day. The frost makes everything dazzle. I grope my way to the car and fumble for the sunglasses in the glove-pocket. It gets light far too early in the morning and dark far too early at night.

Story of my life.

A quick shower, and then I'm off to Lambourn most mornings to ride out or to school. I usually take Claire's Renault. It's only a twenty minute run from our house at Blewbury. I drive an XJS the rest of the time. Sounds grand, but you need a good car in this business. I covered over sixty-two thousand miles last season.

I've had this retainer with Jack Carlton for four years now. I try to ride out as often as possible, as much for my sake as for his. I like to know the horses that I'm to ride and, in particular, to school the young ones. They're all so very different. Jack's an old friend. We used to ride against one another, so he knows the ins and outs of the jock's trade ...

'Where the frigging hell were you last night?' Jack doesn't even bother to look at me as he storms out of the front door and down the moss-blotched steps. He just stands over the car and bellows up at the distant downs. He's every inch the country gent these days in his boots, jodhpurs, Barbour and checked tweed cap. He taps his calf with his whip. Not exactly *avant-garde* stuff. Effective though.

'I – er ... I – what – um ...' I snap back at him, quick as a flash. 'Well?'

'I stayed in Bath,' I slam the car door and push back my hair with a fluttering hand. 'I just met some people at the sports – some friends. We had a drink or two, that's all. Can't afford to lose my licence, you know, so – well, so I stayed.' I shrug in a *soigné* sort of way and remove the sunglasses so that I can swing them a bit. Not such a good idea. I get just one swing in, then put them back fast.

'A drink or two,' Jack hums. His eyebrows tangle in the middle. The corner of his thin lips twitches twice. 'Since when have you been capable of having a "drink or two", Georgie? Mmmm? And why the hell are you white and shaking like a shorn teg – just look at you, man – eyes like piss-holes in the snow – after a "drink or two" Georgie? And why didn't you bloody well ring Claire and, for that matter, me, to tell us what was going on? Or was what remains of your brain too addled by this "drink or two"? Well?'

It should be noted that the casual passer-by would have understood little or nothing of this speech. It was delivered in an undertone through clenched teeth and seemed composed entirely of consonants. What vowels there were came out as 'ee' or 'er' – 'Thees dreenk er tee ...'

'I did ring Claire,' I blurt, then, 'at least, I tried.' I lean on the car roof and gaze casually about the maroon and white yard. A quick cold breeze squirts into the yard, picks up my hair, puts it back again and runs on to play in each of the empty boxes in turn. Hooves clatter and slip on every side. 'I tried. She was engaged ...'

'Oh, sure, sure,' Jack hits himself hard. 'Oh, sure.' He sniffs, swings round and strides off towards the opposite corner of the yard. His arm flaps. 'Sure. Bloody unreliable ... did ring, my arse ... doesn't want the rides, doesn't want the wife ... dunno why she puts up with the little bugger ... Jesus!' Some twenty yards away, he swings round, points with his whip and bellows, 'Might as well mount down here. If, that is, you remember how. Get on Vantage. I'll take Ginger up with me.'

I sigh as I shrug off the camelhair and fish out my skullcap. There's little else for me to do but sigh. I could, of course, inform Jack that I've been giving away stable secrets to Monty Alvin. Seven or eight years ago, after all, Jack himself was no stranger to Monty's place. There was one delightful, restorative night that the two of us spent with three very friendly girls in and around the indoor swimming-pool, for example, and that sort of good clean fun doesn't come free. But all is flux, and if Jack Carlton the trainer had the least idea that I had been doing what Jack Carlton the jockey used to do, there'd be raw Georgie Blane fricassée spattered all over the newly-swept cobbles.

Ginger's waiting with Vantage in the corner. He grins and winks and flicks me up into the saddle. As soon as my feet are in the irons, I feel a whole lot better. My spine seems to straighten, my shoulders to go back of their own accord.

'Right, let's be away,' calls the headman. There's a deal of stamping and snorting then as we form up in line. Vantage moves nonchalantly, almost lethargically over to the others. We take our position one from the back. There's a chorus of, 'Morning, Georgie.' I nod and grunt a bit. Our breath bounces back at us on the cold clear air. So, plumed with steam, the slouching squadron of skullcapped dragoons clatters out onto the road, up the steep dirt track and onto the springy virgin turf of Mann Down gallops.

Jack awaits us up there. For all the jodhpurs and the whip, he travels by Range Rover these days. We who rode against him know why. Six years ago, on a very useful animal called Navarino, he took on the great Harlequin. It is generally deemed to have been a very romantic and a very silly thing to do. I was engaged in that contest and, like all the other lads, had no intention of busting a gut in a bid for the impossible. Second by a distance was the best that anyone could hope for.

Jack's owners thought otherwise. They instructed him to go like the clappers from the off, set up an enormous, dispiriting lead and

41

then hold on for dear life in the hope that Harlequin wouldn't catch him.

It was a three miler, and Navarino was essentially a two mile horse, so it wasn't difficult for him to build up that lead they wanted. At the start of the back straight, there were four obstacles and about sixty lengths between Navarino and the rest of us, who were plodding along in a normal, businesslike sort of way.

Then Jessie Jordan said, 'See you, lads,' sat down, and shifted Harlequin into overdrive.

It was bloody terrifying. He moved away from the rest of us as though he were just starting and we were left at the gate. A few farewell divots spun up in our faces, and Harlequin was gone.

As we cleared the big open ditch we could already see that Navarino had blown up and Jack was struggling. We could also see that beautiful monster Harlequin drawing in the rope. I've seen the video a hundred times. Navarino went backwards. He'd given everything. He'd already covered over two miles at a relentless lick. He'd done enough to win every other race in his life by twenty lengths or more, but Jack was still asking more of him. And now, incredibly, the poor, courageous sod saw Harlequin cruising upsides at an effortless gallop. It was too much for him. Jessie must have seen that Navarino was blown. He even took a pull to avoid half-lengthening him. They met that plain fence neck and neck.

Navarino met it dead.

The heart attack must have hit him one stride off. He ploughed into the solid planks and the three-foot-thick birch twigs. His legs flew up straight and, in a movement as elegant as a gymnast's floor exercise, he somersaulted. Jack had flown forward on the first impact. He landed with a brain-rattling thump and opened his eyes to see eleven hundred pounds of prime horseflesh and bone swinging through the air towards him like a headsman's axe.

It hit him dead centre. It knocked all the wind out of him, of course, but he was conscious again within seconds. The horse was still on top of him. They remained like that, like sated lovers, for another half minute or so as we passed over. I saw him looking up at us. His expression was that of a puzzled puppy, unafraid yet bewildered, curious as to where the next, final blow would come from.

He was experienced enough to know something of the extent of the damage. When at last they pulled him out from under the steaming corpse, he could see a bit more. Not the shattered ribs, of course, the punctured lung, the ruptured spleen, but he yapped and screamed as he emerged, and blood dribbled from his nose and his mouth. Three splintered spars of broken bone emerged from his right thigh like an old shipwreck from the sand. That was enough. Nature's anaesthetic knocked him gratefully cold.

They patched him up well enough. He even rode again at top class. His colleagues wished that he wouldn't. There are few things more sickening to watch or more dangerous for all concerned than a rider who has lost his nerve. God knows, it is nothing to be ashamed of. It could happen to any of us. It happens to most reckless women riders when they have their first children. That sort of natural, chemical thing. But Jack couldn't accept it. For a season and a half we steered clear of him as he leaned back, clutching at the air for support, lips drawn back, eyes bulging, infecting his mounts with his panic, forcing them by a terror-stricken tug on the reins to put in a short one and meet their fences all wrong, and woe betide anyone directly behind them.

It was that spleen which finally let him out. The doctors told him straight. One more internal injury and he'd be begging for the ride on Pegasus.

He still hasn't accepted it. Whenever a whingeing boy claims that some horse is unmanageable, Jack has to prove himself once again by sneering at the boy's gutlessness and climbing on the poor beast's back. There is a complaint in the equestrian world known as 'an electric arse'. Those who suffer from it make their mounts all hot and excited as soon as they sit in the saddle. The best advice that can be given to such people is, 'try tricycles'. It's usually innate, but Jack, who used to be one of the boldest and best, has acquired it. Horses feel his hatred, his resentment, his panic. They move beneath him like faithless firewalkers. Only his enormous strength and his experience have saved him from fatal falls. He proves his pointless point and dismounts as fast as ever he can.

This is the best part of the day. The downs are lovely now, and all the smells – the wet turf, the dung, the leather – and the sounds – the creaking saddles, the clinking bits, the ill-oiled larks, the grunted, shorthand conversation of the lads – they all seem very intense and intoxicating when everything's so cold and clear and still . . .

Yes. Well, it's true today. It really is the best part of the day, the time in which, for a few minutes at least, I can believe again in fairies and in Georgie Blane and in the future. And it's all thanks to this animal beneath me.

He's neither pretty nor showy. He'll attract no cooees from the debs and the pony-club matrons in the paddock, but he's put together right. A horseman's horse.

He arrived in the yard in April, but I didn't get to ride him until September. For the benefit of those who are interested in such things and might have forgotten the details, Vantage was born in Tipperary's Golden Vale, the son of the great champion stallion, Deep Run. He inherited the deep bay of his dam's Bright Cherry family which has produced, amongst other distinguished sons, Arkle, whom God recalled to do the summer solstice run as soon as he'd finished racing. At three, Vantage was quietly broken and won the Champion's rosette at Doncaster's Sunday show of potential National Hunt stock. He failed to reach his 30,000 guinea reserve, but Harry Beeby reported a genuine bid of 25,000.

Back in Ireland, he won a two mile bumper at Limerick, then a novice hurdle at Fairyhouse. His sticky jumping of hurdles at speed made it clear that he was a 'chaser. He was well schooled by Tim Beaumont, his owner's amateur rider son, and started favourite for his first novice 'chase at Navan in January of his fifth year. He put down at the first. From what I can gather, he never even left the ground, just did a forward flip, smashing up poor Tim's left leg in the process. He learned his lesson. He has never fallen since.

According to Tommy Morris, who took over the reins, it took Vantage some time to adapt to the forceful handling of a pro. Mistakes cost him a lot of ground, but he took two novice 'chases and then moved up a grade when he romped home in Leopardstown's Sandymount Chase.

Like James Joyce, like me, like any self-respecting Hibernian with talent, he had to move his campaign to the English front. He started hot favourite for the Kim Muir Memorial Challenge at the Cheltenham National Hunt Festival. I watched that race from a bed in the General Hospital just down the road. Vantage was only six. The pace up Prestbury Hill was too much for him. He blew up and was pipped a length and a short head by Cliff McGann on Double Check and Sam Richards on some grey animal that used to burst blood vessels. Can't remember its name.

Tim Beaumont was a big gambler. He'd been going bad for a while, and Vantage carried the last of his credit on that day. This one horse, it seemed to him, had given him a permanent limp and had lost him a fortune. All Tim's fault, of course, but racing people are superstitious. I can't blame him for thinking that his young jumping star must be jinxed. Drunk and disgruntled at the Lygon Arms that night, he sold Vantage to one Major Frank Smythson, late of the Blues and Royals, for 60,000 guineas.

Smythson is a prick. He even looks like one. He has no shoulders to speak of, but he pulls them back and stands rigid. His face has the colour, shape and texture of sub-preputial membrane. He is also a pain in the fundament. He is one of Jack's luckiest owners. He arrived in the yard with Vantage just a couple of days after the Cheltenham race. Jack showed himself in his best colours that day. He eyed Vantage up, nodded and pronounced, 'Yup, he'll do. I'll keep him, let him down, blister him and turn him out.'

Smythson's eyebrows meshed. 'No, no, Carlton. Absolutely not. Still three months of the season to go, you know. Horse is fit. Good prize money to be picked up. Not wasting that.

Jack nodded. 'OK. You want to train him, it's fine by me. Take him away and do your best. You want me to train him, I'll train him. My way. Better make up your mind.

So I didn't see the horse until the end of July when he came up from grass to start roadwork. He looked super. We didn't even start to steal him into his fast work until September.

I remember that first day. I was just told, 'Try this new bay. He's from Ireland.'

I turned round. Little Ginger saluted and flung open the bottom half of the stable door with all the flourish of an illusionist's assistant. I strolled over as he led out this big trace-clipped creature and turned him broadside on for inspection. I inspected.

And I found myself nodding slowly. Nothing ecstatic, I've been around too long for that. Just a slow, appreciative nod. The horse has a heavy, slightly common head with a white blaze down a nose from one of the more refined suburbs of Rome. Plenty of width between the eyes; good, big honest ears. A thoroughly good sort. Great bone, a well-developed second thigh which should launch him into the stratosphere and, above all, phenomenal depth. If a palaeontologist found the rib cage, he'd think for a moment that tyrannosaurus was still about. It makes his legs look short. They're not.

I reached up gently and patted his neck. 'Hello, feller.' He turned a big dark eye on me and we shared an Irish secret or two.

''E's lovely, in 'e?' Ginger trilled in a proud falsetto. 'Whoah.'

'He's all right,' I nodded. 'He's very all right. You ridden him, Ginger?'

'Yeah,' he said. 'Just cantered 'im. Lovely.' Ginger liked the horse, and Ginger's no pushover. He keeps the bits they cut off for his breakfast. ''E's all yours today, Georgie. Tell us 'ow 'e feels.'

We came in from an uphill gallop and a school over Jack's four fences and I told him, 'Look after him, Ginger. I won't swear to it, but I think he's the best I've ridden for a long, long time.'

45

I've been on him six times since then, and won on him by a leisurely five lengths at Wincanton, then two lengths in the Mackeson at Cheltenham again, and I haven't changed my mind. Either I am growing old and loopy or my senses are short-circuited by the booze and the Sonia/Tanias, or this Vantage – the lads call him 'Ripper' – has all the makings of a truly great steeplechaser.

It's not just the speed; it's the *feel*. I've met it only three times before, and never, I swear, has it been so intense.

It's this extraordinarily powerful awareness not so much of what he's giving as of all that he's got in reserve; the certainty that I have just to click my tongue, give him a little squeeze, and I'll have twenty times the horsepower between my knees. I get the feeling too that he and I both want the same thing. He pricks his ears as he approaches an obstacle, keeps them pricked as we go over, and I've still got a double handful as I gather up the reins. He loves this game. He's already dreaming of glory and he trusts me to take him there.

And just for a moment, here, crouched over his neck, feeling the warm vapour from his nostrils on my lips, my cheek, watching the crisp grey grass dragged back below, feeling the churning and the swell of his stride, I get to forget who I am, forget about last night and all the nights before in which I've been seeking just this sort of oblivion. I'm young again and unthinking, just an active part of a far, far greater force than I, giving myself to it totally. Like a soldier, or a lover.

Don't get me wrong. I'm not anthropomorphising. Horses are very, very thick, and this one, I'm sure, is no exception. They understand little more than loyalty – tenuous loyalty at that – to a pack leader that they can trust to be calm and strong in crisis. Whatever this feller is doing as he clears each fence with a yard or more to spare, he's not really dreaming of Cheltenham Gold Cups. But that's like saying that puppies or lion-cubs aren't dreaming of antelope hunts or fights to the death as they practise for them in their rough and tumble games. It's true, of course, but instinct makes them practise, instinct makes them play. That it serves an end is inevitable, that's all. They wouldn't do it otherwise, just as I'd find no pleasure in screwing an oestrogen-steeped Sonia/Tania if there were no such things as babies. That's practise too, so nature makes it jolly.

But, in this animal, those instincts are powerful. Very powerful. He knows that, young as he is, he is destined to be a leader. He's preparing to take on the old chiefs and to beat them, and he knows that he needs my help.

Then it's back to the house for breakfast. I'm lucky. I don't really have to watch my weight too much, and anyway, jump jockeys don't have to ride at pulletweight like their flat-race brethren. This is the best meal of the day, when you've worked up a good appetite with a gallop. A trainer's house is one of the few places where you still get a proper English country house breakfast – silver-covered trays on the sideboard – eggs poached or scrambled, beautiful sausages, kippers, kidneys, bacon, sometimes kedgeree. The works, and lashings of hot coffee and orange juice too. This is when Jack and I get a chance to discuss the progress of the animals and the entries that he's made ...

Jack might say 'Pshaw!' when he reads this. He might say 'Phooey!' He might even say 'Gawd, what a load of bollocks!' He is not very refined.

To start off with – although it's true what I say about weight – I cannot eat much on a racing day; a boiled egg or two, a slice of toast, that's all. A fall on an empty stomach is bad. A fall on a full one is like every shock you ever had distilled into one neat draught. Furthermore, Jack does not discuss entries with me. His wife Marigold makes them. Jack simply informs me of them.

He doesn't talk to me at all today. He talks to Marigold a bit – affectionate niceties like, 'Where's the butter?' and, 'Bloody miners', but at me he just sighs and rustles his *Sporting Life* in a vicious manner.

By the time we get down to the toast and marmalade, I'm sick of this. 'Darling!' I gulp. Jack jumps. 'I can't stand this silence anymore! Is there . . . is there . . . someone else?'

Jack lowers his paper, frowns, says, 'Hmph,' then goes back to his reading. Marigold's expression of bewilderment changes quickly to a sneer. I grin at her. She gecks. A 'geck', according to a Gaelic dictionary I once read, is 'a wanton toss of the head'. I think we need that word. Please use it. Marigold gecks a lot, and wags her dyed blonde ponytails.

Marigold, yeah, well. That's a real rags to bitches story. In her youth, she screwed jockeys and the Household Cavalry. That was just practise. She was a natural. Tipped for the Olympics, but turned pro young. Got a job as PA to the chairman of a big bloodstock agency. He was married to an amateur and had three amateur children. No contest. She 'married' him, as they wittily call it these days. Two years later, she ran off with young Lord Northop. She got her come-uppance there. He was more experienced and single-minded a performer than she. She found herself in hock and in pup somewhere in New Mexico as Rollo Northop walked up the aisle of Winchester Cathedral with the ever so suitable Lady Charlotte Brodie.

Tee hee, the racing world chortled as one, but Marigold is made of the steely stuff of champions. The pup was mysteriously lost, an Argentinian breeder got her out of hock and into ocelot, and the next we knew, she was back again, ten years younger, sparkling with health and diamonds with poor old Jack Carlton on her arm.

Carlton may seem a strange choice to those unaware that he is the heir to a substantial building fortune and to those who believe that dear Marigold has retired. 'Pshaw,' say I. I am known for my refinement. Trainers have owners. Owners are very rich, cosmopolitan people. Marigold spends the close season on yachts with Albanian or Greek flags on them. She's got lots of books on mythology and shipping and I swear that she's going wide behind these days.

'That, by the way,' I say casually, 'is the best animal you've ever had in this yard.' I flourish my knife. Marigold glowers at the gleaming gob of marmalade on her tablecloth. 'I reckon we'll take the George VI easy. Then, next year, the Gold Cup.'

'Ah. Oh. Well.' He lowers the paper fast. Interesting business, aesthetics. Poets spend their whole lives seeking this or that felicitous combination of words, yet there are times when the words 'Public Convenience' can be lovelier by far than any Shakespeare sonnet. To Carlton, words like 'Gold Cup' possess a beauty which outstrips that of all the verse in the world. They galvanise him. They put a sparkle in his eye. It's lovely to see. 'You really think he's that good?'

'They all go fast past posts and bushes,' Marigold quotes a weary saw. I ignore her.

'He gives me a feel, Jack, a hell of a feel. Know what I mean? A once in years – maybe a once in a lifetime feel. I sure can't remember anything stronger. He's got it. You know.'

'Yeah,' Jack smiles. 'Yeah, I know.'

'He'll piss it on Boxing Day, no matter what the opposition.'

'I think so.'

'Dear God,' I sigh fervently. 'I hope that I'm right about him.'

'So, I assure you, do I.'

'And I hope I'll still be around to ride him in the Gold Cup.'

'Largely depends on you,' Jack says gently. He pours coffee. 'I hope so too. There aren't many who know their way around as well as you. But you know ...'

'Yeah. I know,' I nod rather ruefully. 'Warning heeded, Jack.'

'I should hope so too,' says Marigold. She taps sweetener into her coffee. Both Jack and I turn on her. Jack's frown turns quickly into a meek, conciliatory smile. Mine stays where it is, where it is rapidly joined by a scowl as I swallow back the remark which springs, acrid and unbidden, to my tongue. Jack is my friend. He can say what he likes. But no jumped-up floozie talks to me like that. She's ridden a lot of things in her life, but never four and a half miles around Aintree, never a Gold Cup winner. We have.

It's one of my best scowls, but it doesn't seem to hurt her much. She smirks. Hiding, no doubt, her inner anguish.

'Well now, I must be getting home, mate,' I push back the chair and throw down my napkin. 'I'll see you at the sports.'

Each day for us of the Worshipful Company of Topers and Inebriates is a microcosm of a life. The hardest bit is dragging yourself from the warm womb of the continental quilt into odious iodine light and the mechanical, unsympathetic clatter of This Great Hospice They Call The World. You want to go back where you came from, but there's always some kind soul to welcome you with a sharp spank on the rump. Mornings are inarticulate and fumbling. By midday, you're well into the pangs of adolescence. The afternoon flies by too quickly. You hit your prime, all too briefly, around eight in the evening, then it's back on the primrose path again. You're gibbering and senile by midnight. In the wee small hours it's time to collapse with a grateful sigh, and to expire.

I'm about to adolesce again, and I'm not looking forward to it. I actually have to stop the car on the crest of the hill above the house in order to consider the responsible, adult role which I now have to adopt. Something in my stomach twists like plastic in the fire. I don't want to be grown up. There's going to be hurt down there, and I hate hurt. The landscape spins a couple of times as I draw deep on the first cigarette of the day.

Don't get me wrong. I love my wife. I love my children. It would all be a damned sight easier if I didn't. It's just the adaptation that I can't stand. The racecourse, the gallops, the bar – they're all carefree familiar playgrounds in which I have a preordained role to play. No one asks me to think or feel. I just have to have a few quid in my wallet and then I can be Georgie Blane, jockey, the sassy, sharp, bobbing and weaving survivor or, with such as Jack, the naughty boy with 'a problem'. When I go home, they want me to be a certain constant thing called 'father', to face up to my responsibilities and my mortality. That's not so easy.

It's always been the same. When I was at prep-school, as Conor is now, I could never write letters home. My mother didn't understand. It hurt her. I felt accordingly guilty. She did not realise that Georgie-at-school was bullied, witty, defensive. He had a precociously powerful personality, unrelated to that of the easy, affectionate child that his mother knew. At a push, I suppose, he could have managed something like, 'Dear Mummy, We won the match 3–0. The film was *We Were Not Divided*. It was boring. Jones let off a stink-bomb in the changing-room and got six. I masturbated four times last night. One of the boys has got 'flu. Matron O'Reilly snogs with Mr Watt in the car right outside our window at night. It is very funny ...' To have written anything which I felt to be worthy of my mother's eyes would have been to write a studied lie and to remind myself dangerously of silly, vulnerable, childish Georgie-at-home. I was safer, if not exactly happier, in my shell. I still am.

I release the handbrake and let the car free-wheel down the hill towards the house. It's a nice house. It's white and it's got a thatched roof and a nice big brown and fawn drawing-room with French windows opening onto a terrace and stroked green lawns. There are dinky little attic rooms with circular windows for the children and there's a huge kitchen complete with food processors and electric oven and gas hob and all that because Claire is a brilliant cook. She used to make a living at it. We bought the place with the earnings from two races that I didn't win, what remained of my National money and a generous present from Claire's parents.

The car crunches on the gravel but makes no other sound. I shut the door quietly. I don't want to give them time to prepare their opening lines. I go in by the kitchen door. Joanna's doing something to a lettuce. Her back is turned to me. She's barefoot and wears knee-length Huck Finn pink trousers. She's very tall for her age, Joanna – only six inches shorter than I – and she has long, long beautiful dark hair and soft brown eyes that would not disgrace a doe.

She turns her head as I walk in and just says, 'Hello, Daddy.'

'Hello, darling.'

I swagger over and kiss the back of her neck. The sunlight has warmed her skin. Her smooth dark cheek has a half-moon of soft light about it. She spins round with her back still pressed hard against the range. She shakes her extended hands. 'I'm all wet, Daddy,' she says, then, with a frown, 'Listen. *You* have been very, very bad. Mummy was *so* worried last night. So was I ...' She sidesteps away from me and reaches for a tea-towel. 'You could have rung!'

'I did, love,' I sigh. 'I tried. You were engaged.'

'Not all the time, Daddy. You could have tried again. Really. Up to any time. We sat up for hours!'

'Sorry, sorry ...' I wave the pain away. 'I got involved in some business and couldn't escape. I'm sorry, darling, really. Any chance of some coffee?'

'Yes, OK,' she walks briskly over to the kettle and stabs the tit with her finger. 'Well, you *could* have escaped, Daddy. You know you could. Whatever the business.'

'Yeah, yeah. OK. I will in future, promise,' I say hoarsely. My mouth is very dry but my trachea is full of thick liquid. 'Where is Mum, anyway?'

'Out in the garden.'

'Oh. OK, I'll go and find her.'

'Hm,' says my daughter.

I ignore that and stub the cigarette out in the clean ashtray. That depresses me too. Everything is spotless till Daddy comes in and leaves his detritus around. And the worst of it is, they all tolerate it.

I barge back out and round the back of the house. My shoulder brushes a shower of icy diamonds off the fuchsias by the door. Splayed, dripping grass cools my feet through the thick jodhpur boots. I duck under the apple boughs and crush windfalls underfoot. Vandal, my black collie-cross lurcher, realises at last that I'm there. At least he's glad to see me. He illustrates his delight in muddy hieroglyphs all over my breeches.

Claire is bent over the flower bed. She has a lot of Michaelmas daisies and gladioli in the crook of her left arm. She's wearing jeans and a brown sweatshirt with foliage embroidered on the back. She's very slim and tall and beautiful and I ache to be with her, especially when I'm with her.

'Oh. Good of you to turn up,' she tells a rose, then cuts its head off.

'I'm sorry not to have got through last night, love,' my hand rises in a long-distance caress. 'I tried, but I got in with all the press boys and couldn't bloody escape. You know what they're like. Trevor wants to do my life, and we had to discuss it – terms, you know, all that – and the drink flowed a bit too freely, and every time I tried to ring you were engaged until it was too late ...'

She whistles, three times, very deliberately, grits her teeth and snips with the secateurs as though her mind were on other things but flowers. She straightens and turns and barges past me, eyes set on the corner of the house. Wet petals stick to my sleeve.

51

'Claire, look, I'm sorry ...'

'Yes,' she sings. 'Yes, you're always sorry. Frankly, Georgie, I have had enough of your being bloody sorry. Enough, enough, enough!' She stops in order to snarl the last 'enough' at me with sufficient force, then walks on. 'Just pay the bills on the desk before you go again, please.'

'Claire, look ...' I have to take two strides for every one of hers, which doesn't contribute to my sense of dignity.

'You look!' she turns again, trembling. Her head is framed by sparkling blue hydrangeas. Her eyes gleam hard as marbles. 'The bank manager, incidentally, is going to bounce the cheque I wrote to Saint Mary's, which'll make life just lovely for Joanna. I can't give him any bloody assurances. I can't even ask him to talk to you because you're never bloody here to talk to. We have no hot water in the house because the oil-tank is empty and because the last two bills haven't been paid, so they won't come out, and you, meanwhile, are spending what little money we have on piss-ups in expensive hotels with your infantile chums and their tarts. Jeremy Berisford rings up to offer you rides and I have to tell him to offer them to someone else because I don't even know where you are. How the hell do you expect us to live like that, Georgie? Hey?'

'I'll ... I've got cheques coming in this week. The bloody bank man knows that. The Weatherby's cheque hasn't come in yet, for God's sake! And this autobiography ... Look, I'll talk to him.'

'Oh, Christ!' she constricts the shriek, but it's still a shriek. She storms into the kitchen, barging down an imaginary door. 'Jesus Christ save me from such crap!' She dumps the flowers onto the tabletop.

'Here you are, Daddy,' Joanna says quietly at my elbow. She seems to take this sort of conversation in her stride. Vandal and I are the ones that cower.

'Thanks.' I take the coffee mug and a deep breath. 'Look, Claire,' I say for the umpteenth time, 'you know perfectly well that a jock's income is sporadic. You've always known that ...'

'Sure, sure! Which is why most riders set something aside for the days when they're injured or dead or when the winners aren't coming. But not you. You're immortal. Nothing could go wrong with you. You'd rather invest in whiskey and whores like some bloody eighteen-year-old let out for the first time. To hell with the fact that you happen to be a husband and a father. Well, if that's the way you want it, OK. To hell with the fact that you're a husband and a father. You don't have to be. I have had you and your whining excuses up to here!'

52

She strides over to the sink and turns the tap on full blast. I have to raise my voice above the thudding of the water. 'The season's only just begun, for God's sake! Anyhow, there's Vantage. You'll see ...'

'Fuck Vantage!' She turns off the tap. The words echo in the sudden silence. I sip my coffee. Joanna doesn't even look up from the serious business of breaking a Rubik's cube's bonds. 'Another bloody champion in the making! Another bloody some day my prince will come! I'm not talking about the vague possibility that this horse or that may net you a few thousand here or there, I'm talking about security, which your daughter and I have a right to expect. I'm talking about a man, a man who takes his responsibilities seriously, a man who comes home of an evening or at least lets us know where he is, a man who pays the bloody everyday bills first and thinks about his infantile showing-off sessions afterwards.' She wrings a tea-towel's neck and throws down the carcase. I put my forefinger in one eye and the thumb on the other, and moan.

'All right,' she says, 'you just listen, Georgie. Just listen, and I mean it this time. You have one month. One month in which to set things straight, one month in which to sort out your problems and start behaving reasonably, or I swear you'll come back here and find this house on the market and your family gone. Understood? I mean it. In a month from today, I want to see the bills paid and an insurance policy taken out on Joanna's and Conor's education. I want everything straight. Otherwise, I'll find myself a proper man who can look after me and the children properly, not some whimpering, clapped-out eternal bloody teenager who – damn it, even Joanna has to bloody look after you. I did not marry you to have every standard in my life destroyed – eroded – by you and your sordid bog ways. Right. Understood? One month.'

'For God's sake!' I thump the table. Neither the table nor Claire shakes visibly. My hand does. 'I didn't marry you to have all this bloody middle-class nagging whenever I come home! I am a jockey, a horseman. One of the very best. You knew who I was, what I was when you married me ...'

'I didn't know I was marrying a drunken sot ...' A vase hits the tap with a clunk.

'I am not a drunken sot!' I risk a roar. 'I still like a good night out. Who the hell doesn't? Especially if you know that you're going to return to a lifeless, antiseptic, middle-class, money-grubbing miniature Ideal Home Exhibition! Jesus! Wouldn't a saint need the odd piss-up if that was all he could call home!'

53

It's neither fair nor original, but it'll do for now. A man's got to assert himself, after all.

Claire just says, 'One month, Georgie.'

'One month!' I mimic. 'One month! What happened to good old human emotions like love, hmmm? What happened to "For richer or for poorer"? What it all amounts to in the end is "either you are rich or I don't love you." Is that it? There's a name for that sort of deal.'

'As no one knows better than you,' she hums casually. She leans on one hand at the far corner of the table. 'Listen, I don't know what's wrong with you, Georgie, and frankly I don't even care any more. It's not that I don't love you. You know damned well I do. But for the past year, you've been worse than ever. All right, so you had your big moment of glory years ago and you can't forget it. Think you're bloody Peter Pan. All right, perhaps you're on some sort of guilt trip and are punishing us as a way of punishing yourself. I don't care. I am talking about practical things like survival. I'm talking about my life and my children's lives. I don't believe in fairies any more, Georgie, and I'm not going to be your bloody safety-net any more, always forgiving, always forgetting, always allowing you to push me further, testing, testing. Forget it! If you're going all the way down, you're going all the way down. Perhaps you'll bounce, perhaps you won't. But you are not dragging us any further down with you. Got it? You have one month. See a doctor. Give up the booze. Do whatever is necessary, but if I haven't got money in the bank and a husband in the house by this time next month, you are on your own, Georgie.' She pushes back her hair. Her eyes are wet. She says, 'Sorry.'

'Mummy, shall I do some of those flowers?' Joanna asks coolly.

'Thank you, darling. Yes. Then we must get Benbow tarted up for the show.'

I sit silent, shaking my head and looking fetchingly rueful. Two speckled brown slugs are copulating on the window, twining around one another in sheets of slime. The kettle boils again. Balls of steam barge one another up the misty pane. The world is doing its thing and it's doing it without reference to Georgie Blane. I drain the coffee, slam down the mug and say, 'Bloody marvellous!' I push back my chair and storm from the room, slamming the door so hard that it bounces open again. Behind me, two female voices talk blithely on about flowers and ponies and everyday things. I feel very small and tearful and alone. The horrifying loneliness of Copernican revelation. The world wasn't made for me; I stand at the centre of nobody's universe.

I collapse like a stringless puppet in the swivel chair before my desk. I pick up the bills and fling them into the bin. 'One month,' I mutter. 'One month. OK, so I'll show her . . .'

The bright blue morning has changed into a cool grey afternoon. There are great swagging, lead-coloured clouds above the stands, and the roofs of the houses beyond the back straight are dabbed with thick flake white. There's no smell of rain. Good riding weather, all in all; good going too, which'll suit Gothic Rose. Old Yellow Jersey would prefer a bit more cut. He's a mudlark. It won't hurt him though. He's well in at the weights and has nothing to beat. The chill watery wind is a bonus too. Cuts down on the pressing need for deodorants after two and a half miles at the gallop.

Thanks to my vagrancy, I haven't a ride in the first, so I dump my effects in the weighing-room, change into the blue and yellow stripes of Toby Jansen, Gothic Rose's owner, throw on a covert-coat and stroll out to join the Seething Public.

For shortarses like me, the Seething Public is largely a matter of textures and powerful smells. Lots of sheepskin rustling like Christmas parcels, camelhair, British Warm wool, tweed, quilted green nylon. Above these are bristling whiskers and complex road maps in red and purple on weatherbeaten cheeks, spun silk hair and tighter grey or greying bubbles. The scents are always the same too – tweed seems to hold the smell of cigars whilst beer lingers on huskies and raincoats. Soft clouds of Arpège are jostled along by acrid whiffs of wet dog, wafts of sweet saddle-soap.

I have a fair tour today. Five or six people call out, 'Hello, Georgie!' I barely recognise them, but they're all accompanied. Maybe they just wish to be seen to know Who's Who. I hail four or five more and dodge a snub-nosed redhead named Susan, a trainer's secretary who backed me on a 16–1 winner at Lingfield the other day, then got so pissed that she wanted a bit of backing herself. I too was somewhat less than sober and duly obliged. She's been leaving me little notes ever since – things like 'Why me?' and, 'I'm so ashamed. What will your wife say?', gradually modulating to 'How could you use a poor maiden so?', as though it had been my idea in the first place.

I only get cut by two people in my wanderings. One is a Birmingham businessman who is wrongly convinced that I pulled his animal in a big race at Newbury. He sniffs and shakes his jowls at me as he passes. The other is the sweet, gushing, middle-aged daughter of a rustic peer. She's all muesli and chiffon and bangles and she buys horses because they're so sweet, so – so *masculine*, if you know what I mean. She asked me what she should do with dear Mossy as I dismounted from him about an hour after the other jockeys had weighed in. I just pointed at a sausage magnate standing nearby and said, 'He might have some good ideas, ma'am.' It took her the better part of twenty minutes to work it out, then she decided that she didn't like me any more. She trembles from head to toe as she sees me and lopes by like Groucho Marx with her nose in the air.

I find a decent position three steps up on the grandstand. It'll be five minutes or more before the runners in this, a novice hurdle, leave the paddock and canter up. Meanwhile, it's good just to look around.

Ever since I was a small child, I have loved the seamy glamour of the racecourse, the bustling vigour of it all, the uncertainty which infects everyone there. For us, the jockeys, trainers, lads, spivs and punters, it is a matter of survival. The bookies are the sharks, constantly circling, looking for victims. It's not just the racing that the spectators come to see, it's the gladiatorial business done here on the stands and in the ring.

Yes. Well. The bookies are still there, the tic-tac men and the lords and ladies. There's no shortage of crooks either, but it's all become so big. Now it's the crooks who lord it while the lords and ladies are rather pathetically pompous and down at heel. The rogues aren't lovable any more; they're big soulless syndicates to whom racing is just another source of revenue, not a loved, if much abused way of life; a whore, not a wonderful, weary old mistress.

Here though, glancing over his shoulder with each stride, comes a relic from the old days. His name is Bertie the Spiv. I suppose he once had another name, but it's long since been forgotten. Bertie the Spiv has become a title, like The McGillicuddy of the Reeks or something. Bert was a fixer in the old days – a small-time crook who always seemed worse than he was, a gofer, a procurer, an all round agent. He used to sell tips, of course, but I can't imagine that that earned him much. Bert, with his simian cranium, his bulging brown eyes and his permanently blue chin, could scarcely have competed with Monolulu in his prime. No. Bert is just a typical racecourse villain. He's always had an inside pocket full of dirty pictures, for example, but who needs him now when the high street newsagent's is packed with far more lurid stuff? In those days, too, you'd approach Bertie if you wanted a girl, a boy, a pep pill, a Spanish Fly or a Mickey Finn. Now pimps and dope dealers are spotty faced kids with millions in the bank and hitmen guarding their backs.

The whites of those swivelling eyes are very grimy and the pupils have lost their lustre. He grunts and puffs as he pulls himself up the steps. His skin is translucent as fine porcelain. I reckon he's dying.

''Lo there, Georgie boy.'

'Good day to you, mate. How's it goin'?'

'Oh, great, great, my old son. Never better. You know. Worse the old economy gets, better it is for the skilful entrepreneur, you know?'

'Sure, Bert, sure,' I smile. 'There's a shortage of everything except suckers.'

''Ass right, Georgie, 'ass right!' He slaps me on the shoulder, then fishes his racecard from a pocket. He pretends to study it, but his eyes are still shooting all over the place. He looks like a paralytic at Wimbledon. 'Er – you got any winners for us today, then, Georgie boy?'

'Sure and you know better than to take a jockey's tip, don't you, lad?' I catch sight of Polly Waller coming round the corner. I wave, 'We're just the fellers as sit on top.'

'Yeah,' Bert shrugs and makes a sort of wriggling movement as though to pull up his trousers with his elbows. 'Yeah. Still.'

'Well, Yellow Jersey should win easy enough.'

'Yeah,' he nods glumly, 'Yeah, s'pose so. Odds on, mind.'

'For sure. Sorry, mate.'

Polly bounds up the steps and engulfs me in pale blue silk, pale blonde hair and pale pink flesh. Like many a fat woman, Lady Polly Waller has lovely legs and sprightly action. She used to be a Gaiety Girl in her youth. Her kiss is very wet and warm. I extricate myself floundering, grinning. Both my Gold Cup winners, Holy Moses and Ice Nine, were Polly's.

'Hello, you old sod,' she chortles. 'How's yourself?'

'None too bad, Pol. How's the old peer?'

'Whose old peer?'

'See you, Georgie ...' Bert says glumly.

'Yeah. See you. Good luck, Bertie. No, I heard Percy was having back trouble.'

'Like his front, poor old sod,' she sighs. 'Gone, gone. How's Sleaford's girl?'

'Oh, she's fine,' I grin. 'Thanks for Joanna's birthday present.'

'Dear God, did I send her one? Gettin' soft. Good brat, though. Must send her over to me one day for some education.'

'She's a little young yet for your sort of tuition, Pol,' I laugh. 'Horses doing all right?'

'Oh, I suppose so, I suppose so. They could do with a little assistance from on high, in both senses of the expression. Wish I could have you on them instead of this bloody Wilcox man ...'

'Steady, girl,' I soothe. 'He's all right, Chas. He's learning. One of these days ...'

'One of these days! One of these days! I'll've hopped the perch by the time the little bugger's learned to ride a finish. I want it now!'

'You always did, Polly,' I shake my head. 'You always did.'

'Too right, boyo. He'll never be more than a workman at best, anyhow. Christ, man, I wish to God they'd taken you to the vet as soon as they dropped. I'm afraid Coco'll never forgive you.'

'I know,' I say grimly. 'I know.'

The crowd is thickening about us. There are soft bubbling waves of Irish sound and slapping great breakers of open English vowels above the constant deep growl that seems to make the earth hum.

We both turn to watch the runners, exchanging the normal sort of short-hand observations – 'Nice low action', 'God, what a pig', 'Bit peacocky', 'He's long, like him, though'. I make the judgments and murmur these words of wisdom without really thinking. I'm too busy thinking how much I too would like to be riding for Polly and for her trainer, Coco Collins.

For ten years, Coco and I had a friendly and successful working relationship. We took those two Gold Cups, two Champion Hurdles, a first and a second in the National and two King George VI 'chases. I was champion four times. Coco was champion trainer three times.

Then five years ago, during an injury-plagued season, three hot favourites with G. Blane aboard got mysteriously stuffed in the space of two weeks. One of them was, in fact, a straight race – an ungenuine brute that simply had nothing in the tank that day – but no one's going to believe that when two fancied runners have already gone down in a week. I knew damn well that I couldn't get away with it. I was testing my success and Coco's trust, seeing just how far I could push both before they broke. I was also being greedy. There were a lot of rumours – mostly smoke from other people's fires – I use smokeless fuel – and, just to top it all, I'd been giving a rub of the old relic to Jessica, Coco's voracious daughter. Coco would probably have forgiven that; he'd probably have seen me through the drinking, but professional treason was the unforgivable sin. He booted me out with the casual ruthlessness with which an assassin slips the *navaja* between the ribs. The letter arrived on the first of March. The best of the season was yet to come. Coco didn't care. He left me to explain it to the press and the public as best I could, to sue if I would. I did neither. I licked my wounds and unjustly cursed him. Coco, to his credit, has never said a word about me to anyone. I like Coco.

Polly, of course, stayed loyal to her trainer. She and I still love one another, but Coco, I'm afraid, nods politely when he sees me and walks quickly on. You shouldn't make enemies in racing. It's much too small a world.

'They're under starter's orders ...' says the adenoidal course commentator. I reach for the binoculars at my hip.

A rolled racecard taps me twice on the shoulder. I turn, unwinding the leather strap. What I see makes a rock barge into my bowels.

'Quick word after this one, Blane,' the man with terraced red hair speaks briskly. It is an order, not a request. He raises his binoculars to his eyes and pays no further attention.

Something wriggles through my gut. It whimpers as it goes. 'And they're off!' calls the commentator. I keep my glasses trained on them, but scarcely bother to pick out separate runners as they jump off and swing right-handed towards the stands.

The man behind me is one of the new-style villains. His name is Oliver Parker. The Honourable Oliver, to be ironically precise. He's the youngest son of some obscure baron. He started his education at public school – Harrow, I think it was – then Daddy went bust and the Hon. Oliver was transferred to a Wiltshire comprehensive. Some people in such circumstances would have defended themselves by adopting their new found culture with exaggerated pride, scorning their former ways. Not Parker. He is an offensive snob. He simply scorns everyone and everything. From Harrow he took the accent and the autocratic air, both of which he overdoes. From his state school playground he took the unscrupulous ambition and resentfulness of the back-street gangster. This questionable but rare combination of talent first found its *milieu* with a high-flier bookie called John Crayke. Crayke had a curious habit of offering very long odds about certain big-race runners for which other players showed rather great respect. He employed Parker as his front man.

For a while, they seemed to have the luck of the devil, but then, the devil makes his own luck too. Parker, with the highly developed instincts of generations of rats, resigned from Crayke's organisation just one month before the ship sank, taking a lot of cash, useful documents and contacts with him. If Crayke ever suffered from a profound need to be wanted, he's got his wish. The British police want him badly, which must give him a nice warm feeling as he basks on his yacht or potters off to the golf-course from his villa in San Pedro d'Alcantara. He's warned off every racecourse and every training establishment for life. Bet he weeps in his jacuzzi.

Parker turned up next with a new record company, doing, I assume, much the same sort of work. It's not a subject I particularly like to think about. Like God, Parker moves in a mysterious way. I don't really know whose interests – aside from his own – he now represents.

I'd just walk away from the man if I could – if, that is, I were brave, rich and bidding for beatification. But Parker pays for services rendered, and, once you've been fool enough to do his dirty work, it's as well not to put his back up or to draw attention to your association with him. I have even had cause, when in desperate straits, to borrow money from Parker's organisation. It's all been paid back by one means or another, but these men are professionals. They keep their records well.

Lean, lank Tommy Perkins wins the race with three lengths to spare. The long animal that Polly and I liked is moving like a train at the finish, but ran green. Better luck next time.

'Er, see you later, Polly?' I ask glumly, reflecting that the transition from lovely, fat, healthy Polly to drawling, snide, sadistic Parker is the story of my recent life in microcosm.

'Yes, Georgie,' she smiles warmly. I wish she wouldn't. I'd like to tuck myself up in that smile, but if I let go for a moment now, I let go for good. She lays a hand on my arm. 'Let's meet for a drink. Later. After the last or something.'

'Lovely,' I nod, 'or before, if you like. I'm not riding in the last.'

'OK. Look forward to it.' For a moment she looks into my eyes, then she sees someone beyond me and hollers, 'Geoffrey! Geoffrey! I've a bone to pick with you! Come here, you idle old bugger!' She charges past me. The crowd opens up and swallows her.

The stand empties fast. Everyone bustles off down the steps, headed for the paddock or the bar. The little groups that remain are always of people wearing hats. Don't know why. 'Yes, just a quick word, Blane,' Parker drawls behind me. His voice has a very tinny tone. I glance quickly back at him. Parker studies *Timeform* as he speaks. I cannot see his eyes. He has a very white face and very dark red hair. He wears a camelhair coat and glasses with thick black frames. His hands are white and soft. He often wears gloves. I turn back to the course.

'Yes, couldn't reach you on the telephone last night . . . It's Yellow Jersey. There's three and a half in it for you.' He speaks as though asking a casual question.

'Oh, *shit*,' I whisper.

Yellow Jersey's a big, boisterous brown gelding, a bit of an overgrown baby, really. He has no real turn of foot, but he's honest as the day is long and jumps staidly and safely. These last two or three weeks, he has hit form and the handicapper has yet to catch up with him. On the book, there's nothing to touch him today. His owner is an old, one-eyed Devon beef farmer. He's certainly no pauper. He has several thousand acres and one of the finest herds of pedigree Herefords in the country, but Yellow Jersey is his only racehorse and his hobby. He's terribly proud of him. He gave me a monkey as a thank you present when we won at Thirsk the other day.

Aside from all that, of course, Yellow Jersey also carries several hundred thousand thirty-pence bets, God knows how many little old grannies' tenpence each way yankees and so on. About a quarter of the Great Train Robbers' haul, all in all, I'd guess.

But he's also carrying Georgie Blane, and Georgie Blane could use three and a half grand.

'All right, Blane?'

I say nothing. I'm too busy licking my lips, clearing my throat, gulping.

'That's all right, isn't it, Blane?'

'Yes,' I rasp. 'Yes, all right.'

'Good, good.' Parker steps down past me. There's a strong smell of peppermints as he goes by. His lips are puckered as though to whistle, but no sound comes out. He despises me, of course. I'm Irish. I'm a jockey – a professional at that. Precisely what right such a man, who has devoted his whole life to the acquisition of money at whatever cost, has to despise anyone for being a professional, I'm not quite sure, but Parker despises everyone. He doesn't even love a lord, as one might expect, because he could show the whole effete lot of them how to use their privilege and their breeding if only he had had their advantages.

I curse again several times, then shudder and slouch slope-shouldered off towards the weighing-room. I feel very tired.

I win on Gothic Rose out of sheer bloody-mindedness.

I don't know that I'd have bothered today if it hadn't been for Parker and the knowledge of what I must do on Yellow Jersey. Gothic Rose is lying fourth out of ten as we turn into the home straight. It's taken a deal of concentration just to get him this far. He's a slow beginner, so he can't lay up in the early stages. He's also a lazy jumper. Now he's hanging to the left, but I'm just not going to let him concede ... I pull the stick through and give him

61

a couple of quick ones down the near flank. There are two ahead of us and two upsides as we hack up to the second last. The horse has no desire to jump it. He'd very much prefer to run out, projecting me over it, then run off and find a nice deep clover bed somewhere. I squeeze hard and push him on and yell, 'Garn!' and Gothic Rose wakes up. It feels as though I'm picking him up and pulling him over. One way or another, we're a stride up on the other two as I pick up the reins and start to ride him out.

We're galloping through treacle now, but there's just one more plain fence and two tired nags still to go and I've made up his mind. We're going to win. Tommy Perkins' grey mount is going quite easily. The other contender, a washy bay ridden by Polly's *bête noir*, Chas Wilcox, is deeper in quicksand than we. His ears are drooping and Chas is drooping with them. He flaps about, wasting energy and making the job a lot more difficult for his horse. The art is to stay firm and still when your mount is foundering, just pushing him on. Watch me. This is how.

I take a pull to collect Gothic Rose as we approach the last, then sit down like a show-jumper, give him an almighty crack on the 'quarters at take-off point and bounce him over it. The birch crackles. I bang my jaw on his neck and get a mouthful of mane, but everything else seems all right. The washy bay goes down with a rattle and a thump. I don't give Gothic Rose time to think. I just sit down and start riding hands and heels. Tommy Perkins' creature corkscrewed over that one. We're ahead now and we've got to stay that way. If we're caught, we'll not come again.

So, yelling, kicking and shoving, I get him there with half a length to spare. The horse reels as we pass the post, but I reckon that I've worked a deal harder than he. I trot him out, though. Too many breakdowns start with cowboy-style emergency stops.

We return to a polite patter of applause. Toby Jansen, the owner, is a young stockbroker who doesn't really know which end bites or kicks. He plays it cool. We racehorse owners, you know, we're used to this sort of thing. He just says, 'Jolly good! Well done!' as though I were in the early stages of potty training. No presents there. But someone yells, 'Good on yer, Georgie!' from the crowd, and Jack claps me on the shoulder and says, 'Nice one.' Those are compliments worth having.

It's a lot colder when we all walk out to the paddock for Yellow Jersey's race. The old owner and his wife are waiting with Jack. They watch my arrival with embarrassing and undisguised admiration. I'm a jockey, a member of a glamorous fraternity, an athlete. They are pleased and proud that I am riding for them.

'Sod it,' I mutter.

I give them a quick nervous grin and look at my boots quite a lot as Jack goes through the unnecessary routine of instructions for their benefit.

It's obvious that I must take a tumble. There's no alternative. Yellow Jersey has no finishing speed, so Jack would smell a monster rat if I were to wait and come too late, which is the classic method. Getting left at the gate won't do either, not on a hot favourite. Both the horse and I are old pros. Old pros don't get left. We've got to fall.

I jump him off in front. The pace is slow, and Yellow Jersey is not afraid to get his nose cold. I'm only doing what Jack and the knowledgeable public would expect.

On the first circuit I trust to fate. Maybe the horse will meet one wrong and peck on landing, and I can throw myself in a graceful parabola over his head. Fate, unsurprisingly, doesn't reward my trust. He's running smoothly, ears pricked, as we pass the stands, and he's jumping like a studious stag. Which means, basically, that I'm going to have to risk my life, and that of the horse, for the sake of that cash.

He runs up towards the first open ditch on the back straight like a puppy runs up to its dinner. I can't see anything very attractive about it. It's five foot, two inches tall and very fat – an overall spread of seven foot or more. The horse seems to think that it's just the loveliest little obstacle he's ever seen. He can't wait to get at it. Just as his back end drops for the takeoff, I give a quick hard tug on the reins and whisper a prayer in no very lively expectation of an answer. The poor bemused animal has to put in a quick one and try again. He's right on top of the ditch when he takes off. From my position, the fence looks huge.

Only thanks to the horse's courage do we get over it at all. We plough through it, taking a lot of it with us. Yellow Jersey sprawls. His hind legs buckle, his nose hits the ground, then, incredibly, he's scrabbling to regain his footing. It's too late though. I'm already wrapped rather fetchingly around his neck. The press would call it a 'miracle recovery' if I were to regain the saddle now. There are going to be no miracles today. The horse grunts. I grunt back at him and roll forward.

Like we said, your man's a stylist.

So then I roll up into a tight ball and think of warm beds and icy champagne as the rest of the lads thunder over. One hoof strikes me a glancing blow to the shoulder and nearly rolls me over, but in general, racehorses are surefooted and you're safe as long as you stay still. I've known animals to execute routines of which Gene Kelly would be proud in order to avoid prostrate bodies in their way. Fifteen seconds later, I drag myself to my feet, dust down my breeches and curse convincingly. The rest of the field, with Yellow Jersey loose in amongst them, is approaching the next one. They rise with the usual ragged chorus of oaths and exhortations, then they're lost from sight.

I pick grass and mud from my lips. It's suddenly very cold. I shiver and duck under the rails. 'It's a funny old way to make a living ...' they'll quote me in the *Sunday Times* tomorrow. Funny peculiar, that is. They'd love it on *What's my Line?* 'And Georgie Blane's profession is – Throwing Himself Off Horses at Speed.' The ha-ha has gone out of it now.

To the casual critic, it no doubt seems that I am but a crooked, amoral, ill-educated, clapped out old drunk. This is not quite true.

First, I am not clapped out. Not entirely, anyhow. I would go so far as to say, indeed, that, on the good days at least, I am still among the four best riders in the country, which puts me well up in the world's top ten. Like many an Irish jump-jockey before me, I have the advantage that I was a horseman before I became a jockey. I learned my trade on the hunting-field and in the show-ring. I'd never claim to possess that weird gypsy magic that men like Lester Piggott or Michael Beary, for example, have possessed, the ability to strike up a rapport with any animal and, or so it seems, to talk horse. Such men can have real problems sometimes simply because horses regard them as friends and equals rather than as their masters. Michael, for example, used to give some of his rides hard races. They'd come back cut to ribbons. And afterwards, whenever he entered the yard and the horses heard his voice, they'd climb the walls of their boxes to get at him. He had betrayed them and they hated him. It would take four lads to hold them down as Michael mounted, but as soon as he was up again and crooning in their ears, they'd go sweet and kind and willing as police-horses in a heatwave.

No. What I've got is simply the means and the knowledge and the strength to make a horse work for me, to con it, coax it, coerce it or force it to give its best. I learned timing from Irish banks and finishing from Irish bumpers. Perhaps because of my experience in other disciplines, I have a reputation as a stylist, which basically means no more than that I sit into a jumping horse and use my legs to supply guidance and impulsion instead of bouncing about like a pea on a drum as most of those taught in racing stables do.

Look. Horses – my apologies here to all twelve-year-old pony club members who would like to think otherwise – horses are not exactly the intellectuals of the animal kingdom. They are, in fact, very seriously stupid. No discredit to them for that. It's just that individual intelligence never played much of a part in the evolution of the horse. It might, indeed, have been a considerable hindrance to survival. The horse depends on the pack. He is the victim of predators, not a predator himself. He has no cause to reason, only to conform and to obey. The horse which falls behind the pack or is separated from it is dead. For ninety-nine per cent of horses, therefore, happiness consists in being able to trust the leader, to obey without question or fear. If the leader is weak or fearful, the horse becomes unhappy and, quite rightly, seeks to take charge himself. That's why horses won't work well for anyone who is frightened, anyone who becomes angry and brutal. It's not the pain that they object to; it's the weakness, the panic, the loss of control.

The true horseman knows damn well that any pony – even a tiny Shetland – is stronger than he. No man can control a rogue horse by mere physical strength. But you can control a horse by confidence and cool, by judiciously applied force, by showing that you are a worthy leader. That's why the first thing I was ever taught to do with a foal was to take it into frightening and unfamiliar situations – take it into the house, show it big lorries, barking dogs, anything – just to demonstrate that I was calm and strong and would lead it safe through to the other side. Of course, the odd colt wants to take you on, assert his own right to lead. Some concede more readily than others. One of the services that I perform for friends in the summer is giving a good sorting out to mishandled or over-ambitious animals. I take a running jump – real Lone Ranger stuff – and then, as coolly as I can manage on a bucking, rearing, squealing brute, I lay about me until the would-be pack-leader has got the message: not yet, my old son. There's still someone bigger and more potent than you around here.

Well, that, I suppose, is what I'm good at, aside from the purely technical business of timing and the experience which enables me to know what horses are thinking before they think it. I con them into the belief that I'm a good and worthy boss. Horses, like I said, are very stupid.

When I came over here it seemed preordained that I should succeed. I was the boy most likely to and I did, lots.

There you are. I was surrounded by rich owners and rich owners' wives and rich owners' daughters and rich owners' drink and helicopters and cars and all that. Only thing was, I never became rich myself. It took me a long time to notice that. That's the trick. That's the way with the rich. That's how they stay that way. You or I spend money and have nothing to show for it but memories. They use money and the trappings of wealth as a lubricant – a spot here, a spot there, just to keep the engine running smoothly. And as soon as we, the cogs, get used to our function, we wear out or we are superseded and the oil is applied to a new wheel instead. Money achieves nothing in itself. It's just part of a far greater power. It gets people working for you, but true wealth never gets transferred – just taken occasionally, by those with the luck and the nerve.

I didn't know that at the time. I thought that I was really about to become rich. In reality, I was just a clown, a liveried entertainer. They let me play the game of being rich. They gave me money, but never wealth.

Look. I have a friend called Bobby Beasley. You may have heard of him. He was one of the best and bravest and most beautiful of all steeplechase riders. He comes from a great racing family. If a young Beasley doesn't win the National, they assume there's been a mix-up in the maternity ward and they call for a blood test. Bobby too was educated by Irish Jesuits. He too came over to England and did well. He too found the drink copious and the girls available. Do I have to enumerate the others who, by reason of natural talent, have recently followed the same path? Barry Brogan, Georgie Best, Johnny Lehane, Alex Higgins ... Anyhow, Bobby too drank the champagne that they gave him and played the conventional role. The drink got to him. Something had to. He took some crashing falls when smashed or hung over. Fred Winter probably saved his life by dispensing at last with his services.

After a spell trying to sell insurance in Leamington, Bobby ended up with the following daily timetable: 1100 hours: get up, stagger down to the shops, buy a bottle of Cyprus sherry and a copy of *The Sporting Life*. 1130: return to bed, drink the sherry whilst reading about his friends, pass out. 1800: get up again, shave. 1830: down to the boozer. 2300: pass out.

He had brains and guts. With the help of AA, he dragged himself back into the light. A couple of years later, he rode Captain Christy to victory at Cheltenham. I'll always remember Bobby's words to me as we leaned on the bar at Chepstow one day in my first year over here. 'You can take the boy from the bog,' he said, 'but you can't take the bog from the boy.' At the time, I thought it a maudlin old saw from a weary man. I know better now.

*   *   *

'Quite, quite brilliant,' drawls the Hon. Oliver. 'Really splendid stuff.'

'Thanks,' I snap. 'That's actually the sort of compliment I can do without. Money, please.'

We're in his room at the Coach and Horses just outside Newbury. He's sitting in an armchair just ten feet away. He has a dry Martini with a sliver of onion in it on the windowsill at his right, a long cheroot in his hand, a Davidoff box on the bedside table at his left. *Fancy Tales of Smoke,* it says in copperplate. He's taken his glasses off and he blinks pale eyelashes vulnerably over pale, pale eyes.

'You really are getting a little jumpy in your old age, Blane,' he twangs. He leans back, crosses his legs and puffs a series of smoke mushrooms at the ceiling. He stays like that, pouting upward like a nymphing trout, long after the last wisp of smoke has twisted up his nostrils. At last he shakes his head and snaps out of it. 'No, I was just saying how really impressive I thought you were. If I hadn't known better, I'd have sworn it was an accident. Lovely to watch, lovely. These young boys have none of your finesse.'

'Lucky them,' I step forward and stand over him, hand extended. 'Money, please.'

'We have another one for you, by the way.' He holds a fat brown envelope above my palm. 'Lots and lots of money.'

I grab the envelope and shove it with some difficulty into my breast pocket. 'Yeah, well, I don't want it, thanks.' I always say things like that, just as a bitch always yaps and spins and puts her ears back and skitters away from a dog – and always comes back for more. The dog's not much discouraged. Nor is Parker.

'Oh, I think you will,' he says, 'when you hear about it.'

'No, there've been too many. People start to notice, then I'm no darned good to you or to anyone any more.'

'Don't worry, dear boy, don't worry. After this one, you won't be needing another job for years. There's sixty grand in it for you.'

I gulp a lot of air. My hand reaches of its own accord for the chair behind me. Downstairs, strings start sawing at *Good King Wenceslas.* 'Sixteen?' I stammer.

'Sixty.'

'Six-Jesus!' My mind is whirring like a fruit machine. Everything's coming up bell-fruit and daffodils. Clunk. There's Conor's and Joanna's education sorted out. Clunk. The house, the car, even the deposit on a small farm or training establishment in County Tipperary. Sixty thousand. Beep beep. Clunk. Claire's happy, secure, admiring, astonished smile. 'What ...' I start, then have to clear my throat. 'Er, what the hell is it?'

'Vantage,' he says quietly, and sips his Martini. 'In the King George VI.'

'No.' The word has come out before I've thought. It comes out quietly, but very decisively. It shocks me slightly, like a freakishly brilliant child, but, on reflection, I'm quite proud of it. A poor thing, but mine own. 'No, no, no, no, no,' I say, just in case there should be any misunderstanding, 'sorry, no.'

'Sixty grand, Blane.'

'Yeah, I know, but no.'

'Oh? And why not, mmm?'

'Because he's the best novice I've ever ridden and he loves his business and if I did that to him, it would shatter his trust and his will to win and his confidence and no.'

'So why not sing me *Galway Bay,* Blane,' Parker's voice is gloved in velvet now, 'whilst we're in this sentimental mood, I mean? You are a man, aren't you, mmm? And you have a wife and children, no? And this – this Vantage – he is a horse. And we are offering you sixty thousand pounds for this horse to have a slightly easy race. That is all. Now.'

'You don't know shit about it,' I spit at him. I walk over to the window. Down there in the car park three children bicker happily as they climb from a Rover. A little girl with a bang of bright gold hair beneath her duffel-coat hood trots to catch up with the fat au pair girl and to grasp her hand. Mug punters. 'There's only one way he'll have "an easy race", as you put it, and that's with me leaning back over his 'quarters and tugging hard all the way. That horse would win with – with you on his back. He finds his own way.'

'So just topple a little,' says Parker as though explaining something to a child for the twentieth time. 'Jockeys do, you know. You're rather good at it, as a matter of fact.'

'No,' I turn. 'No, Parker, I'll not do it and there's an end on it. Any other horse, maybe. I'm hard up, I won't deny it, and I can't go on for ever. But not that one. It would be rewriting the history books. I've waited for this feller all my life.'

'Cue violins,' the Hon. Oliver smiles sweetly. He tips ash delicately from his cheroot into the ashtray, then, 'There are, after all, other, less edifying means to the same end ...'

I get an attack of the raging heroics at that. In three strides I'm on top of Parker. I put my hands on the arms of his chair and push my face up close. 'You even think about touching that horse – you just think about it and I'll beat you into a pulp and feed it to the pigs, if they'll have it. I swear it. Do you understand me, you jumped-up, dirty, little parvenu?'

That gets to him. Something flickers through his eyes. They narrow and film over. His right hand grasps my wrist. 'Get your filthy, bogtrotter hands off me,' he spits the words out like grape pips. Soft puffs of peppermint and tobacco touch my lips. 'Now, or you will die. And unlike you, I do not deal in empty, impotent threats. And kindly remember, if we can't stop the horse, we can always stop the jockey, can't we, Blane, mm? Your replacement would be rather cheaper, too ...'

My breathing is suddenly quick and heavy. My cheeks prickle. I feel faintly foolish. 'All right,' I release him and dust off my hands, 'you do what you like, but just remember, I'll not do it. Tell your good masters that, would you? Anything but that. And threats don't bother me, OK?'

'Tough boy,' he lovingly smooths his lapels. He wears a large black agate signet ring on his left little finger.

'Yeah, well,' I shrug, 'I risk being beat up as bad as your boys can manage six, seven times a day. Why should I worry?'

'Because,' Parker tells my back, 'there are always some things you haven't been through.'

Blood leaves the cheeks as quickly as it can mount to them. All that heat that was there a minute ago is suddenly gone. It feels as though someone is slowly pulling away the skin over my cheeks, my neck, my chest. It's very cold without it. Strangely, though, my arms stick to my sides. Something trickles down my spine. I find it difficult to walk straight to the door. Only once I've got there and opened it, only once I'm sure that I can make an exit without stumbling do I turn and sniff and say, 'Yeah, well,' again. It's the best that I can contrive in the way of defiance.

I trot down the red-carpeted staircase, past the Christmas tree, through the empty hotel lobby. There's trotting troika music from the bar behind me, guffaws and noisy gossip. What Parker says is true, of course. With a £60,000 budget, he can well afford to nobble the Ripper without my compliance. It would be riskier, of course, but he can do it. He can also quite seriously nobble me, as a measure both pragmatic and punitive, at a cost of two or three grand, buy off Paul Martin, the stable's second rider – poor Paul has never smelled or seen ten grand in a career as long as mine – and still have some loose change to jingle.

'Well, let him try.' I thud the steering wheel and turn the key. The door slams. 'Let him bloody well try.'

I get the engine to growl a bit in sympathy and to execute an exemplary emergency stop as I emerge from the car park onto the dual carriageway. A Porsche flashes by, making a sound like a zip. I draw out more soberly. After a few miles, the anger has died in me. Fear is waiting to take its place. Not just physical fear, the fear of pain – 'though I suffer from that as much as anyone. But pain has limits and I have explored them extensively. No. I am afraid above all of yielding control to others, of being taken over and coldly destroyed without the chance to fight back. I am afraid above all of fear itself.

All in all, I wouldn't offer long odds on my remaining heroic for long.

No one's home when I get back. I'd feel resentful if it weren't for the chronic terror that I should know where everyone is; gym-night, perhaps, or a parents' meeting, a party. Something like that.

The kitchen striplights blink and buzz at me. I blink back. There's no message on the memo board. Nothing that you could call a message. Just old postcards of France and Happy Valley and Conor's latest letter from prep-school and a strange scrawled list in purple and green felt-tip:

> Coffee
> Bog paper
> BRAHMS 2Bb Serkin/Solti
> Pickling spice
> Oil tank
> Dolcelatte
> Damn

I pour a modest slug of Scotch and snap off the lights again. The hall is lit only by the soft shimmering glow of the Christmas tree lights. I potter into the office like an old man. It's very cold, and the thought of sixty grand and that big black slab of agate makes it a lot colder. There's a leather jacket on the back of the chair. I put it on, flick on the desk spotlight and sit down in the yellow mantle of light. I sip. A nice tit-tautening shudder shakes me from head to hip. That's the fun of drinking over for tonight.

Bills now. I fish them from the bin, the chequebook from the drawer and I start writing. In five minutes, I sign away £1,374.56. The cheques go into suitable envelopes. I leave the envelopes unsealed.

Duty done. I lean back and switch on the wireless and the Ansafone. The wireless is one of those big wooden Bush things with

Allouis and Hilversum and BBC 3rd written on it. It takes two minutes to warm up, and then, joy of joys, it's *Down Your Way*. Ghosts reside in that wireless, forever broadcasting in their dinner jackets in 1936.

The lifeboat coxswain selects *For Those in Peril On the Sea*, which is as it should be, and the first caller on the Ansafone is a girl with an adenoidal Midlands drone. She'd loik a job in rycing, she says. She got my name and number from someone called Clement whom I've never heard of. Don't know what she thinks I can do. I wouldn't moind a job in rycing myself.

Another woman rings, does some breathing, says, 'Um ...' then, 'Oh, damn and blast!' and rings off. I'm not sure, but it sounds like Bob's wife, Susan. I'll call her later.

Then as Brian Johnston wishes goodbye to the charming and hospitable little seaside town of Padstow,

'Errrrrr ....'

I grin as soon as I hear it. Your main man.

'Er, yeah,' Bob drones. 'Hello, Georgie. Bob. What the hell you want to tell me your number for on that damned message thing? I just rang it, didn't I? Brain's getting soft. Listen, mate. I'm doin' a sort of show thing, guest in a television, this afternoon. Can you – d'ye think you could get up some time? CBO theatre, I'll be here till, I dunno, half-eight, nine? Thought perhaps we could have a jar or two, some dinner or something after, you know. Please – yeah, please try to make it, will you? I really could do to see you. Few problems. Yeah, well, bye. Bye.'

The machine switches itself off. I look at my watch. Twenty-five to seven. I could make it by eight, eight-thirty. I haven't seen Bob since I drove the kids down to Cornwall in August. 'Yes, OK, my old son.' The sound of my voice makes me jump. 'I'll do it. Why not? Could do with a night on the town ...'

It takes me all of five minutes to cajole the CBO theatre stage door number from directory enquiries, another ten minutes – or so it seems – before at last I get through to Bob.

'Speak to me,' he snaps.

'Bob.'

'Hi. G.'

'Yeah. Listen, reckon I can make it tonight. I leave now, be with you in, what? Hour and a half? 'Pends on the traffic.'

'Great. Sure. Thanks, Georgie.'

'Problems, hey?'

'Yeah. Big bad variety.'

'So give me some idea. Know whether to bring a gun or a bottle.'

'Both,' he laughs faintly, 'both. It's Susan.'

'Not ill?'

'No. Well ... No. Gone.'

'What?'

'Buggered off. 'S'morning. Got a man.' His voice is flat, expressive only by its lack of evident emotion. He's reverted to plain chant.

'Bloody hell, Bob,' I burble. 'Gotta be some mistake.' The gravity of other people's dramas is always inconceivable at the first. Bob's sorrow gives him centre stage. I'm trying, almost instinctively, to retain my position there by minimising it.

'No mistake, Georgie. Look,' he sniffs, 'I've got to be off. Don't know my stuff. See you. OK?'

'Yup. OK. I'm on my way.'

I leave the cheques and cash to cover them on the kitchen table. 'Bills paid,' I scribble on a sheet of Joanna's Snoopy paper, 'and here's a bit extra for Christmas presents or summat. I've had to bolt up to London. Bob's in some sort of trouble. See you later. All love, G.'

I count out another twenty twenties, think better of it, and take three back.

I draw a new bottle of Bushmills from the winerack. I pull on my gloves, set the burglar alarm and stroll out onto the drive. It's a cold starry night. Black clouds shift across the moon. I whistle some tuneless tune to the rhythm of my feet as they crunch in the wet gravel.

'Christ!' My stomach contracts and a huge gout of cold air jolts into my lungs. My body jackknifes and I crouch, panting, behind the car. I lick rubber dry lips. There's someone out there in the darkness, not thirty yards away. I heard a breath.

It's a split second only before I check reflex with reason. My heart starts to beat again, and it's making up for lost time. I straighten and sigh. The someone out there sighs back. He also snorts as though he found the whole thing very amusing. It's Joanna's old cob, Benbow.

I pinch the bridge of my nose and practise deep pranayam breathing for a while as the fluttering in my gut dies down. Then I hiss, 'Shit,' brush gravel from my knee and climb into the car.

I look up at the stars as though showering in their cold light, then back, rather wistfully, at the long black mass of the house. I slam the door. The wheels kick up a wake of gravel.

Four minutes later, I pass Claire and Joanna in the Renault. My foot hits the brake-pedal, then rises again. There's no point. I'm more popular in my absence.

72

The CBO theatre looks like a cross-section of honeycomb set on a low white table. There are pink lights along the tabletop. I lock the car and shoulder the bottle and stroll over towards them. Laughter from within sounds like the rasp of the needle on a Caruso record.

At the foot of the steps, I stop and look up and say something like 'Sheesh!' The lights say, 'TONIGHT, KIKI TABOR, GUEST STARS BURMESE DAYS BOBBY BLANE FRAN CARTER'. It's a hell of a haul from Ballymena and a showband called the Lilywhite Boys.

I swagger through the plate-glass doors. Swaggering, like skipping, does wonders for the soul. Mine, at present, needs all the help that it can get.

It's very bright in here. There's a clogged burst of laughter as I enter, a sudden splash of brass blasts. Everything echoes like in a public swimming-pool.

'Yes, can I help you, sah?'

I turn. A commissionaire with a face like a padlock sidesteps out from behind his horseshoe desk. His hat lies on the desktop, but he's still wearing enough scrambled egg to outshine a Ruritanian field-marshal. 'Oh. Yep. I'm Georgie Blane. My brother's working here this evening.'

'Yes, yes indeed, sah.' He is suddenly avuncular. I'm used to this. 'Of course. We were told to expect you. He's on stage at the moment, actually, sir, but I was instructed to direct you to his dressing-room.'

'Thanks. Yes.'

'So,' he comes up close up behind me and points over my shoulder with a white-gloved hand, 'it's through that door there, sir, straight down the corridor, then left at the door marked *Private* just below the stage, all right? Down some steps to your – right, yes, then it's first, second, third on your right, sir.'

'Got it.' I shoulder the bottle again and set off at the march.

'Umm, bad luck today, sir.'

I grin back over my shoulder. 'Yeah, well. Thanks. 'S the way it goes.'

'I was on Ice Nine in the Gold Cup, sir. One of the best days in my life.'

'Glad you did well. Constant mystery to me, you know. Seem to have made or lost fortunes for half the world and its wife. Never made one myself somehow. Still.'

He chuckles politely. I count under my breath, 'Five, four, three two . . .' as I click across the foyer and open the door. On 'Blast off!' he clears his throat.

'Er, wouldn't have a tip for us, would you, sah?'

I shrug. 'Never ask a jockey for tips. Best tip you'll ever get. Still, try Glendower at Towcester on Monday. Each way. If there's a bit of cut in the ground, he'll be there or thereabouts.'

'Right, sir,' he affords me a conspiratorial wink. 'I'll do that. Thank you very much, sir.'

I nod and step through into a dark tunnel. The darkness is brown not black. The door marked *Private* is down on my left, but at the top of the stairs on my right, there's a half-open door through which Bob's words and every thump on the stage come very loud. I tiptoe up the steps.

I'm in the wings. Ahead, on dusty bleached boards, Bob stoops and crouches, huge hands painting pictures in the smoky pink and purple air.

Look.

It's that loping, stooping, bouncing gait that first you notice about the man. He's very thin and his legs are very long. He wears a sloppy grey sweater and brand new blue jeans. Both arms are bent at hip level. Both fists are clenched. His steps are directionless and very rapid. They must be a nightmare for the men behind the cameras. His head is pushed forward, his bottom backward. He bobs continually from the waist.

He's like a man that just got up from the electric chair. Every muscle seems to strain and tremble against another.

Then his nose. It has to be the nose next. It's a great bony beak which sets out straight and broad, is interrupted a third of the way down by a large ridge, then curves inward and outward again to end in a bobble. It is a unique, instantly recognisable conk, an Olympic Downhill piste for fleas.

The rest of the face is long and thin and always very pale. Deep grooves run from his nose to his lip, from cheekbone to jaw. His hair is colourless, thin and scruffy. He is just thirty-eight.

'... mind,' he is saying, 'salvation has a price. Oh, yes. Lord, man, but you should've seen the way we were brought up. You lot – the damned – you have it easy. At school, for example, in Ireland. The dances, where the holy fathers wander around making sure there's a clear six inches between you and the girl. Straight up! Promise you! I never did understand that. Why six inches? Why not three? Why not a foot? Never could work that out. Oh, yeah, and wearing knickers in the bath. That's another beauty. ''S'true! On my life!

Good Catholic boys wear their swimming cozzies in the bath so as God can't see their shame! Hell, I mean, even Superman has x-ray vision, but a pair of Y-fronts is sufficient to thwart the Supreme Being!'

As he says, "S'true. On my life,' a girl with tight dark curls stands just five yards ahead of me. She leans on a rope, watching. She wears a little black waistcoat, a man's white shirt rolled up to the elbows, and very tight faded jeans. I tiptoe further in.

She turns, looks up at me, smiles. 'Hi,' she whispers.

'Hi.'

'You meant to be here?' She is pretty. She has large black eyebrows and wide brown eyes and a large mouth which shows a nice little gleam of white at the centre.

'Shouldn't think so,' I tell her. 'I'm his brother.'

'Oh. Oh, great.' She turns back to the stage with a sort of implied shrug. 'He's been in a bit of a tiswas, I'm afraid.'

'Yeah. I gathered.'

'He's doing OK, though.'

'Winging it. He'll still be OK. He's a pro. So when's he come off?'

'Should be – well – shouldn't be more 'n another – what? – five minutes? He doesn't exactly stick to his script. Hard to know. He'll need a lot of editing. That's OK.'

'Oh,' I say. 'Good.'

'. . . course all Catholic girls are virgins. Dunno what you're laughing about. It's true. All Catholic girls are virgins almost all of the time. Especially our mothers. My mother, now, she comes home and she says to her ma, "Ma," she says, "I think as I'm pregnant." And her ma says, "Are you sure it's yours, dear?" No, look. Catholic girls don't sin; they just get sinned with. My wife, now, my wife she's a good pure girl from down Mullingar, went to a convent and all that. Just before the wedding, she says to me, she says, "Bobby, should I wear white for the wedding?" So I tell her. "Well, the tradition is, if you're a virgin, you wear white, and if you're not, well then, you wear blue." So the big day comes, they're playing the wedding march, and I turn round and I look at her, and there she is all blushing and blooming and beautiful and decked out in this long white dress . . . with little blue spots here, here, here . . .'

'Seems to be going down all right,' I murmur.

'Yeah,' says the girl, 'but he's sort of nasty sometimes. Should've heard him earlier.'

'So what happened?'

75

'I dunno. Some gag about an Irish bloke, comes in and finds his wife humping away with her lover. So he pulls out a gun and puts it to his own head. And his wife starts laughing at him, and this Irish guy ...'

'This Irish guy,' I supply, 'says, "Don't laugh, you're next."'

''S'right. And your brother seems to – I don't know – to get lost. Doesn't seem to know where he is. Just stands there blinking at the audience and repeating, "Don't laugh, you're next. Don't laugh, you're next. Don't laugh, you're next." And then he sort of shouts it. He had to come off for a minute or two. I dunno. Maybe he's high on something. Lot of 'em are. Hey?'

'No.'

'Well, maybe it was just a brainstorm, forgot his next gag or something. But it was – it was weird.'

I nod for a while, which is a fruitless exercise. 'Ah, that's just Bob,' I tell her. 'Great moralist, our Bob.' Her hair touches my lips. She does not move away. Used to be a Jesuit seminarist, you know.'

'Heard that. That for real, then?'

'Yup, That's for real.'

'And you're a jockey, right?'

'Uh huh.'

'Hmm.' She turns. Her eyes are flawed and milky amethysts in the light from off the stage. 'Interesting.'

'Suppose so. If you call getting cold, wet and muddy six times a day interesting.'

'Well, you obviously do,' she hums. She is unimpressed by everything. Particularly apology.

'True, O wise one, true.' I flash my expensively crowned teeth. 'Well, I'd best be getting down to the dressing-room, I suppose. You going to be busy all evening?'

'Probably, yes. Why?'

'Get a free moment, come down, have a drink.'

'Don't know. Might.' She too smiles, just a little. 'See how it goes.'

'Right. Great. OK. See you later.'

It's a habit, that's all.

Bob's dressing-room is much cleaner and slicker than others that I've seen in the clubs and university theatres that are his usual stamping-grounds. The furniture, however, is much the same.

Your man marks his territory. There's the granary cob and the Stilton on the table, the bottle of Black Bush and the papers –

Times, Mirror, Private Eye and *Sporting Life*. I sit in one of the blue-grey moulded plastic chairs and pluck the photographs from the mirror-frame.

There's a very stark black and white portrait of Susan with long flat blonde hair looking characteristically and fashionably bored but showing her dimples, and a very dramatic Gerry Cranham number of me going over Becher's on Secret State. I'm looking more terrified than I remember feeling.

It's cold. I kick the tit on the convector heater. It starts to purr and rub itself up against my trouser-cuff. An intercom fizzes and farts in the corner. Bob is singing an old favourite, *An Oxford Love Song*.

> Though I may lack *savoir faire*
> I have lately been aware
> Of a subcutaneous tingle
> And an urge to intermingle
> Limbs with you ...

It's one of the first songs that he wrote when he came over here. It comes off the second album, *Hero Dust*. It's more suitable for television – even on the late night Kiki Tabor show – than most of his material, which is either sombre, acerbic or filthy. Television producers have taken a liking to him recently. He's risqué, has a youthful following and an ethnic accent, but is regarded, it seems, as essentially safe.

They wouldn't have thought of him as safe ten years ago.

Bob started writing doggerel when he started drinking. He must have been eighteen or so when, presumably after an enthusiastic experiment with gin and lime or something, he shoved this well-nigh illegible minor classic beneath my bedroom door.

THE CAT SAT ...
Yes. But.
Wast a plush and purring Persian
Or other of that ilk?
And did he make a feline beeline
For a carpet spun of silk?
Or wast a meagre, mangey moggy
Sat gingerly upon a proggy?

77

It was, in fact, the latter
(for I observed the matter);
A tabby ratter, after ratting
Sat on tatty tatting matting.

Yes. Well. Fish gotta swim and birds, in general, show an inclination to fly.

What would you?

Anything, anyhow, will do just now. Anything but think of Vantage and of that moist badger-dropping, Parker.

Oh, I know that I'll hook the poor beast. I know that I must. I just don't want to think about it until the very last minute. That way it won't hurt so much.

Have you ever seen a child hiding by covering his own eyes?

That's me all over.

The door opens behind me, slams shut, rattles, shuts again.

'Hey! Hi! Georgie, my old son!' his hand clasps my shoulder before I can get up. 'Georgie, hey, great!' I look up at him in the mirror. His grin draws a big diamond on his face. He looks tired. He turns quickly away from my gaze. 'Jaysus, yup. Glad you could make it.' He turns to the table, unscrews the bottle-top, gulps and makes a noise like an astronaut's sigh. 'There now. D'ye get some of that pap, then? Thought I'd forgotten that poor foolish Irish stuff. Comes back though. Yup. Just shove my fingers down my throat and – it – all – comes – back.' He whistles and perches on the corner of the table. Still he does not look at me.

'Seems to be going down all right,' I shrug, 'the bit I saw, any road.'

'Yeah, yeah,' he swats away reassurance, 'good house. Have to go a bit easy on 'em, you know, but.'

'OK, Bob,' I turn, put the glass down and push it across the table. I slap my thighs and stand. 'OK, so you're into being a big star. So I'll tell you what. Whyn't I go down the pub and wait till you come back to earth, hmm? Or are you going to talk to me?'

'Yeah, well. Haven't got long.' He stands upright again, bows eagerly three times and sweeps past me to sit in the chair which I've just left. He makes a quick three bump turn and then, with his back to me, taps out a cigarette. He bums it, lights it with a quick click and hiss, and concentrates on smoothing the make-up at his right eyebrow. I can see just half of his face in the mirror. The cigarette waggles on his lower lip as he mumbles, 'Yeah, well, OK. Not really – there's not really that much to say. She's gone. That's all.'

Very casual. Just a little tremor as he gulps up the last word with a mouthful of smoke.

'When? Why?'

'When?' he exhales two long jets of smoke which break up on the mirror. 'This morning. Left, I mean, officially. Been going on for months – six, nine, Christ knows.'

'Hold it, Bob. You're jumping ahead of yourself. She leave or did you push?'

'I pushed,' he says sullenly, 'least . . . bit of both. She knew . . . I mean, she knew she couldn't stay. A policeman,' he gives a little half laugh. 'Would you fucking believe it, mate? A lawman. What effing law does he represent, I'd like to know? Eh? What sort of law where basic social contracts, fundamental . . .?' His mouth stretches in a broad rictus. He shakes his head fast. 'Blessed is he who comes in the name of the law, hey?'

'Don't, Bob, don't,' I sigh. 'Jeez. I'm sorry. I really am. But listen. You sure . . .? I mean, of course it's serious . . . I don't mean . . . But are you sure that it's for good? I mean, she . . . I dunno.' After this eloquent exposition of the Case As I See It, I dry up somewhat. Bob sits still, frowning through the smoke. He's making me sweat.

I try again. 'Look, what I'm trying to say is, you're a pretty impossible man, Bob, and you know it. So things go wrong and there are rifts, separations and that, but she – you know that she loves you, don't you? She'll be back.'

His shoulders hunch. His head sags. 'Shit, G., I could never have her back. You know that. She's gone. She's dead. She's gone to the bleeding underworld.'

'Ah, come on, man,' I rap, 'don't be childish.'

'I'm not,' he tells his solar plexus, 'I'm not being childish.' He sighs, blinks up at the ceiling, then makes that three bump turn again. He leans back to retrieve his glass, always keeping his eyes averted from me. He gulps whiskey and slumps forward so that I'm looking at the thin, stitched white line of his parting. We wait a full minute like that until the purr of the heater acquires a rhythm in my ears.

At last he looks up and his pale grey eyes are wide and very wet. 'They just don't understand, Georgie. The total destructiveness of it. Whatever the . . . It's death, Georgie boy. It's one of the very few irrevocable and so – and so unforgivable things you can do. Like a killing, you know? It's changed her state beyond remedy or recall. They just don't realise, with their fine liberal theories, they just don't realise what violence they do. Georgie. You know, I really don't know how I can live without her – what she used to be – but

79

I sure as hell couldn't stay five minutes with what she's become. The idea – the stench of the idea.'

'Yeah, sure,' I soothe, 'sure, but in time, you know ... I mean, you can't possibly see why it happened? You couldn't come to terms with it? I mean ...'

'Don't be fucking stupid,' he snarls.

'I'm only trying to think of – I don't know – solutions.'

'There are no solutions, man, and what solutions could there be in the Lord's name? She's walking around with this vile, stinking ... What solution would you? A bath in hydrochloric? A total transfusion? I can never so much as look at her again without ...' The powder pink lining of his lip gleams above his teeth. 'I'm going to ...' he stands. He wipes his eyes with the length of his sleeve. Again he blinks up at the light. 'God, I don't know,' he keens. 'Sometimes I'd like to ...'

His fingers tighten on the glass until the knuckles seem old ivory. He reaches for the bottle and tips it up. 'It's – it's like grief, G., that's the thing of it. It touches everything, makes everything poignant or squalid. Thing is, with grief, it's important that you put the carcase somewhere. Bury it, cremate it, but put it somewhere, right? Burial is a kind of full stop, and people who lose their loved ones at sea or something, they never have that full stop. It's an open-ended pain. Worse, it's an open-ended worry, and worry just eats up the soul. It's like that, this business, for the rest of my days, she goes on somewhere, and I'm going to be tormented by worry and pain and doubt and disgust and there can be no relief, never, never, *never*, and murder seems kind of logical. It's an end, a full stop to all the fantasies and fears, you know?'

'Yeah, I know right enough,' I nod, 'but you wouldn't ... I mean, that's just sort of ... You know, like in a play. How d'ye get rid of the hero and the villain, how d'ye sort out your plot? Have a shoot-out. Bump somebody off. But you're not so dumb as to do anything like that, are you?'

'Shit,' he slumps down again. 'I dunno. I mean, no. I'm not going to go out with a blade or something, or anything, but, Christ Jesus, it seems – it seems the only rational end, the only creative ... and the pain, Georgie, the impotence! You just – can't imagine the *pain!*' His clenched fist trembles. His mouth stretches wide.

And then a darling little man with sandy hair comes dancing in to tell Bob that he's marvellous and me that he's thrilled to meet me. He summons Bob back on stage for a duet with the good Ms Tabor, because this is one of your recorded almost-live type shows where the seams all show.

So I potter off down the pub along the road where I try to drink ale slowly and reflect on Bob's problems and try not to reflect on mine.

The trouble with Bob, I decide, is that he, who has always laughed at the *laissez-faire*, theoretical morality of this adopted land, had never really understood its implications. The boy from the bog is as bewildered and shocked and hurt as the Moor amidst the intrigues of Venice.

An innocent abroad.

And later, walking back to my car in the lamplight, he's really letting go. 'Oh, Jesus, man, I can't take it,' he yaps suddenly. He doubles up. Then he's up again, pacing, striking his left palm with his fist.

'Bob ...' I warn. It's like watching a little boy holding his breath.

'... bucking and sighing and panting over her lips, lips. Stubble rasp on smooth skin then and Jesus! Oh, Jaysus,' he sobs. He leans his head against the damp brick wall. 'I'm burning up, Georgie. I – kissing – I – really – don't think – I can take it.'

'Ah, for God's sake, man,' I tell him. 'You're spritzing, that's all; winding yourself up with images that come only from words. Sure, you can imagine that's happening, and you'll always be thinking the worst. I could do the same before a day's riding – imagine, I mean – and if I did, I couldn't ride one side of a fucking seaside donkey 'cos I'd be thinking fractured skull and crushed spines and brains spilling on the turf and that. No!' I spin round and bark at him. '*You* wait, Bob. Just shut up for one moment, would you? Think about it. I don't go fracturing my skull that often and Susan on my oath doesn't spend every minute of the day humping. Fact, I reckon she's unlikely to be doing much of that sort of thing for some time. She's not enjoying the situation either, Bob. She's probably sat there all cold inside, her stomach churning, worrying about you and what she's done. But oh no. You'd rather she was permanently on the job. That fit in with what you know of your wife, does it? Does it?'

It is dark here and his face is smoke, but I can hear his heavy breathing, see his shoulders shifting. For a moment, I think that he might be fool enough to take a swing at me.

Then the shoulders droop. A car speeds by with the noise of an angry cat. The lights for a second show Bob's face. In Dublin there's a crypt where the air preserves carrion, and there's a holy Crusader down there whose hand you can shake if you want to back a winner.

81

Bob's face is still and gaunt as the holy Crusader's. His eyes are closed. The corners of his lips sag. His face recedes into darkness. He swings round and rests his head on his forearm against the wall.

'Look, Bob, I'm sorry.' I lay my hand lightly on his right shoulder. 'But you wouldn't indulge yourself like that with anyone but me, and no one but me'd tell you to leave it out. There's just no point, you know?'

I feel his head nod twice. There is moisture on the back of my hand.

'I really am sorry. I know what it's like. Something, anyhow. Tell you what, whyn't you come home with me? Get things in proportion a bit.'

He shakes his head and sniffs deeply and deliberately. 'Can't,' he mumbles, 'I'm playing the Battery midnight.'

'Jays, man, take it easy, would you? How about Christmas? Any plans?'

Again he shakes his head. ''N't be very good company 'm afraid.'

'Ah, bollocks, man,' I swallow. 'We'll expect you. Give us a bell. We'll arrange it.'

''Kay.'

We walk across the road to the car park in one of those foot-dragging silences in which words would be like farts at a funeral. Bob is a sombre figure – almost entirely tubular – in his long tweed Ulster. I unlock the car and open the door. I turn. His face is streaked with tears.

'Bob,' I say.

He resists for a moment, then suddenly tweed rasps against my cheek and his rough face is warm and wet against my temple and his right arm holds me so tight that it shakes. 'Oh, sod it, G.,' he says with a little laugh.

'You'll be all right, Bob,' I croak. 'Just take it easy. Be patient. Get to bed in good time, that sort of thing. Ease up on the booze.'

'Yeah,' he stands back, blinking, 'yeah, I will. Thanks, G., thanks for coming. I'm sorry.'

'Don't be a prat.' I climb into the car. My voice wavers a bit. I find it difficult to complete a full sentence. 'Let's be seeing you. Soon.'

'Sure,' Bob waves absently, 'sure. You will. Promise. Go on. Bugger off.'

He grins and turns away. When I drive out onto the street, he's already a hundred yards away, a thin dark cylinder, no more.

It makes me sad that he should have to be seen like that. Believe it or not, Bob really is a charming, complex, funny man, frequently exasperating, always exhausting, a great companion provided that you have nothing else to do.

And yes, OK, he's childlike. Like a child, he demands attention and affection. Like a child, he fears rejection. Like a child, he loves absurdly. But his charm too is childlike, his sense of fun, the disturbing clarity and simplicity of his vision. Oh. I can see why Susan would leave him. Matter of fact, I can't see how she stayed with him for seven years. He's aggressive, argumentative and generous to a grave fault. He'll give you a present if it makes you smile, but he'll not pay the bills. By the same token, he'll shower a stranger with affection and gifts while totally ignoring the people whom in fact he loves best. He's also a manic depressive and a drunk.

Hardly the sort of rooster that gets the hens clucking and knitting egg-cosies. But we've been through it all, Bob and I, and you'll just have to take my word for it that your man can make the sun come out with one smile.

Listen.

Our da was a GP in Dunboyne, just north of Dublin, until he retired seven years ago. Never really retired, of course, but he'd only treat old patients. And their children. And their friends. And their friends' children. A darned good GP he was too, by all accounts, as ready to pass a patient on to a psychoanalyst as to deliver a stern lecture on the virtues of self-mastery. He was short and round and cheerful and he always wore a black waistcoat and a fob watch. He had a hell of a twinkle and a fund of stories and limericks and songs. He died three years ago.

Our mother came from a 'good' family from Co. Cork. 'Good' in this context means there were a lot of English corpuscles in her blood. Her father, in fact, was an English admiral. She killed him by her own soft-heartedness, which may account for some of her later problems and her ambivalent guilt feelings. She never really knew whether she was a tender, sensitive female or whether she regarded tenderness and sensitivity as unforgivable weaknesses. I'm told she had Nazi sympathies until 1940. Figures.

What happened was this. Funny story, really. My grand-dad was fattening a turkey for Christmas. Come the time for this bloody great bird to be executed, my mother, then just six or seven years old, kicked up an almighty fuss. The sweet little gobble-wobble turkey-wurkey was her friend. Daddy couldn't be so mean as to chop its head off. Well, Daddy was a sentimental old sod and he didn't want to upset his little Maggie, so off he went down the pub to ask his mates how to dispatch the poor beast without bloodshed or evident violence.

'Simple,' says one of the lads. 'You force a large scoop of brandy down your bird's throat, then chase it like the clappers till it has a heart attack and drops down dead.'

So grand-dad did just that. Poured the booze down the bird's gullet then flapped his arms and yelled at it and chased it round the garden at a spirited canter. Trouble was, the bird showed no inclination to die. It made good speed, if teetering a bit. It even turned on him occasionally with an aggressive glint in its bleary, beady eye. Round and round the lawn they went, and every so often the good admiral has to stop to restore his strength with a snort of the brandy he left on the windowsill.

Fifteen minutes and a brisk six furlongs later, the rat-arsed turkey was still going gobble gobble gobble and doing a little victory dance like a ululating Comanche, and my puce grand-dad was gurgling his last on the lawn.

She was OK generally, my mum, till she got older and got worried about it and started taking pills and then she went peculiar because her body wasn't designed to operate on that sort of high octane fuel. Her brain in particular started to malfunction, so she'd fight with someone. Sometimes that someone was me. Usually, perhaps because I was a cocky little man and scared her, it was Bob. I was eleven, twelve at the time. Bob was thirteen or fourteen. So she'd scream and grit her teeth and shake all over and snarl and make claws of her hands and scratch at the air around my face and the tears would dribble out like juice from a lemon and I'd feel frightened and embarrassed. I'd retire into a cold little shell of contempt – contempt for a member of my clan who was weak, contempt for an ideal that had betrayed me. She smelled and sounded as animal as I in my secret indulgences amongst the damp leaves in the woods.

As for Bob, he had no such shell to protect him. These scenes hurt him very much. He did not have friends amongst boys of his own age and depended upon a mother's love far more than I. He spent many hours crying alone in his room, uncomprehending. Where I had scorn, he had compassion, and compassion hurts. That, I suppose, was when I started to feel responsible for Bob and to hate his enemies. I'm told that one day I flew at our mother, fists flying, while Bob sat curled up and weeping hopelessly in the corner. 'Leave him alone!' I shrilled. 'Leave him alone, you witch!'

Once, too, right at the beginning of all this, when I was only thirteen, I suppose, I yelled in her face, 'Go and fetch my ma! I want my ma! She'll stop you all right!' which was kind of cruelly astute for a plump little brat. She shrieked like an air-raid siren and shut me in the broom cupboard. Really. Then she went out. When she got back it was night and she was full of cooing maternal affection and concern only she couldn't remember where she'd put me. Thought I'd been kidnapped. I just stayed mum there in the darkness, hugging my cruel satisfaction to myself. I let her cry. That's called growing up or, more precisely, becoming a man.

She had curly yellow hair down to her shoulders and a long horse-face. She called it a horse-face because of the large features. She was proud of her horse-face. Attractive, I think. Everyone says so.

She wasn't getting funny pills from my father. She was getting them from another doctor, name of Gilbert Merton Bryant, who just happened to be our dad's junior partner. Bastard wanted to get into her knickers, I suppose, or maybe just to hurt the old man. He succeeded in the second aim. God knows how he fared as to the first. She wouldn't have noticed by the time he'd finished with her.

Dad cottoned on in the end. Took him time because it had never crossed his mind. Someone had walked into his surgery looking and behaving like that, he'd've sussed it straight off, but not his Maggie. Still, he worked it out in the end. He couldn't have Gilbert Merton Bryant struck off, of course, because of the publicity. He could not have stood the shame to his wife, his family. So he behaved typically. He horsewhipped your man in the surgery waiting-room. Literally. He took this bloody great lungeing whip and thrashed Gilbert Merton into Stroganoff-size strips. He then kicked him down the front steps and made a few telephone calls en-suring that Bryant's professional career, in the British Isles at least, was finished.

Funny thing about Bryant. He couldn't find a practise here, so he joined the Red Cross. They sent him to Rhodesia. One day some black guerrillas came along and chopped him and nine members of the hospital staff into very small pieces. There's a ward named after him in a Geneva teaching hospital now. He's a hero and an inspiration to us all.

Sometimes Gilbert Merton's son sends letters to Bob or to me. Sometimes he sent letters to our dad. They all say that he, Newton Merton Bryant, intends to put a hole in our vital organs or a vital organ in our holes so soon as he can get round to it. He says that he wouldn't sleep too deeply if he was us. He says that he has bought a sawn-off .22 – there's an Irish gunsmith for you – and a long knife and a cheesewire and a meathook. He's going to kill us with all of them in turn. That way, it'll really hurt.

Newton Merton Bryant is a dental hygienist.

Whenever the doorbell rang in the old days, our father would say, 'Oh, lor, it's Newton Merton. And about time too.' He stopped saying that towards the end. I think he really hoped that it might be Newton Merton, complete with cheesewire et al. He thought that it was much nicer to be killed than just to sink and die.

Our mother did a bit of both. Early on Christmas morning, just two years after Gilbert Merton had been booted out, she went for a walk through the town. Everyone else was in church or preparing their turkeys or geese. She had the itch for something, and she didn't know where to scratch. Some people might have thought that that something that she itched for was sex or fear, but our mother never did like sex much and she must have had enough of fear – fear of losing things she never had, fear of her own malfunctioning body, fear of her children, fear of sex and age and death – so when she got the itch for something, she thought that that something was the funny pills that Gilbert Merton used to supply.

My father kept his drugs tightly locked up, and, because it was Christmas, there was no chance of obtaining anything from any of her other sources, whatever they may have been.

There was mud-mottled snow all around. Christmas must have looked long and cold and horrible to her.

It so happened that the local vet, George Danby, my godfather and one of my father's oldest friends and drinking companions, was spending his Christmas morning with a spaniel puppy that had eaten its present. Its present was a rubber bone made by Glendale Petcorps of Pontefract. I was to meet Mr Glenn of Glendale many years later. He made six million pounds out of his rubber bones and a thing called Doggy-Dri-Lawn. Doggy-Dri-Lawn was a sort of mat covered in green nylon fronds. You put it down in your living-room. The idea was that your dog, impressed by the incredible *greenness* of this thing, would instantly piss on it. All the dog-piss would then sink through the mat into a special deodorised foam. That way you never had to take him out to be run over or poisoned by carbon monoxide.

It was a brilliant idea. It didn't really *work* because dogs have noses and there are precious few of them so stupid that, when confronted by a green nylon mat, they think, 'Whoopee! The wide open spaces!' But it was a brilliant idea and it made Mr Glenn millions of pounds of which he spent three hundred on having me open a Glendale Pet Shop in Belfast, so good luck to Doggy-Dri-Lawns.

Anyhow. This puppy had chewed up its rubber bone and its owners had beaten it for being so ungrateful as to chew its nice present, and then it had sat down and started to die of acute rubber-in-the-gut. And George Danby was called out.

And he left his near rear window open.

My mother recognised the car, of course. She looked in and she saw a long thin cardboard box marked Physeptone. That's a methadone. It was in ampoules of a size to get horses stoned, but presumably she just hoped for the best. She reached in and she took it. She returned home to pick up a syringe, then she too went to church. She must have come in through the crypt and climbed the spiral staircase to the bell-tower. She had no time for religion but she always loved carols. When she got there, she sat down, looked out of a loophole, and shot up.

She had been seen walking through the graveyard. She was found just ten minutes after the service ended. Her skirt was rucked up above her waist. Her right hand was clamped between her legs. Once, when smashed and maudlin, the old man told me, 'The writer chappies in the penny dreadfuls, they're always sayin' as how men look as though they've seen heaven when they've passed on, you know? And true it is, and if I've seen twenty I've seen a thousand and when old Rick Sardonicus arrives they do indeed have a look about them as if they've seen something wonderful, and maybe they have and maybe they haven't, who knows? But your mother, Lord save us, she looked as if she'd seen the devil himself, the devil himself. And the worst of it is, she looked as if she liked what she was seeing ...'

The terrible thing is that I was excited rather than distressed by this development. I wish I'd been distressed. I've punished myself a fair bit for that first sense of elation. But at the time, her death won me presents and attention from a host of well-meaning would-be surrogates and full-time widow-consolers, respect from schoolmates (the sort of respect they might give to a ghost, but respect nonetheless) and an easier, more 'manly' way of life at home. I seemed to acquire instant equality with our da. A manikin. I was older than other boys because my mother was deader than theirs. I'm not saying as it didn't hurt me. I think it did, but like most great hurts it took time, and for the moment I defended myself with an easy, unselfconscious, confident manner. Bob had no such ease. He was gawky and nervous and, perhaps, rather effeminate in that he never felt happy with other boys and men but developed uncritical and agonising passions for every young woman that smiled his way.

Poor George Danby blamed himself. He drank himself to paralysis and then to death within four years. He left £12,000 and his library to Bob, £12,000 and his hunter, Blorin, to me.

That puppy has a lot to answer for.

Funnily enough, Bob wasn't really a clown at school. People laughed *at* him because he's got this big beak and wore opera cloaks and all that. He invited their jibes. Maybe that helped later on – the fact that he actually came to enjoy hostility and coping with it on his feet. People laughed at those quick, damning one-liners that he used to produce, but he never actually got up and told jokes or anything. He was a good mimic. That comes naturally. But it was very rare that ever he let down the inhibitions enough to show just how good he was.

Strange, that. Maybe comics learn their trade simply by being solitary and defensive. It is the loneliest job in the world.

Me, now, I was different. I was stocky, gregarious, rebellious, inclined to form gangs and to look for trouble. I loved to be loved and always grew depressed when I hadn't got a medium – when I felt stupid and couldn't make people smile, when I was broke and couldn't make people happy. I'm still the same. If I have no clever words on me, I can't just shut up and accept that people might quite like me. I have to keep gibbering. When I run out of money, I can't just be poor; I have to draw cheques on empty accounts, just so as I can have power, just so as I can control my circumstances.

Anyhow, Bob left school at last and became a Jesuit and was packed off to Trinity, Dublin, where he discovered that he saw things funny. He also discovered Giordano Bruno, who became a hero, and decided that after all he wasn't cut out for a life of celibacy, prayer, obedience and intrigue. I, meanwhile, cut a dash with George Danby's money, rode to hounds all over England and Ireland, was champion amateur three years running and then, when the money ran out, took out a professional rider's licence.

It was inevitable that we should both come to England in the end. There's nowhere else for Irishmen to go, save hell or America. Bob practised his new trade on tour with a showband called The Lilywhite Boys, narrowly missed getting blown up in a Craigavon pub and wrote *Street Song* which was a hit on both sides of the water. He came over just a few days before his twenty-fourth birthday and set off on the first of his tours with the one man show. Every year since then he has cobbled together a new show – songs, monologues, stories – which he takes to university towns and festivals, and each show becomes an album and one number off each album becomes a single, and one single in five seems to become a modest hit. The biggest single successes so far have been *Street Song* and a rock number called *Black Diamond Doors* and a little love song called *You Matter to Me*, which has been covered by a lot of big names.

There you go, then. That's the Blanes for you. We've both come a long way from Dunboyne, a long way from knickers in the bath in Ballymena. But if the way up seemed quick and easy, coming down again was a doddle.

Home again. The house is in total darkness. No candles burn in the window against the traveller's return. A wind has got up and the trees are dancing like heavy-metal freaks. Claire must have gone to bed.

I tiptoe in through the garage. Vandal whimpers and wriggles and widdles his welcome. 'Hush up, you daft old mutt,' I whisper. 'Shh!' He seems to think that's funny and jabs a cold nose in my eye. I stand and shoo him through the door. He bounds out, laughing, spins round on the gravel and stands, haunches high, nose between extended forelegs, challenging me to a race. 'Get on with you,' I tell him softly, and he's off like the shadow of a train.

I turn wearily back into the house. I kick over some gumboots and squat to set them upright again, only each time that I set one up, another goes down. The moonlight casts guillotine blade shadows on the tiled floor of the kitchen. A tap plays a dead march. My feet naturally move to its rhythm as again I walk through to the study and switch on the desk-lamp. Again I turn towards the Ansafone.

Then I stop.

First a sort of keening sound seeps from my lips, then a sort of stammer which sounds like an old VW starting up. Then I manage to get a whole word out, huskily but with heartfelt emotion.

The word is 'Shit'.

I reach for the support of the desk like a blind man. Instant angina grips my chest and squeezes.

A long cheroot lies in the silver ashtray on the desk.

A framed photograph is missing from the wall to the right of the desk, above the Wellington.

About an inch of the cheroot has been smoked. Two cylinders of silver ash have been neatly tapped off.

The photograph is lying face up on the rug. It is a picture of Claire and me with surfboards in Hawaii. It has not fallen. The glass has been broken, but tidily and from the centre.

I stand like an idiot looking from the cheroot to the photograph and back again. Then fear hits hard. My heart yaws. 'Joanna ...' it comes out as a whisper, then my head's down and I'm charging for the stairs. I take them three at a time. I bounce off the landing walls. 'Joanna! Claire!' I yell. 'Darling! Joanna!'

I come to our bedroom first. Claire has already turned the bedside lamp on. She sits up in a smocked white cotton night-dress and blinks at me, bemused. I don't bother to talk. I just turn and clatter up the uncarpeted attic stairs. Joanna's waiting for me on the landing. Her eyes are clear and bright. She wears a big Bob Marley tee shirt. Her legs are very tanned.

'What is it, Daddy?'

'I ... I was just ...' I pant. 'Oh, Lord,' I lean back against the wooden wall and gulp. 'Nothing. I was scared that something ...'

'What the hell's going on?' Claire's head emerges above the top step. 'You scared the life out of me, Georgie.'

I nod often. 'I'm sorry.' I hold out an arm in invitation. She comes to me. My arm curls about her waist. She does not lean against me but then she does not resist either. 'I'm sorry, darling,' I kiss her cheek, 'I got back and ... and there was this broken picture on the floor and ... I just over-reacted, that's all. Suddenly thought there'd been burglars, you'd both been raped and murdered, that sort of thing.'

'Just for a broken picture?' Joanna giggles. 'Daddy. Really.'

'Yeah, well,' I shrug. 'Sorry.'

'If you want my opinion,' Claire is magnificent, 'I reckon that daddy went to sleep in that chair of his once again and his conscience gave him a nightmare. And serve him right too.'

'No!' I start. Then, since she's still smiling and talking softly and her body is warm against mine, 'Well, I suppose as you might have something there, come to think of it. Picture's still broken, though. That's for real.' A shudder shakes me.

'Which picture?' demands Joanna.

'One of mum and me. You know? With surfboards and broad smiles. Honolulu.'

'Oh, that!' she is dismissive. 'It probably just fell off the wall,

90

Daddy. Really.' She rolls her eyes heavenward, despairing of the silliness of daddies in general, hers in particular.

'Yeah, well, like I said, sorry. Silly. Listen, no one came here tonight, did they?'

'What do you mean, came here?'

'No one visited. No one dropped in for a drink. Vandal didn't bark?'

'Vandal always barks. Daft dog. He's barking now. Listen.'

'Yeah. OK. I'll let him in,' I am suddenly very tired. 'Sorry. Come on. Bed time. Anyone fancy a cup of tea, Horlicks, something?'

'Not for me, thanks,' Joanna reaches forward and kisses me. It's like being touched with wet grapes. 'Night.'

'G'night, love.'

'Well, I'd love a cup of tea,' Claire announces. Together we turn and walk to the head of the stairs. 'I'm going back to bed. I don't know,' she sighs, then chants, 'Pity the poor man for he is demented.'

Fear is an aphrodisiac, but it's not going to do me any good tonight. By the time that I've made the tea, bedded Vandal down for the night and swigged a nightcap or two from a bottle of Tesco's dry white in the 'fridge, Claire is asleep. I climb into bed beside her and press myself against her curled back. My hand starts slowly stroking her thighs. She groans a bit and for a while I think that it's all going to be all right, then, in my urgency, I do something wrong and she says 'Ow!' and 'No!' and slaps me away.

I roll over onto my back and sip my tea. The usual numbness at rejection seeps through my limbs like embalming fluid. She knows it, and her hand fumbles back to grasp mine in tactful reassurance.

She's right, of course. I had merely wanted to exorcise the ghost of Parker with a woman, any woman. Sometimes that's enough for Claire, but I know that ultimately she wants more. She wants something that I cannot give her any more. She's snapped and snarled at me and withered my precious vanity too often. She's hurt me too often by forgiving the hurt that I have done her.

I switch off the lamp. As lust fades, anger replaces it.

Most horses run faster for a couple of cracks of the whip. A few, however, are bloody-minded. Soon as you hit them, their ears go back and their tails go up in protest and they actually go slower rather than quicker.

Me now, I belong in that bloody-minded class. I suppose the first thoughts of any human being are 'What the hell am I doing here?' followed closely by 'Where's the tit, then?' One way or another, I don't seem to have moved on much since then. But I did get just one stage further. I got as far as, 'Shan't.'

Cajole me, sure. Bribe me, seduce me, coerce me, please. But don't push.

I'm a perverse little sod that way. I'm inclined to push back.

There's not much in the way of racing as Christmas draws near. Today it's Towcester, which is no cause for cheering. On the other hand, if fog or blinding rain had caused racing to be called off, I, in common with the whole fraternity, would have spent the day in cursing and kicking things. Lord knows, the prospect of pushing staggering horses through the mud up that filthy Towcester slope is unattractive, but that of sitting at home watching the weather is infinitely worse.

I arrive back from schooling youngsters and am about to open the back door when Claire emerges carrying two large canvas and leather suitcases. She walks straight past me. She and Joanna are off to Somerset to pick up Conor. They'll stay at her parents' place in Dartmouth for a couple of days, and return on Christmas Eve.

'Here, let me help you with that,' I grasp the handle of the larger suitcase.

'No, thanks,' she shakes my hand off. 'I'm balanced, thanks. It's OK.'

I follow her to the car. 'Get the dough yesterday?'

'Yup. Thanks. Where'd that come from, then?'

'Oh, nice little present from Toby Jansen, Gothic Rose's owner.' I improvise.

'Hm,' she opens the hatchback and heaves in the cases. 'Well, there's no need to look so darned pleased with yourself. What if he hadn't given you a present, hey?'

She leans in and shifts grey and gold gift-wrapped parcels.

'Yeah, well, he did,' I say lamely. A change of subject seems a good wheeze. 'Susan's left Bob,' I tell her, 'run off with some policeman.'

'Yes, I know.'

'You know?'

'Yes,' she slams down the boot, 'she rang last night. She had no choice, you know. The man's a sod. Permanently pissed, filthy temper. She was being driven stark staring mad by his bloody black moods.' She dusts off her hands and turns back towards the house.

'Yeah, but he was always like that. She knew that.'

93

'No, Georgie,' she says over her shoulder, 'he's got much worse over the last few years. Poor Sue was just – oh, darling,' this to Joanna who had just emerged, laden with boots and coats, 'you'll have to put those in the well at the back, the boot's packed.'

'OK.'

'No, but the poor girl was just so *lonely*. Thanks.' We pass into the house again. 'And this David sounds just what she needs. Reliable, generous, thoroughly boring, thinks the world of her ...'

'So does Bob.'

'Huh. Not so's you'd notice.'

'Christ, you should've seen him last night.'

'Serves him right,' she says crisply. 'I'm sorry, love. I know you love him, but I don't think you have a clue what it must be like for a woman to have to live with a man like that. I mean, it's bad enough being a bloody depressive moralist without having to be a drunken libertine as well. One or the other, please.'

'All very well, doll,' I smile, 'but she married him for better or for worse. A contract's a contract.'

'Not if it's an unconscionable one it isn't. Anyhow, he's the sod who went off screwing old dames.'

'Laura is hardly an old dame, darling. She's a hell of a looker.'

'An elegant bitch, Sue said. Sort that eats the likes of Bobby for breakfast.'

'Fair description.'

'Has Bob been having it off with her ever since they were married?'

'No, no. He was going out with her when he met Susan, but he gave her the push. Didn't see her for – I don't know – three, four years. He's a pet to her, that's all. She's sophisticated and older and clever. Sue's gauche and young and ... I dunno.'

'I'll never understand you Catholic bastards,' she walks into the drawing-room at the end of the house and sits at her bureau. 'Where did I put those photographs ...? No, I mean, you get your knickers in a twist about the sanctity of marriage and all that, but you conveniently forget the "forsaking all others" bit.'

'Yeah, well,' I clasp her shoulders and massage them gently. Her head goes back and she sighs. 'Marriage is a social contract and should be binding. Just don't believe in monogamy, that's all. Unnatural and none of the law's darned business. Better be married and stay married to two or three if you can afford it than have intrigues and lies and broken homes, that's all. You wouldn't mind a wife number two to help with the infants and the rutting, would you?'

94

'Mmmmno, but ... lower. Between my shoulder-blades. Ooh, that's it. Mmm.'

'Well, that's all there is to it. I reckon as I'm married to you for life no matter what. Even if you went screwing around, I'd still be married to you. Wouldn't want to have much to do with you, but we'd still be wed. Less pain and fear that way.'

'I dunno. Maybe. I've seen some pretty unhappy couples limping on.'

'Probably because they married because they were in love. Only one way to go from there, and that's down.'

'Oh, yeah?' she laughs. 'So you weren't in love with me when we were married?'

'Matter of fact, I was, but that wasn't why I married you. Incidental, that's all. I married you because we got on, because we liked the same things, because I wanted children with you – and 'cos I fancied you something rotten.'

'And now?'

'What about now?'

'Do you still?'

'What?'

'Fancy me.'

'You know darned well I do.'

I kiss the top of her head and squeeze her ribs tight. I close my eyes and, for a moment, just breathe in the scent of that X-certificate sex-aid which is her hair. Her right hand comes back. Her palm rests for a moment against my cheek, cool as china. I kiss it, I reckon she's got her eyes closed too.

'Mummy?' Joanna strolls casually in. Rows and kisses, they're all the same to her. 'Have you packed my binoculars, because I can't find them *anywhere*.'

It's Kellow Hoyle day at Towcester. Every race is sponsored by Hoyle's Turf Accountants Ltd. Kellow's ingenuous, bearded face beams at us from the hoardings as we ride by. *Hoyle's Credit Betting – The Easy Lay* is the choice legend emblazoned along the back straight. *Hoyle's – We Bet* is the message at the home turn and on the racecards. Odd to think that, just ten years ago, Hoyle Leisure consisted of two Putney betting shops and a disco on the Upper Richmond Road.

Kellow is one of those phenomena that seem to pop up in business just once or twice in a decade. A tall, tanned cockney with the keen air of an engineering student, he can only be thirty-six, thirty-seven now and he looks thirty. He's inclined to wear moleskin trousers, tee-shirts, leather jerkins and trainers to the sports, which doesn't endear him to the Powers That Be. Last year he turned up at Ascot in a sky-blue morning-coat.

He's one of those people who has an incomprehensible passion for making deals. Over the past few years, he's indulged that passion plenty. First he bought a chain of amusement arcades, then a load of run-down seaside hotels which he turned into leisure centres, then Joe ('Even your daughter can bet with Joe') Hibbert's chain of Northern betting-shops. Somewhere along the line, he has also found time to do a lot of surfing, para-gliding, deep-sea diving and Formula Ford racing. He has given a new lifeboat to Clovelly, started a project to motivate young cricketers in the inner cities, and attends a lot of parties with pneumatic singer/dancer/actress/models on his arm. The millionaire recluse he ain't.

It's strange, really, that no one ever thought of it before. In the old days, your rails bookie was always a flamboyant type. If Honest Joe wore a louder suit and a broader smile than Scrupulous Sam, Honest Joe got your money. In recent years, however, the big bookies have depended on massive impersonal corporate advertising rather than on individuals. Kellow Hoyle has reversed that trend. Punters consider it a privilege to lose money to him.

The other thing which has made your man a real force on the turf is that his proud claim, *We Bet*, actually seems to be true.

The big bookies are public companies. They're not meant to make a loss. They take that obligation very seriously. They've invented a thousand rules to ensure that the punter can't come out on top. They fix measly odds and, when caught with their drawers around their ankles, run screaming to mama. Not Kellow. In last year's Derby, for example, he laid heavily against Richard Heron's hot favourite, Russian Dancer. He got a lot of publicity – and a lot of bets – by offering 7–2 at the off when all the others were quoting evens. He proved right. Russian Dancer didn't make the trip. He blew up two furlongs out and staggered in seventh.

Then there was the Jailbird affair.

My old mate Robin Nuttall, now managing a stud in Ireland, together with Jimmy Ryan, Dermot Newton and a few other sporting rogues from the land of the free or bloody cheap, pulled off a complicated little coup with a jumper named Jailbird from which they stood to make some £600,000. The coup involved a lot of perfectly permissible smoke-screens and disinformation and the breaking of a couple of National Hunt rules which should have rendered them liable to a £100 fine.

It was clever and it worked. The bookies refused to pay up. They called it fraud. The Director of Public Prosecutions disagreed and chucked the case out, but bookmakers have a powerful lobby. The case came to court. The judge summed up in the defendants' favour. He praised them for their sportsmanship in coming over to England to face trial. He called the affair by its rightful name: 'Just an old-fashioned coup.' The jury ignored him. They found the whole gang of them guilty.

It shows what the judge thought of the verdict that he fined each of them £1,000 and gave it as his opinion that 'no disgrace should attach to them.'

Kellow Hoyle emerged as the hero of the day. He was into the Irishmen for £130,000. He not only paid up, he also, with a deal of well-orchestrated publicity, paid their fines.

'Well, that's what it's all about,' he declared. 'They bet with us, we bet with them. It's all risk and tryin' to be one step ahead of the other mug. We win as often as not, but this time we got done. Fair enough, say I.'

Jacobs were subjected to a campaign of attrition. Every night, righteously indignant punters filled the locks of their offices with superglue. A lot of people shifted their accounts to Hoyle's.

I get to talk to Hoyle today because he presents me with a silver-mounted engraved claret jug for winning the Hoyle's Sevenplan Handicap 'Chase on a grey who hangs to the left like a wonky supermarket trolley. The horse's name, incidentally, is Banana Blancmange, because his owner, a cheerful, hugely fat young merchant banker named Kelly, wanted to hear Peter O'Sullevan and Dan Knight struggling – 'And as they come to the last, it's Banana Blancmange, Balana Bramange by a length, Birana Blange ...' It works too.

The applause is thin and desultory like the patter of wet cement. The small crowd slopes away. Jack isn't here today, so I have a silver-mounted engraved claret jug in either hand.

''Ere, let me give you a hand, Georgie boy,' Kellow grins. I've known him vaguely since he was just a common or garden millionaire. ''Ow's it goin', then? Joints must be creakin' a bit by now, aren't they?'

'Nah. The pauper's burden is light,' I tell him. 'From what I hear, 'tis you as should be worrying. Jetting here and there, fighting off the floozies and the paparazzi – stressful stuff, that. Tell you what, I'll take the burden off your shoulders and you can live happy and healthy and carefree and ride in the last.'

'Always were a considerate lad, weren't you, Georgie boy? No. You can keep your bleedin' gee-gees. Never did like the beasts, truth to tell. Bite, kick, buck an' fart, 'ass all they ever seem to do.'

'And make tons of the folding stuff for the likes of you.'

'Yeah, well, there is that of course, but you should've got the message by now, Georgie. Closer you get to the beast, the less spondulicks you make. Lads get sod all, jockeys five bob a day, trainers a couple of quid, punters on the racecourse sod all, punters off the racecourse a few thousand and bookies – bleedin' millions.'

'Yup,' I say cheerfully. 'There must be a lesson there somewhere. Roll on the Tote Monopoly, eh?' Then I look across the enclosure and the chuckle dies on my lips and a sort of growl rumbles up from my gut. 'Uh oh.' I turn my back and concentrate on replacing claret jugs in their blue velveteen cases.

The Hon. Oliver is over there. He leans forward, one leg crossed over the other, his forearms resting on the white enclosure rail. His lips are pursed speculatively as he reads *Raceform*, but I know that he is half watching me.

'Whassat, then?' Kellow frowns.

'That bastard Parker,' I mutter.

'Who, Olly boy? Aaah. What you got against poor old Olly boy, then? 'E's all right. Bit lahdidah, but gets results. Gets the troops movin', does our Olly. Few kind words from the Honourable Olly and welchers pay up sweet as pie. Better'n all that old-fashioned rough stuff, eh? Useful sort of chap, Olly.'

'You mean ...' I swing round and look up at his smiling face. I swallow the implications in one hard-edged, foul-tasting chunk. 'You mean Parker works for you?'

'Course, Georgie boy!' Kellow booms and punches my shoulder. Not a friendly thing to do to a jockey who's broken his collarbone, to date, sixteen times. 'Thought you'd've known that. Yep. Our Olly is under the protective umbrella of Hoyle's, Turf Accountants Extraordinaire.'

'Right,' I say quietly.

I now do something very childish. I'll rue it before the day is done, but just at the moment I'm shaking with fury. I pick up my new silver-mounted engraved claret jug, hold it out at the full extent of my arm, and drop it. It rolls on the suede-smooth grass and does not break. 'Thanks a ton, Kellow,' I snarl. I pick up Jack's jug in its case and shove it under my arm. I turn. Kellow's hand grasps my shoulder. He inclines his head towards me with a soothing grin, a wrinkled brow, the sort of expression with which you appease a potentially dangerous but pitiable lunatic. I pull away, raise my booted foot above the gleaming glass and bring my heel down and then up again, hard and fast. 'Thanks a bloody million.'

Behind me as I stride, head down, up the steps and into the weighing-room, Hoyle's voice calls, 'Georgie...? Come on, Georgie ...' then, more querulous, 'What the fuck's the crooked little bugger think 'e's *doing*?'

I barge past a couple of surprised faces and into the changing-room. Even Hoyle can't follow me in here. I throw myself down on the bench, close my eyes and try to breathe slowly and deeply.

Yes, it makes sense all right. The Hon. Oliver can afford to indulge his natural nastiness just that little bit more with the might of Hoyle's behind him. And yes, Hoyle could do with the likes of Parker to arrange things if he's to continue to lay long odds against favourites and maintain his heroic status. And is it entirely a matter of happenchance that Parker turned up when he did, or does Kellow think that I'll take Parker's threats more seriously if I know who's behind them?

If so, he's dead right.

For a moment, such is my loathing for tinpot saints, my mind fills up with absurd vindictive ideas such as, 'Why don't I reveal all to the Sunday funnies? Why don't I show them just who and what the sporting, dashing Mr Hoyle really is?'

The answers are not long in coming. They run:

1. Because no one would believe you.

2. Because Hoyle or Parker would at once reveal your past little transgressions.

3. Because flickknives make nasty leaks.

After the last, as ever, we sit half-dressed and weary in the changing-room while the valets bustle around us and the crowds outside disperse. We munch equally weary smoked salmon sandwiches and drink laced or unlaced coffee and talk of the Profounder Mysteries, such as horses, women, restaurants and speedy means of transport. When at last I leave, dusk has charred the edges of the sky. The air is icy.

The racecourse at this hour is always strangely eerie and depressing. I love it. Even a pisspotical little 'course like this one is amongst the most haunted places on earth.

The caterers are still about, tying up black bin-liners crammed with uneaten sandwiches and salads, empty bottles, paper plates. Elderly men in kennel coats wish you good night and wander listlessly on across the lawns, spiking screwed up betting slips and muddy racecards. On the gloomy grey steps of the stands, a few empty glasses gleam.

The ghosts are out. Not just the ghosts of today – the echoes of laughter and curses and cheers – but also, it seems to me, out there on the 'course, the ghosts of brave men and horses who have sweated their guts and strained muscles and nerves battling with the fences and with one another. Jack Dowdeswell's out there, Bryan Marshall, the Beasleys and the Molonys, Dick Francis, Dave Dick, Fulke Walwyn, Fred Winter, Pat Taaffe, Josh Gifford, Terry Biddlecombe, Stan Mellor – even, somewhere in amongst 'em, riding an endless race against phantoms and eternally cursing that bloody hill, the ghost of one G. Blane.

There are, after all, just two things that they can't take away from me. My name in the record books, of course. That matters. But above all, the fact that I'm one of that phantom field out there, and ever more shall be so.

My fanciful intimations of immortality are interrupted when a shadow crosses mine on the grey grass. I don't even need to look up to know to whom it is attached. The impeccable grey trouser-cuffs which just break over burnished oxblood brogues would have given me a 10–11 chance of being right. The noise which emerges at my left shoulder makes it a stone cold certainty.

'Aaaair . . .'

It's a sort of wavering, tinny bleat which starts with a glottal stop. I can only think that it's the residue of a stammer. Captain Rory Fitzroy-Haigh, steward of the National Hunt Committee, late of the Blues and Royals, starts every sentence like that. 'Aaaair, Blane. Good.'

'Evening, Cap'n.' I don't check my stride. He falls in beside me.

He's a good-looking chap is Rory, short and slight with those Bob Martin's good looks which can come only from nannies and nursery teas, rice-puddings and rugger fields. You can't buy high, fair colouring like that, and the flash which comes off his buffed golden hair cannot be reproduced even with a whole fruit salad in your shampoo and conditioner. It's the Croesus glow. He's forty maybe.

'Aaaair, Blane. Yes. Been waitin' for you. Just wanted a quiet word. Are you doin' anything? Now, I mean?'

'Er, no,' I frown, 'no. Claire's away. Why?'

'Aaaair, it's just, a few of us rather wanted a chat with you. Thought you might just pop over to John Stratton's place. Just down the road, don't you know. Have a drink, aaair.'

I'm mildly bemused, but I shrug and say, 'Yeah. OK. Who's us, then?'

'Oh, aaair, just a few of the stewards, don't you know. John Stratton, Benet Kilcannon, that sort of thing. Little confab, you know?'

'Not entirely social, then, sir?'

'Well, aaair, bit of both, bit of both. Always delighted to see you, d'ye know.'

We're out in the car-park now. Herringbone tracks criss-cross the ground. There are just twenty or so cars left scattered about. 'That's me over there.' Rory indicates a dark red BMW motor-cruiser. 'D'you want to follow me?'

'Yeah, OK,' I duck under the rails. 'This won't take too long, will it, sir?'

'No, no. Just a drink, you know? Half an hour or so? Good. Excellent. See you there, then.'

By the time I'm behind the wheel of my own car and have turned the key in the ignition, his has bumped in a half circle across the car-park and awaits me at the gates. I follow.

Everyone seems to want something of me these days. I wish they'd just leave me alone.

First, I confess, I'm apprehensive. My mouth is dry quite simply because I don't like being bearded by stewards in any circumstances. The old 'see you in my study after prayers' syndrome.

Second, however, I'm downright confused. I've never been much of a chess player. I'm always too preoccupied with death or glory charges to consider the apparently infinite options open to my opponent. People like Rory Fitzroy-Haigh, however, for all that they give the impression of being Grade A Supreme Champion Show Twits, are canny and devious.

It's plain that this is no disciplinary matter. They don't dole out the spotted dick and the double damask when they're slapping down the bad boys. So what in God's name does a gaggle of senior stewards suddenly want with me?

I rapidly rule out the possibility that they've all experienced a spontaneous upsurge of affection for poor misunderstood Georgie Blane. Stewards may nod in our general direction from time to time by way of acknowledging our existence, but they don't hobnob with professional jockeys. The Marquess of Stratton and Kilkhampton, furthermore, to whose stately gaff I am bidden, has had me up before him on two occasions and has done nothing to conceal the fact that he regards me in much the same light as a dog-turd on his heel.

101

Rory Fitzroy-Haigh, like most cavalry officers that I have met, drives fast, smoothly and carelessly. He barely bothers to indicate before swinging to the right into a concealed entrance. We pass between two imposing gateposts, then dip downward through a dark stretch of wood. As we emerge in an avenue of naked poplars, I see the house for the first time.

It's not what I expected. Unlike most stately English homes, it doesn't sprawl over a vast area; in fact, it is taller than it is wide. Nor does it declare with wings and dovecotes and orangeries and ornament and extensions built for the Prince of Wales, just how very grand it is. It's grand sure enough, but in the elegant, simple style that you might expect of an eighteenth-century ambassador or well-travelled merchant. It's of dark red brick with white cornices and keystones and shutters and other bits whose names I don't know. It's Frenchified and very pretty.

Rory doesn't bother to ring the doorbell. He just trots up the steps and leads the way into the hall.

A butler emerges from the shadows behind the Christmas tree.

'Evening, Carless,' says Rory.

'Evening, Carless,' say I.

Carless mumbles something butlerish and opens the door at his left. Rory leads me in at a brisk quick march, which is a pity. There's a huge painting above the hall fireplace which just might be a Surtees. I'd like to have taken a look.

We're in a morning-room whose walls are lined with buttermilk silk. The high curtains in the curving wall opposite are of gold. A big tapestry covers the wall at my left. There's some sort of stormy Dutch seascape above the prancing fire.

'Ah, Rory,' the Marquess of Stratton pulls himself to his stockinged feet. He plainly has not been at the sports today. He's in baggy tweed breeks and a knobbly green sweater. He's a burly, coarse-looking man with an oarsman's build and a bullet head. White floss swirls like wisps of smoke above a very pink pate and face. 'Good. You found him. Come on in, then, come on in. Sit down.'

Two other men have also arisen from their deep, powder-blue armchairs. I know them both, like them, even, but I'm not overjoyed to see the chap on the right.

'Ah, Georgie,' Lord Kilcannon, the spry old man on the left, is, as ever, a model of courtesy. He extends a beautiful hand. 'Nice to see you. Well done today.'

'Thanks, sir.' His hand is warm and dry.

'And we've got Brigadier Grey here, as you see,' Stratton waves dismissively. 'Know him well enough, I should say, Blane.'

'Not as well as he knows me, I'll be bound.' I grin a little nervously and shake Hugh Grey's hand too. It's his job to know me. He's the head of Racecourse Security.

I ignore the armchair indicated. I walk around the tea-table to perch on the bumrack by the throbbing wood fire. I want to be able to see all of them, all the time.

Kilcannon is now sitting in the chair hard at my left. He has a long, distinguished face and high cheekbones and pewter hair. He also happens to be a Brigadier, and a very senior Knight of Malta. His fingertips are joined, Sherlock-style. A small smile tugs at the corners of his lips.

Rory has pulled up a high-backed Chippendale chair from before the bureau. He is almost straight ahead of me, his legs carefully crossed so as not to crumple those trousers. His socks are of black silk.

Then there's Hugh Grey to my half right. He's a slightly dumpy, grizzled sort of chap who seems to do everything very slowly, very quietly, very thoughtfully. He's wearing a scruffy salt-and-pepper tweed suit and a paratroops tie.

Stratton, meanwhile, has gone for a stroll. He stands with his back to me, his saveloy fingers tightly linked over his bum. He gazes up at the tapestry.

It's a lot to gaze at. On a cream background amidst cascades of flowers, swans, blue-tits, finches various, a kingfisher and various other birds, all vividly portrayed, feed and play informally in a glorious formal pattern.

I decide to get things going. 'That's a wonderful thing, sir.' My voice echoes. The carpet and curtains quickly hush it.

Stratton says, 'Hmph,' which, loosely translated, means, 'Who does the little oik think he is, squeaking before he's squoken to?'

I'm not going to give up. 'I've always coveted a Soho. They're such lovely light, decorative things. Never did understand all the fuss about Aubusson.'

'I agree,' murmurs Hugh Grey, as though quite pleasantly surprised.

Stratton, on the other hand, swings round looking apoplectic. 'Yes, well, we're not here to discuss tapestries,' he announces brusquely. He barges through the unresisting air and throws himself down in the armchair at my right. He resents my elevated position on the bumrack. I can feel it. I'm glad.

'Now, fact of the matter is, Blane,' he explodes, 'English steeple-chasin's been damned good to you, and you haven't always exactly been good to it in return.'

'John!' Kilcannon reproves.

'No, no.' Grey sadly shakes his head.

'Now, there's a fascinating thought to be having, sir,' I say politely, suddenly all Irish and ingenuous, 'but I'm not exactly sure as I catch your Lordship's drift. The way I see it, I ride races and that entertains people, so they pay and I benefit and racing benefits. I don't exactly see as how I'm in debt.'

'No, no,' says Kilcannon. 'Of course you're not. Can we leave this to Hugh, John? You're about as diplomatic as a wild boar.'

'No point in beatin' about the bush,' Stratton fumes.

'None at all,' I agree amicably, 'but we need to be precise. That's the thing of it. I haven't long, you see, sir.'

'I'm afraid we've pretty much devastated the tea,' says Kilcannon quickly, 'how about a drink, Georgie? I know I could do with one.'

'Yes, thanks. That'd be nice.'

'John, ring for Carless, would you? Mine's a stiff whiskey and that's spelled with an "e" if you please. You, Georgie?'

'Oh, champagne, please.' Well, and isn't this a Marquess's house, for heaven's sake?

'Of course,' Kilcannon's eyes glint. I can well believe the *on dit* that many an ex-debutante's or dancer's eye mists over at the mention of his name.

It seems that champagne is a popular idea with everyone but Stratton, who perversely and pointedly demands beer. When the Bollinger has been distributed and Carless has effaced himself, Hugh Grey leans forward, his forearms on his thighs.

'I understand,' he says slowly, 'that you had a little contretemps with Kellow Hoyle today?'

'Yeah, I suppose so.'

'Would you care to tell us what it was about?'

I shrug. 'Bit of a disagreement, that's all.'

'All right, Georgie. Now, I don't want you to be offended or anything. We're not watching you. We're interested in one or two other people, all right? Now. Yesterday evening, you visited the Coach and Horses at Newbury where you saw Oliver Parker. Could that have anything to do with your barney with Hoyle?'

The bumrack may have psychological advantages, but it's too close to the fire. I'm sweating. 'Now, hold hard here, sir,' I croak, then clear my throat. 'My barney with Hoyle, as you call it, is a personal affair. If you want to make a disciplinary matter of it, you'd better do it through the usual channels.'

'Don't think we couldn't,' puffs Stratton.

'John. . . .' Kilcannon warns.

'All right, Georgie,' Grey soothes and smiles, 'we'll leave that alone for the moment. Now. Georgie. You're – what? Thirty-six, thirty-seven now? Thirty-six. You've maybe two, three years more at this game?'

'Something like that,' I murmur, and wonder, not for the first time, how all those years managed to telescope like that.

'OK, and you don't particularly like Hoyle and Parker and Co, but you've been – well in with them, shall we say, in the past. You have a reputation, shall we say, and I'm sure it's totally unjustified – for – well, say someone asks you to give a novice hurdler an easy race – I mean, I'm sure we all would – but – well, let's say you're not generally thought of – probably quite wrongly, as I say – as the most saintly of riders.'

I flush. It's not that it's untrue or anything, but a man has his pride. 'I don't know what makes you think that,' I mumble sullenly. I take a gulp of champagne. 'Still, all right. Go on.'

'Well, the thing is – you may have noticed – the thing is, there've been a lot of races recently, not particularly involving you, but there've been a lot of suspicious races, many of them involving a great deal of money, and there are a lot of rumours, a lot of circumstantial evidence, nothing firm, you understand . . .' he trails off, exasperated by the convolutions of tact. 'Well. I can see that I'm going to have to lay my cards on the table. Hoyle's are getting big. Very big. They'll be going public soon. And we think – and this is very much off the record, mind – we have a suspicion that they are responsible for a very serious outbreak of race-fixing in the past year or so. We want to stop them.'

'I don't know anything about it,' I say with all the conviction of a recorded message.

'No, well, be that as it may, you're an established jockey and you're just the sort that they might approach. As you'll appreciate, with word-of-mouth cash transactions, we find it nigh on impossible to establish proof. Now, having seen your – your rather public demonstration of distaste for Hoyle, we were hoping that you might – that you would stay chummy with the likes of Parker and Hoyle, keep your eyes and ears open and report back to us. We'd like to catch them *in flagrante* as it were, and you could be – well, an enormous help.'

Rory stands and pulls the dripping bottle from the ice-bucket. He fills my glass first. He is bent over Grey, obscuring my view, as I answer. 'I don't think you really know what you're asking,' I say slowly, then, 'You say Hoyle's is getting big. I say that from where I stand, Hoyle's is already bloody big, and from where they stand, I reckon I look bloody small. Sure, and just suppose as it is Hoyle who's doing the fixing and I do find out something or other and I shop him. Suppose I do give you the weapon you need and he and Parker go down, d'you seriously think these people don't guard their backs? I don't want to be melodramatic, gentlemen, but this is a world of vigorous physical competition at close quarters. One wrong move by someone that dislikes me and I could be seriously maimed or seriously dead. You know that.'

'All right. Yes, it's risky,' Grey nods, 'but no one need know save the five of us. We could find a way of keeping your name out of it.'

'A sure-fire way,' I laugh, 'and what way could there be, for Christ's sake? This is a very small world. Rumour spreads faster than athletes foot. Nah. There's no way.'

'It doesn't strike you, I suppose,' rumbles Stratton, 'that you might in common decency have an obligation to racing?'

'No, sir,' I say blithely. I stand and place the glass on the table. 'No, it doesn't. See, I'm an Irishman. Whatever you may think, I reckon I've given to the game and taken from it in pretty fair proportion, but I've got no extra obligation to the old school tie or principles of fair play or the sacred flag of the British gentry. As you've made pretty clear from the outset, sir, this isn't my place. I'm not a part of it all, so why should I fight for a country that doesn't acknowledge me as a citizen? I'm sorry. It may be incomprehensible to you, but I don't see why I should put my career and possibly my life on the line in the cause of your common decency or your fair play. I'm sorry.'

'We could make life seriously difficult for you, young man,' Stratton waffles, 'we've had our eyes on you for a long time ...'

'Oh, don't be a cunt, John,' drawls Kilcannon wearily.

Everyone freezes. Somehow, such a word on such noble, high-Christian, meticulous lips becomes hysterically funny. Rory almost chokes and disguises an outburst of laughter with a coughing fit. Grey's lips twitch. His open hand wipes away a smile. Stratton, astounded, stammers, 'Well, I'm sorry. I didn't realise. Well, if it's going to be like that ...'

'Let me see you out, Georgie,' Kilcannon stands and lays a hand on my left shoulder. 'Thank you so much for coming ...'

'I'm sorry I couldn't be more helpful. Thank you for the drink, sir,' I bow. Stratton says rhubarb.

Kilcannon leads me out into the hall. 'I'm sorry about that,' he says softly as he shuts the door behind us. 'He cares very deeply about the Right Thing, you know, but too much of this exclusively rural living narrows one's views a bit; doesn't make for subtlety. Have you seen Charles recently?'

'Not since he thrashed me at poker last Dublin Horse Show. Is he well?'

Charlie Vane is Kilcannon's only son, got on a lovely woman half the old man's age a mere twenty-three years ago. He was a very bad amateur until last year.

'Oh, fine, fine. Pretending to run the stud, but seems to spend most of his time riding to hounds or playing cards. Jousting with JCBs is, I understand, the latest diversion out there. You should go and see him when the season's done. He'd be glad to see you.'

'I'd like that.'

I frown up at the painting above the fireplace. It is an elegant, very stylised view of a meet in front of a tall house. In the foreground, a bay colt stands pissing. Behind him at various distances other horses gallop *ventre à terre*, their riders stiff and perpendicular. 'Hey,' I whistle, 'that's *here*. Surtees came here!'

'Hmm,' Kilcannon speaks quietly at my side, 'wonderful, isn't it? Look, old chap, if there's any way that you can actually help us – a quiet tip-off, you know, something like that – we'd be very grateful. It's really getting very bad, you know. We're not just talking about the usual quiet little fix up at Cartmel or Market Rasen; we're talking about big races, lots of money. It has got to stop.'

'Yes, sir,' I sigh. 'If anything comes up, I'll do my best to let you know. I'm not such a total shit as everyone seems to think.'

'No,' Kilcannon smiles and ushers me to the front door. 'No, I know you're not, Georgie.' He opens the door. It's dark outside now. 'I know you're not. Good night, then. Good night.'

The door hisses shut behind me. For a moment I am in darkness, then the light in the porch comes on. A few snowflakes bob in the light like seagulls on a swell.

It's absurd and I know it, but those few words of polite reassurance – coupled, perhaps, with the melancholy beauty of the snow – bring tears to my eyes.

Lord Kilcannon doesn't think that I'm a total shit.

Whoopee.

For that I'd wag my tail and bring him his newspaper.

Hell, I'd like to do what they ask. I'd like to have the approval and protection of the establishment. I'd like to ride Vantage to the victory that he deserves.

I'd also like to have a clear conscience, to own a palazzo in Italy and a beach house in the Marquesas, to draw like Picasso and to sleep with Hedy Lamarr fifty years ago.

It's just those niggling practical details which get in the way. Like if I shopped Hoyle and Parker those tapes would finish my distinguished career in seconds. Like I need money. Like I'm afraid of dying. Silly, trivial little things like that. There should be a sage proverb about it, really; something like, 'There's no dessert at the devil's table,' or, 'Mephistopheles won't go home on Monday morning.' Or, for the less whimsically minded and educated – flat jockeys, for example – the would-be virgin's proverb, 'Once you're fucked, you're fucked.'

I'd quite like to be a virgin again, but frankly, begging your pardon, ma'am, I'm well and truly fucked.

'The problem is,' this girl is saying, 'I really like them. They're really nice, really sweet people. But they never bothered to renew the original holiday let. They just let things run, you know? And it's been over four years now. So here I am, sitting in a cottage which must be worth – what? A hundred? A hundred and ten thousand? – and I've got sitting tenant's rights so I could just stay there for three generations. Well, not me, but you know what I mean. And one day soon, the old boy's going to want to sell, so what then? Do I just do the decent thing and move out, or do I sit and use my right to buy the place at half-price or something?'

She's sitting in the corner of the pub beneath a picture of Mandarin (F. Winter up) and a strand of red tinsel and a cardboard cut out of a Christmas tree with parcels on it. A scroll beneath it says *Seasons Greetings* and *Joyeux Noel* in golden Gothick.

It's Sunday morning and I've just finished singing the *Missa de Angelis* and I'm perched on a bar stool applying organic emollients to the tonsils. Johnny Mathis seeps from the speakers behind the bar, but the final hymn still sounds louder in my head.

> *Dear Lord and father of mankind,*
> *Forgive our foolish ways!*
> *Reclothe us in our rightful mind,*
> *In purer lives thy service find,*
> *In deeper rev'rence praise ...*

She's quite pretty, this girl, in a peaky sort of way, but you'd have to tether her in a strong wind. She's all got up in Laura Ashley flowers and frills and thick woollen tights. The young city type beside her quaffs his ale in the approved Victorian Hunt Breakfast manner. He sighs and punches away the foam on his upper lip with the sleeve of his Barbour. 'Sit tight,' he says, 'I would.'

'But I'd feel so *shitty*.'

'So do it through an agent.'

I like that. It's like the anti-hunting brigade: 'How can you be so

109

cruel as to kill a living being? Another slice of scrummy pre-packed pre-drawn battery chicken?'

The girl just says, 'Yes. But.'

'Honest, Soph. I mean, I hear what you're saying. I understand the problem, but you've got to take advantage of the lucky breaks as they come. The law says you have the right, so take it. Ten years ago, no question. I'd've said sure, do the gentlemanly thing and get out. Not today though, with property values what they are and so on. Things have changed . . .'

I had a good draw at the back of the church, so I broke with the leaders and got a clear run. Now the rest of the congregation is turning up and the tinsel creeps along the walls like a caterpillar possessed as the doors thud open and shut, open and shut. A few of Jack's lads are in amongst them. I say hello, Titch and hello, Belfast and hello, Billy 'iggs and so on. Not that Billy 'iggs is really called Billy 'iggs or anything. Things aren't so straightforward in these parts. Billy 'iggs just happens to look like a lad of twenty years ago who was also known as Billy 'iggs because he looked like an old-time jockey who really was called Billy Higgs. Obvious, really. Other lads are known by the usual nicknames – Titch, Slim, Chalky, Irish and such – or more usually by the name of their cities of origin. There must be ten Dublins in Lambourn alone.

A couple of jocks are in too – Pat Kersall, almost as aged as I and one of the most skilful yet consistently unlucky riders I know, and lean, hungry, tough Jimmy Knight. We may be intimates in the changing-room, but here we just exchange greetings and go about our business, ignoring one another yet constantly aware of one another's presence, a bit like schoolboys eating out with their parents on exeat day. Pat's with his wife Jodie and a couple of friends. Jimmy's got a trainer's son and Trevor Newport, the journalist, with him. They're making a lot of noise.

I've got a sleeve sodden with beer.

> *Drop thy still dews of quietness,*
> *Till all our strivings cease;*
> *Take from our souls the strain and stress,*
> *And let our ordered lives confess*
> *The beauty of thy peace,*
> *The beauty . . .*

'Excuse me,' says a firm female voice at my back, and suddenly there's a breast pushed up against my upper arm. I move the arm and shift to one side. 'Thanks,' says the girl.

Girl, I say. In fact she must be almost my age. She's taller than I and sort of biggish but slim, like a swimmer or something. She's got shoulder-length mousy hair and a strong, resourceful, sympathetic face. Not exactly pretty, perhaps, but halfway to being beautiful. She wears tan boots and jeans, a white shirt and a white angora sweater.

'Bloody Mary, please,' she tells Tony. 'Correction: large Bloody Mary with half a gallon of Worcester sauce.'

'Ice and lemon?'

'Ice, good idea. What in hell'd I want lemon in it for?'

'Chasing away the demons, are you?' I grin up at her.

She turns. Her eyes are very pale, very clear grey. They are extraordinarily beautiful. 'God, you don't know the half of it,' she laughs, 'and I didn't even enjoy it. At least, I don't think I did.'

'Here,' I slide off the stool and push it towards her. 'Invalid's rights.'

'Oh, thanks.' She sits. As she counts the coins and hands them to Tony, she says casually, 'You're Georgie Blane, right?'

''S'right.'

'Hi. Patsy Bryce. I thought jockeys couldn't drink nasty fattening things like beer. One glass of champagne and a lettuce leaf. Isn't that the sort of thing?'

'That's the flat boys. They just have to sit there. Me, I work. I need the nourishment. Can I take it that you're not the world's greatest expert on horses and racing?'

'You most certainly can. That's why I was knocking it back so much last night. Everyone was talking horse horse horse till it was coming out of my ears. If I'd ripped off all my clothes and danced a gay fandango on the table, they might just have noticed for long enough to compare my rump with some filly or other.'

'Hmm,' I nod, 'there is a tendency to single-mindedness round these parts, I'll grant you that. So what are you doing here?'

'You mean anyone who doesn't know what won the Derby in 1922 should be driven out with bell, book and candle and yells of "Unclean!"?'

'Nah. Very good to have a change, far as I'm concerned. It's just – in that case – how d'you know my name?'

'Aha. Faces are my business,' she says portentously. 'No, I take photographs, so I'm down for a few days to do the standard strings-of-horses-in-the-morning-mist and honest-sagacious-wind-whipped-wrinkled-faces bit.'

'For a magazine?'

'Maybe,' she shrugs. 'A book, even. Who knows?'

111

'Drink?'

'Yes,' she says slowly, as though surprised at herself. 'Yes, thanks. I'd love one.'

'Same again?' I gaze straight into those mountain spring eyes. She does not blink or look away. Her lips curl into a little smile.

'No. Reckon I can just about move on to white wine now. I gather the whole town falls asleep of an afternoon, so there's nothing for me to do anyhow, is there?'

So Patsy Bryce and I talk and laugh and my eyes linger on her lips, flicker occasionally and very evidently to her crotch, and her retinas do not contract in reproof. Her smiles are warm and playful and fearless and innocent as, paradoxically, adult eyes can only be in this business of sex.

Can I excuse myself on the grounds of fear or loneliness? Neither, I suppose, counts as much of an excuse. Not that I see the need for one really. I'm not hurting anyone after all.

'It's immature,' is the best that the accusers can muster. So what, pray, save in a cheese, is so darned wonderful about being mature, and what do the sanctimonious carpers mean by the word? So far as I can see, if you're enjoying yourself and the puritan can't quite see why it's sinful, he resorts to good old, reassuring, self-defining 'immature'.

It's just that some, like Kellow Hoyle, get their kicks by making deals, some by stalking deer or pursuing the great wave. Me, I find that frisson of power and liberty only in the great game of seduction: the thrill of anticipation as each circles the other, the first touch, the first smile returned, the blissful, heartstopping moment when the light rushes up in her eyes like a silver salmon to a fly.

And then – oh, then, you're away, and she, ideal, mysterious worshipful woman says in a thousand ways, 'Don't be ashamed. Don't be afraid. I, godlike, will share your lust, your feebleness, your nakedness and, by sharing, forgive.'

Every lover for me is a Christ crucified, a world redeemed. *Domina, non sum dignus intrare . . .*

> *Breathe through the heats of our desire*
> *Thy coolness and thy balm;*
> *Let sense be dumb, let flesh retire;*
> *Speak through the earthquake, wind and fire,*
> *O still small voice of calm!*
> *O still small voice of calm!*

Or there again, maybe it's all to do with knickers in the bath.

As my good friend Patsy says, Lambourn is a ghost-town of an afternoon, so when we notice that everyone has drifted away and that Tony is pointedly dusting tables and clattering ashtrays, I suggest that she come home with me.

It's a filthy dark grey afternoon and the roads shine brighter than the sky. Faces in the cottage windows are scattered as we walk to our cars. Hers is a scruffy dark blue VW Polo which chatters a lot as it starts up.

'You're married, aren't you?' says Patsy casually as I unlock the front door and show her into the house.

'Yup,' I throw the keys down on the hall table. 'You?'

'I was. Where's your wife?'

'Away for a couple of days. And?'

'And what?'

'And what happened? To your marriage, I mean.'

'It didn't work, that's all.' She wanders around the drawing-room touching flowers, glancing up at paintings. She picks up a vellum-framed photograph of Claire on our wedding-day. 'She's lovely.'

'Yeah,' I tip peanuts into a bowl and put them on the coffee table. 'So who was he?'

'American. Writer of sorts. War correspondent. Dour macho thrillers. Liked drugs and more than the statutory two in bed.'

'Other girls?'

'Other men.'

'Oh, tricky. More wine?'

'No. Just tea, please if I could. So it's OK if it's other women, is it?'

'Yeah, well, less destructive. We lesbians have got to stick to-gether.'

'Ha ha.'

'Children?'

'Nope. Wanted them at first. Decked out a Moses basket, bought hundreds of little antiquey sort of smocks and things, had a bassinet busting at the seams with old toys and Chilprufe liberty bodices and Lord alone knows what. Had a miscarriage first, then changed my mind pretty quick when dear Martin started playing his little games.' Suddenly, gracefully, she pirouettes and collapses into an armchair. 'Long time ago,' she smiles, 'all a long time ago.'

'I'll make the tea,' I say feebly.

'I'll give you a hand.'

Tea is made and crumpets toasted. The Scrabble board is brought out. *It's a Wonderful Life* is on the television. I cry. She just blinks and once, surreptitiously, wipes her eyes.

She trounces me at Scrabble, not least because she insists that 'Frisbee' is a bona fide word. Evening settles in like a sulk. Twilight always depresses me. I tell her so.

'Me too.' She stands and closes curtains and switches on lamps as though the place were hers.

A holiday programme starts on television. I go to turn it off, but Patsy says, 'No. Leave it. Please. It's pure pornography for me. That and seed catalogues.'

She is on the sofa. I laugh and join her there and kiss her. Nothing too lingering, forceful or demanding; just a minute or two of darkness and soft sensation. Then she pushes me back, sits up, kisses my cheek and says, 'Hush. You're disturbing my programme.'

I lean back. My hand rests in hers on her thigh. 'Why d'you like it so much, then?'

'I told you. Pornography. Sun and sea and sand and all things bright and beautiful. I haven't even been to the sea now for two, nearly three years, and as for the sun ... I haven't even had a decent car for – I don't know.'

'Ah, well, now, if there's frost tomorrow, you could at least come to the sea,' I tell her. 'Get some good photographs too.'

'Yeah?' she turns briefly away from the azure waters and golden beaches of Crete, half-board from two hundred and seventy-nine pounds. 'How come?'

'This time of year, there's snow or the ground's too hard, we take some of the animals that need work down to Minehead. Gallop them on the strand. You could come down with us.'

'Could I?' she's totally adorable. Her smile is broad and uninhibited. She clutches both my hands and kisses me with a loud 'Mmmah!' then, 'Oh, God, let the ground freeze to diamantine hardness, let it snow till the whole world is fat.' Again she turns back to the television. They're in the Maldives now.

A moment later, she throws herself back and stretches luxuriantly so that my hand on her thigh arises of its own accord to somewhere about the bikini line. She doesn't seem to notice. 'Oh, Georgie, Georgie,' she sighs, 'take me somewhere East of Suez where the sun blazes like that and the sea is clear and blue like that and ... ooh, I sometimes really find myself literally aching for the touch of the sun.'

'I'd like that,' I kiss her temple. 'So why've you stayed away so long?'

'From the sun, you mean?'

'Yup, that and.'

'Simply because of a paltry, squalid little thing called money. Or

114

rather because of a still more paltry, squalid thing called lack of it. Can't get very far on a dole cheque and what I make out of my pictures.'

'No alimony then?'

'Not a farthing.'

'Shit. No sugar-daddy?'

'Nope. Don't get many Rollers in Ladbroke Grove.'

'That where you live, then?'

'Yup. It's not too gruesome, but the natives don't do much in the way of scuba-diving.'

'No. Don't suppose so. Family?'

'One charming but impoverished father who lives in Budleigh Salterton with a cat and a lot of *Punch* almanacs and old pictures of himself in white tie and tails, and one pompous barrister brother who disapproves of both of us.'

'Not good,' I nod, 'not good at all.' And all at once I'm thinking how much I'd like to spoil this girl. I'd like to buy her presents, take her to restaurants and race-meetings, whisk her off for a fortnight to the Maldives, full-board two thousand, eight hundred and ninety-nine pounds per person. I could do it too with the Hon. Oliver's assistance.

At eight o'clock I suggest dinner. We're in the hall and I'm hollering to Vandal who has vanished into the next county, when the telephone shrills.

'You get it,' says Patsy, 'I'll get him in.'

I walk quickly through to the study and pick up the telephone like an executive in the movies. 'Yeah?'

'Blane?'

'Yeah.' Instant dysentery symptoms as I recognise Parker's voice. 'I'm just going out, actually. Talk to you some other time.'

'Blane, I just wanted to say one thing.'

'So say it, and fast, and by the way, Parker, if ever you enter my house uninvited again, you or your effing gorillas, I'll turn the blank white canvas of your face into a bloody Jackson Pollock action painting. Got it?'

Parker laughs. Least ways, I think that's what he does. 'Her her,' he says, then, 'You've been reading *Towards More Picturesque Speech* in your *Reader's Digest*, haven't you, Blane? I thought I'd already told you about pathetic little empty threats. They don't do anyone any good, you know, and they are rather laughable. Now, yes. You were very foolish and rude at Towcester yesterday. Very foolish. Very rude.'

'Good,' I snap. 'Just fuck off, will you, Parker.'

'Now, now. I just wanted to know whether you'd sorted out your ideas about our little sponsorship deal,' he continues in the same bored tone.

'You mean about hooking Vantage in the King George VI?' I shout into the receiver. 'Yes, Parker, I told you what I think about that. I'll not do it and there's an end on it.'

'I have no idea what you're talking about, Blane,' Parker says quickly. 'I suppose you're drunk as usual.'

'Well, that's what you asked me to do, isn't it? Pull Vantage, right?'

'Let's not be ridiculous, Blane,' Parker raps. 'I never mentioned any such thing and well you know it. We are talking about a little sponsorship on Boxing Day. I really think you ought to take a couple of Alka Seltzers and retire to bed. Too tiresome, all these silly fantasies and scenes. I'll expect your decision when you're sober. Tomorrow evening at the latest. It won't wait. All right? Good. Splendid. I'm sorry to find you in this unfortunate condition. Hope you're better tomorrow. Byee.'

My right hand grips the receiver so tightly that it visibly shakes. 'You just listen to me, Parker,' I yell. The tears of frustration and fury in my eyes are those of a child teased beyond endurance, 'You can take your fucking "sponsorship deal" and ... Oh, *Jesus!*' I pray as the telephone clicks and purrs at me.

I blink up at the light, then slam the receiver down hard. 'Jesus, Jesus, Jesus.' I slowly hit the desk with my clenched fist. Every muscle in my body is tensed. 'I want to kill that bastard. I want ...' But no one has yet invented sufficient vocabulary with which to express the things that I want to do to Parker and all that he represents in my existence. I end up producing nothing more than a high-pitched squeak, a sort of natural fax signal containing vivid descriptions of every torture yet conceived and several as yet unconceived which I'll get round to when I've got a moment.

It isn't fighting or losing that I object to. It's impotence that drives me mad.

Patsy insists on a change of clothes, so I spend half an hour on the white candlewick bedspread in her room in the Red Lion. I pluck imaginary gloves from my fingers as she does mysterious things in the bathroom.

She sings *Paper Doll* as the taps thunder and splutter. She sings *Blue Moon* as the still bathwater laps and gulps and splashes. She sings *Satin Doll* as she pads about the bathroom afterwards.

She emerges in a black and grey silk jersey number which clutches her *mons veneris* as she walks and stops just two junctions north of the knee. Her thighs are long and strong, her knees slick and shiny, her calves tight and smooth as mussel shells under black stockings.

'Do me up, would you?' she holds up her hair. It's only now, when fiddling with zips and hooks and eyes, that a quick pang of guilt makes my lips stretch and my vision blur. This everyday ritual of intimacy has far more of betrayal about it than anything we might do in bed. Fucking is always different. This – the touch of smooth warm skin on a knuckle, the hamfisted fumbling – this is always the same.

I run my fingernail up her spine and banish all thought by leaning forward and nuzzling her shoulder, the nape of her neck.

'Oh, Christ, come on,' she says, suddenly impatient, 'I'm hungry. Let's get a move on.' She scratches her neck where my lips have just been.

We dine on decentish winter fare at a nice little pub out Kingston Warren way. There's seafood platter – a few prawns that taste of scrapbooks, a few *crevettes crevées*, a few tiny rolls of smoked salmon, three mussels and a queen scallop shell filled with unidentified pulverised piscatorial particles Mornay, all balanced precipitously on rather tired *feuilles de chêne* – then a noble pie of steak, kidney and prunes stewed in Guinness. We drink an overpriced Beaune and then, with crème brulée and fruit salad, champagne.

Some sort of childish madness possesses us both tonight. It's compounded, I suppose, of sexual tension and, on my part at least, the desire to be free of all responsibility, all thought as to cause and result.

I start by telling Patsy the life-story of the poor bloody lumpsucker and how it sits on the bottom of the sea desperately and devotedly guarding these eggs which adorn our scraps of smoked salmon. We move on to the subject of the basking shark and how he ejaculates seven pints and what sort of life that must be – basking, ejaculating, a bit more basking . . .

There's a bit of sighing and tutting from the table behind us, which provokes us a bit more, so I tell Patsy about a girl I once knew called Mavis Trout who mistook her hair lacquer for her vaginal deodorant, spent the next twelve hours swinging from the light and has remained a virgin ever since, for all the efforts of her friends. I swear it's true. She doesn't believe me. She has a point.

I ask her to tell me a joke.

This is her joke: 'There were two teddy-bears in the bath. One

117

says to the other, "Pass the soap." The other says, "No. Who d'you think I am, a typewriter or something?"'

For some strange reason I find this cripplingly funny. I cackle so much and for so long that she gets the giggles too. Our fellow diners regard us with concern. Even when the fit has passed, I merely have to catch her eye and we're off again.

Over coffee and brandy I begin to spin fantasies. We talk of plays and dinners and holidays and things that we will do together. She shares the fantasies. Sex, it seems, is accepted as one of the things that we will do together, in amongst these adventures in the unfailing sunshine.

I hold her hand a bit. Our eyes play tag a bit. I tease her a bit. Really there's nothing much to say about this sort of dinner. We've all had them, the world over. No one remembers a single word that was said because the words are just the music to the dance.

One way or another, by the time we get up and return to the car, I'm feeling warm and proud and more than a little in love with Patsy Bryce. It's been a long time since I got feed-back like this.

'We'll have to start early tomorrow,' I tell her as I pull up outside the Red Lion.

'What sort of time?' Her face is in shadow.

'I'll be here – what? – six-thirty?'

'God in heaven. OK.'

'Do I ring you or nudge you?'

'Ring,' she says softly, 'this time.'

'OK,' I nod and grin, 'I like that.'

'What?'

'That "this time". Very hypodermical, that.'

'Yes, well, don't let it go to your head, Georgie Blane. You're a respectable married man. Well, I'm going to have to get some sleep.' She takes my hand. Suddenly her face is close to mine, her breath on my cheek. 'Thanks, Georgie. It's been years since I had a proper dinner like that.' She kisses my cheek. 'It was lovely.' She kisses my lips.

I suppose that the rest is just instinct. I'm not aware of exerting any muscular pressure which makes her turn over and lie in my lap, her head supported by my left arm. This, evidently, is what I missed in my Irish adolescence – the words whispered lip to lip, the amplified crackle of tongues, the panting, the heaving, resistance, yielding, resistance, the first touch of a naked breast which, like a new book, will never again seem so smooth, so cool – and then the pushing hands. 'No, Georgie. Not now. I must be going.' She kisses me quickly and it all starts again, then, again, this time mock exasperated, 'No, no, *no*! Good *night*, Georgie. I'm *going*!'

She buttons her dress, kisses me chastely and opens the door before she can reconsider.

I watch her to the hotel door, then wave and start the car up. If I were in a Western, I'd be whooping. I reckon I'm in love.

You've got to understand. In the first years of our marriage, Claire and I had a few nights of jollity with a visiting American girl called Toni and then with a rather gorgeous Italian *au pair* called Alessandra, but Claire tired of that game when the children arrived.

Aside from those, I've never been unfaithful to her in thirteen years of marriage, unless you count the floozies thrown at me by punters and the odd groupie here and there when I'm staying far from home. You may count them. I don't. And who asked you anyhow?

She hugs herself. Her hair is painted across her face. The speckled wind from off the sea makes her cord trousers struggle. Beside her, Jack leans over to shout something in her ear. He points at us. She nods, then reaches down into the pale blue grip at her feet.

I turn Canardeau. He's one of my oldest chums, a good looking brown animal with lop ears and a lovely eye. He's won nineteen races all told, on the flat, over hurdles and over fences. I've ridden him in some thirty races and he's as genuine as the day is long. He's running in the last at Kempton on Boxing Day.

On either side of me, Sandra and Dominic also swing their mounts round. Sandra is black and chubby-faced and has a smile like a strip cartoon. Dominic, who's on a young, free striding grey whom I've schooled and tried to teach manners over the past few years, is long and thin and loose-limbed and looks like the scarecrow from *The Wizard of Oz*. We've tooled these animals around for the past half hour, just to get their backs down. Now we'll take them for a sharp six furlong canter upsides on the harrowed sand.

To our right, the sea is indistinguishable from the sky. Everything out there is uniform grey. Closer in, the waves crisp and crinkle like tinfoil, suddenly accelerating as they climb the beach, beaded with yeasty spume. The water creeps almost up to the horses' hooves, then slithers back like folds of silk.

'OK?' I grin contentedly at Sandra and Dominic in turn.

'Wiv yer, Georgie,' Sandra grins.

'Let's jump 'em off quickish, then.'

119

And we're off, the hooves pounding on the hard sand, the horses' regular breathing providing a counter-rhythm to the regular rushing and hushing of the sea. 'Elbows outside your knees!' I call across to Dominic. 'You'll find it easier!'

As we draw near the cars, I look up. Patsy's on one knee now, the motor-drive on her camera clicking and squealing, clicking and squealing as she follows our path.

We pull up by the black rocks at the southernmost end of the strand and walk the horses slowly back through the water, letting the sea soothe and cool their tendons. They enjoy these trips. Anything which relieves the disciplined monotony of their lives can put an extra spring in their steps, an extra inch on their strides. That, really, is the point of these outings – that, and giving Jack the chance to give a slip o' the kipper to Diana Brockbank, one of his owners who lives down here.

Patsy's camera keeps on clicking all the time as we stroll back, and even as I pull up and dismount, she's scurrying around, looking for a better angle on this or that.

'Get anything worthwhile?' I ask.

'Marvellous. Absolutely marvellous. Stay there. Just talk to him. Great. And again. Lovely. Damn this wind. No. It was great. I could really get into this racing business.'

'Yeah. Kind of contagious,' I smile. I hand Canardeau over to his lad and turn to her. She takes three quick mugshots of me, then at last lowers the camera. Her eyes sparkle. She plucks hairs from her eyes. The wind at once whips it back again, resentful of her interference.

'Is that it, then?' she asks.

'That's it, I think. Nothing more, Jack?'

'No, no. You two get on. We'll just get 'em all loaded up and we'll be off.'

'Don't want a spot of breakfast or something, Jack?' I tease. I know full well that he's itching to be off with the good Mrs Brockbank. She is rumoured to drain strong men and leave them, like the vampire's victims, bloodless and tender and pleading for mercy.

'No, no,' says Jack again, 'you just be on your way. Nice to have met you, er ... Hope you got some good pictures.'

'I'll send you some,' Patsy shakes his hand. 'There must be something good in amongst all that lot.'

Jack turns away to supervise loading up. Patsy and I are alone on the dunes.

'Well,' I say.

'Well?'

'What next? What'd you like to do?'

'S'pose we'd better be getting back,' she shrugs.

'Yup. S'pose so. Wouldn't like a bit of breakfast first?'

'Well . . . Coffee, certainly. Yes. OK.'

So we hammer on the doors of two or three down-at-heel promenade hotels, only to be told that it's out of season, and at last find one landlord who's prepared to rustle up some coffee and a croissant. We sit in a sort of glass box extension and look down at the beach. It's littered with blue and orange binder-twine, plastic bottles, a plastic milk crate, a lorry tyre onto whose tread a host of half-developed mussels cling ('Oh, look, tyred mussels,' says Patsy). The sea is having its usual effect. We don't talk much, just sit, and drink, and watch, each isolated. Last night's feverish fumblings seem unimportant and ridiculous.

Things perk up a bit as we drive back. The world about us is up and doing. The morning's stillness is past. I switch on the wireless, just to banish the silence with mindless chatter and treacly Christmas songs. I even open the window on my side, trying desperately to awake us from this fit of sanity which possesses us.

In three days' time, when I have sixty thousand pounds in my pocket, there'll be no more sanity.

'You drive,' I say suddenly.

'Yup.'

'Like to drive this?'

'Oh, God, I don't know. I'm out of practise. Pretty powerful isn't it?'

'Yup. Like to have a go?'

'Well . . .'

'Which means yes. OK. I'll enjoy being a passenger for a change.' I pull into a gateway and, doing everything very fast now, walk round to her side. She slithers across into the driver's seat as best she can.

After a few miles and a few quickfire, pertinent questions, she begins to enjoy herself. I sit back, watching her affectionately out of the corner of my eye. She drives studiously but well.

'Tell you what,' I tell her as we near the Baydon turn off, ' 'Stead of turning down Lambourn way, follow the signs for Baydon.'

'Why? What's there?'

'I want to look at a car. All right with you?'

'Sure.'

Ray Yately owns Baydon Motors. He sells new Jaguars and used just about everything elses. He also owns a few handicappers of the sort which annually win a couple of quick races before the official

121

handicapper can catch up with them, and then run as regularly down the field in preparation for the next year's campaign. He has nothing to do with jumping, but I've bought my cars from him for the past ten years and he looks after them well in exchange for the odd tip.

He's a balding, fat little man whose brown or fawn suits are always too small for him. He is always chewing too, and his round pink cheeks bob up and down like bingo balls.

''allo, Georgie,' he greets me, ''allo, Mrs ... Whoops, it's not. Well, 'allo, any'ow, darlin'. What can I do for you, then? Car goin' all right?'

'Fine, fine.' I nod. 'Never been better. Just wanted to buy something used. Reliable, quickish, not too smart. Useful for getting about town, bombing to the shops, that sort of thing. Enough room not to be too tiring on long trips.'

'Know exactly what you mean, Georgie. Should be able to fix you up. Now, then,' he waves a cigar-box hand at the ten or so cars on his forecourt. 'Try the Polo. Reliable. Good engine, promise. Been over it myself with a fine tooth comb. Plenty of space – well, you know all about it.'

I stroll over and examine the little blue car. 'Lot of miles for a lot of money, eh, Ray?' I call over my shoulder.

'Yeah, well,' he shrugs, 'we can discuss that, of course, Georgie. Only one owner, mind. Reliable chap. Deals in antique clocks, matter of fact. Knows how to take care of a delicate bit of machinery, you know?'

I like that one. It has the ring of complete untruth.

'What else is on offer, then, Ray?'

'Well, let's see, there's the Fiesta. Nice little car that. Low mileage, extended warranty ...'

My eyes light on a lovely long low shape which reminds me of happy days. 'What about the MG?'

'Well, yes, of *course*,' Ray waddles over and strokes the sand gold roof. 'You know I love these. Drive one myself, don't I? Lovely car. New sills, beautiful nick. A little more expensive, of course ...'

I glance at the sticker on the windscreen. £3295. More than I can spare. 'V reg,' I muse, and open the driver's door, '86,000 on the clock. We'd have to discuss prices quite seriously, Ray.'

'But it's a collector's car, Georgie! Be worth – ooh, five grand in a few years time, you know that. Don't make 'em any more, dear,' he explains confidentially to Patsy, 'closed down the Abingdon plant. Tragedy. Everyone loves these cars. Make people smile, you know? Sporty without being flashy, you know?'

'I know all about it, Ray,' I hum, strangely content to be sitting once again cramped in that little bucket seat.

When first I arrived in England, I had two of these. The sudden surge of speed with which to dart through an opening suited me. The grace of the lines pleased me. It was a selfish time. They are selfish cars. 'Give us the keys, Ray.' I hold out my hand, 'We'll take her for a spin.'

I drive on the outward journey. Patsy takes over, amidst many protests, on the return. I teach her how to double de-clutch, how to shift out of overdrive in third in order to get the sudden kick in the back which carries you past many a more powerful motor. She enjoys it. She likes the speed and the sunroof and the stereo.

Back at Ray's garage, Patsy sighs deeply as she pulls herself from the car. Ray sits like a frog behind a desk too large for him.

'All right, Ray,' I tell him, 'I'll take it if the price is right and we get a twelve month warranty, and I don't mean one of those warranties that just covers you if the engine blows up. I mean a proper warranty. With that, I'll give you two seven-fifty.'

'Ah, no, no, no,' Ray sighs. 'Sorry, Georgie. Do anything for you, you know that, but we're talking about a collector's car, a vintage car in the making. Top quality, super condition. I'd keep it myself if I hadn't got my own already. Sorry, Georgie, but we're not speaking the same language.'

He's right, of course. He's speaking used-car-dealer, a subtleish language for forked tongues. I'm speaking Irish horse dealer. We've had a few centuries more practise. He groans a lot, sighs a lot, swears that I'm a thief, but settles for three grand with a twelve month warranty, which is what I was looking for. Still more than I can afford, though.

I exchange a currently worthless cheque for the documents and the keys. The cheque will not be presented until the day after Boxing Day at the earliest, and by then ...

I've burned my boats.

'No, Georgie, I *can't*! I *won't*! It's ridiculous! You've only known me for twenty-four hours and ... Oh, for Christ's sake ...'

'Look, doll,' I say with exaggerated patience, 'this is a selfish Christmas present, OK? I want you to be able to get down here. I want us to be able to go away for weekends and things. I want you to be able to get to the races sometimes, you know? OK, so incidentally it also means you can get to places of work or to the seaside occasionally, but first and foremost, I'm thinking about me, OK?'

We're standing on the gravel outside the house. She leans hunched over the MG's roof, her back to me. She is trembling.

'Look, Georgie ... Look, it's very sweet of you, but no. I mean, I can't ...' she struggles '... you just can't expect me to take a thing like this from a total stranger! It's crazy, Georgie. I mean, you've got a wife, and children and ... I mean, are you mad or something? I really think you must be mad. I mean, you're not bloody Elvis Presley or something! We're talking about serious sums of money.'

'Sort of money can be made with one small bet,' I shrug, all casual. I don't convince me much.

'Yes, but ...' She swings round now, exasperated. 'No, Georgie. I'm sorry. I don't know you and you don't know me ...'

'You weren't saying that last night,' I tell her with a nervous smile.

'Oh. Oh, so that's it.' She struts. 'Now I get it. A couple of kisses and I'm the established mistress. Sure you don't want to set me up in a nice little flat off Piccadilly, Georgie? Provide me with a maid and a poodle, hey? Or is this just meant to be the bribe to seal the bargain? Isn't three thousand a bit much for a quick screw, Georgie?'

'OK, OK,' I flap my hands feebly and turn away. In between momentary upsurges of indignation, I feel bloody stupid. 'OK. I'm sorry. Forget it.'

I trudge to the front door with a certain amount of resentful mumbling and a good number of sighs. I kick the boot-scraper, which doesn't argue, and fling open the door, which decides to have a go at me and narrowly misses me on the rebound. I fling myself down on the sofa and think the bitter, lonely thoughts of the spurned and frustrated lover. Life is unfair. Patsy is unfair. Nobody loves Georgie Blane though he's the nicest of nice guys.

Like the Irishman in the joke, it's not that I am out of step; it's the other fellers.

The front door clicks shut. I close my eyes. Patsy's footfalls click on the hall parquet, pad on the corridor carpet. Then her hand is stroking my forehead. Her lips kiss my cheek. 'I'm sorry, Georgie,' her voice is deep and soft. 'I shouldn't have said that.'

I open my eyes. Patsy kneels at my side, her chin on her left forearm which rests on my chest. Her right hand still strokes my brow, soothing. I muster some sort of uncertain smile. 'Ah, don't worry,' my voice fails. 'You're right. It was a mistake. I just wanted ...' I shrug and gulp. A tear slides down my left temple, 'bloody silly, really. I just wanted to give you something as would help out, you know? I know it's crazy, and maybe I'm cracking up altogether. Jesus knows, sometimes I think I must be, but . . . Oh, I don't know. It's been so long since I felt like this about anyone. It's crazy.' I laugh.

'No, it's not,' she leans forward and kisses the moist corner of my left eye. 'You're a really sweet guy and it was a lovely thought. Stupid, but lovely. But you don't understand, Georgie. With a present like that, you're not just giving; you're taking too. You giving so much so soon is putting an incredible amount of pressure on me. Do you understand that?'

'Yup,' I nod and clasp her hand. I kiss her palm, then lay my cheek in it. 'Yes. I understand. Sorry, love.'

'Oh, damn you, Georgie,' she kisses my lips. 'You're such a nice sort of mess. Tell you what we'll do. Neither of us knows what's going to happen tomorrow or the next day or a month or a year from now. I'm making no promises and you're not in a position to do so. So. I'll take the car with many thanks, but it's yours, all right? I'm just borrowing it for as long as we're . . . well, for as long as it takes, but there are no guarantees, all right? You might get the keys back tomorrow morning, all right?'

'All right,' I grin and pull her head down on my chest. 'I notice you say "tomorrow morning". I'll not get 'em back tonight, then?'

'No,' she mumbles into my shirt. 'Not tonight.'

For a while we just lie here. My breathing steadies. I kiss the top of her head. My hand strokes slowly up and down her rib cage. Some gland or other pumps out a warm substance which suffuses my brain like a blush. She turns her face up to mine. We kiss again, lie back again. Her hand starts moving. It opens the buttons of my shirt, runs flat over my nipples. I kiss her again. That hand emerges from under my shirt and roams downward, stroking my cock through the thick twill. Then we're rolling over so that she lies beneath me, legs splayed, and she groans as I run my hand over the warm welts between her legs. Her kisses are desperate now and demanding. I kiss her face, her ears, her throat, her breasts – and again she checks me, and this time I can smile down on her where she lies, her face streaked with saliva-soaked hair and more beautiful than ever.

'Not here,' she breathes. 'Oh, no. Not here. Let's go back to the hotel.'

'I want you,' I kiss her eyes. I then repeat this somewhat obvious statement several times, just in case she hasn't got the message.

'I want you too, damn it.' She arches her back, then hits me hard on the breastbone. 'Come on,' she pushes me off her and sweeps back her hair. 'Let's go.'

Now. I suppose it's time for the precise and breathless description of our activities – just what Patsy or I do with our mouths, our hands, our genitals this afternoon in our bedroom up there in this little old hotel overlooking the church, just what words are used to stimulate, what *soi disant* perversions we practise as afternoon turns to evening.

Yeah, well. Forget it.

There are moments of luxury, moments of pain, moments of delirious pleasure, moments of anxiety, moments of brutality, moments of exquisite tenderness, but all that matters is that it's Patsy and it's me and we're both at a particular moment of our lives in which we need each other and the freedom which each can bring the other.

Is it significant that as she sits on my face she shouts with real anger, 'Damn you, Georgie, damn you, damn you, damn you!'? Does it mean anything to anyone else that, on the first occasion, I can't even get it up, or that when I do and I come for the first time inside her after very slow and gentle lovemaking, her tears drip onto my face? Does it matter to anyone that her left nipple is inverted or that she sometimes likes to be punished and that I am happy to oblige? Judgments are made about such things: this is sadistic, this is masochistic, this is rude, this is immoral, this is erotic. There are no judgments. Not where we are.

We make love, that's all. We also sometimes fuck. It feels bloody marvellous. For today, I am home again and at liberty.

So instead, I will give you a bit of Socrates.

See, Socrates had a teacher called Diotima. She told him this. She said that we humans were once androgynous creatures, but that then we sinned and God split us clean – or almost clean – down the middle. So, according to Diotima, we spend the rest of our lives desperately searching out that other half who will make us whole.

And that's where I am for an afternoon and an evening. Whole, and home.

We dine in the restaurant downstairs, then drive up onto White Horse Hill in the MG. It's cold and clear and what clouds there are

126

shift rapidly across the face of the moon. We stroll for a few hundred yards along the old grass gallops.

'Walk on this,' I lead her to the side of the track.

'What?'

'Here,' I guide her. 'Just walk here.'

'God!' she laughs. It's like moonwalking!'

'S'right. Virgin turf. Never ploughed. You can put your hand right down into it – I dunno – eight, nine inches before you touch the ground.'

'Wow,' she leans back against my chest for a second and her hair whispers against my lips, my cheek, then, 'When does your wife get back, then?'

'Tomorrow.'

'Yes, well, I've got to be away tomorrow too.'

'Where'll you be for Christmas?'

'Oh, down in Devon. Daddy likes his Christmases.'

'When'll I see you again?'

'Dunno,' she shrugs. I kiss her crown and hug her to me. 'When you like, really, now that I've got proper wheels.'

'How 'bout Boxing Day? Kempton races.'

'I used to go racing with my father when I was a child,' she muses dreamily. 'Don't know whether I'll enjoy seeing you breaking your neck.'

'Yeah, well. I have no intention of doing so. Please come. I'd like you to be there.'

'All right,' she says quietly. 'If you want me to.'

I turn her round to me and hug her close and kiss her. The wind wraps around us. Once again I feel tears on her cheek.

'What is it, love?'

'Nothing,' she sniffs, 'just me being silly.' She gently disentangles herself and steps backward. 'Come on,' she gives a little laugh and wipes her eyes with her sleeve, then looks up at the sky. 'Come on. Time we were back in the warm.'

'Just one moment,' I tell Patsy when we're established at the bar with a drink. 'Got to make a quick call.'

I telephone Parker. He is obviously waiting for the call. The telephone rings just once, then 'Yes?' he says curtly.

'All right, Parker,' I tell him, 'you've got a deal.'

'Good boy,' he drawls, 'delighted that you've seen sense. Absolutely no need . . .'

I'll never know what there's absolutely no need for. The man's very voice makes my teeth ache. I quietly replace the receiver and, after telling myself under my breath what I would like to tell Parker, I return to buy another drink for my lover.

I can afford it, after all.

Somehow it's plain that tonight is for sleeping. In the morning, we make love, but all that we're doing now is fighting the inevitable. Outside, hooves clatter as strings pass by on their way back from work. Cars sound like cellophane as they sweep by on the wet road.

Baths, packing, make-up, the dreadful formality which prevails when another human being has invaded these private and solitary rituals, and so to a quick kiss goodbye on the landing.

I trot down the stairs and leave first. I feel cold and tired and empty as I return to the town where people regard me as a jockey, a husband and a father.

Fat lot they know.

Midnight mass is over. Christmas is come. We've sung *Adeste Fideles* and *Silent Night* and exchanged happy looks of love, and outside in the church porch I've hugged Claire and Joanna and Conor and wished them all a happy Christmas. Everyone has wished us a happy Christmas too as we walked back to the car. Then after Horlicks and excited giggles at the kitchen table, the children went off to bed. We waited half an hour or so and I drank a few large whiskeys, then we went upstairs to their rooms. While Claire kissed them goodnight, it was my job to replace the empty rugger stockings on the bed with others already full to bursting with tubes of Smarties and chocolate coins, handkerchiefs, socks, comical books, toys, gimmick pencils and such. Both children know the truth, but they have elected to preserve the illusion. To my mind, that makes them very bright children.

The turkey is stuffed. The chopped potatoes lie in a bowl of water with a lump of coal. Piles of gaudy parcels are stacked beneath the tree. All is ready.

Today will be as it always has been. The children will come early into our room to empty their stockings. Claire will put on the turkey. The morning will be filled with carols. The same decorations will be on the dining-table. There will be roast potatoes, brussels sprouts, bread sauce, cranberry sauce, bacon, chipolatas, grape stuffing, sausage meat stuffing and fried chestnuts, then three-year-old plum pudding and a great deal of brandy butter. There will be champagne, of course – Taittinger, this year, thanks to some generous sponsors – then port and crystallised fruits and orange and lemon slices and dates and nuts.

The tree comes after lunch, the exchange of presents and thank you kisses and expressions of delight, then a walk, a Christmas cake which will barely be touched, a snooze in front of a movie, cold turkey and ham and mince pies and so to bed.

We have often asked the children if they would like anything different just for a change. They say no. They like things as they are. That too, to my mind, also makes them very bright.

I cannot sleep tonight. Maybe because I am conditioned from

childhood to expect a miracle this morning, maybe because I long to talk to Patsy and to wish her a happy Christmas, maybe because of Vantage and tomorrow's hateful task, maybe even because my mother is calling from somewhere out there. She always made a big effort at Christmas. It was a symbol, to her, of the happy family which she had visualised and could not quite reconcile, in the usual run of things, with the real family that she had. She believed in making it an extra special day. She did that all right.

I stand at the window enjoying the touch of the cold air on my naked body. Beneath me in the paddock, Benbow snorts and stamps and snuffles on the frost-fused grass. Behind me, Claire lies sleeping peacefully, one long arm flung out where I have been lying. Her dark hair is splashed out on the pillow which seems cold blue and cubist in the reflected moonlight. I make a resolution, as so often before, that I will make this a happy Christmas, a happy year.

The telephone rings. I jump like a rabbit. I throw myself across the room and snatch it up before it can awake Claire. 'Yes?' I whisper urgently into the receiver. 'Who the hell is it?'

There is no reply. I can hear a rustling sort of sound and what might be breathing. That is all.

'Hello!' I croak again. 'Hello, hello, hello! Who's there? Look, if this is some kind of a joke...' There's something about the telephone which brings out the clichés.

Again that rustling. Whoever it is is in bed. Then a deep sigh, a click and the telephone says 'brrr' to me.

I replace the receiver very gently, but Claire is awake. 'Whozat?' she groans into the pillow.

'Dunno,' I frown. 'No one. Go to sleep, darling.' I lean over and kiss her temple.

'Bloody people,' she mumbles.

'Yeah.' I get up and walk over to the window again. 'Go to sleep.'

Then suddenly, almost before I know what I'm doing, I'm getting dressed. I pull on boxer shorts and trousers, throw my shirt over my shoulders and pick up my boots and socks.

'Georgie...?'

'Go to sleep.'

'What are you doing?' She's fully awake now.

'Nothing. Just going downstairs to make a call. I think it might be Bob. Go to sleep.'

'So what if it is Bob?' she snaps. 'For Christ's sake, it's after three o'clock on Christmas Eve! He's just drunk again.'

'Maybe. I'm just going to check.'

'It could be anyone, for God's sake, Georgie. Don't be absurd.

130

It could be any old drunk in Lambourn having some weird little joke.'

'Yeah, well, maybe. I think it was Bob.'

'You're being ridiculous. Really. You'll wake the whole house up.'

'No, I won't,' I tell her sharply. 'You might if you carry on like this. Hold on. I'll try his number.'

I switch on the bedside lamp. Claire groans and blinks at me, then rolls over and bangs her head into the pillow hard – 'Oh, for God's own sake...'

I dial Bob's number in London. I count twelve rings. No reply. I give it another five. Still no reply. 'Damn it.'

I try his cottage down at St Genny's. Nobody home. 'Right,' I reach down to pull on my socks, 'I'm going to have to go up there.'

'You're mad. Stark, staring...'

'Yeah, well, OK, so I'm mad, but I've got to back this hunch. Bob's depressed, he's alone, it's Christmas...'

'Balls,' she says flatly. 'He's probably stuffing that Laura woman.'

'Good thinking,' I sigh. I pull open the bedside-table drawer and fish out the address-book. 'Pullen, Pullen...' I dial with my right hand whilst buttoning my shirt with my left. 'Come on...' I breathe into the telephone. I reach for the cigarettes. 'Come on...'

'Hello...' a voice as cross and bleary as Claire's creaks at me.

'Laura?' I light the cigarette and exhale through my nose.

'Who is that?'

'Look,' the cigarette sticks to my lower lip. Smoke makes my eyes water. 'Look, sorry to ring you at this ungodly hour, love. It's Georgie. Georgie Blane. Is Bob with you?'

'No,' she sounds mildly surprised but she has regained her self-possession. Her voice is once more the well modulated coo of the fantail. 'I haven't seen him for a couple of days, actually, Georgie. What's the matter?'

'I don't know. I got a call ... Look, I can't explain, but I think something might be badly wrong. I may be making a fool of myself, but – do you think – could you possibly get over there?'

'What, now?'

'Yup. Sorry. He's badly depressed, you know, and I can't raise him on the 'phone. I've got a nasty sort of feeling about it. Please, Laura.'

'Oh, shit,' she stretches and sighs. 'OK. I'll get a taxi.'

'Great. Thanks. I'm setting off now. If anything's wrong, stick a note on the door. I'll not be more than an hour or so. OK?'

'Oh, God save me from emotional cripples,' she breathes, but already the rustling and rattling beneath her voice tells me that she is on her way. 'OK, Georgie. I'll expect a rather nice present from the Celtic twilight twins for this one, and nothing less than dinner at Nico's if you're wrong.'

'If I'm wrong ...' I start, then, 'Go on, get on with you, girl.'

'I'm going, I'm going. Happy bloody Christmas, Georgie.'

'And to you.'

I get up, switch off the lamp and head for the door.

'Georgie . . .' There is a warning note in Claire's voice.

'Sorry, love. Got to go. Get back to sleep. I'll be back in time for breakfast. Don't worry.'

'*Georgie* ...'

But I've shut the door behind me and am halfway down the stairs before she can muster another logical word.

'And all for the sake of that sausage,' purrs Laura behind me.

I turn away from the drawn, open-pored face on the pillow. Bob's hand is heavy and clammy in mine.

'Sausage?'

'That ridiculous gawky little Susan woman.'

'Ah, come on,' I smile, 'she's not that bad.'

'Oh, God. I wish she were. Bad Bob could care for, but not timorous and bossy and middle-class and – I was going to say "moralistic", but of course Bob's the moralist. She thinks morality means keeping things the way mummy liked them. She spent the first few years nagging poor Bob about being a responsible citizen and making lots of money. Then when he's done his best to be a boring old fart of a TV hack, she complains that he's not the man she married and she runs off with a bloody policeman.'

'Yeah, well, I reckon as he sort of wanted that sort of thing when he married her. Live on *foie gras* too long and a sausage can look quite attractive.'

Foie gras takes it as a compliment and slowly smiles. Her gloved hands fold precisely in her lap. 'A balanced diet,' she says, 'is what is needed. Bob throws out squibs and flares and she's like – I don't know – a solar panel. She absorbs all the light and stores it for her own inner source. She gives nothing back. No sparkle, no enthusiasm, no admiration, nothing. She's a black hole. Bob can't live with that sort of thing.'

For a woman who's been dragged from bed at a quarter past three of a Christmas morning, Laura Pullen looks pretty darned good. A few more wrinkles than usual are visible around her eyes and her mouth, perhaps, but then this has been an emergency. All told, she can't have allowed herself more than fifteen minutes for make-up. Her sleek black hair is swept up, smooth as dolphin skin. Her high brow is polished, her thin lips glossy pink and perfect. She wears a full black skirt, a tight, tailored black and white hounds-tooth jacket – and those gloves, for the Lord's own sake. A very elegant lady is our Laura.

She sort of took Bob up about nine years ago. She indulged him, paid his bills and showed him off to her *demi-monde* friends. Bob's lazy. He was happy to get his oats and his dough from the same source and perhaps, too, he liked to play the talented, indulged child to his sophisticated mother figure.

The hand in mine moves. A deep clogged sound like a long burp shakes Bob's chest. His hair sticks out in spikes. His eyelids are veined and waxy. His skin has the texture and colour of suet pastry. A tube runs from his nose, another from the drip feed at his left arm.

Outside, the light is growing. The sky is tarnished silver. Soon dawn will come with its tin of Goddard's. Here inside the hospital, the striplights hum. Already things clatter and clank beyond the screens which surround us. It's Christmas morning.

Bob never fully lost consciousness, so Laura says. When she found him, he was dopey and more than a little drunk, having chased an improvised cocktail of Paracetamol and some sort of sleeping pill with three quarters of a bottle of whiskey. 'I'd seen him worse than that before,' she told me smoothly, 'I mean, at least he was still excited enough to groan a bit and swear at me. The pill bottles were artfully arranged. There were stacks of letters – just in case anyone coming on the scene should get the wrong idea. Bit on the hammy side, frankly.'

Laura knows human idiocy. Her scepticism might be mistaken for hardness. I don't think that she's hard. Childless years as a rich man's mistress have merely stripped her of self-deception and romanticism. Like a worldly wise and weary mother, she sort of loves in others the aspirations and pretensions which she no longer possesses.

Bob's eyes flicker open then sink back again. 'Oh, Jesu, Jesu,' he moans. 'I've got a hell of a head on me.'

'Serve you right,' I tell him.

'Georgie,' he says definitely, 'how d'you get here?'

'You summoned us, remember? Laura had to lose her beauty sleep to play Superman. Bloody marvellous Christmas you've given us all.'

'Sorry.' He drools as though his tongue were too large for his mouth. 'Sorry, Laura.'

'Ah, don't worry, Bob, dear. It was going to be a very boring Christmas anyhow. You've done nothing to change that.'

'Should've left us,' he mumbles.

'Ah, for Christ's sake, cut the self-pitying crap, would you, man?' I snap, though my hand tightens about his. 'This is a very old scene, and unless you can think of some new and interesting dialogue, I'd rather you just shut up.'

His shoulders jerk upward at that, though whether it's a sob, a laugh or mere flatulence, his face does not tell.

'Blick ...' he dribbles.

'What?'

'Black cock,' he enunciates clearly, and a large tear spills from his right eye.

'*What?*'

'Black cock,' he shakes his head three times. His eyebrows arise at the centre. His lips turn downward, 'Oh ...?' he squeaks, the tears dribble down his cheeks. His shoulders shake and he turns his head into the pillow. I can just squeeze his hand and wait.

I know what he's thinking of. A long time ago, when Susan and he were engaged, she had an attack of food poisoning. Susan was a rookie journalist on a newspaper in Frome in Somerset. She had her own flat there, but her parents – a retired bank official who had worked in Kenya and his ever so respectable wife – lived a mere half hour away near Bath.

Anyhow, on this day, Susan went to a dinner party at the house of some avuncular closet queen old family friend. He served a soup of blackcock, which is some sort of grouse.

When she returned to her flat, things started happening to her. Her intestines started playing trad jazz, her heart heavy metal, her head psychedelic electronic stuff. She was freezing but dripping sweat. Someone was pushing a pillow down on her head and little bright tropical fish swam behind her eyelids.

She managed to swim through milk filled with these fish to the telephone. She managed to dial nine nine nine.

'All right,' the ambulanceman told her, 'drag yourself to the door if you can. We'll be there within five minutes.'

She did as she was told. By the time that the ambulance arrived, she was ga-ga. The ambulancemen's faces loomed out of the haze at her. 'What have you eaten?' they demanded. 'What-have-you-*eaten*?'

And all that her feverish mind could hold on to were those two grotesque words. 'Black . . . cock,' she murmured, 'black . . . cock.'

The last words that she heard before lights out were, 'Gor, we've got a right one 'ere.'

Bob gulps down a couple of tritones and opens his eyes again. 'Sorry,' he croaks, then he clears his throat and says it again. 'You know,' he says, 'if I'd known what it was like – the stomach pump and that – I'd never have done it.'

'I suppose you realise what you're saying?' I growl.

'I . . . well,' he blinks sheepishly, 'it was really horrible, G. Honest.'

'Yeah. Well, thanks for a lovely Christmas present, Bob. You've really cheered things up. I'm off home. Talk to you this evening. OK?'

'OK.' He looks puzzled and hurt like a puppy that's swallowed a wasp.

I bend and kiss him quickly, then turn away. I kiss Laura too. 'Stupid self-centred bastard,' I tell her. I don't lower my voice.

'I know,' she nods, 'I'll give him a right royal bollocking for this when he's up and about again.'

'You do that, and add a few choice phrases for me, would you? I don't trust myself to talk to the poor bloody invalid just now,' I direct my remarks clearly at the poor bloody invalid on the bed. 'I just might wring the poor bloody invalid's neck.'

I cast a quick last glance at Bob where he lies propped on the pillows. He just watches me from under heavy eyelids with an impassivity which seems insolent.

I'll wager that Regulus's last thoughts were of identical vestal virgin twins with busts like junket and inner thighs like nacre. I bet that in those final moments he dreamed of Numidian nymphets and of sinking his muzzle into Punic pubises as deep and dark as the oblivion into which he was falling.

Sleeplessness, I am trying to say, makes one inordinately concupiscent, and I'm feeling raunchy as hell as I head back out of London in the slate grey light. I want to see Patsy, and Patsy's flat can be no more than a few hundred yards away as I drive down an empty Notting Hill. But Patsy is in Devon, and I've got to get home.

I nonetheless grant myself five minutes' indulgence. I find the house where she lives. It's a once-elegant little terraced place with cream paint peeling from its facade. Two battered Ford Zodiacs stand in the patch in front like dusty barracudas in a museum. There's a lot of dog shit on the pavement, and even as I look, a grey creature with the look of an old paint-roller waddles deliberately across the road and squats and strains.

Hardly lilac trees perhaps, but I sit there for a minute or two anyhow, doing a Freddie Eynsford-Hill and feeling happy because soon, I know, we'll share some good times up there on the second floor behind the net curtains.

A few minutes of such reveries have a regenerative effect. I'm feeling positively vigorous as I set off again, singing the appropriate song with a degree of power and sincerity which would make Jeremy Brett consider taking up mime, could he but hear me.

Back at home, I ignore Claire's accusing questions save to murmur, 'He tried to top himself. Nothing serious.' I then plunge wholeheartedly into the business of Christmas.

St John's College choir and Bing Crosby alternate on the record player. After breakfast, we present each of the children with just one present to keep them occupied while lunch is prepared. For Joanna, it's a home computer, for Conor, his first fly-rod.

Now, a computer to me is an artefact a little less exciting than a swiss roll, but Joanna seems delighted and rushes off to her room to play with it. As for the rod, it's a carbon fibre beauty which'll serve for trout or small salmon. I picked it out myself. So I teach Conor how to tie the figure of eight and the half blood, stick a large Green Highlander on the end of the cast and take him out to practise casting.

This is fun. Conor's enthusiastic and receptive and has a deal of patience. I'm happy to have him back with me and I'm happy too to be out on this frosty morning, hearing once again, out of season, the reel's complaint as line is stripped off, the song of a shooting line.

Conor's a fine feller. He has dark hair of course, and a lot of my natural stockiness and strength, but he's taller than ever I was at his age and he has his mother's large dark eyes. From me, if you believe in ascribing such things, he's acquired stubbornness, persistence, belligerence and an affectionate nature, from Claire a degree of restraint, cool, poise and considerateness. He'll make a gentleman by the time he's done.

None of the snow so far this winter has remained, but somewhere around midday a few flakes skitter around like gnats. This is a further cause for celebration. The bookies lay long odds against snow on Christmas day. I hope that Hoyle takes a caning. There's always the distant possibility, too, that the snow will fall so heavily that racing will be cancelled.

I'm positively cheerful when at last we're summoned in to lunch. We troop in with the ritualistic solemnity suitable to so aged a convention, so sacred an altar.

The golden turkey gleams and steams on the sideboard. Every silver charger is filled with food. 'Ah, now, there's a fine bird,' I sharpen the carving knife with a flourish, 'a noble bird as lived well and died happy. Shall we avenge great-grandpapa on this proud gobbler?'

'Aye,' say Joanna and Conor in unison.

'And I say "aye" and all. Bird, thou standst condemned.' And I plunge the fork into the great bird's breast.

But no sooner are the plates charged, the knives and forks raised, than a car engine sounds like a distant wind and tyres crunch on the gravel. I look up. 'Who the hell is that?'

I stroll around the table, taking the opportunity to give Conor's shoulder a quick encouraging clasp as I pass. I peer through the frosty window, through the strobe light snow.

A grey Vauxhall stands arguing with itself beneath the hornbeam. The passenger door opens. The sleeve of a cream husky emerges, then a leg in loose black denim, a head of shoulder-length blonde hair. She straightens and opens the back door. She leans in for a second and talks to the driver, then emerges again with two large flat parcels in her hands. She pushes both doors shut with her hip and turns towards the house.

'Oh, bloody hell,' I say grimly.

'What is it?'

'Susan,' I say, and the word tastes sour.

'Auntie Susan?' Conor's knife and fork clatter on his plate. His chair puffs as it is pushed back on the carpet.

'Stay where you are, old son,' I say more sharply than I had intended. 'Get on with your lunch.'

'But Dad ...'

'Yeah, yeah, all right,' I open the door into the hall. 'Don't whinge. I'll see what she wants. Back in a second.'

Moans from Conor and Joanna follow me through the front door. Susan is just five yards away as I step out. The snowflakes are large now. They swirl slowly, like the stars in the darkness when you've landed on your head.

She stops when she sees me, and for a moment we just look at one another. She has dark eyes and a full mouth which is normally curled into that blasé, pseudo-cynical semi-sneer favoured by nicely brought-up schoolgirls who want to be thought sophisticated.

I've never liked her much. I thought when first Bob introduced us that she would be good for him. Bossy, perhaps, but that was not necessarily a bad thing. I thought that she might supply him with the motivation and the security that he needed whilst he would give her fun and – well – education in the ways of humans. But it didn't work out that way. These formulae never do.

I never liked her because she seemed bright and knowing but I suspected her of being vacuous. I never liked her because, when you smiled at her as you do smile at pretty girls, her pupils contracted like Rediffusion stars. She was nice enough, but I never could see beyond the smoked glass windows and find out who, if anyone, was driving.

'Hi, Georgie,' she steps towards me. She obviously intends to kiss me. Something in my eyes changes her mind for her. 'I'm so sorry to bust in on you like this, but I just ... er ... I had to find out ... Can I come in?'

'I'd rather you didn't just at the moment, love,' I tell her. Then, taking pity on her, 'They're all having lunch, you know. Let's go for a walk. I can't be long. Who's that in the car?' Sudden anger puts an edge on my voice.

'Oh, that's Olly. You remember? He used to work with me. You can't believe how sweet he's been.'

'Well, that's all right,' I sigh. I remember her friend Olly, a tall, lean, bespectacled nodding-dog. He thinks that Susan's arse is the Orient.

I look down at the parcels in her hand, now flossy and spangled with snow. 'Those for the children?'

'Yes, I thought...'

'Thanks. I'll take 'em if I may.'

'OK,' she says sadly. Snowflakes snag on her eyelashes. She blinks them away.

I take the parcels from her and lay them on the bench in the porch, then turn back to her and take her elbow. I guide her back up the drive.

'How is he, Georgie?'

'Oh, fine, fine. Bad hangover, that's all. That and a great deal of pain and confusion. Otherwise fine.'

'Oh, God,' she shivers. 'Don't be too hard on me, Georgie. You don't think I wanted to do this, do you?'

'Yeah, well. Funny, that. There's a school of thought says you can only do what you want to do. There are at least two options in every circumstance. You could have stayed. You could have said "no" to your little friend.'

'Yes. I know. I could have done. I could have gone on putting up with your drunken brother and his self-centred ways until I went mad, but I have only one life, Georgie.'

'So has he, and as I understood it, you'd committed those lives for better or for worse. Obviously my understanding of the language is imperfect. Just what do you people mean when you say those words?'

She holds up her hands. She bites her lip. 'All right, Georgie, all right. I didn't come here for a fight and I don't expect you to understand. I only wanted...'

'Georgie!' Claire calls from the front door.

'What?'

'What are you up to? Bring Suzy in. Don't keep her waiting around in the cold! Hi, Suzy.'

'Hi, Claire, love.'

'We're all right here, thanks,' I call back sternly. 'We've got a couple of things to discuss.'

'Oh, don't be ridiculous, Georgie. Suzy's a member of the family and as long as I'm around, she's always welcome. Come on in, Suzy. Pay no attention.'

Susan turns uncertainly towards the house, then glances back at me. 'You'll not be thinking,' I say softly, 'of messing my family about any further?'

'That's bloody unfair, Georgie. You just don't know what I've been through.'

'Nor do I care, doll. Oh, sure, you could tell me a hundred tales of Bob's sins, and I could sympathise. Christ knows, I *do* sympathise. I'd find it difficult to live with the man, but I didn't choose to. I'm his brother. I may want to tear his throat out at times, but I can't make myself any the less his brother. You think marriage is about love and individual happiness. I don't. I think it's about commitment and bloody hard work and growing up through each other's sins. I see it as a contract for the good of society, just like – I don't know – a commitment to a country, and to hell with the individual, but maybe I'm just an ignorant, old-fashioned little shit of a bogboy and you're a highly-sophisticated intellectual. I dunno. All I know is, you've broken a contract with one of mine, so sympathising with you would just be a needless complication. You're the enemy. That's all.'

'Simple as that, is it?'

139

'It has to be.' I shrug.

'*Georgie*,' Claire's exasperated voice makes me spin round. She stomps up the drive, a mere shadow at first on a malfunctioning television screen. When she emerges, she looks furious. She's put on boots and a sheepskin coat. 'What the hell do you think you're doing? The children are longing to see Suzy. Hi, Suzy.' She kisses her with unaccustomed warmness. 'Come on inside and pay no attention to him. We've laid a place for you. There's masses of food.'

'No,' I give anger its head, 'there's no place for Susan at my table, and there's an end on it.'

'Don't be so fucking rude and ridiculous.'

'Rude?' I laugh. 'Rude? This woman, my brother's wife, has been rutting with some goddamned policeman, Bob attempted suicide this morning and you tell me that *I* am rude?'

'It's all right, Claire,' Susan says quietly. 'I'll go. There's no point.'

'No, I'm damned if you will,' Claire grinds her teeth. 'Of all the hypocritical crap...'

'It wasn't a real attempt at suicide anyhow,' Susan drawls casually. 'From what I can gather, he notified half the world and its wife of his intentions. He was just posturing.'

I stare at her bland face, stupefied. 'Dear God,' I breathe, 'you don't know the man at all, do you? You don't understand a feckin' thing, do you? Yes, sure, he was posturing, pathetically posturing, and, do you know, I'd almost rather that he had actually topped himself. Don't you see what it means when a man like Bob ends up doing a thing like that? Ha, he's alive all right, but he's lost his vanity. He's lost his sense of humour. *He's not funny any more.*' I take a deep breath and steady my voice. 'Now, go please, Susan. I've got nothing against you personally. I don't blame you. But just don't turn up here expecting to be welcomed. You're not one of us any more. That's all there is to it.'

Claire tells her to pay no attention. She begs her to stay. She glances accusingly back at me a lot. She says that it's her house as much as mine and that anytime Susan feels like dropping in, she's welcome. I say nothing. Susan has at least some sense. Her cheeks are bright red. Her formerly apologetic expression becomes more and more self-righteous and indignant but, with the odd sneer in my direction, she at last slams the car door. The silent, shadowy driver starts up the engine and, just ten yards up the drive, the Vauxhall vanishes.

'Well, well done,' Claire jeers. 'Big man.'

'He's my brother,' I snap as she stomps, head down, towards the house. 'OK, so there's nothing logical about it. There it is, that's all. Someone shits on him, that someone gets as assegai up the arse from me. All there is to it.'

She stops, turns. 'We're not bloody cavemen, Georgie,' her voice shivers up a chromatic scale, then, 'at least, some of us aren't. Susan's had a hard time, for Christ's sake! She's a human being!'

'Sure she is,' I lick snowflakes from my lips, 'and so'm I and all, and human beings survive by making allegiances – clubs and classes and nations and families and so on. And they all battle against one another and that way there's some sort of balance, right?'

'One can change allegiance,' she says. Her eyes flash snowlight.

'Oh, sure. You can move to a new club and face the consequences, sure you can. But you can't just cop out. You can't just say "OK, so my nation or my family's given me loyalty and life but as an individual I don't find it particularly nice or convenient just at this moment, so they can get stuffed". You and the children are starving one day. The woman next door has food. You can't say "Ah, poor little diddums will suffer if I nick her food". You go out there and you cut the bitch's throat if necessary and to hell with the selfish luxury of a bleeding-heart conscience.'

'Jesus,' Claire stares, 'you really are out of the bloody ark, aren't you, Georgie? You and your brother.' She shakes her head with pitying condescension. 'I don't know, I really don't. If I'd known . . .' She turns back towards the house but remains standing still.

'If you'd known what?' I say softly.

'What it was like to be married . . .'

'Yes?' I lay a hand in the crook of her right elbow. 'Go on.'

'To a bloody Irishman!' she shakes off my hand. 'If I'd known . . .'

'You'd never have done it, right?'

'Too bloody right I wouldn't. You're savages as near as makes no odds, both of you!' Her voice is without rage or rancour.

'I see,' I sigh. 'Because we're loyal, we're savages, right?'

'You? Loyal?' She chips off a chunk of fossilised laughter, 'You and Bobby? You with your two bit tarts and Bobby with his rich bitch Laura? Loyal, you? Don't be ridiculous, Georgie.'

'Oh. Right. Yeah.' I shrug, 'But then we don't get divorced like you sweet, kind, understanding English, do we? And we don't let people fuck around with our wives or our children or our brothers. You English, think you know about family, don't you? We all sit there by the bleeding Christmas tree and sing carols and play at being nice little Victorians and that's *it*. Then we go off and if we happen to feel a little uncomfortable or frustrated or aggrieved or

141

something, what the hell? That's not family. That's not marriage. That's fucking play-acting, no more. Niceness. Hell, anyone can afford to be *nice*. Nice is cheap. Nice never troubles your conscience or gets you into the wars. OK, so fine. Let's go back in there. Let's all be nice together. Let's understand the bastard who rapes Joanna or murders Conor. Let's ask him in to tea and find out what went wrong with his potty-training. Come on.'

I push open the front door and hold it open for her. She sweeps past me like a princess.

Any hopes that the sports might be called off are quickly dispelled when I peer blearily out of the window this morning. The sky is a shocking blue. Snow lies like sunlight on eaves and windowsills and in crisp neat patches on the lawn and the fields.

I should be excited, looking forward to winning one of the biggest races in my career on the finest horse I've yet ridden. Instead, I drag my feet as I descend the stairs and make myself a cup of coffee.

Claire is upstairs pretending to be asleep. I tried to jollify the proceedings when lunch was at last resumed yesterday, but Claire was in a serious vengeful sulk. Joanna saved the day by ragging us both, but then, what with one thing or another (it didn't help that Conor gave me a sculpture that he had made – and quite a good one at that – of his brilliant sporting hero father taking a fence on Trufflehunter) quite a fair amount of wine and then whiskey found its way to my complaining gut. Booze means weight, so then I had to take four piss pills and spent half the night disposing of unwanted fluid.

Piss pills are effective enough. A few Lassix or Hydra-Saluries can take five or six pounds off you in the course of a night. They also, of course, have their side effects. Cramp is the least of them. Your hands lock, your legs swell up, breathing becomes painful and the least effort can prove exhausting.

One way or another, I'm not feeling at my best this morning. But I'm going to meet Patsy. I concentrate on that, and I'm eager to be off. In fact, so soon as I hear a footfall on the landing, I rapidly drain my mug and get going.

I long to talk to my wife and children, to be at ease with them, but I haven't the time or the energy to play more than one role this morning. Joanna is hunting today. Conor and Claire will watch the race on television. Children get bored at the racecourse, says Claire. She's probably right.

My gloved hands flutter and flap on the steering wheel as I slip onto the M4 and head Londonwards. I'm apprehensive, as though today were a day of beginning or ending. The worst of it is that it is neither. I'll come home tonight and things will be as they always were. I'll be richer, that's all. There'll be no glory, no magic, no miracles, just a workaday bit of villainy. The thought depresses me. Somehow, somewhere inside me, I'd like a beginning. Or an end.

The man on Radio 2 says he reckons that Lightning Bar will take the big race, but look out for that phenomenally talented novice, Vantage. He then plays a song called *You Really Got a Hold on Me*. Somebody knows something.

There's no point in taking two cars to the sports, so, after much argument, I've arranged to pick Patsy up in London and take her to Kempton. At first she said no, she'd meet me at a pub near the course. Then it was, OK, she'd wait at Hammersmith tube. I said no. Hell, it wasn't much further to Ladbroke Grove and why should she wait outside in the cold? And anyhow, I'd like to see her place so that I could picture her there in days to come when we were apart. At last, very reluctantly, she conceded.

We've got plenty of time, so I lock the car when I arrive, anticipating a cup of coffee at the least, a restorative tumble at most, but I haven't even crossed the road when she emerges, obviously bustling, at the front door.

'Georgie,' she effuses across the road. A lorry rumbles past, picks up my name and runs away with it. Then she's by me and kissing my cheek, smelling of wool and powder and L'Heure Bleue. For a moment she holds her cheek against mine, then she gives me a quick squeeze and says, 'Mmm.' She steps back.

She's in a classical, slightly too sculptured number in green silk. A black coat hangs over her arm. She says, 'You made good time.'

'Yeah,' my hand lingers on her arm, 'I thought we could have a cup of coffee, something. Set us up.'

'Good idea,' she walks round to the near side of the car, 'but not here, please, Georgie. I can't wait to get away from here. Depresses me.'

'OK,' I shrug, ' 's go, then.'

She chats well nigh non-stop on the way to Kempton. We stop at a hotel for a cup of coffee and still she witters. She's sparkling, she's witty, she's silly, she's excited about the day ahead. If we were at a dinner party, I'd be proud of her. As it is, I feel lonely.

We arrive at Kempton soon after eleven.

It's not my favourite course. It should be like its lovely sister just down the road at Sandown, but somehow it never quite makes it. It's got a lot going for it. The obstacles are big and stiff and well-banked. The gravel subsoil means that the going is never heavy.

Under its new management, it's been tarted up a fair bit and the facilities are now OK. They've also got rid of the bitch of a fence on the back stretch which some genius placed right by the path back to the racecourse stables so that your horse had its mind on bed when it should have been thinking about jumping.

It's just that somehow it's an impersonal place. The contests are too far from the crowds and there's always a pervasive smell of London about it all.

'So what now?' asks Patsy as we step from the car.

'Well,' I pull on my covert coat and reach for my trilby. 'First thing is, I abandon you and go to the weighing-room. Shouldn't be more than twenty minutes, but I've got to talk to my valet.'

'Your *what*?'

'My valet. They're the fellers look after the kit, clean your breeches and boots, lay out your colours, things like that. They also tell you what you're riding.'

'You mean you don't know?'

'Not entirely,' I sling my binoculars over my shoulder and shut the car boot. 'I mean, I know what it says in the papers, but there could be extra rides, changes of plan, you know. My valet'll know all that. Then I have to sort out the tack with him. You know, which animal needs breastplates and blinkers. That sort of thing.'

'And he's your personal valet?'

'Ah, no. On the average day, the poor sods have to look after perhaps eight of us. On a day like today, though, when you've got ten meetings or something round the country, there'll probably just be two of them here to look after all of us. It'll be chaos. That's why I'm glad to be here early.'

'OK,' Patsy flicks her hair back over her broad black collar, 'then what?'

'Well, when we've got all that sorted out, I change into my colours for the first and come out and join you. We can walk the course if you'd like.'

'Sounds cold.'

'And wet, I'll be bound, but educational.'

'I might take a rain-check on education just this once,' she grins and takes my arm.

We stroll across the car-park. Tam Maclellan pops out from behind his Rover. 'Mornin', Georgie,' he leers suggestively at Patsy.

'Good day, Tam.' I scowl and move on fast. Various other people hail me as we pass.

'Well,' I continue, 'I'm afraid you're going to have to spend the rest of the day as a spectator. I'm engaged in all six contests today.'

145

'Do I back you in any of them?'

'If you like. I'm in with a squeak in the second, and I'll be there or thereabouts in the last.'

'What about Vantage in the big race?' We duck under the rails.

'How d'you know about him, then?'

'Oh, I've been reading the papers a bit since we met.'

I like that. 'Nah. Not worth your hard-unearned money. He's a great horse, but only a novice. He's got a lot to learn. He's inclined to put down.'

'Put down? English please, Georgie.'

'Sorry. Yeah. A free-striding novice comes charging up to a fence and he gets it wrong, so he puts in a quick one and gets too close. Hits the fence with his chest and goes A over T. Or at least, if he doesn't, you do.'

'Isn't that what you're meant to do? Put him right, I mean?'

'Yup,' I grin, 'in general I can judge an approach ten strides off, but you can't mess around with an animal like the Ripper, and even if I've got it right, he may not think so, so he puts down regardless.'

She shudders. 'There must be a better way for a grown man to make a living. Like being a mercenary or a Kamikaze pilot or something.'

'Yeah,' I agree ruefully, 'there must be.'

At the entrance to the winners' enclosure, I take her hand. 'Meet you out here in – what? Twenty, twenty-five minutes. OK?'

'OK. I'll get a cup of coffee and warm my toes. Good luck, Georgie.'

'Thanks, love.' I kiss her lips as warmly as the public nature of the place allows, then swing jauntily around. As I trot up the steps into the weighing-room, I see Polly Waller on the other side of the enclosure. I smile and wave and take a couple of paces towards her, but she just looks at me. One corner of her lips is tugged back in an ironic grimace. She slowly shakes her head and turns away.

It's already chaos in the changing-room. The only three valets are rushing hither and yon, desperately trying to keep everybody happy. I'm greeted with the usual cheerful chorus of 'good mornings' from those who aren't too busy with dirty stories or gossip to notice my presence.

'Gawd, you look bloody terrible, Georgie,' chortles Tim May, a bold blond farmer's son who was champion last year.

'Thanks, mate.'

'Don't mention it.'

146

'Who's the bird, then?' calls Chris Young.

'Did 'e come with a bint then?' Jay Cullinan raises an eyebrow. 'Didn't see 'er. What's she like?'

'Tasty if you like 'em big. Posh sort.'

'Ooo, hold your hand out, you naughty boy.'

'Let us know if you need some help, Georgie!'

'I'll manage, thanks.'

'All fucking goats, these Irish buggers. Did you hear about the Irish chemist called Flynn? Busy bonking his Swedish assistant in the back room when the shop bell rings. Rushes out with his wedding tackle still sticking out, and there's the parish priest Fr O'Reilly standing there waiting for his aspirin. So Flynn doesn't know where to put himself, but the till's open, see. So he shoves his pecker in the till and slams it shut, right? And Fr O'Reilly sees Flynn standing there all bright red and he says, "What's up with you, my son?" and Flynn says, "Sure and you're not going to believe this, father, but I've just come into rather a lot of money." '

The laughter is general and ironic. 'Doesn't improve with age, Tim,' I tell him.

'Who does, mate? Anyone heard about Pete?' – a reference to Peter Straker, who was leading in this year's championship table when he fell at Worcester and had his face trampled by a clumsy nag.

'Yeah. Saw him last week,' says Jay.

'He's out of hospital, then?'

'Yeah, but they're going to be patching him up for years to come. Split his nose, knocked all his teeth out, broke his cheekbone. He's thinking of buying a little place in Covent Garden. Beneath the opera house.'

'Might be an improvement.'

'Couldn't be much worse.'

'Poor sod. He'll be back some time next month.'

The conversation continues like that: here a joke, here a solicitous enquiry about the health of a wife or a child, here a ribald jibe: the conversation of barrack-rooms and changing-rooms and clubs world wide. A feminist with no taste for precision would no doubt sneer and call it 'macho'. She'd be wrong. As wrong as if she called the everyday boys-and-make-up chatter of disco-girls 'bimbo'. We all form associations, that's all, and are strengthened by them, and each of those associations has its own carefully worked out internal hierarchy: nations, classes, clubs, religions, all have their rituals and their sub-culture language and their uniforms designed to alienate others and to give us, the members, a nice warm feeling. We belong. We have a family.

'Er, Georgie?'

Tam again.

'Hello, my old son. How's it goin'?' I raise my bum from the bench in order to pull on the breeches.

'Och, fine, fine. Nice bit o' cuff you got out there.'

'Ah, sure and she's a charming lady, Tam, charming lady.'

'Listen, mate,' Tam punches my right shoulder conspiratorially. He sits beside me and breathes jellied eels and toothpaste at me as I pull on the boots. 'Listen, Georgie,' he glances nervously from side to side. 'Just wanted to ask you. Just for interest's sake, you know. I've been wondering, see. Thing is, when you ... I mean, when a man, you know, does it ... well, how much should it be?'

'Depends,' I hum, 'I always charge a tenner myself.'

Tam wriggles. 'No, seriously, Georgie. I mean, how much, do you reckon? Would you say a level teaspoonful?'

I frown. Simplicity can be very confusing. At last light dawns. 'Five mililitres?' I give it the expert term and adopt the expert expression. 'Sounds about average to me, Tam.' I stand and pull on my red sweater. My mind is shying away from the image of Tam concernedly measuring such things. 'Yeah. Something like that. Don't see as you could get a heaped teaspoonful, anyhow.'

'No.' He too stands. His smile paints many broad diamonds on his face. He pats me on the back. 'That's a good one, that is, Georgie. Heaped teaspoon. Nice one.' He laughs, which in his case means going 'Hng' and having a quick writhe.

'Yeah, thanks, Tam. Must be going now.'

'Right. 'Course. Nice bit o' cuff. Heaped teaspoonful, eh?' He giggles.

I smile tolerantly, then turn my back and grimace. One day someone's going to hit poor Tam out of sheer disgust.

I'm impatient to be back with Patsy. I've had a quick word with Johnny, my valet, I've had the fourth piss of the day, I've counselled Tam and I've changed, all within twelve minutes.

I stroll out of the weighing-room and into the icy air. I look around the enclosure. Patsy isn't there. She said that she wanted a cup of coffee. She'll be in the bar. I wander across to the nearest one. No Patsy.

Maybe I should return to the weighing-room. She'll be back in a few minutes. But why make her walk all the way back in the cold? Better to find her, wherever she is, and share a warm drink with her.

I walk round to the stands. I check the Seafood Bar. Already a

148

thick strand of smoke divides the room. A few punters huddle over their drinks and their newspapers, plotting. No Patsy.

Of course, she could just be in the loo. I'll get back to the weighing-room as soon as I've checked the Jubilee Bar.

I trot up the steps of the stand.

Half way up, the piss pills hit me. At least three invisible Zorros lunge at my chest with razor-sharp rapiers. They hit their mark. I stop. I screw up my face against the pain. I half turn and I clench my fist and I rest my forearm on my thigh. I wait for it to pass.

It's only a second before the oxygen forces its way through my lungs again. I breathe out, straighten, and blink burning eyes at the blue sky. 'Jesus,' I mutter. I swing round to continue my climb.

And then I see Patsy.

She's down on the grass by Tattersalls. She's talking to Oliver Parker.

I am a powerful engine starting up. I know that from the noise which rumbles its way from my gut to my lips. It starts as a low purr and changes rapidly into a snarl, then a full-blooded roar. And as it increases, my speed increases too. I leap down the steps two at a time and then I'm springing across the grass, jinking to avoid the strolling punters.

Even as I run, Patsy turns back towards the weighing-room. Parker walks through the gate into the ring, and vanishes into the milling mass of bookies.

My business is with Parker. I want to rip his throat out. But I reach Patsy first. 'Georgie!' she gasps as I charge up to her. 'What is it?'

I grasp her hands and clutch them hard. 'That bastard,' I pant, 'that filthy bastard in the camelhair. What did he want?'

'Oh,' she shrugs, 'nothing.' But those gin clear eyes show worry, even fear.

'You've got to tell me,' I squeeze her hands still harder. 'You've got to, Patsy. I need to know. What did he say to you?'

'He just thought he recognised me, that's all.'

'Oh, sure.' I snarl in the general direction in which Parker disappeared, 'Oh, sure. He just thought ... What did he say to you? Exactly.'

'Nothing!' she squeaks, then I look down into her eyes. Her whole body trembles. She wrenches her hands from my grip and pushes past me. 'For God's sake, what is this? "What did he say?"' she mimics, '"What's going on?" Oh, shit, I knew I shouldn't have come!'

Her voice wavers. I pursue her. I know now that, if I go on, I am

149

going to hear something very horrible. I have to persist.

'What are you talking about, you shouldn't have come?' I demand. 'What's going on, for God's sake? Do you know Parker or something?'

'Leave it, Georgie,' she snaps. She bends beneath the rails and stumbles across the course, 'Just leave it alone, all right?'

'No, it's not all right!' I roar at her back. 'What the hell is happening? What ... ?' My vision blurs. I follow her into the centre of the course. I have to gulp a lot. Terror chills my veins like embalming fluid. 'Patsy, *please*,' I beg, 'please *help* me. I have to know.'

'No, you don't. Just forget it,' she is crying now, but her voice is still hard, 'forget the whole thing, Georgie. Here,' she fumbles furiously in her bag. 'Here,' she flings something bright onto the grass. It clinks. The MG keys. 'I told you. Now just go, Georgie.'

'Patsy...'

'Fuck off, Georgie!' she howls. Then she stops. She covers her face. Slowly she sinks until she's on her hunkers and her shoulders shake and heave.

I'm blinking away tears myself as I stroke her hair. 'Tell me,' I order.

It takes time. It takes time for her to check her heaving chest and to wipe the tears away. It takes a little longer for her to gain control over her voice. Then she wants to escape again, but this time I grab her and shake her and demand that she explain.

She does, and each sentence is a punch in the gut.

'Parker – he paid me.'

'To do what?'

'Not ... just to be nice to you. That was all. See if I liked you. I did, Georgie. I really did.'

'Sure, so he paid you. How much?'

'You don't want to know all this.'

'I do. Tell me.'

'Five hundred.'

'Five hundred. Oh, dear Lord Jesus, help me. And for that you were to screw me, make me fall for you...?'

'No!' she yelps. 'No, Georgie, no. Don't do this to yourself. I'm sorry. I'm so, so sorry.'

'So you're a whore. Right?'

'No! Please, Georgie, I promise you. There was nothing said – I – I didn't have to do anything. It was like an escort job, he said. It was up to me. I didn't mean ... I *liked* you, Georgie. You were

150

k-kind. I was sorry for you. I – I really wanted to ... to make love with you.'

'Is this what you do, then? For a living?'

'No! Oh, for God's sake! I never lied to you, Georgie. Everything I said was true. I do live where I said. I do live alone. I am divorced. Everything. I made a point of ... Oh, God, I wish I could die. I meant it when I said I'd go on holiday with you. If this hadn't happened – I don't know – it might have gone on for years. I'm sorry, Georgie. I'm sorry, sorry, sorry.'

By now I can only mask loneliness with cold fury. 'You're sorry. So every time we fucked you rang Parker and told him, "It's OK, he's hooked," did you? Does that shit know every detail of what we did, every damned silly joke I made? Christ, what a prat I've been! Let me buy you a car. Let's go on holiday. I was in *love*, woman. I was seriously in love. With a goddamned whore.'

'No!'

'Oh? So how did Parker pick you out, then? Advertise the job in *The Times*, did he?'

'Oh, God,' she shudders, 'all right. You might as well have it all.' Again she reaches into her handbag. Her fingers shake as she plucks a scrap of paper from her purse. 'Here.'

I blink down at a tiny scrap of glossy paper. 'I was lonely, Georgie,' Patsy says as though from far away. 'I was lonely and I wanted some unhypocritical fun. I didn't know ...' her voice tails off.

I read:

> *X3597 Attractive educated girl, 34, seeks good company and sexy fun with sensuous male. Sense of humour, cleanliness and discretion essential. Photo, phone no. ALA LONDON/ ANYWHERE.*

I stare at her. She just looks straight back at me. The tears spill from her eyes and drip from her jawbone. Her lips tremble and work.

'Like I said,' I say harshly, 'a whore.'

'All right,' she gulps, 'so I'm a ... a whore if you like, Georgie, but I got paid and I did what I was paid for. I'm ashamed, but only because I care for you and I've hurt you. But I've never lied to you, Georgie,' she blurts. She is almost screaming now, her arms extended to me as I turn away, 'I never broke my word! I never broke my word. I never ...'

And when I glance back through a lens oiled with tears, she's on her knees in the dirt, hugging herself and rocking. Her body heaves as though she were choking and she keens as though asking a question. 'I never broke my word ... I never...'

'Georgie and I have discussed this, Frank,' says Jack, 'and we reckon the best thing to do is to hold him up. He'll jump better settled and we know he's got the turn of foot. They'll be expecting us to jump off and go like hell like last time. We'll give 'em a bit of a surprise, eh?'

'But what about thingy?' Smythson points with his umbrella, 'Lightning Bar. He always comes with a late flourish, doesn't he?'

'Yeah,' I say glumly. 'Tim's flash that way. Likes to lie out of his ground and come with a wet sail. I'll try to slip the field four furlongs out. We'll just not come back to 'em.'

'Well, I'm not sure,' Smythson waggles his moustaches, 'not sure at all. He's a tried and tested front runner. Why change a successful formula? That's what I'd like to know.'

I sigh and tap my boot with my whip. Jack also sighs but tries to be diplomatic. 'He's a tried and tested front runner, sure, but in essence he still thinks he's hurdling. He's too much on his forehand. We've been putting a lot of work into getting him back on his hocks, but Georgie still feels that he needs settling if he's to concentrate on his work. These are stiff fences, Frank. Not much margin of error.'

'Well,' Smythson waves dismissively, 'on your own heads be it. Must say, I'm disappointed you haven't got him better schooled yet. Still.'

Jack casts me a quick glance which seems to say, 'Don't hit him. That's my privilege.' I smile wearily. I'm numb and dumb and on automatic pilot. I just want to get this over with and to return home.

At long last comes the order to mount. Ginger leads Vantage over. The rug is pulled off. The horse looks frankly magnificent. His mane and tail are plaited – an old fashioned Carlton touch which I approve of. I am surprised again – as ever – by the depth of his girth and the great pair of breeches on him. He tosses his head as though, like me, he's anxious to be getting on with the business.

Jack flicks me up into the saddle. I wink down at him. Smythson calls, 'Well, good luck then, Blane.' I nod and steer Vantage into his place in the line.

I'm alone now, thank God, with an animal that I love, an animal that will not argue with me or cheat me. The sense of fellowship that I have with him merely serves to intensify my loneliness and sense of rejection. That, and the fact that I must reward his trust with betrayal.

It's all very well, but there is no choice, is there?

I mean, I have a family. Isn't that where my first obligation lies? And anyhow, now that I've given my word and Hoyle has laid heavily against us, there's too much money involved. All the other bookies must have been laying off with Hoyle, and still he has us on offer at fours. There are millions riding on this, and for millions, people will do all sorts of things, including murder.

Oh, I'd love to rub their faces in it, but not at the cost of my career, my health, even my life.

And it's all very well to spout the old 'Thou must thy trouthe holden by my fay' number at me. The man who takes that as his motto, in the City, say, can kiss goodbye to the Porsches and the country houses.

But I'm not in the City. I'm an Irish lad who loves horses and racing.

Sure, but even we're allowed to survive aren't we?

OK. Let's look at the options: I pull this horse. He loses a bit of faith and his slot in Ruff's Guide – always supposing that he actually can win after all this. A few thousand people lose their money and curse me a bit, then forget it all. I pick up £60,000. Everybody at home cheers and thinks I'm wonderful.

Or: I win this race. Everyone pats me on the back. I earn 7% of £25,000. I am forced into early retirement, well nigh penniless and disgraced, and run the risk of more serious retribution to boot.

Consider. Moot. Discuss. With diagrams where necessary.

We canter up to the start and the cold air which splashes over my face refreshes and wakes me. This, I think, not for the first time, is what I was born to do. Here, alone on a fast horse in the open air, far from the lies and intrigues, the flattery and coercion which constitute the 'social skills' of the City or the grandstand over there, here I belong and am in control.

People bemuse and scare me. At least horses just kick or bite.

Tim May is already up at the gate on Lightning Bar, a showy dark brown with a white blaze who looks supremely wound up for today. Tam is on Musk Orchid, a long-backed, pale bay runt with a hell of a pop in him. Jay Cullinan has what would have been Pete

Straker's ride on last year's winner. Oblomov's a beautiful, burly, seventeen-hands gutsy grey with feet like dinner plates. Tommy Perkins looks taller than ever on my old friend Sundance, a light-framed rich chestnut with four white socks that used to win a lot on the flat – and so on. There are twelve of us in all. I know all the riders, all the horses.

We mill around as ever and Tim calls up to the starter, 'Don't bother about me, sir. I'm in no hurry. I'll just drop in behind them.'

'All right, my old son,' I think, and grin, 'and we'll just drop in behind you and hitch a ride, thank you very much.'

The tapes spring up and I do just that. Tommy Perkins finds himself, much to his surprise, having to set the pace, while I tuck myself in on the inside at the back and we just bowl along behind Tim. Vantage snorts a bit and wants to be ahead, but I just tell him to wait a while. It's all right. His time will come.

And as soon as he is balanced and going well, I too attain a mysterious calm. Most professionals, whatever their game, will, I think, recognise this. You've worked and trained and practised for this moment of action. You've envisaged it many times. Now at last it has come, and you thank God for it.

I experience it to some degree whenever the tapes go up. You can't ride a good race, after all, if your mind is a box of fireworks accidentally lit, shooting off emotional squibs and rockets every which way. Some controlling part of you has to be still, ready at any moment to deal with this problem or with that as it crops up. Fear, grief, resentment, anger – all these things are irrelevant. They'll wait. I rode a treble on the day after my father's death.

It's as though an orchestra back there in the cranium had been having high jinks with John Cage improvisations all day. Now the conductor has picked up his baton and they are all in perfect harmony. They are playing Bach.

'I am in heill, and in gladnesse . . .'

At the first, I pull him out a little. He bounds impatiently up to it and over it and shakes his head like he's just had the first scoop of the day and is saying, 'Boy, did I need that'. At the second – an open ditch – and the third too, I give him enough room but not too much, and he gets back well and launches himself like a good 'un. As for the first stride away from the obstacle, my principal problem with this horse is not gathering up slack and picking him up; it's keeping up with him. He's so darned intent and quick away from them that he might leave me behind if I'm not sitting tight at the time.

No need to get excited. We're having fun, aren't we, boy? A day out together. Been looking forward to this. Pace is a bit too steady, isn't it, feller? We might have to slip 'em a bit earlier than we thought if that Sundance isn't going to run away with it off the pace. Yeah, well, I'm sure you can take him with one leg tied behind your back, but nonetheless, just in case.

There are six ahead of us, five behind.

Ah, dear God, boy, but it feels grand to be here with you beneath us, the boys around us . . . seven, eight, nine and – hup!

Nice one, lad, but stop racing, will you? There's time enough for that. Just concentrate on getting over them safely for now, would you? That Oblomov is going like a train. Ah, so you reckon he should be pulling a dray, do you? All right, my cocky friend. You just prove it.

Is no one going to take the responsibility for stepping up the pace? Someone's got to break before we do. Ah, good on yourself, Tam Maclennan. That's better. Shit. Who's this fucker right on our shoulder? Could get rough for a second here, my old love. Sit tight.

And if there were a tape-recorder on at the moment, you'd hear nothing but regular harmonium bellows of the horses' lungs, the faint jingling of harness and then a couple of loud bumps and grunts and a dispirited whine, 'Ah, come on, Georgie, giss some light, will you?'

You'd then hear my witty response, 'Sod off, Chas,' before the hooves stop rumbling and the birch crepitates and another open ditch is behind us.

It's sod's law, of course. If I'd intended to win this race, I'd have been brought down on the first circuit. Because I don't, we're going sweet.

This concentration on what I'm doing doesn't prevent images from flashing across my brain as I guide Vantage through the ack-ack volleys of mud over fence after fence. Susan is there, standing forlorn yet poised in the snow, saying, just as I have said to myself about this race, 'Don't be too hard on me, Georgie. You don't think I wanted to do this, do you?'

I let out a reef and move upsides on Tim's outside. We're stride for stride as we take the first on the second circuit.

Joanna presses the tit on the kettle in the sunlit kitchen. 'You could have escaped, Daddy. You know you could. Whatever the business.'

Ah, youth, youth.

'All right, boy. Still full of running? Let's stretch our legs a little, shall we?' I do something imperceptible, indefinable even to me, which makes Vantage move up, past Tim and Lightning Bar, past Jay and Oblomov.

We're third now as we turn into the long back stretch. Tam still leads on Musk Orchid. Tommy and Sundance are a length and a half behind. We're still on the inside, about three lengths behind the leaders.

There's a lot of to-ing and fro-ing going on. Chas Wilcox moves up on my outside on Permesso. He's got no chance, but at least the commentators will mention him for a few minutes. Behind us and to the right, Jay pulls out into the middle of the course, poised. I can't see Tim anymore. He must still be in our slipstream.

And now something incredible happens. Chas tries to do me.

Now, Chas is English and started his brief career on the flat. Whatever Polly says, therefore, he can ride a hard finish. But we Irishmen learned other, more arcane skills while poor little Chas was still in his cradle. In many a bumper back home I've been turned over, sometimes for no better reason than that one of the old sods feels that he could do with a bit of practise. I've turned a fair number over myself and all.

There are several techniques, ranging from the boot raised hard under another rider's foot to the good old, conventional, direct technique of barging violently sideways, taking the feet from under the other feller just as he approaches an obstacle or even forcing him through the wings. This is the technique which Chas favours. With me, for Christ's sake!

He's just ahead of us and we're racing now as we charge up to the open ditch halfway down the back straight. Suddenly I see that certain look on his peaky little face. His mouth is set in a tight nervous line. Some conditioned reflex tells me that this is trouble.

Even as I realise it, he's on me. His chestnut's rump swings across hard, catching Vantage just ahead of the shoulder. We can't swing left without going through the wings. I can't pull Vantage back without ploughing through the fence. I do the only thing possible. I stick my whip hard up under the chestnut's tail, yell, 'Gaaarn!' and kick on. A lesser horse than Vantage might have swung to the left. A lesser horse than Vantage might have retreated from the fence and ended up in a forest of legs beneath the fence. He just grits his teeth, keeps a straight line and charges on like a tank annoyed by a mini.

Chance is on our side too. The combination of my yell, Vantage's brute force and a whip up the fundament makes Chas's mount yield a little to the right. If he'd kept coming in our direction, we'd have been dead. Vantage gets too close. For a moment, everything inside me lurches from its proper position and I think I'm going out through the back door, then, mercifully, the see-saw tilts forward. Vantage slithers. I flounder, but I'm all right. We're both all right.

Chas isn't. It's not easy to concentrate on jumping large fences while being shouted at, barged and goosed with alien objects. It's a confused horse that takes a Louganis-style dive with somersault and half-twist into the unyielding ground.

Chas won't be riding for some time. That'll teach him to take on Georgie Blane.

Quick now. We've lost ground. Come on, my old love. Let's shift. I sit down and soothe him and jockey him along. It's all right. No one's going to try that again. We're going to win this. He is shaken but glad to be running at last. It's like that overdrive in third on that MG. *At least I kept my word...* Damn! This is where he's in danger of putting down. Concentrate, feller. Please. Just concentrate.

OK. Now we're up with Oblomov again. Somehow nippy little Sundance has regained the lead. Tam's animal looks as though the wind has been knocked out of him. He's failing. An animal called Great Snipe has moved up for a crack at the leaders. He's that sort of big boat of an animal which gets round no matter what and wins if the class horses get into trouble. Pat Kersall, my contemporary, has the ride. I still can't see Tim. I have a sickening suspicion that Chas's little enterprise might have brought Lightning Bar down behind us.

Three more fences to go. We're fourth now and motoring. *At least I kept my word...* It's true, I suppose. Parker got what he paid for and more, and I didn't exactly suffer – or wouldn't have, had I not been fool enough to project my fantasies onto her. She was straight. And Susan hadn't kept her contract but you could understand it, but it wasn't interesting that you could understand it because basically it all comes down to loyalty or betrayal. Simple as that, and to hell with the individual...

Simple as that?

It has to be.

We swing round into the home straight. Tam slides gently off at the third last. Vantage says if I can't concentrate on the job in hand, who needs me anyway?

We'll just come a little too late. No disgrace in that.

The rest of the field is beat. It's Sundance, Great Snipe, Oblomov and us. I know that we've got more finishing speed than Great Snipe and Oblomov. In fact, I know that we've got the beating of the whole darned lot of them. If only we wanted it.

From far away, the course commentator calls Vantage's name again and again. I'm tired now. Air rasps like sandpaper through my lungs. My arms and thighs burn. My goggles are misty and spattered. At the second last, Vantage puts in a big one and sweeps past Oblomov.

Great Snipe is still hanging in there but Pat is working hard. Sundance leans to the left. Dear God, but we could take them with ten lengths or more to spare. I laugh, but there are tears in my eyes. Every reflex in my body bids me sit down, push, shove, take it. It's yours.

Every reflex in Vantage is telling him the same thing.

Sorry, lad. So sorry. This is where we have to fight, and I will win, you know. Don't make it too hard.

Sundance arises to the last and seems simply to topple to one side, too weary to hold himself upright. He gets over, but there's nothing left in the tank. Great Snipe takes it with his usual precision and care about two lengths ahead of us. Vantage rushes up to it, ears pricked, aware now that he's got only one to beat.

He puts down.

I'm jerked forward then backward, then violently forward again as he lands, and for a moment I look down and there's nothing beneath me but grass and mud and nicotine-stained snow. Vantage's nose is somewhere between his forelegs and I am leaning forward at an impossible angle. He gets his head up just as somehow I contrive to pull myself back from the brink. We're a good six lengths behind Great Snipe now. There are three hundred and fifty yards to go.

Vantage raises his head, pricks his ears, and, apparently unwinded, bounds off in pursuit.

I raise the goggles and wipe tears from my eyes and murmur, 'Oh, fuck it,' as I feel the power and willingness and urgency – the sheer sense of fun – in his stride. 'All right.'

I crouch down. Tears stream from my eyes but I'm grinning inanely as we eat up the ground between us and the leader, and then I'm pushing forward, urging him on, and I'm yelling 'Go on, my old beauty! Go on, my old darling! Go on! Go on!'

'Winner all right!' calls the Clerk of the scales.

The winner is far from all right. Not only has he just recovered from a bad attack of cramp in his right calf; he is also having serious problems with his breathing and his bowels.

I saw Parker as I unsaddled. He made sure that I saw him. He was very white, and those thin lips were short and tight as a razor-scar. It's not much good my rushing over to him – 'I'm terribly sorry. Don't know how it happened. Something came over me' – Parker just isn't the sort of sympathetic chap in whom you confide your problems.

I saw Rory, too, as I entered the weighing-room. He said 'Aaaair, well done. Jolly good,' and patted my shoulder.

And because I need any allies that I can get just now, I told him, 'OK, sir. I'm on your side. Got to talk to you and Brigadier Grey. As soon as possible.'

'All right. Surely. Let's meet at my place.'

'I'm not even going so far as the car-park till we've talked, sir,' I gulped, 'I'm bloody scared.'

'Oh. All right. Er. How about the royal box? After the last.'

'All right. And Brigadier Grey, OK?'

I ride the remaining three races of the day in a blue funk. It's all very well being accustomed to doing people and to being done, but when someone hates you bad enough to ask another someone to kill you, race-riding doesn't feel safe. It's like boxing. Injuries are a part of the game. Death is usually unacceptable.

Hell. Far as I'm concerned, death is always pretty much unacceptable.

To hell with the individual, I said. Mine own lips have condemned me.

'They even took out insurance, damn it,' I gratefully gulp royal whisky, 'tried to turn me over in the back straight.'

'Who was that, Georgie?' asks Hugh Grey.

'What the hell?' I shrug. 'I sorted him out. He's got his. It could have been any of the boys – well, fifty per cent of them at least. Let it lie.'

Rory has chosen the royal box with good reason. It's empty and it's discreet and it's provided with alcohol. We're in a little room curtained off from the main box. It's white with white icing. There are no windows.

Here, just an hour or so ago, the Queen Mother and her cronies sat guzzling the crumpets and the Lapsang. The table is still laid, and the royals don't seem to be such good doers, so I help myself to a couple of egg-and-cress and a couple of sardine sandwiches.

'All right,' Hugh Grey nods, 'we'll leave that. I gather, by the by, that young Chas Wilcox has a broken pelvis and a hairline skull fracture. Brought down poor old Tim May and all.'

'Tim's OK,' I say, 'just concussion.'

'Yes. Yes, I know.'

'So, aaair, let's see,' Rory, still in his British Warm, taps an arpeggio on the white damask tablecloth. He catches himself at it. After a reproving glance at his hand, he tucks it away. 'Yes. What it comes down to, then, is that you have lost Hoyle a cool million or so and you reckon he's going to want blood, hmm?'

'Don't you?'

'Yes, yes. Absolutely. Almost for certain, I'd say.'

'I'm not so sure.' Grey grasps the knot of his regimental tie and shakes it, 'If you're right, of course, you're hardly going to be in a position to tell us much of their activities in the future, are you? On the other hand . . .' He wraps his left hand around his chin and says 'hmmm.'

'On the other hand?' I prompt.

'Nothing, nothing. This needs thinking about.' Grey pulls out his pipe and squints down the bowl. He puts it into his mouth for a minute and makes popping noises. Then he stands with a grunt and walks stiffly over to the far wall where a picture of Sun Chariot hangs. Slowly and clumsily he starts to fill the pipe.

I take a scone and ask the most pressing question. 'Would there be any chance of – I dunno – some sort of protection?'

'Hmm?' Grey turns casually, one eyebrow raised. 'What's that? Oh. Well, we'll have to see. That would be a police matter. I'll try to arrange something, but round the clock protection – indefinitely too – that's an expensive business. I don't think you can rely on that, Georgie. Still. Can you put us in touch with this girl?'

I hesitate for a second, then, 'Yes, I suppose so, but go easy on her, would you? She's – she's just a victim, that's all.'

'Don't worry, Georgie,' Grey drones absently, 'we're not the

Gestapo. We just want all the information we can get. You see, I think you may be wrong about what Hoyle and Parker and Co will get up to next. That sort of direct thuggery is old-fashioned stuff. Still useful, of course, with large-scale welching punters, things like that, *pour encourager les autres*, you know? But even there, nowadays, if the welcher hasn't shot his mouth off too much, they're more likely to scare him and use him. He can pay off his debt by smuggling some dope or killing someone or something.'

'Great,' I mumble. I can't find a clean knife with which to butter my scone, so I take the nearest used one. Fetishism's funny. A weary old alien like me would think himself immune, but I'm not. Even as I sit here considering whether I'll have any legs by the end of the week, this childish thought flashes across my brain: The progenitor of the Queen of England might have used this knife to apply apricot jam a mere few hours ago. Wow.

Grey at last lights his pipe and tosses the match into a saucer. He gives a satisfied sort of rumble and continues talking through clenched teeth. 'Oh, don't worry, Georgie. They've got better uses than that for the likes of you. You can recoup their losses for them several times over. Oh, they're going to have to prove that they're the bosses, soften you up a bit, satisfy themselves that they've brought you to heel, but they're not going to dispose of what could be a nice little earner. They want you, at least for the moment, alive and riding and under their thumbs.'

'Thanks a ton,' I mumble, 'that sounds like a whole load of fun. I want protection.'

'Oh, no. It's going to be rough, but you knew that, didn't you?'

'I didn't know nothing,' I say glumly. 'I want protection.'

'You see, I see it like this,' Grey is keen now. He pulls out a gilt dining chair at the other end of the table. He sits and leans forward, using his pipe as a pointer. 'One way or another, not many people know about all this. Hoyle has had to be discreet in order to maintain his holier-than-thou reputation. You and Rory and I are the only other people who know about today. So there's no *encourageant les autres* involved, is there? There's no premium in breaking your legs or bumping you off or sending out incriminating tapes to finish your career.'

That makes the third sardine sandwich shake a bit. 'What tapes?' I stop the shaking both of the sandwich and the voice by biting, hard.

'You don't know?' bleats Rory.

'No. What are you talking about?'

'Oh, Georgie, Georgie,' Grey sighs. 'D'ye know? I spent four years at school and at home convinced that my housemaster and my father didn't know that I smoked. Exercise books to fan away the smoke, tube of toothpaste always in the pocket for after, sniffing loudly or pulling at the Izal Medicated to disguise the sound of a match striking – all that intrigue, all that hard work to put one over on them. And they knew all along. Both of them.'

'I still don't understand what you're on about,' I say stubbornly, now dancing cheek to cheek on my chair.

'Let's try again, shall we?' Grey's pipe has gone out. He studies it sombrely. 'You're a Catholic, right? Well, so am I as it happens. And unlike our late unlamented pontiff, I believe in the magic of liturgy as liturgy and to hell with its precise meaning in the ever changing vernacular. I also believe in the saints whether bloody *Paschalis Mysterii* says that they existed or not. Your saint, Georgie. St George. As far as I'm concerned, he may in reality have been a child-rapist and murderer, he may never have existed at all. It doesn't matter. He's still St George, the guy that killed the dragon. It's the only way to cope with the onset of cynicism, Georgie. I know that the people that I admire or care for do strange things in their youth or in the privacy of their bedrooms and I don't enquire into those things. As long as they don't tread on my toes or hurt me or mine, they can do what they like. It's what I see that matters. There isn't a jockey out there who hasn't given information to a birdman or received a thousand in used readies for services rendered. I don't care. For all I know, Rory here spends his leisure hours in buggering the smaller furry species of mammal. I don't care ...'

'I say ...' says Rory vaguely.

'... we could all be blackmailed; we could all be warned off. We're humans, that's all. Venal and fallible. I care only when those minor transgressions become major and start to hurt me or offend me or embarrass me or seriously threaten the people of the sport that I care for. Can you understand that?'

'Yes,' I croak. 'I suppose so.'

'Right. So I know that you – and you're not alone in this, Georgie – have been illegally recorded agreeing to this or that minor transgression, OK? It doesn't worry me, and because they're illegal tapes it never should worry me. They're inadmissible evidence anyhow. It's only when they become public property and bring the game into disrepute, only then do I descend on you like the proverbial ton of bricks. Understood?'

'Yeah. OK.'

'So what I reckon is, they teach you a lesson, then they propose a lot of dirty business to you. You report back. We keep tabs on everything and gather evidence, right?'

I'm on my way to the sideboard for another octave of Scotch as he says this. I just say, 'Nope.' I pick up the bottle.

'What do you mean, no?'

'I mean "no".' I pour and spin the bottle-top back on. 'No, I'm not sitting around just waiting for something to happen and no, I'm damned if I'll co-operate with the stewards if I don't get some sort of protection. If you don't help me, I don't help you. I take my beating and do their dirty work. It's safer for me that way.'

'Aaair, I shouldn't think it'll be you that gets the beating,' says Rory calmly. He swings round to face me, 'Have you thought of that?'

'What?' my voice raps at each of the walls in turn.

'Well, aaair, if Hugh is right, they'll want to keep *you* intact, won't they? Don't want to worry you or anything, but it could be your family, your house, anything.'

I walk back to my chair with the rapidly accelerating gait of the drunkard. This is not because I am drunk but because I realise as I go that my legs are weak and that a great deal of what had been in my stomach is now pressing down on my buttocks. I need to sit. I need to gulp whisky. And air.

'All the more reason why I'll need protection,' I breathe at last.

'Hmm, well . . .' Grey smiles benignly, 'obviously we can't bring in the troops, as I've already said. First, it makes it all too obvious, second, it's too darned expensive and third, it's pointless. You've still got to make a living and your family still have to go to school or to work or whatever they do. Hoyle can hit you on the racecourse or them on the street and there's damn all we can do to stop him. I think you'd best rely on Rory. Thing is, Rory's young and you've ridden in the same races and you live near one another. It's not going to arouse too much suspicion if he's seen calling in or something, know what I mean? He can just be a casual chum, right? If I'm seen around, tongues will start wagging.'

'Aaair, absolutely,' says Rory.

'OK,' I say again. It's strange really, sitting here talking about the prospect of someone doing something personal and nasty to me at some time. To Rory Fitzroy-Haigh and Hugh Grey, that something will just be a means to an end. To me, it might just be the end itself.

'I'm not just going to wait,' I announce bullishly. 'I want to do something. I can stand pain but I can't stand sitting around just waiting and anticipating and . . .'

'There's nothing you can do, Georgie,' Grey has relit his pipe. He puffs philosophically, 'Nothing at all. Hoyle keeps his books clean. All we can do is try to catch him and his minions in the act.'

'What about Wilcox?' suggests Rory. 'He must have been paid.'

'He must indeed, but it'll have been cash and there'll be no evidence.'

'He might have done other services for Hoyle,' I grasp at the idea, 'I might persuade him to tell us.'

'No, Georgie. No private detective stuff, please. With you on our side, we can get Hoyle ...'

'After my house has been burned down or something, sure.'

'Well, you chose to win today.'

'Are you saying as I shouldn't have done?'

'No, no,' Grey is ponderous, 'but you agreed to pull the horse in the first place, then changed your mind. That's where the problem starts.'

'Parker threatened to kill me if I didn't!' I protest.

'Yes,' Grey shook his head solemnly. 'I know. We've got a clean game, basically, but if one big organisation chooses to lean on one small man ... Well, I don't blame that one small man if he concedes. But that's why we've got to do the likes of Hoyle and Parker, Georgie. We've got to show them that God isn't just on the side of the big battalions. That's why you won today.'

'No, it's not,' I drain the chunky glass and stand. 'I told you already. I don't give a monkey's about the good of the game or high principles or anything as big and high-falutin as that. I won today because of one drunken old sod of a man, one poor fool of a woman, a child's sculpture and ... and, well, because of a feckin' horse, and there's an end on it.'

I get them to accompany me to the car because I'm convinced that I'll find a copse of crowbar-wielding thugs waiting for me there. There's not a thug nor a crowbar to be seen. Nonetheless, after a lifetime of Nat Gould and Edgar Wallace, I'm not so easily reassured. I insist that Rory give the car a thorough military-style once over, in search of what the newspapers insist on calling devices. You and I know them as bombs.

It's pointless, of course. Rory wouldn't kneel down to propose until he'd changed into ski-pants. In a suit, a *demi-plié* is the best that he or his tailor could possibly countenance.

Reluctantly, then, I climb into the car. There may be no devices or thugs, but who's going to protect me from the high velocity bullets or crossbow bolts which might at any time jerk my intestines onto the biscuit suede upholstery or pebble-dash the windscreen with my brains?

I drive home fast, unwilling to stop for anyone or anything. On the wireless, Peter Bromley tells the world of Vantage's 'gallant victory' and declares him to be 'the most promising novice that I've seen since Pendil back in '72. Almost anything is possible for this brilliant young 'chaser over the next few years.' He refers in passing to the 'skilful handling of veteran pilot Georgie Blane, whose strength and experience was invaluable in curbing Vantage's youthful exuberance'. Vantage, he reminds us, 'has joined a list which reads like the Debrett's of staying 'chasers, including such as Cottage Rake, Halloween, Lochroe, Mandarin, Captain Christy, Pendil, Mill House and, of course, the great Arkle himself'.

I wish he'd shut up. Perhaps if everyone keeps quiet about it, it'll just slip Hoyle's mind.

The impacted brown snow on the drive steams in the headlight beams as I steer to what should be my haven. A quick glance over my shoulders, a quick glance up at the house to check that everything is as normal.

The drawing-room and the hall lights are on. The red light at the top of the house indicates either that Joanna has returned from hunting or that she has again neglected to switch off before leaving. Situation normal.

I slam the car door and almost scurry to the porch. There's a wicked North Easterly army which sweeps fast and low over the garden. It attacks in waves, gnawing at my trouser legs, sawing for a second or two at the fabric of the house, then bounding on to tussle with the trees beyond. A second or two later, you can hear the next wave coming, pipers to the fore.

I open the front door and step into the hall. It's an army of Jehovah's Witnesses. I need all my strength to force their feet from the jamb. When at last I manage to shut the door, the house seems sepulchral by contrast.

'Hi!' I call casually.

'Hi, darling,' Claire's voice is that of someone otherwise engaged who has no intention of moving.

The drawing-room door opens, however, and Conor comes bouncing through. 'Hi, Daddy! That was brilliant!'

I growl and pick him up and hug him. 'See it then, did you?'

'About twenty-six times so far. Thought you were going to come off at the last.'

'So did I,' I kiss him and put him down and lead him into the drawing-room. The curtains are drawn. The lamps are lit. The room is festooned with Christmas cards hung on ribbons – most of them in aid of the Injured Jockeys' Fund. Conor has spread a minefield of model cars on the carpet. A new board game is laid out on the low coffee-table.

Claire is at her bureau again, writing bread-and-butter letters in her meticulous italic. She says 'Hi!' in a surprised tone, then spends five seconds more in writing before slapping down her pen and standing. 'Well done, darling,' she kisses me, 'that was marvellous. Talk about heart attacks, we were sitting here squealing, weren't we, darling?'

'It was brilliant,' Conor enthuses, 'especially when Daddy nearly fell off.'

'Thanks a million, old lad, I'll try to do it more often for you.'

'You're home early.' Claire is just mildly sarcastic. 'Thought you'd still be celebrating. Cup of tea, or are we on champagne?'

'Tea, please,' I tell her hoarsely. 'Conor, my old son, star in my night-sky, crouton in my soup, would you mind clearing the car-pool out of here while your mum and I have a quick word?'

'Oh, all right. That Lamborghini grand-dad gave me is brilliant. Oh, and you'll be on the news in – a quarter of an hour, just over.'

'Thanks.'

'What did the Queen Mum say?'

'She said, "Well done. Such a lovely animal. That was exciting."'

'That's all?'

'That's all, I'm afraid. Now, get on with the mopping-up operation, would you, son?'

Claire walks before me to the kitchen. Her shoulders are tense. She's a strong, blithe, lovely woman, but somewhere in there, there's a little girl who knows that there's still more hurt in store and just wants to be tucked in and to cry in someone's arms. I love that little girl with all my heart. I want to slap her whenever she shows pain.

'So,' she fills the kettle and leans up against the worktop. The tea-tray on the table has not yet been cleared. They had crumpets and Christmas cake. 'That should pay a couple of bills.'

'Yeah. No presents from that jerk Smythson, though.'

'What's it come to?'

'Dunno. Seven percent of £25,000. What's that? Two grand?'

'And the last.'

'What?'

'The television said you won the last.'

'Hell,' I sigh and make for the 'fridge in search of white wine. I'd clean forgotten the handicap hurdle at the end of the day. 'Yeah. Well, that can't be more than three hundred all told.'

'Still.'

'Yeah,' I pour wine into a tumbler and resort to platitudes. 'Every little helps.'

'You bet it does. I thought you wanted tea.'

'Not much,' I sit on the corner of the table. 'I just wanted to talk to you.'

167

'Oh.' She stiffens. 'What about?'

'Well. Listen. OK. Thing is, we've got problems. Not too serious, but listen. Look, you know I love you, don't you?'

She shrugs and looks down at the kettle. It's not boiling yet, so she has to look nervously back at me.

'Yeah, well, I do. You know that.'

'S'pose so,' she smiles.

I hold out my hand for hers. She takes it almost timorously. I squeeze. She squeezes back.

'This trouble,' I go on, 'like I say, it's not too serious, but I'd ... I'd like you and the children out of the way for the next week or so. Go down to Dartmouth again. Ireland, perhaps.'

Now the kettle boils, so she can release my hand and attend to things. 'Don't be ridiculous, Georgie,' she sings, 'this is Christmas. The children have things planned. Parties, you know. There's no question of going away.'

'You've got to,' I plead. 'Really. I wouldn't say this unless it was necessary.'

'Yes, well, your idea of necessary and mine are very different, Georgie. What is it? Some girl you want to bring here?'

'Don't be absurd.'

'Well, what else am I meant to think? All this melodramatic, conspiratorial stuff. "You must leave ze country and lie low." What's it all about, then, Georgie?' She squeezes out a teabag and chucks it into the flip-top bin. She throws the teaspoon into the sink. Very casual. I'm just a naughty boy who's been watching too much television and is letting his imagination run away with him. 'Well, you might as well forget it, anyway,' her sleeve brushes mine as she clicks briskly to the 'fridge. 'There's no question of our going anywhere, and that's that.'

She underlines the final word by slamming the 'fridge door.

'But you've got to, doll,' I soothe.

'How many times do I have to tell you that I am not a doll? And why have we "got to", Georgie?' She sweeps past me again on her way back to the sink.

'Because I think we may all be in some – well, I know it sounds melodramatic, but – some danger.'

'Don't tell me. You've been a secret agent for the IRA for all these years and now an international hitman is after you. Well, don't worry, we've got Vandal, and Joanna's been taking judo.'

'OK, that's enough,' I say softly. 'Sit down.'

'What?'

'Sit – down.'

To my astonishment, she does so. Not without a tut and a sigh of exasperation, but nonetheless she undoubtedly sits. I follow up my advantage. 'Now listen. I wasn't meant to win the King George VI today.'

'What?' she frowns.

'I wasn't meant to win it. I was offered a large sum of money to hook Vantage and was threatened with dire penalties if I didn't. I didn't. They're going to want to hurt me for that.'

'*Georgie!*' Genuine terror scrubs her face and leaves it clean and flushed and young.

'Yeah, well.'

'Who are these people?'

'Thugs who represent bookies.'

'I thought this sort – I thought all that was a thing of the past.'

'It is, mostly. Just needs one unscrupulous whiz-kid, though, and it starts all over again. They'll get theirs, but in the meantime ...'

'But why – I mean – why did they think you would do it?'

I take a deep breath. It's time. 'I've pulled one or two in the past.'

'What?'

'Oh, for Christ's sakes, love, leave out the shocked disapproval, would you? You knew. Don't pretend you didn't. You didn't think that all this was paid for on an ageing jump-jock's earnings, did you? Oh, most of it, maybe, but there was always more cash in the coffers when it was needed, wasn't there? And it didn't all come in the form of cheques from Weatherby's, did it? When it was badly needed, there was cash. You knew it and you liked it that way, and if now you're going to tell me that I'm the devil incarnate and that you'd rather have lived a pauper's life, pass me the sick bag first, OK?'

My defensive harshness doesn't help. She pulls herself upright. She slams the mug down on the table. She adopts a facial expression from her mother's repertoire. 'I did not know. I didn't even suspect. It's no bloody good you trying to make me some sort of accessory to your squalid little deals, Georgie. You did it, and I hadn't the faintest – I hadn't the remotest clue that you were doing things like that.'

'I wasn't "doing things like that",' I groan. 'Given twelve hours you'll have convinced yourself that I was "always" pulling horses. I did it a few times, that's all, when the money ran short.'

She places her head in her hands and mumbles, 'Oh, God Almighty. I don't believe this is happening.'

'OK, OK,' I empty the bottle of Entre Deux Mers into my tumbler, 'so you never suspected anything and I'm a villain. If that makes you feel any better, so be it. The fact of the matter is, today I rode a straight race and I won and now I want you and the children safely away from here while I sort things out. OK? I don't think it'll be too bad, but things might get just a little bit hairy, so please just pack your bags and go.'

'I don't believe it,' she says again. She raises her head. Her hands have made her face red. She looks at me with incredulous, insulting eyes. She slowly shakes her head. 'I just don't believe any of it.'

She's looking at me like that in order to annoy me. She succeeds.

'Start believing,' I say quietly, 'and just take yourself and the kids away. I love you and I don't want to see you tangled up in all this. Tell them – I don't know – tell them that there was some sort of holiday as part of the prize for the King George. Take 'em to a hotel. Tell them that John and Catherine want to give them a special treat or a party or something. Take them down to Dartmouth. Give them a really good time. Take them skiing . . .'

'With what?'

'We'll cope. Just take them away.'

'We'll cope,' she echoes, and blinks. 'What does that mean, Georgie? Another horse pulled?'

'Oh, Christ,' I close my eyes as much to shut out her accusing glare as for dramatic effect. 'No, no, no, no, no. It means "we'll cope". Somehow. I've always managed up till now, haven't I?'

'I don't know, Georgie,' she says sombrely as though this meaningless remark were the last two lines of a sonnet, 'I really do not know.'

She stands. She flings the mug into the sink from a couple of feet away. It does not break. 'I'm going to have to do a lot of thinking, Georgie,' she hisses at last.

'Good idea,' I say coldly, 'so think somewhere peaceful, somewhere nice, somewhere a long way away. Please, love. I can face all this hassle a darned sight more easily if I haven't got to worry about you and Joanna and Conor. Really.'

'All right,' she snaps, 'we'll go. It'll ruin the children's holiday, but I suppose we must. And you've got a lot more to sort out than just this business before we come back, Georgie. A damned sight more. I told you last week you'd have to change, pay the bills, get some regular money in. And now this . . .'

'*This*, darling, is a consequence of trying to do just that. To look after you and the kids in the style to which you would like to be accustomed. I didn't like it any more than you do now, but then you didn't have the moral problem to face, did you?'

'So – how much did they offer you today?'

'Sixty.'

Her expression changes as rapidly as did mine a week ago in Parker's room at the Coach and Horses. 'Sixty?' she gasps. 'Thousand?'

'Sixty thousand,' I nod.

'But ...' I can almost see the dreams that flicker like a magic lantern across her mind's eye. 'Jesus! Sixty thousand ...'

I laugh. It's not a very pleasant sound, nor a very pleasant feeling, but I laugh. 'Precisely,' I say.

She shoots one quick glance dipped in curare at me, says, 'Oh, God,' swings round and storms from the room.

Ah, dear Lord, but I do love that woman.

When at last she has calmed down enough to come downstairs, stiff and heavy in her armour of reserve and disapproval, she informs me very loudly that her parents have organised a big party for the children. There'll be hunting and more presents and a visit to Butlin's for the day and everything else that her inventive mind can conceive in the way of sops. And seeing as I'm going to be away – at Doncaster, she says, though there's no racing at Doncaster until the end of the month – it seems like a good idea that they should return to Dartmouth for a few days more.

They'll leave tomorrow morning. Tonight, I murmur. Tomorrow morning, she gecks. I sigh deeply. I pointedly lock all the doors and windows.

Polly Waller rings. She says well done today. She also says that I'm a little shit and that she couldn't give a damn what disgusting activities I get up to in the privacy of my own dungheap, but if ever again I make a public display like that with one of my goddamned strumpets, that's it. She'll never talk to me again. I say OK, Polly. Sorry. She says that's all right. I still love you, Georgie, but really.

I'm sat on the carpet playing Clue with the kids and I've just asked Joanna whether Miss Scarlett did it with the lead piping in the Conservatory, when the telephone rings again. Claire's upstairs packing, so I grab my whisky and spring up fast. There's an extension up there in the bedroom.

I get to the office 'phone first, vaguely hoping, I suppose, that it might be Patsy ringing to say sorry. It isn't. It's Parker.

'Blane.'

'Hello.'

171

'Well, well.'

'Well, well what?'

'I didn't think you had it in you.'

'Well, there you go,' I say sullenly. 'I don't respond well to bullying.'

'So it seems, so it seems. That, in fact, is what my masters have been telling me. They are displeased with me, Blane, so you may take it that I in turn am very displeased with you. I always feel so sorry for the people that I am displeased with ...' then, 'You cost us a lot of money, Blane.'

'Ah. Put it down to experience, Parker.'

'Now, now, let's not try to be clever, shall we?' He exhales, then the voice hardens. The words rattle like a slip of scree. 'If I had my way – if I *have* my way, as yet I may – I would send some very nasty coarse people around to deal with you, Blane, after which I'd send those tapes round to the police and the stewards to ensure that you would never again be permitted to wheel your chair onto a racecourse. That is what I would do. Still ...' The smoothness returns suddenly to his voice. It's like riding a switchback in a Deux Chevaux. 'Still, my employer has those tapes at home with him and he absolutely refuses to countenance what he calls gratuitous violence. Such an interesting concept, gratuitousness, isn't it? It's a hymn by implication. It asserts that there is something other. Ah, well. In common with many an intelligent man, he has his blind spots. It seems that I am to be held to blame for your gross impertinence.'

'Good,' I grin. I don't believe a word of all this, but then I don't believe most compliments. Doesn't mean I don't like to hear them if they happen to be passing.

'And the girl, of course.'

'What?' My bowels gulp like a giant clam. Small insects emerge from hiding to run and play on the back of my neck.

'Have a nice time there, did you, Blane?' Parker drones. 'Hmm? Get our little bogboy end away, did we? There's a lucky chap. Still. Yes. She didn't do as she was told. Silly girl.'

'It's not her bloody fault!' I yap, then remember the children next door. 'It's not her fault. Don't you touch her, Parker, d'ye hear me?'

'Giving orders again, Blane? Silly little bogboy.'

'Don't touch her, Parker. I mean it.'

Parker laughs. They say you can tell a lot from a man's sense of humour.

I can stand this no longer. I replace the receiver, gulp down my my whisky and spend the next two minutes with my eyes closed, attempting to breathe slowly and steadily whilst muttering a fervent prayer to a vengeful and mischievous god. Loki, perhaps, could lend me a hand.

Dear God, is it any wonder that we go down with stress-related diseases? I've just had a conversation which should, in any normal, natural circumstances, have seen Parker's whole smirking face turned into a pulsing, bleeding mass of haemorrhoids, instead of which, he's still somewhere smirking and all that I have to take it out on is a grey plastic jawbone and a mahogany desk.

And myself, of course.

The Reverend Green did it, by the way. In the Dining Room. With the rope.

Six times tonight I dial Patsy's number and wait as the telephone rings and rings and rings in that scruffy house off Ladbroke Grove.

'Please God,' I murmur thickly into the mouthpiece, 'let her have gone away ...' The mouthpiece gives back a bouquet of tobacco and whisky.

'Georgie?' Claire's voice on the extension makes me jump. 'Are you ever going to get off that phone and come to bed?'

'Sure,' I lick my lips and prop my head on my hand. The desk top tilts. I blink a couple of times in an authoritative sort of way. It stops. 'Sure and I'll be with you in a second. I'm just trying to raise Bob.'

'You're pissed.'

'No'm not. Just very, very tired.'

'Well, go to bed, then. Do you know what time it is?'

'Yes,' I say equably. 'Thank you.'

'Oh, for God's sake ...' The telephone clatters. Above me, footfalls make the floorboards creak.

A lot of conversations seem to end that way these days.

Things are coming to a head with the consoling inevitability of winter or ejaculation or death. It'll feel bad for a while, but just so long as everything comes to an end, all's right with the world. Just let it come, that's all. I can't stand the waiting.

*   *   *

173

I ride work as usual this morning. Mann Down Bottom is just a bowl of milky mist. Up on top, horses burst out of the grey and white haze at you, suddenly materialising in a roll of thunder like stage ghosts, then as suddenly vanishing.

At one point, Dominic, the *Wizard of Oz* strawman who's as thick as he's thin, causes a fair amount of chaos by 'going to fetch the 'papers'. Anywhere else, this is called 'being run away with' and is regarded with a proper degree of awe, but in laconic Lambourn, time out of mind, as one of their *confrères* gallops terrified by, the lads turn to one another and say, 'See so-and-so's gone to fetch the 'papers'.

Anyhow, Dominic's on this stringy flame chestnut pig called Boulder Dam, and this rip of a brumach has a wall eye and an evil disposition and reckons that conditions are just right for a bit of wanton destruction. So he bucks once, gets his head, and is away like the wind. He charges through a couple of other strings which hardly see him until he's on them. There's a lot of cursing and rearing and squealing.

Boulder Dam was to have run at Cheltenham next week, but he's well and truly left his race on the gallops. Dominic returns to a right royal roasting from Jack just as I dismount and the lads turn for home.

The *on dit* is that Stratford is likely to be called off because of freezing fog. For the first time in my life, I hope that it's true. I hang around at Jack's for a while and don't head homeward till after ten. I'm praying that Claire will already have left. At the public telephone by the bridge, I try Patsy again. Still no reply.

Well, why should I care?

Claire's car is gone. The house sounds and feels very empty as I let myself into the kitchen and open a hot-plate on the Aga to warm my freezing hands. It's a minute or two before I stop shivering and turn away from the stove. I look for the wireless. They've taken it with them.

I see the note on the table and pick it up almost casually. Then I have to sit down, fast.

Georgie . . .

The style is economical:

Georgie

The bank manager rang. £3,000. Thanks a lot from me and your children. I think I've probably just about had it up to here now. Sorry, but even the refugium peccatorum has her limits.

We'll have to think very hard over the next few days. There may be some solution, but I'm damned if I can see it. Anyhow, I'm afraid I'm just too furious to make any sense at the moment.

Claire

Oh, it makes me feel sick sure enough. It brings a tear to my eye. It gives me the usual rejection horrors, but somehow it doesn't really sadden me. I feel a little like a criminal when he feels the copper's hand on his shoulder after years on the run. I've been found out. I can forget the lies. Perhaps Claire and I can even be friends again now that it's all out in the open.

There's an exhilarating sense of solitude and uncertainty, too, that I haven't known since I was eighteen, nineteen. Sure, there'll be pain, regrets and sorrows enough out there in the cold, but at least they'll be mine, not someone else's. I can forget the role now. I can fight my own battles.

She may stay with me. Matter of fact, I'd say that it's a stone cold certainty that there'll be no nonsense about divorce or anything like that. Maybe we'll live together sometimes; maybe not. But however it works out, there'll be no more illusions, no attempts to attain oneness. We'll be two independent people again, and any love there may be will be that of old friends – or old enemies.

And although I cannot look at that note without doubling up, although my eyes burn, an involuntary grin tugs at the corners of my mouth. I'm on my own now.

It's a day for pottering. I chop some wood. I fill the log-baskets. I wander around the house, in theory tidying, in fact just taking valedictory mental snapshots. Every so often, I dial Patsy's number. Still no reply.

It's just after two o'clock when Rory rolls up. He's all casual today in a dark blue cashmere overcoat and button-up dogskin gloves. I show him into the kitchen where I'm halfway through a Findus lasagne.

'Coffee?'

'Aaair, no thanks.'

'Mind if I just polish off lunch?'

'No, no. Please.' He eyes the foil dish with the same sort of benign curiosity with which, no doubt, Sir Richard Burton regarded female circumcision rituals in Dahomey. I eat quickly. It takes him a little longer to unbutton his gloves and his coat. He sits very carefully on the other side of the table.

175

'All well, then?'

'All right, thanks, sir. Yes.' I get up and throw the dish into the bin. Rory eyes it wistfully as though he'd like to study it more closely.

'Good,' he says distractedly. 'Jolly good. Aaair, we found that girl, by the way. Bad news there, I'm afraid.'

I rub a clear space in the frosty window and peer out at the desolate garden. 'What happened, then?'

'Last night. Thugs, I'm afraid.'

'Oh, Jesus,' I close my eyes for a moment. 'How bad?'

'Oh, not too bad. I mean, horrible, you know, but she'll survive.'

'Tell me.'

'Oh, just ... you know ... black eyes, a few bruises here or there, aaair. Don't know if they ...'

'Go on.'

'Well, you know. Get some thugs like that with a pretty girl ...'

A little whimper somehow escapes from me. My fists clench very tightly. 'I know,' I blink out at the garden.

That body which I had kissed and stroked and urged because it shared in a moment the burden of loneliness, that body which now I am sure was freely given to me ... Nobody hurts it but me is the extraordinary form of words which the thought takes in my head. Goddamn it all, *nobody* hurts her but me.

I can feel Rory's eyes on me. I take a deep breath and try to relax my back-muscles as I refill the kettle. 'Who did it?'

'Don't know. Apparently they got her when she went out to empty her rubbish bins. She can't talk much at the moment.'

'In hospital?'

'Yes, aaair, for the nonce. Out today, I should think. Poor creature.'

Creature.

Yes. Not just Patsy Bryce, but one of God's creatures. Funny how that distancing concept makes me feel still closer to her. 'All God's chillun got wings,' I murmur.

'Sorry?'

'Oh, nothing. Sorry.'

'Aaair ...'

'Hmm?'

'Do you really think that Hoyle's going to ...?'

'I think he's angry,' I say, 'and I think he's going to do something. No idea what. Maybe Brigadier Grey's right. Maybe he'll try to bring me to hand rather than trying to hurt me. I don't know, but I know he'll do something.'

'Trouble is, it won't be him. Whatever it is it'll be more paid thugs. The sort that don't talk.'

'I know,' I nod sadly. 'Multi-millionaires don't do their own dirty work. Still, there's Parker. I'll get him before I've done . . .'

The telephone rings. I excuse myself and make my way to the office.

'Hi, G.,' Bob's voice. 'Would you come and fetch us?'

'Where are you?'

'Newbury. Big white hotel in the middle. What's it called? Oh, the Chequers. Yup, The Chequers. Would you come and fetch us?'

'Yeah, OK,' I shrug, 'I s'pose so. What're you doing down here?'

'Oh. You know. Look. I'd better say it quickly here and now while there's just nineteen – eighteen – pence in this box.' A large sniff, then, 'I'm sorry 'bout the other night. Bloody silly. Feel sort of naked talking about it. Dunno what came over me.'

'How're you going now then?' I ask.

'Ah, bit glum, bit embarrassed. Fine, though, really. Bit like a rip-roaring bender, you know? Afterwards the things that seemed so important just look sort of trivial, you know?'

'Yes.'

'It's just – Laura was going to be out a lot and the streets of town got me down and I couldn't stand just sitting there and thinking, and Laura reckoned the best thing to do was come down and take some exercise and see some places as don't remind you so much, you know? So here I am.'

'OK, Bob,' I sigh. 'I'll come now.'

'Sorry I didn't ring before,' he says.

I make two unpremeditated calls on my way into Newbury. The first, on impulse, is on the church. It's empty but for the little winking red flame of the sacristy lamp.

I kneel and I pray, just because it affords me a moment of stillness and makes me feel better. I pray for Claire and for the children. I pray for Patsy and for Bob. I pray for the welfare of my immortal soul. For the rest of me, I do not pray. I feel like a Crusader pledging his service, and having felt that, I feel absurd.

Lambourn church is just the standard English RC hut (and if everyone's so darned keen to give the Greeks back their marbles, please could we have Durham and Wells back too?) but, unlike most of its kind, it has a legend attached to it – a giant builder, its very own saint.

Every brick of this hut was laid back in the 'forties by one Fr Taylor. There are a hundred stories about your man. How he abandoned his congregation in the middle of mass to hammer on the doors of lads who hadn't bothered to attend, even, on occasion, climbing ladders to their bedroom windows; how, at election time, he would announce, 'Now, it's not my place to tell you where to cast your vote, but this much I will tell you. If you vote for the fellow in the red tie, you'll go to hell'; how, when Stalin died, he announced in reverential tones, 'There he lies, flowers at his head, flowers at his feet, flowers on his either side ... and a ruddy great fire under his tail by now.' The lads lived in awe of him and adored him.

I genuflect and cross myself and feel stronger as I return into the now dazzling light outside.

The second call is on a newsagent on the outskirts of town. I buy a *Times* and, having checked the typefaces under the disapproving gaze of the old biddy at the counter, a dirty magazine called *Vibrations*.

Bob sits disconsolate, his upper lip flecked with foam, his chin thrust deep into the collar of his Ulster. His arms hang loose between his legs. The muscles of his face too are relaxed. His eyes stare dully ahead. His lower lip sags. He'll not want to be seen like that, so I announce my presence very loudly from the door of the bar. 'Bob!'

He looks up. His mouth snaps shut, then stretches in a broad grin. His eyes wrinkle up. 'Georgie, my old darling!' he stands and embraces me. 'Good to see yez, it really is. Right, then, what'll it be? Will you join me in a pint of ale? 'Tis well! Sit you down. I'll get it.'

He pushes me into a chair, swings round and walks to the bar. Aside from a few businessmen who susurrate no louder than the fire in the grate as they nurse their half pints, the low dark room is empty. Bob's voice is clearly audible as he rattles on.

'The finest of ale in abundance. Come, landlord, fill the thingy bowl. *"Beer! O, Hodgson, Guinness, Allsopp, Bass! Names that should be on every infant's tongue!"* Yes, indeed. Bass will be splendid. Two pints, if you please and – are you chasing, G.? No? Milksop. Ah, well. Two pounds and sixteen – two pounds and twenty pence. I thank ye, squire. May all generations call thee blessed.' He turns with the two pints. 'Here you go, Georgie boy, here you go. *"Shoulder the sky, my lad, and drink your ale."* Now,' he sits, 'tell me all about it. How goes it?'

'Oh, all right, thanks, Bob.'

'Glad to hear it, glad to hear it. Saw the race yesterday. Fine stuff. And how's the queen consort?'

'Gone back to Dartmouth with the children. Fine, though, fine.' I don't want to discuss marital bliss, as much for his sake as for mine.

'So we're all alone?' Bob nods eagerly.

''S'right. Now. Tell me. How are you?'

'Ach, never better, Georgie. Still a bit of a hangover, but otherwise fine, fine. Just need some fresh air, bit of peace and quiet, you know? Maybe even do some writing. I've got some really neat ideas.'

It can't last, of course. The exuberance rapidly fades as we drive back. Once again the face and the shoulders sag and he sits like a very old rag doll gazing blearily ahead. Grief, anger and vanity are at least egotistical, but even they have gone now. Save in the odd moment when he manages a tolerable imitation of his old self, he seems drained of all energy and all self-esteem.

He acknowledges as much later as we trudge past the great house at Ashdown. Dusk draws in and it is bitterly cold.

'Oh, hang it, it's no good, G.,' he slumps down on one of the many volcanic rocks which litter the valley. 'I don't even understand me any more. I hate self-pity, yet I'm stuffed full of it. I feel – well, *nothing*. I feel like those smart-arsed kids pretend to feel, you know? Nothing moves me. Nothing hurts any more. I look at that house. I know it's lovely, but it doesn't hurt, you know? Airey Neave lived there, didn't he?'

'That's right.'

'Well, there you go. I know he was murdered, but I can't even work up enough outrage or anger to make a joke about it.' He looks down at his groin as though it might hold the answer. 'I just don't understand it, Georgie,' he thuds, 'it's as though nothing in the world matters any more. Shit, I can't think of a good reason to get up in the morning. I can't think of a good reason to do anything. Pretty bloody pathetic, eh?'

'It's called depression, Bob.' I grasp his shoulder, 'It happens, and it passes.'

'Does it?' he looks up at me with wide wet eyes.

'Ah, sure it does. You can't do it all by yourself. You'll need

179

help. Don't worry, mate. We'll sort it out.' The wind buffets me like a whip. 'Come on, Bob,' I shudder, 'let's go home.'

We watch videos of races, then *Singin' in the Rain*. Bob sits listlessly staring at the television. Whenever I laugh, he musters a faint echo of a smile. When I tell him of a horse, 'He puts in a big one here,' he nods intelligently and murmurs, 'big one'. When I express my astonishment that so much of *Moses Supposes* was shot in one take, he says 'one take'. We both sink a lot of Scotch. He drinks without aggression or interest, just tips up each tumbler and gulps the whisky as though it were water.

As discreetly as I can manage, I once more lock the doors and check the windows. I also, perhaps ridiculously, put a slug into Conor's air rifle and slip it behind the curtains in the dining-room, then I dig a couple of steaks out of the 'fridge, smother them in pepper and grill them. We eat them between slices of Hampstead Homepride. The ticking of the clock is very loud.

And suddenly Bob perks up. He licks blood and molten butter from his fingers and leaps to his feet. 'Right,' he says, 'what's going on, G.?'

'Hmm? What do you mean?'

'Ah, come on, man, I may be crazy but I'm not dumb. Something's up. You've been jumping around like a prawn on the hob. All the doors and windows locked, and you a fresh air fanatic. Poor old Vandal shut out in the hall. Glancing over your shoulder and jumping everytime a branch taps the window. Not like you, my old marra. Not like the cool, carefree sportsman we all know and love. Come on, now. Tell Uncle Bob. What's it all about?'

'Nothing, Bob.' I chomp. Blood-soaked bread tumbles down my chin and onto the plate. I dab my lips with kitchen-towel. 'Just a bit nervous is all.'

'Ah, leave it out, Georgie,' Bob's hands flap. He is assertive and nervous again. It's good to see. 'There's something stinks round these parts.'

'Ah, for God's sake, man, shut up and eat your steak.'

He swings round at the fireplace. He grins. 'I'll sit, and I'll eat all my greens, auntie, but only if you'll tell me the how and the why of it.'

'All right, all right,' I smile. There's life in the room again. 'I'll tell you the how. The Lord Himself doesn't know the why, mechanistic, teleological or any other bogging way.'

I tell him the story. He frowns where others would grin, grins his comprehension where others would frown. That's brothers for you, I suppose. He paces a lot, occasionally punches his palm. Occasionally his cheeks jerk back in that characteristic nervous *rictus*. Occasionally too he sits down and takes a bite at his steak, because I order him to. His plate is bare when at last I lean back and say, 'Well, that's it.' He whistles. He slaps his thighs. There's a glint of that old anger in his eyes. I'm looking at a happy man.

'Ah, Jaysus, man, and there was I feeling sorry for myself. Why didn't you tell me, Georgie? Why didn't you tell me? Any minute now, the house may blow up! Sheesh!'

'Great,' I say, 'glad it cheers you up.' I stand and pick up our plates. Vandal cowers as I walk into the hall. He thinks he's done something wrong. I toss him the steak fat.

Bob follows me to the kitchen. 'Those bastards!' he squeaks. 'Those bastards! And what the hell's the Ice Queen doing pretending it's all news to her, I'd like to know? Goddamned self-deceptive, father-fixated English girls. Every time they open their legs a little light comes on. Only ambition's to be screwed by the Unknown Soldier. OK. So what do we do? How do we hit this man Hoyle?'

'We don't,' I say wearily. 'There's bugger all we can do. He's a famous, well-protected millionaire. Best I can hope is that somehow we can get enough on his minion Parker to discredit him a bit. Hoyle's style of bookmaking won't work if the public don't trust him. Oh, and I intend to smash Parker to a pulp. Best I can do. The little man conquering the big corporations is a myth. It doesn't work that way.'

'It can. It could.'

'Uh-uh.' I shake my head and run the hot tap briefly over the plates. 'You just tell me how, Bob.' I shake my fingers. 'The stewards may just be able to amass enough evidence to get Hoyle warned off one day. Best I can do is contribute to that.'

'It can't be like that!' Bobby looks as though life were a long-lost friend who had cut him.

'Yeah, but it is. Sorry, mate.'

'But he's hurting you, hurting this girl ... I mean, people can't do things like that!'

'Oh, yes they can,' I tip three piss-pills into my palm and cram them into my mouth. 'It's like a prostitute,' I say, only it comes out as 'shlike a proshtew'. I run a glass of water and gulp. 'It's like a prostitute saying, "He promised me a tenner, officer, and he only gave me a quid!" Everything's cash. Everything's word of mouth. There's no real evidence, so law just doesn't come into it. There's bugger all I can do, Bob, except wait and hope that they make a mistake.'

It's as though I'd started his bed-time story and shut the book when I was on the penultimate page. Quixote has had windmills explained to him. 'Well,' he says sulkily at last, 'just let 'em come here, that's all. Just let 'em try anything while I'm around ...'

'Come on, Bob,' I smile. 'One more jar and let's go to bed.'

Sleep is, to say the least of it, sporadic when the piss-pills are at work. Twice now I've got up, padded to the bathroom and thrown myself back into the double-bed. Twice I've lain there staring at the shadows of the bare wisteria branches shifting on the wall. Twice I've felt a pang as I look at the virgin pillow beside me in the moonlight and I've banished remorse with excited thoughts of the future. If there's going to be one. Twice, having swept over me and receded, the waves of sleep have picked me up and carried me unresisting away.

This time, it's different.

My bladder is full, sure, but not so tight as to have awoken me, yet I am awake. Wide awake. I glance at the clock. Seventeen minutes past three.

Something's wrong.

The wind still pushes enthusiastically at the windows. The wisteria still taps at the panes and twines on the wall. The moon seems to be travelling at thirty miles an hour.

Something's wrong.

There's a scraping sound outside. It lasts for a split second and is barely audible beneath the shoving and panting of the wind. I frown. I know that sound. It comes again, then there's a long, low snort.

I jump out of bed and stride naked to the window. I force my eyes to focus. The lawns, the little stable block, the copper beech are all the pale greys of an ageing photograph. Clouds cover the moon and everything sinks back into two-dimensional blocks of black, but not before I've seen the horse standing loose there on the cobbles.

I switch on the bedside lamp and fling on a towelling dressing-gown. I stride out onto the landing. 'Bob!' I call, 'Bob!'

There are a couple of muffled thumps from the spare room at the end of the landing. I'm halfway down the stairs when Bob emerges in a gold silk dressing-gown. His hair is like storm-smashed hay. His eyes are surprisingly clear and intelligent.

'Whass up?' he croaks and swallows.

'Benbow's loose.'

'Benbow?'

'You know. Joanna's cob.' I have to raise my voice because Vandal is sounding the alarm. A little late in the day.

'Oh,' says Bob dully, 'OK. I'll give you a hand.'

Whilst he descends the staircase, I dart into the dining-room and grab the air rifle. It's not powerful enough to kill a pigeon, but moonlight plays funny tricks. It is at least a gun.

Bob steps back from the dining-room door to allow me out. 'You think it might be those buggers?'

'Might be,' I nod. 'One way of getting us out in the middle of the night, isn't it? Look. I know it sounds silly, but you just stay here in the doorway, right? Know how to work this thing?'

Bob looks down at the gun. 'Bloody well should do.'

'OK. If you see anything move out there, shout the place down and fire at whatever it is. It won't do me a blind bit of good, but it'll give me a moment while they work out what's happening.'

'Right,' Bob hefts the rifle. It looks more than ever like a toy in his hands. 'What about Vandal?'

'Nah,' I shoot the bolts on the front door. I turn the key. 'Daft dog'll be shot or poisoned before he knows what's happening. And if it really is just a loose horse, we'll have to chase it into the next county with him making that racket. OK.' I place my hand on the door handle. I'm pretty sure that I'm going to feel very silly after this is over. 'Ready? One, two, three and – '

I pull the door inward and run out as far as possible like they do in the movies, crouching and weaving. I reach the corner of the house and stand for a second, breathing heavily, my back against the wall. Then I swing round. The wind sees me and pounces and gives me a big gloved punch that darned near picks me up. It makes my eyes water. The horse is still there, facing away from me and standing stock still on the cobbles. The loose boxes are to his left, the paddock rails to his right.

'OK, boy,' I soothe as I near him. 'Easy now. Easy...'

And then things start to cohere in my mind. This horse is bigger than Benbow, for one thing. Benbow's head sticks out of the last box for another.

I frown and take a few steps nearer. My heart starts pounding very hard at my chest walls. The wind freezes the sweat at my sides as soon as it breaks from the pores, but the sweat keeps coming. Still the horse doesn't move.

'Oh, God almighty, no,' I breathe. This time it certainly is prayer not profanity. 'Please God, no. I can't stand it...' I swing round

to the right so that the horse can see me approaching. 'Please...'
My voice raises to end on a little whipcrack. I extend a hand towards
the animal's neck. He turns to look at me. He gives a little snort of
interest or recognition.

The moon comes out in that moment.

Vantage.

A racehorse should be moving. He should be skittering and
dancing and high-stepping on the cobbles. He's not. He just stands
still and gazes at me with eyes which sparkle very faintly from their
pitch-black sockets.

'Oh, Christ,' I pant, 'Oh, Christ, oh, Christ, boy.' I switch on the
stable light. The house and the trees vanish. I throw my arms
around his neck and sob into the slick, greasy warm fur by his ear.
'What have they done to you, lad?'

He shakes me gently off and puffs out air. His brown eyes are
very sad, very curious. I've seen that look before. I step back. My
eyes flicker quickly over his forelegs. I sob, and overpowering anger
shakes my whole body. 'How can they? How can they? The filthy,
fucking *bastards*! How can they?'

Something – probably a hammer – has smashed his off fore
cannon bone. Not just once, but several times, until the matter is
beyond doubt, until gleaming crimson tissue and splinters of bone
can be seen through the ripped and bruised hide. Someone with
more evil in his heart than I could ever imagine has repeatedly
struck with all his might in order to reduce this powerful and
beautiful animal to a trembling, hobbling cripple. And they've done
it to punish me.

'Bob!' I shriek, and he's there, the air rifle hanging limply from
his hand.

'What is it?' he whispers. 'What is it, G?'

'V-V-Vantage.' I stammer. I have no control of my voice now.
A huge sob forces its way upward like an airlock. My shoulders
shudder violently. 'The bastards have...' I retrieve my breath and
let it all out in a torrent. 'Get back. Call the vet. Tell him to bring
a hum ... a hum...'

'Oh, God.' Bob snarls. 'They can't...'

'A humane killer. And Jack. Call Jack Carlton,' I bellow, 'tell
them to come *now! Now*, do you hear me? And the police. Hurry,
Bob. Please, hurry...' my voice tails off and I hide my face once
more in the uncomplaining horse's neck. I'm still saying, 'Hurry,
please hurry...' long after Bob has gone.

Somehow I get him into an empty box. Somehow with coaxing and cooing I get him to lie down on the bed of shavings. Somehow, because he needs it, I quell my anger. For now, I sit at his head, stroking and murmuring encouraging nonsense. 'Who's a brave feller, then? Who's the best feller? There's a lad. Easy, now. There's my bold lad . . .'

Then the cars start arriving, roaring and crunching, their head-light beams sliding around the box walls. The police make it first, but I tell them to go away, go to the house, talk to my brother. I don't want them here.

The vet, praise God, arrives mere minutes later. I've known Trevor Jellinek for ten years and more. He's smooth and he can't be more than forty but he's good at his business. He bustles in briskly and efficiently. He takes one look at Vantage, nods and starts to set up his equipment. Aside from, 'Don't worry, Georgie, you can stay where you are,' he says not a word.

A minute later, those huge muscular legs stiffen and tremble. That huge head jerks upward, hitting my knee. The lips roll back off his teeth. The soft dark eyes glaze over.

Thirty-six hours ago, this mass of meat and fur was Vantage, the 'brilliant young 'chaser' for whom 'almost anything is possible'.

The possibilities just ran out.

He should have stayed in Ireland.

That makes two of us.

'I just don't *understand*!' Jack strides back and forth on the drawing-room carpet, 'Why should *anyone* . . . I mean, he was a *horse*, for God's sake! Why . . .?'

'Because they wanted to get back at me, Jack,' I say softly. 'Somebody out there knows me a darned sight too well. They want to hurt me, they kill your horse.'

'And you say, Mr Blane,' interrupts the detective constable who sits on the sofa nursing a mug of tea whilst we sup whisky, 'that you were approached by Parker before the race on the 26th?'

'Yes.' I nod.

'And he asked you deliberately to lose the race and promised you sixty thousand pounds to do so?'

'Yes.'

'And you quite properly refused and reckon that this is Parker's revenge?'

'Yes.'

'Hmm,' he runs his forefinger round the collar of his pink shirt. He's young and blond and smug, and I don't like him. 'I see

Mr Carlton's point. Why attack the horse? Why not punish you directly?'

'I don't know,' I say sullenly. 'I have no idea. I'm not a bloody psychologist, officer. Ask Parker.'

'Oh, we will, sir,' says his partner solemnly. I don't like him any better. Where Number One is slick and quick and thinks he's God's gift to policewoman cadets, Number Two wears a moustache and a tweed suit and thinks he's on the way to making Chief Constable.

Maybe I'm being unfair. I don't like anyone much, tonight.

'So they take the horse from your yard, Mr Carlton at – what?'

'Can't have been before midnight,' snaps Jack. 'My head lad lives above the shop and was awake till eleven or thereabouts. The closed circuit cameras should tell us all that.'

'And they deliberately bring the animal down here, break its leg and – how do they get it down the drive without you hearing, Mr Blane?'

'They walked him,' I sigh impatiently. 'There's a grass verge. You don't have to touch the gravel if you don't want to.'

'Right,' the man in the pink shirt nods. 'We'll check that. Should be prints. The horse could walk, then?'

'In pain,' I say, 'yes. He had four legs.'

'Did you hear a vehicle – a horsebox, say, during the course of the night?'

'Nope,' I drink whisky and shudder. 'There was a stiff wind, the road's a good ninety yards away and I was asleep. Aside from that, they're more likely to have used a car and trailer than a horsebox.'

'Why do you say that, Mr Blane?' Number Two leans forward eagerly.

'Because a horsebox is a pretty obvious bit of kit, that's why. A hundred people could have seen it between Lambourn and here, even at this time of night. A car is just a car and a trailer is anonymous. By now they could be miles apart from one another and nothing to connect one with t'other. Pretty darned obvious, I'd've thought.'

'Thank you, Mr Blane,' says Number Two indulgently as if he'd known it all along but had just been testing. He glances to his partner. They both nod. They both stand. 'Well. I should think you'll be wanting to get to bed. Thank you for your assistance. We'll call on you tomorrow morning, Mr Carlton. Can you be there, Mr Blane?'

'I usually am.'

'Good, good. We'll have to talk to your head lad, Mr Carlton, and his wife if he's got one, and of course we'll want to see your closed circuit film. Meanwhile, we'll try to track down our friend Mr Parker.'

'Trouble is, of course,' Number One muses, 'it's not a very serious offence. I mean, stealing, of course. Serious enough, but that's it, really. Just stealing. There won't be many charges to cover breaking a racehorse's leg. Malicious damage, I suppose. Nothing which really carries a sentence commensurate with the sort of money you were offered, Mr Blane.'

'You mean they'll have paid some thug a few grand and he'll have taken it knowing that he'd only get a couple of years or something?'

'Probably, yes. And tying him up with your friend Parker may prove very difficult. Very difficult indeed.'

'All right, officer,' Jack snaps. His first response to grief or pain is always anger. 'Thank you for coming so promptly. Good night.'

When they have gone, Jack strides brooding back into the drawing-room. He helps himself to half a glass of scotch, knocks it back in one and pours another large one.

'Bloody hell,' he growls and sits on the sofa.

'Yup.'

There's a long silence.

'Why the hell didn't you tell me, Georgie?'

I shrug. 'What'd you have done if I had? If I'd lost or fallen, you'd've thought it was done a-purpose. No point. I told the stewards.'

'Maybe right,' he nods slowly. 'God, this is seriously rough stuff, I mean, you and I, we know it happens. People want favours pulled. You say, "Yes, I'll do it" or, "No, I'll not". Maybe they start spreading rumours about you if you refuse. Maybe you get put through the rails. That's normal, but *this*. This is bloody terrifying.'

'I know,' I sniff, 'this is the brave new world, mate. There's money in it, so, according to current theory, Parker and Hoyle are the cleverest guys around. Anyone as doesn't play dirty must be a berk.'

'Vantage.' Jack throws himself back and closes his eyes. 'Oh, God. The best horse I ever had.'

'The best I ever rode,' I say quietly.

'Smythson'll blame me, of course.'

'For sure.'

'Jesus. That horse could have done anything.'

'Yup.'

'Oh, bugger it all, Georgie.'

188

'Pretend he fell racing and broke his neck.' I shrug. 'It's all there is to do.'

'I suppose.' He empties his glass and shakes himself. 'It still hasn't sunk in.'

'I know. Incredible, the whole darned thing.'

I follow him to the back door. Vandal tap dances excitedly at my heel. Jack turns at the door. 'You be OK here on your own?'

'Sure,' I lay a hand on his shoulder and gently push him out into the freezing wind. 'Bob's here – you know, my brother.'

'No, he isn't,' Jack turns to me. He blinks. 'I saw him when I got here. He just said "hello" and jumped in your car. Drove off like he was in a power-boat. Showered me with gravel.'

'*What*?' I gape, then my skin starts to crawl. 'Stay there!' I swing round and barge through the kitchen door, down the hall and left into the dining-room. Nothing has been moved. The table is bare. The curtains are still drawn.

The drawing-room. A quick scan of the bookshelves, the sofa, the chairs. Nothing. Just the empty glasses, the full ashtrays, the squashed cushions which suddenly seem an accusing mess.

'Georgie?' Jack's voice echoes in the kitchen.

'Hold on!' I call back. I push the office door open. The air rifle lies on the desk. Beside it, *The Directory of the Turf* lies open:

HOYLE, KELLOW FRANCIS. Born 14 February, 1952. Educ. St. Peter's College, York. Chairman and Managing Director, Hoyle's Leisure Enterprises Ltd, Hoyle's Turf Accountants Ltd; Patron and Chairman, Inner City Youth Cricketers' Trust ...

There follows all the stuff about his recreations – hang-gliding with the Pope and all that – then *Best Horses Owned* and, last, *Home Address: Roundway Place, Newton Valence, Alton, Hants.*

'Stupid bastard,' I hiss. I snap the book shut.

'Georgie ...?' Jack appears in the doorway.

'Lend us your car, Jack.'

'What?'

'Your car.'

'Er, well ...'

'Come on. Let's go. I'll drop you off at home. Bob's gone after Hoyle. He's mad.'

'Well, good on him,' Jack scurries sideways down the hall to keep pace with me. I push past him into the kitchen, 'But look, Georgie. About the car ...'

'It's insured isn't it?' I hold the back door open for him. 'Listen, Jack,' I tell him as he steps onto the gravel, 'my brother has just set off like a loon to attack a man twice his size and with a thousand times his money. If he succeeds in killing him it'll be just a little bit worse than if he fails. He's in a fast car and he hasn't driven for over eight years. I'm taking the Range Rover whether you like it or not, so shut up, will you?'

'OK,' he says equably. He walks round to the passenger door. I lock the house and whistle up Vandal, who bounds into the back, panting happily. Twenty minutes later, he's in the seat beside me as I swing the car onto the motorway and put my foot down hard.

Through Newbury. Past the ghostly church at Kingsclere where the Tetrarch – the spotted wonder – is commemorated in stained glass. Round the great *Close Encounters* spaceship of Basingstoke, then into the rolling, gentle downs of Hampshire.

It's still dark when we reach Alton. Look. The streetlamps show a one street market town which climbs a steepish hill. There's a Victorian museum and assembly rooms at the top, then the usual shops and terraced houses. At the bottom, there's a big green. Not a soul is abroad.

I've looked at the map. Newton Valence looks to be a tiny village just four miles away. It could take hours of toddling around to find Roundway Place at this hour of the morning. I need a guide.

I'm hoping to find a milkman or something. Instead, the police find me. A white Range Rover stands propped on the pavement in a thick cloud of white smoke. A uniformed officer steps out and waves me down. Perhaps he just wants to compare cars. I pull in ahead of him and hope to God that he won't bring out the breathalyser. The diuretics will help – my bladder is bursting again, my feet tapping fast – but I'm definitely over the limit.

'Morning, sir,' the policeman smiles amiably enough. His eyes flicker over the interior of the car, taking in Vandal, the skull-cap and headcollars in the back. Vandal growls.

'Shut up,' I tell him. 'Good morning to you, officer.'

'Looking for something, were we, sir?'

'Yeah,' I grit my teeth and try to stop my right leg from jiggling. 'I'm looking for a chap called Hoyle, Kellow Hoyle. Place called Newton Valence.'

The policeman frowns. 'Don't I know you, sir?'

'Dunno,' I shrug fetchingly, 'Georgie Blane.'

'Of course!' he beams, well pleased with his powers of detection. 'Saw you on telly – what? – yesterday? Day before. You lost me a bomb a week or so ago.'

'Sorry.'

'Yellow something or other. You jumped off.'

'Not voluntarily,' I lie. 'Yellow Jersey. Tell you what, you try it next time.'

'Wouldn't mind a go, I must say. Very slowly, though.' He snaps out of the reverie. 'So, you're looking for Mr Hoyle. There has to be a story here, but it's none of my business, I suppose.'

'Nothing exciting, I can assure you. We keep the same sort of hours, you and I. Got to be up on the gallops by seven-thirty.'

'Nice chap, Mr Hoyle,' says my new-found friend, 'always good for a bob or two. Gor, what I wouldn't do to have some of his cash, eh?'

'Yeah. Me too. So,' I say loudly for fear that he's slipping into another little dream, 'it's down this way isn't it?'

'Oh. Oh, yes, sir. Straight down here, onto the by-pass...'

What you do is this. You turn left at a white pub called the Horse and Groom, and you follow a deep, freestone, tree-covered lane up to the village. I say 'village'. It's just a few scattered workers' cottages really, for typical Hampshire workers with £250,000 to spare. Anyhow, you pass through the village and the hill dips downward and you take a right along a narrow bumpy path and there you are.

Yes, but I expected electronic gates and guards and all sorts of arguments and fights and suchlike jollity before I could even get to the front door. Not a bit of it. That's not the English way.

So here I am, outside Hoyle's house at six o'clock of a winter's morning. There's no sign of the XJS.

What now?

It's light enough to see something of the house. It's very big and it's red brick and the architect would have described it as 'in the Georgian style'. It's Churchillian Georgian, however, where the real thing would have been Burke. It's burly and squat and assertive. The dovecote on top merely serves to stress the sense of parody. Strangely, too, for so evidently a rich man's house, the builder has skimped by using the eaves as lintels on the top storey. It looks like an amateur's portrait, with the eyes at the top of the head. In there is the man who beat up Patsy, the man who killed Vantage, the man who feels that I owe him a million pounds or more. He's a big man, a powerful man, and he is not well-disposed towards me. So perhaps I try some impromptu breaking and entering. Little boxes on the walls declare that the whole place will jangle like a headache if I so much as raise a window-sash.

So I wait and stake out the joint, pounce on Hoyle as he leaves

191

and demand that he returns me one brother, used, some damage. Not good. Hoyle will have staff in there. Expert staff, accustomed to doing his bidding. By then, too, Bob could be dead or brain-damaged and the car could be full fathom five down in the Bristol Channel.

So, still shifting from foot to foot like a circus elephant because I forgot to ease the bladder on the way, I adopt a novel, inventive course of action.

I ring the doorbell.

And again.

And again.

It makes a noise in there which makes the bladder problem still worse, but I steel myself and keep ringing. A light comes on above my head. I step back. I can see cornflower blue walls, a white ceiling. Another light comes on up at the left hand corner of the house.

I keep ringing.

Soon there are sounds from inside. There are whispers and soft footfalls, faint thuds and creaks as the house stirs and stretches.

I'm shivering, and it isn't just the wind.

At last yellow light shows in the two small windows on either side of the front door. A carriage light in the porch comes on, momentarily dazzling me. Shuffling steps draw nearer. The light dribbles down the two steps and lies in a puddle on the gravel. I step further back so that whoever it is will not see me before I can see them. The bolts grind and bang. The key goes 'clunk'. The door opens inward.

I don't know exactly what I'm expecting; a couple of grinning leather jacketed jobs, perhaps, or an older man with hair like a stoat, a nasty expression on his face and a sawn-off shotgun in his hands. Something like that. Whatever I have visualised, it sure as hell isn't this.

A little woman in a checked flannel dressing-gown and fluffy bedroom slippers peers nervously out into the darkness. 'Yes?' she trills. 'Who is it?'

I say, 'Er.'

'Who is it, please?' she calls again. Her voice is tremulous, 'Hello? Hello?'

I summon anger to overcome any mild momentary embar-rassment. I step quickly up the two steps and into the doorway. Instinctively, she tries to shut the door in my face. I'm too quick for her. Some hero, this Blane. I push the door back. She staggers backward with a gasp but keeps pushing.

'Excuse me,' I slip past her.

'Mr Fleming!' she calls in a good strong voice. 'Mr Hoyle! Mr Fleming!'

There's a lot of movement upstairs. 'It's all right,' I tell her. 'I want to see Mr Hoyle. My name's Georgie Blane. It's urgent.' My voice echoes around the hall, rattles along the gallery rail, rings in the great baronial fireplace.

'Well, can't you wait on the doorstep like anyone else?' she demands. 'Mr Fleming!' she calls again.

'I'm sorry,' I nod, 'I just had to get in.'

'Do you realise what time it is?'

'Yes, I know. I'm sorry. It really is urgent.'

There is a movement on the gallery. I look up, alert. A man emerges, also in a dressing-gown. His thin, sprayed-on dark hair gleams as though he's just left the swimming-pool. His eyes have heavy bags beneath them, but they're wide and bright. He somehow contrives to keep his face set in the dignified butler cast whilst very clearly displaying intense irritation.

'What is going on?' he stage whispers as he descends the uncarpeted stairs, dewlaps juddering. 'Do you know what time it is?'

'We've been through that,' I tell him. 'I have to see Mr Hoyle. Now.'

'Mr Hoyle is asleep, sir. He will be awoken as usual at half past seven. I can see no possible excuse for disturbing him at this hour.'

'He pushed his way in, Mr Fleming,' says the woman.

'Oh.' Mr Fleming grasps my arm and tries to spin me round towards the door. 'Well, in that case, young feller-me-lad, you can leave right now, and think yourself lucky I don't call the police.'

I wrench free and push him back. There's a bit of undignified jostling. 'Kellow!' I shout. 'Where in hell are you?'

'None of that,' Fleming grunts in my ear. We are locked in a sort of Sumo shoving match. He has his arms around my chest, I have my hands on his. We're not making much progress either way. 'Mrs Travers,' he croaks, 'call the police.'

'Kellow!' I yell again. The carved wood sings back at me. The butler gets his hand over my mouth and pushes my head back hard.

''Allo, 'allo,' says a high-pitched voice from above, 'what the bleeding 'ell is going on 'ere, then? Leave 'im be, Duncan. It's all right. I know this feller.'

Fleming releases me and steps back, red-faced and panting.

I wipe my mouth on my sleeve and look up, and there, leaning on the banister rail in a dressing-gown of pale grey silk, is Kellow Hoyle.

'So,' he says before I can recover my breath, 'what's all this in aid of, Georgie, eh?'

It's his grin which does it, his broad, innocent, trust-me-I'm-a-nice-guy placard grin. I'm remembering the bared teeth of a horse, the beaten face of a pretty girl, whilst he is grinning a moist, red-lipped grin beneath that sandy beard.

I take one deep breath like you do before you dive, and I charge up the stairs at him. 'You bastard!' I yell as I run. 'You fucking bastard!'

That's the trouble with battle. You learn about strategy. You learn about tactics. You know that it's silly to attack an enemy on higher ground, but by the time that a battle's worth fighting, all that sort of thing just evaporates and you just want to tear the other feller's throat out.

I run into a forearm as firm as a beam. I contrive to grab a silken sleeve, that's all, before Hoyle's knee jerks upward. It misses my balls but hits me in the solar plexus, none too hard. I almost wish it had been the balls instead. Somehow I manage to control my sphincters, but cold sweat bursts from my brow and I double up, groaning. Hoyle just pushes me away with his bare foot. I slither down a couple of steps and gasp Janis Joplin chords.

'What in God's own name are you doin', Georgie boy?' Hoyle squeaks. 'First you smash up a perfectly good dooverywhatsit at the sports, then you go charging at me in my own 'ouse like a bleeding bull. What's up with you, man? You off your trolley or what?'

'Where's my brother?' I pull myself up and blink away the mist.

'Your brother,' Hoyle considers. 'No, leave him be, Duncan.' Only then do I notice that Fleming has trotted up the steps in my wake and intends to bundle me away. 'It's all right.'

'Shall I call the police, Mr Hoyle?' calls Mrs Travers in a tone of profound satisfaction.

'No. No, not yet. Get up, Georgie. Duncan, Tessa, would you leave us? No point in going back to bed. Might as well get dressed and make us both some breakfast.'

'You're sure, sir?' Fleming sounds resentful.

'Yeah, yeah. Course I'm sure. Don't worry 'bout a thing.'

I get to my feet and stand flattened against the wall as Mrs Travers and Fleming climb past me, pressed hard against the banister.

'Look, damn it,' says Hoyle, 'you've torn my bleeding dressing-gown.'

Travers and Fleming, each with a worried backward glance, vanish into their bedrooms.

'Where's my brother?' I pant. 'Where is he, Hoyle?'

'Where's my sister, Georgie?' Hoyle asks calmly. 'Look! This cost me four hundred quid! What do you wanna come here ripping my dressing-gown up for, eh?'

'What do you mean, where's your sister?' The whole world is plainly conspiring to mock me. There's a universal joke, and I'm the only person not in on it. 'I've never met your sister!'

'Same 'ere, Georgie,' Hoyle strolls down past me, 'I've never met your brother. Pity, really. I like 'is records.'

'He – he came here tonight.' I trudge downstairs after Hoyle. 'He wanted to kill you.'

'No way to treat a fan.' Hoyle pads across the worn flagstones and sits at one of the two tasselled dark red damask sofas in the hall. He leans back and crosses his bare tanned legs. 'What have the clan Blane got against me, then?'

'You bloody know.'

'I bloody don't. Wish I did,' he gives the Jewish shrug, palms upward. 'I don't mind being hated *per se*, but I do like to know why I'm being hated, you know? Call me a sentimental old fool, but there it is . . .'

'Ah, leave it out, Hoyle, will you?' I sigh. Concentration has now become impossible. 'Listen . . .'

'Yeah?'

'Well . . .'

'Ah, come on, Georgie.'

'Where's the goddamned loo?'

All right, all right. Hardly a heroic performance so far, but have you ever tried to assert yourself when you're wriggling and writhing like Cliff Richard on noonday desert sand? How come people never snipe at James Bond when he's got a bad boil on his bum or he's carrying two gallons of shaken Martini in his bloated belly? How come the good guys don't inherit when it comes to the thousand natural shocks that flesh is heir to?

Me, I was a favourite son in that regard. I got the lot.

There are still no thugs when I return, still no guns or high-tech thumbscrews in evidence, just Hoyle sprawled on the sofa. He has found a rug which he has slung over his shoulders so that he now resembles a mid-sixties Californian guru. He has also managed to rustle up coffee from somewhere.

'Sit down, Georgie,' he indicates the sofa which faces his.

I consider saying, 'I'd rather stand,' but it's always been a petty line. I sit.

'Coffee?'

'All right. Black.'

He leans forward and covers the handle of the silver coffee-pot with a napkin. He pours.

'Right,' he picks up his own cup and discreetly rearranges the skirt of his dressing-gown. 'So tell me all about it. First of all, what's all this about your brother?'

'He came here,' I say shortly. 'Tonight. This morning.'

'If he did, he came here very quietly, Georgie. You're our first intruder so far tonight. What makes you think he came here?'

'Well ... he'd looked up your address and then hopped into the car and driven off. Given his state of mind, I'd say he meant to come here and have it out with you.'

'Well, he may have set out for here, but he sure as hell never got here. OK? Maybe he got lost. Maybe he broke down. Maybe he saw sense and headed home again. I don't know. All I know is, he's not been seen here. OK, so that's that,' Hoyle sweeps on, 'now would you mind telling me just what he wanted to have out with me and why kind, Christian Kellow doesn't appear to be flavour of the month with the Blanes?'

'You know,' I am bullish, 'don't play me for a fool, Hoyle.'

'I don't, son. I won't. I know that you're anything but, but all the same, I can only swear to you that I don't know what I'm meant to have done. On my mother's life, Georgie.'

'So when did she die?'

'No, no,' he grins. 'Still alive and well and living in Whitley Bay, God bless 'er. Seriously, Georgie,' his voice becomes deeper and slower. Suddenly I can understand why he's got where he has. 'You'd better tell me. Something's obviously gone badly wrong. It affects me. I want to know what it is.'

'So you're telling me you don't even know about the King George?'

'I know that I lost a packet laying against you.'

'And why did you lay against us, then?'

'Same reason as ever,' he replies swiftly, 'information received.'

'From Parker.'

'Yeah, as a matter of fact. He's always been right in the past. He says, "Word has it that Georgie's not going to win on Vantage." I say, "Are you sure?" He says, "Certain". That's good enough for me. I back my hunches, Georgie, and my information. That's what bookmaking's all about far as I'm concerned. What's wrong with that?'

'Nothing. Only that Parker offered me sixty grand to stop Vantage.'

Hoyle frowns and leans forward, his forearms on his thighs, 'You're kidding.'

'I'm bleeding well not.'

'Well, well. Now we are getting somewhere...' I can see his mind performing some complex calculations. 'Go on.'

For the second time in one night, I recount the whole sorry story. With Jack, I omitted most of the Patsy element and the inconvenient fact that at one point I had agreed to Parker's proposal. With Hoyle, I omit nothing. Very coolly, very cleverly, he guides me backwards or forwards, getting me to fill in gaps or explain this or that minor detail. It's like watching an actor rehearsing every line until he's got it pat. By the end, as the sun comes up over the valley, he could tell the story as thoroughly as I.

'Jeesus!' he whistles. 'Young Olly has been a busy little bugger, hasn't he? No bloody wonder you wanted to have a go at me. God almighty, I wonder how many others there must be out there plotting their revenge on me! Probably half the bleeding jocks are dreaming of disembowelling us when they get a chance.'

'So you are telling me that you really didn't know a blind thing?'

'Georgie,' he flings off the blanket and stands as though to proclaim, 'I am many things, but I'm not a bully. I'll send a man round to intimidate a welcher, sure. You'd do the same if you were owed a lot of bread by some polisher, but you won't find me beating up women and dumb animals. Believe me or not. I don't give a monkey's, but that's a fact.'

I believe him. I still want to hit him because there's no one else to hit, but I believe the man. My wariness does not totally desert me. Kellow, after all, is a clever man, and more than one trusting guest in my nation's history has tucked into the turtle soup and the stewed pike only to find the steak knife planted between his ribs. Nonetheless, my fantasies of the monster in his high-tech palace of evil have fled with the darkness and now seem far-fetched and absurd. Goldfinger did not employ the likes of Mrs Travers as his front-line security staff.

'Let's think about this over some breakfast,' announces Hoyle, and then, as if reading my thoughts, 'I'll have Tessa stand by the table to test your food if you like.'

'Nah,' I growl and grin, 'I'll take my chances.'

Breakfast at Hoyle's is as you'd expect: opulent but ever so healthy. A buffet is laid out on the Smallbone Provencal-style sideboard: different varieties of mix'n'match muesli with nuts, prunes, figs, sliced bananas and dried fruit, all set out in separate bowls, then a magnificent fruit bowl, huge pitchers of fruit juices, a platter of Havarti or whatever the darned stuff is called, and finally the silver coffee and teapots on the hot plate. I content myself with an ugli fruit and more coffee while Hoyle eats a bran mash which would make a carthorse groan.

We eat largely in silence because he's busy flicking through files. Occasionally he gets up, murmurs, 'excuse us, Georgie' and moves next-door where either a sink is overflowing onto a concrete floor or he's got a computer keyboard. Each time, he comes back with sheaves of print-outs and resumes his eating whilst marking the print-outs in pencil.

His secretary arrives. Now this is very much more in the Goldfinger mould. She has coiled and shiny Bob Martin's blonde hair and a smile that makes the tonsils tickle. She's dressed in molten sapphire which flows up and down and in and out without apparent interruption. She sits and crosses legs gloved in nylon stockings. They hiss at me. I find myself hissing back.

Hoyle is now on the cordless telephone, speaking in what sounds to me like a numerical code. He covers the mouthpiece briefly to say, 'Georgie, Katrina. Katie, love, give yourself some breakfast and start collating all the transactions that I've ticked here, would you?'

She nods, spares me a brief smile and shifts from 'play' into 'fast forward'. It's an impressive sight. In Ireland, they'd think it obscene. She wastes not a moment nor an effort. I just sit there and drink coffee and look as though I'm interested in Messrs Smallbone's joinery while Hoyle and Katrina perform their own mind-popping dance to a faultless rap from Hoyle. When Mrs Travers comes in to clear away the breakfast, I cough a bit just so that she knows not to put me down the waste disposal.

'Christ, Georgie, this is bleeding serious!' Hoyle squeaks at one point. 'We're in trouble, mate. You and me both. They've stitched us up good and proper. Not your fault, but – Jeez!'

'What's it all about, then?' I ask nervously.

'I dunno yet.' He frowns and picks up the telephone again. 'Jacobs' are in on it in a big way. A few small-timers too, running errands, cashing in, generally confusing the issue. Monty Alvin knew what was going on. Freddy Sheil, Sam Travers ... I'm gonna have to do one hell of a lot of bobbing and weaving to wriggle out of this one. You'd best watch your back too, Georgie,' he stabs at numbers on the receiver, 'we're talking a lot of dough here. There's not much some people won't do for ... Hello? Frank? Kellow. Drop everything. I need to know who placed the following bets. Ready?'

And he's off again, rattling off figures like a cokehead bingo-caller.

His few well-chosen words have done nothing for my state of mind. Jacobs' are not just big; they're bloody enormous. Casinos, offshore banking, bookmaking, hotels, steakhouses – you name it, they've got anything from a pinky to a fist in it. And somewhere in that giant corporation, there is a cell which has been manipulating me to its own mysterious ends.

My stomach rumbles a lot. I walk quickly across the hall, glancing apprehensively this way and that, to take another much-needed piss. I back away from the windows. Having Hoyle as an enemy felt bad. Like being the only British soldier in Port Stanley the day the Argentines arrived. Having Jacobs' as an enemy feels worse. Like being the only Argentine soldier a couple of weeks later.

It's a quarter past ten and I'm thinking, with no great enthusiasm, that it's time I was setting off. It's cosy in here. There's a pretty girl and a steaming coffee-pot, and no one's shooting me or drip-feeding me gin or whatever the state-of-the-art murder-method happens to be. Out there, it's cold. I'll be on my own.

'Right, my old son,' Hoyle thumps the table. I jump. I haven't exactly got a headache, but every circuit in my brain is very close to another, uninsulated, live and humming. The slightest sudden movement can cause a rather nasty flash and bang. 'We're getting there.'

'We are?'

'Yup. Not too difficult, really. Just a matter of seeing who's been hedging his bets most, isn't it? I've gone back over Parker's brilliant ideas in the past twelvemonth. Most have worked out. A few have come a cropper. So who, for example, knowing that Vantage would win . . .?'

'They didn't know he'd win.'

'Oh, yes, they did, Georgie boy. Jacobs' knew. Leastways, they had a pretty shrewd idea. Think Parker cornered that girl just when he did by accident? Not Parker. That fucker does nothing by accident. You were meant to see 'em together. Think Parker didn't know that you're the sort of stubborn little shit that goes the wrong way when you're threatened? Course he did.'

'What about Chas, then?' I demand. I can't quite bring myself to believe, still less to like, the implication that I've been so evidently manipulated. 'They took out insurance. They tried to do me.'

'Bollocks, mate,' Hoyle laughs. 'Little Chas Wilcox turn you over? Don't make me laugh. I don't know shit about race-riding, but even I know that you could ride Wilcox into every bleeding trench on the Somme if you had a mind to. Nah. Don't you see? They try to do you in the race, they let you know the girl's a plant, they beat the girl up, they kill the horse, Parker rings up occasionally just to insult you. They don't do anything logical like actually hurting *you*. What's the common factor, then, Georgie? What's the one thing that all these things achieve?'

'I don't know,' I sigh, then, 'They make me bloody angry.'

''S'right, Georgie boy! They make you bleeding furious. That's what they're meant to do! That way you swear that you'll do me no matter what. You go to the stewards. Perhaps Parker sets you up with another of my employees in a pay-off, something like that. Perhaps Parker himself is set up with you. Little sods like that are expendable. A few other odds and sods in the game get wound up and start complaining too, and goodbye, Mr Nice Guy. Don't you see, Georgie, they're out to get *me*! They can't get real evidence against me, so they manufacture it, start rumours. Racing's becoming a cesspool and it's all 'cos of Hoyle. Oh, he hasn't been done, OK, but a few of his top employees have been warned off. Do you see what that would mean to me, Georgie? It means I'd be blocked from going public next summer, so I'd never have a chance to compete with the other bastards. It means that a carefully constructed image on which I've spent millions gets blown apart and that's the last time Hoyle buggers up their starting-prices and steals their trade.'

'Makes sense,' I say grudgingly. I still can't come to terms with the idea that someone knew me, my strengths and weaknesses, well enough to use me as an instrument of evil. We men like to feel that we move things, not the other way round. Silly, but there it is.

'Course it makes sense,' Hoyle barks, 'and it means we've got serious problems. Come here, Georgie. Take a look at these. If these guys know that a horse'll win or lose in the course of their little plot, they'll want to cover their costs, even make a tidy profit at my expense, right? So who laid off most punts on Vantage, for example? Well, let's check through. A lot of 'em are disguised this way or that – a few thousand laid off here and there by small bookies in exchange for favours – but the bulk of the money is Jacobs' all right. Look. Listen. . . .'

And at this moment, there's a loud bang from the hall. The wind flings open the kitchen door.

A man's voice calls 'No!' and then, 'Please. . . .'

Katrina frowns. Hoyle starts and looks up. I swallow a gallon of air and fling back my chair. I try to say 'Jesus!' but it comes out as though I'm chewing gum. I grab a large Sabatier knife from the magnetic strip on the wall and retreat to the furthest corner. I crouch behind the dresser.

'Sir . . .' Fleming is the first to enter the room. He looks as though he really couldn't apologise enough for the disturbance. Then comes a white-faced, orange-haired boy in the uniform of the Royal Mail. Bringing up the rear, wild-eyed, shock-headed, his face daubed with shoe-polish, his trousers and black tee-shirt stained with mud and grass, is Bobby Blane.

He carries a long, black-muzzled handgun. He looks very stern when first he sees Hoyle. He looks faintly embarrassed when his gaze falls on Katrina.

I straighten. An irresistible urge to giggle makes my lips twitch.

'Oh,' says Bob.

I stroll back to the table and pick up my coffee cup.

'Oh,' says Bob again, very sadly. His shoulders droop. 'Shit.'

202

'Well, how was I to know?' Bob, now cleaned up and dressed in one of Hoyle's Lovat sweaters, sits beside me in the front of the Range Rover. Kellow will bring the XJS over this evening for the meeting. Fleming will drive the Rolls. 'I mean, it took time, didn't it? I had to go up to town to get the gun. It was in a trunk in the basement with all my other old things – teddy bears and what not – and I couldn't exactly wake up the caretaker at five in the morning to unlock the bloody basement, could I?'

'No, Bob.'

'Right, so I had to break in, which was difficult, and the light wasn't working so I couldn't see what the hell was happening and every darned trunk and picture-frame and tea-chest pounced at me as I went by. So at last I get the gun and set off again, only I miss the turn-off and end up somewhere called Preston something or other and could I find a map in your car? Could I hell. All you keep is smutty magazines. Didn't know you read those things.'

'I don't, often. The map's under the driver's seat.'

'Oh, great. Thanks. So then anyhow I get here in the end and I do all the right things – blacked up my face like they said in the OTC, parked the car up the road and used great stealth – great stealth – to get up to the rhododendrons in front of the house. And there were lights on everywhere, weren't there? So I could hardly just barge in and expect a warm welcome, could I? So I thought, "I know, I'll wait. They'd not let me in, but they'll let the postman in, won't they?" So sure enough he comes along on his bicycle and I jump out, knock him off and tell him he's to hammer on the door, pretend to have a registered letter, and if he doesn't I'll shoot him, right? So I hide with my back to the door, and as soon as it's open, I force the poor sod through. Good plan, eh?'

'Very good plan, Bob.' My eyelids are heavy. I have to keep shaking myself and blinking to stay awake.

'Yeah. Well. I thought so. And then you go and mess it all up by sitting there all chummy with Hoyle and his fancy floozy. I mean, how was I to know?' He fiddles moodily with the cigarette lighter.

'You weren't,' I console him, though even now laughter threatens to bubble up inside me. 'You weren't. Honestly.'

'I suppose you reckon as I've made a bit of a prat of myself.'

'God, no!' I flick him a packet of Marlboro, 'You were bloody magnificent. Jaysus, man, but you could've been killed!'

He nods, reassured. 'It was bloody cold too.'

'Must have been freezing.'

'It was, but, you know, I was just so bloody furious.'

'I know. So was I. Thanks, Bob.'

He cheers up a little. He's proud enough to look modest as he lights two cigarettes and passes one to me. 'Did the postman a good turn too.'

'You did indeed.' I wind down the window, 'Hoyle won't miss a grand.'

'No, and the kid can get wed now.'

'I'm sure he'll be undyingly grateful to you, when he gets over it.'

'So you're really certain Hoyle had nothing to do with it all?'

'Yup. I'm certain.' I yawn and force my eyes to focus on the car ahead.

'So, who ...?'

'Leave it, Bob. Not now. All will be revealed later. Hoyle's still got some work to do.'

'Getting evidence?'

'Yup,' I yawn again, noisily, 'or manufacturing it. He's all right, Hoyle. For all the "butter wouldn't melt in my mouth" stuff, I reckon he can be as ruthless and unscrupulous as the other buggers when he needs to be.'

'Aaaaair, who? Sorry. Oh, of course, sorry, Blane. Yes. Couldn't hear. Blasted dogs, you know.'

I've had a quick shave and shower and, if still a little past the sell-by date, am feeling at least a little fresher. Bob's gone to bed. I've got twenty minutes or so in which to telephone before setting off for Plumpton.

'Right. Listen.' I tell Rory, 'Hoyle's not guilty.'

'What? Really? I mean ...'

'Hoyle didn't set up this whole thing. It's been a deliberate attempt to discredit him and his organisation.'

'I say, really?' Rory's voice is like a bored dog's yawn, 'Extraordinary. Who's responsible, then?'

'Jacobs', principally, but they won't have done it on their tod. Others will have been in on it for certain.'

'Good heavens above. You mean that all these races have been stopped and, aaair, simply because Jacobs' wanted Hoyle out of the way?'

'That's right. I was just a . . .' I look for another word but can't find it, 'just a patsy.'

'Barely credible. Oh, do shut up, boy. Sorry, Georgie; listen, I mean, can you prove this?'

'Probably not enough to get a conviction in a court of law, but enough to get a fair number of people warned off, yes. That's what Hoyle's up to today, going through the books, mobilising his spies, all that.

'Extraordinary, aaair. Quite extraordinary. I mean, you know, Sir Ernest Jacobs, well, I can't believe he'd've had anything to do with a thing like this.'

'Well, someone pretty darned high up must've known. We're talking a hell of a lot of money. You can purge the bastards now, clean the whole darned business up.'

'Absolutely. Yes. Splendid. Well now, listen, are you going to be there for a while?'

'No. I'm off to Plumpton. I'll hope to see Brigadier Grey there, put him in the picture, then I want you and everyone else involved to come round this evening. Seven, say. Hoyle will explain everything.'

'Aaair, yes. All right. Jolly good. Glad you got to the bottom of this. Thing is, Georgie, don't mention a word of all this to a soul, eh? Very important, that. If what you say is true, these people could cut up very rough, you know? They mustn't know that you even suspect the truth.'

'Yeah, right.'

'Extraordinary thing. Quite extraordinary. So. Seven o'clock, you say? Fine, fine. I'll have a word with Benet Kilcannon. He'll want to be there too.'

'Sure. The more the merrier. Look, I've got to get going . . .'

'Aaair, of course, of course. Please remember, though, Georgie. It's really important. Not a word about this to anyone. If you're right, things really could get nasty. Very nasty indeed.'

'Yeah,' I shudder, 'they already did.'

Dear X3597, I write quickly, boy, is this your lucky day! I've got nine inches of quivering gristle and a collection of Monkees records. I am also interested in ecclesiastical vestments. If you want a good time, please be in touch soonest. Seriously.

G.

I fold the letter and put it into an envelope with the MG keys. Then I set off for the sports.

I take Vandal to the races for company, and with some vague idea that he might deter assailants.

It's a good day in that I do not see Parker. Or Tam. It's also good in that I do see Polly, and both Robin Nuttall and Charlie Vane, both of whom have come over to spend Christmas with their fathers. Kilcannon, however, is not here today. Nor is Hugh Grey. I also fail to trouble the judges in all three contests in which I take part. I'm too darned jittery to ride one side of a seaside donkey.

Charlie, however, is on good form. You haven't met Charlie before. He's one of those jolly late developers in which the English specialise. He's slightly overweight, has high colouring and permanently dishevelled pitch-black hair. An idiot would think him an idiot, because he loves to drink and to witter about horses and he is always ready to concede to those who believe themselves to be cleverer than he, but Charlie's the sort that chortles and plays dumb and ends up apparently inadvertently ruling the world.

'Hello, venerable bogtrotter,' he greets me outside the weighing-room. I've just ridden a spirited hands and heels finish to come in last in a two mile handicap hurdle. I haven't a ride in the next.

'Charlie. Hi.'

'See you've lost none of the magic.'

''S'right. Why they call it a handicap, isn't it? What news from over the water?'

'Oh, it's green, you know, that sort of thing. Lot of rain. Life's bloody expensive, but we still manage to get in a bit of gas.'

'Your dad was telling us that you've taken to jousting with JCBs.'

Charlie frowns. 'How the hell does he know about that? Anyhow, yes. Passes the time. Horses are all right too. Got a really nice Sharp Venture colt should pay a few household bills next year. If the aged progenitor will sell him.'

'And Eledi?'

Charlie examines the toe-caps of his brogues. 'Oh,' he shrugs, 'fine. Busy.'

'Yeah. Saw her in that sitcom – what's it called?'

'Yes. She's doing well. Only get to see her once every six months. Sod it.'

Eledi Donovan is a very pretty young actress with freckles and saffron hair. She and Charlie met when they were both undergraduates at Cambridge. He's been proposing to her at regular intervals ever since.

'So,' Charlie says after a pause, 'all well with you, Georgie?'

'Sort of. You know.'

'Saw you in the King George. Very impressive. What's this I hear about you doing that little swine Wilcox?'

'Yeah, well, he tried to do me, didn't he?'

'Did he now?' Charlie grins. 'I thought as much when I saw it on video. Thought that's dangerous driving if ever I saw it. Still. So he got his come-uppance, did he? Good. Why'd he want to do a damn fool thing like that, then?'

I glance quickly over my shoulders. No one seems to be within earshot. Most of the punters are already up on the stands for the big race. 'That's what I'm hoping to see your dad about this evening. Seems I've exposed some pretty mucky corruption in low places. You remember Parker?'

'The Hon. Oliver?' the Hon. Charlie snorts. 'Yes, well, we didn't need you to tell us that he was a corrupt little so and so, did we?'

'No, but it's not just him,' I say softly. 'He's just the front man. See . . .' I've got the whole sentence lined up and eager to come out. I have to gulp it back like bile.

Close behind me, a voice says 'Aaaair.' It then says, 'Blane. Good. Charles. Hi. Nice to see you,' and Rory Fitzroy-Haigh shimmers into our midst.

'Rory,' says Charlie.

Something's amiss. I won't claim to be Charlie's oldest and dearest, but I've ridden against him, drunk with him, even regarded him, perhaps presumptuously, as something of a protégé – because I liked him, I suppose, because I liked his father, because he was such a lousy, exuberant rider, because of the Irish thing – I don't know. Anyhow, one way or another, I reckon as I know your man a bit. And although he smiles at Rory in the accepted manner, he has stiffened at his arrival. His eyes are suddenly cold and shifty. He looks like an ardent adolescent who has just got his hand on it when his parents walk in. Polite enough, but tense, guilty even.

We Irish have a reputation for garrulousness. Totally unjustified, of course, as the perceptive reader will have observed, but Charlie's reaction makes me glad that Rory turned up when he did. I like Charlie, and maybe its just fatigue and paranoia that are affecting my perceptions, but it's just possible that Rory has saved my life.

207

I ask Polly to accompany me back to the car. Only an Iranian on pre-med would even think of attacking me with Polly at my side.

All right, so I'm excited. I'm driving home to a conference at which I will play a leading role. I'm going to ensure that Parker is smashed and, with a bit of luck, that a lot of ugly heads at Jacobs' also roll. A few of the revelations may be just a little bit on the embarrassing side, but basically I'm the hero of the hour. It's an unfamiliar feeling these days. I like it.

The traffic's bloody awful and I reach home just before seven. Somehow, I'd expected the likes of Hoyle and Grey and Kilcannon to be extra punctual, so I'm faintly surprised not to find a bevy of gleaming Rollers hobnobbing on the drive. There's not a car in sight, not a light on in the house.

Bob must have slept all day. Good.

I let Vandal out of the car and whistle *My Funny Valentine* as I stroll into the kitchen. I switch on the lights. There's the usual moment's pause as they decide whether they feel like coming on or not, then they think OK, ... well ... yes ... are you sure? At last they sigh and yield to my will but they hum, just to show that they're not that impressed.

There's a note on the Memo board from Bob.

G. Buggeration. Have had to go up to town for an audition. A sitcom, would you believe, so I'll miss the fun and games tonight. Knock 'em dead. Back sort of nine-ish or so, if I bother to come back at all.

Yours per om. saec. saec. Amen,
Bob.

I'm still whistling as I walk down the corridor to the drawing-room. I pause to switch on the Christmas tree lights because we might as well be cheerful and because I remember that I didn't see a tree at Hoyle's place and I feel sorry for him.

Hold it. *I* feel sorry for *Hoyle*? Ah, well, there it is.

Your looks are laughable,
Unphotographable

208

My thanks and abject apologies to Rodgers and Hart, but that's the way it comes out.

There's something about the very fact of life where you don't expect to see it. Your mind is programmed to see a certain consoling pattern of inanimate objects. You turn on a light like I do now as I saunter into the drawing-room, and there's something animate in there too, and the very fact of life seems terrifyingly vivid in that second. Even a tortoise on the armchair would have given me a turn.

This is no tortoise.

My perceptions run something like this. There's a live human being in here.

And it's Parker.

Then comes: God, I hate that tight terraced hair and: why is the little bastard smirking at me?

Only then, when the shock has made my heart strike my chest like a shotgun blast, only then do I notice the gun in his hand and start to be seriously scared.

Parker's pleased with the dramatic effect he's had. His lips contract and expand like a worm in a hurry.

The gun, it should be said, is not a large one. Just a small squat sort of thing which probably couldn't make a hole bigger than a five penny piece in human flesh. Bob's gun this morning was much more impressive. But Bob's gun was a Diana repeater air pistol modelled to look roughly like a Colt .45. This little implement, I suspect, is the real McCoy.

And I don't know if you've noticed, but, in television programmes and films and things, people walk and talk in a sort of *soigné*, careless way when they've got guns pointed at them. Either I'm odd, or they ought to go back to the Strasberg school and polish up their method. Because me, I find that the knees become very weak indeed. My mouth dries and I have to support myself on something, quick. I choose the stereo stack at my right. I say, 'Ah ...'

'Good evening, Blane,' Parker twangs cordially. 'Just thought I'd pay you a little visit.'

I say, 'Ah ...' again.

'Meddlesome little bogboy, aren't you?' Parker smirks. 'You know, I really would love to hurt you, Blane. I really would. It's something I've been longing to do. I dream of it. I don't know what it is about you, but you just have that effect.'

This time I manage an 'Er . . .'

'Oh, I *would* like to,' Parker says through gritted teeth, 'but I suppose not. Mustn't leave messy evidence around, must we?'

I get some words together. 'In a few minutes,' I croak, 'there are going to be people arriving.'

'No, no,' Parker says as though irritated by a querulous brat, 'of course there aren't. Your brother's been sent off to an audition. Genuine audition, actually. Starline television. Hoyle Leisure's a major shareholder and our cockney friend Kellow is on the board. Astonishing, really, the oiks these people appoint these days . . . Oh, and your nice little steward friends. I'm afraid they all have prior engagements. As for Hoyle, well . . .' He shakes his head. 'No, Blane, you and I are all alone.'

'You're still done for, Parker.' *Now* is when you move into the *soigné* bit. I actually make it to the sofa and rest my bum on its arm. 'I'll give evidence against you. The stewards know all about you . . .'

'Ah, yes. Of course they do,' Parker grins. 'You will give evidence, you say? A discredited, disgraced little bogboy's evidence harm me? Those tapes, I'm afraid, Blane, are even now with your chums the stewards. And with the racing press. Every racing journalist in the land is at this very moment tut-tutting as he hears Georgie Blane agreeing to do some very, very naughty dishonest things. Hoyle? Well, poor Kellow was getting seriously above himself. He won't be troubling anyone. So you see, there *is* no evidence against me, Blane. No, no. It's you that's in trouble. Big trouble.'

I shiver and try very hard not to look at the gun.

There are different forms of fear, different brands of courage. I've been described as a brave rider, but that's just the hot-blooded bravery of the warrior. This demands something different: the cold courage of the bomb disposal man, the ability to cope with the prospect of sudden, incontrovertible annihilation. That hooked white finger just has to tighten and the celestial DJ will be saying, 'And that was . . .' just as the tune is getting good.

Whatever the variety of courage necessary, I ain't got it. Parker knows it too. He smirks, though his eyes look anything but amused.

'So what do you want, Parker?' I ask nervously.

'What do I want?' his eyebrows arise. The crenellated skullcap of his hair slips backward. 'Ah, what I want . . . What I want, Blane, is to shoot your kneecaps off and to watch you lying writhing and, and screaming and whimpering and jerking and. And then I want, I want to blast your filthy genitals and watch the blood spurting and you, your eyes as you realise that this is it. The end. No more

210

smutty activities, no more clever clever bogboy wisecracks, no more. That's what I want, Blane, but I suppose ...' He shakes his head sadly, then frowns. The gun barrel arises. 'Oh, I don't know. I still could. What do you say, Blane, hmmm? Why shouldn't I take you somewhere nice and quiet, somewhere out in the country, on the downs, something, hmm?'

'No,' I croak. I'm eager to say nothing which might offend him. 'No. Someone's bound to see us.'

'Think so?' Parker muses. 'Yes, maybe you're right. Ridiculous things these, really,' he looks wistfully down at the gun, 'just brought it along, keep you under control. You've shown a rather vulgar tendency to act first and think afterwards. These weapons induce pensiveness. Also useful should you decide to call that nasty dog in or something. Contrary to popular opinion, shooting people is a singularly messy and amateur business.'

'Good,' I gulp, a little, but not much, reassured.

'No,' Parker stands, 'I just thought I'd drop in to tell you not to bother to wait for your friends, that's all. And to see your face. That was worth it.'

Fear is slowly fading. As each image of that little gun spitting lead into my body grows fainter, it is replaced by another, more vivid, more enduring: Patsy's face, puffed up and bleeding like some overripe plum; Vantage, staring betrayed and bemused at his shattered, useless leg. Anger is on its way back, and with it, it's own brand of high octane fuel. It warms me. By comparison with the cold stuff which was there before, it makes me feel positively good.

'So,' Parker almost wriggles with delight at his own cleverness, 'I'll be off now. I do hope you've learned from this experience, Blane. It's not good for little bogboys to try to be clever. Other people do the thinking in this life, and it's best to accept that as the law of nature, you know? I'm sorry that your career has to come to such a messy and undignified end, but you really did ask for it.'

Parker's amused eyes never leave me as he opens the door and backs into the hall. I follow him at some five yards distance. If I tried to rush him now, he would almost certainly be startled into shooting even if, as he claims, he is reluctant to do so. Bide your time, Georgie. He's yours. Just wait a little longer.

'When we get to the door,' Parker says crisply, 'you'll be good enough to call that dog of yours and tell him what a dear friend I am, otherwise I shall shoot him. I do hate to hurt defenceless animals, you know.'

I nod. Parker backs into the kitchen. 'In fact,' he says, 'you'd

211

better go to the door ahead of me if you wouldn't mind.' He gestures with the gun. I obey.

I open the door, praying that Hoyle will be there, or Rory. Where the hell *is* Rory, come to that?

There's no one there. Just a big silly dog whimpering in the darkness, just a cold breeze with a scent of snow. I scratch Vandal behind the ears and tell him that he's a good boy and not to worry. He licks me and, aside from a cursory growl for form's sake, ignores Parker.

'Right,' says Parker lightly. 'Good. Now, stand back a bit, Blane. That's it. Sorry about all these broken appointments tonight. Still. Life is like that, isn't it?' He raises his gloved left hand. A yellow mini backs out of the trees up by the coal shed, reverses at speed onto the lawn and bounces back onto the gravel. Although he is on my side, I cannot see the driver. A scarf is wrapped around the lower part of his face, a tweed cap pulled down so that his eyes are in shadow.

As the car draws near, Parker gives me a last smug grin. His left hand falls on the door handle. He pockets the gun.

He's perhaps eight yards from me and suddenly I have a very silly idea. It's not so much that I'm thinking in terms of capturing him or anything tactical like that, more that I am desperately anxious to hurt him, but those eight yards and that gun prevent me. If I had a gun, I would use it. If I had a whip ...

And that's when the daft idea comes. See, with a whip I could – no exaggeration – knock the tip of your cigarette off at five yards. The whips, alas, are in the front hall. But close at hand there is something else with which I can attain a reasonable degree of accuracy. Every summer of my adult life, as others, contrary to logic and nature, have headed southwards in droves, I have headed northward – to Iceland, to Scotland, to Norway, to Labrador – where the days are long and the gnats are many and the salmon run. Now, I can place a fly over a fish at fifteen yards, say, with ninety-eight per cent accuracy. And Conor's rod is still standing where I left it on Christmas morning and there's a big double-hooked fly on it and the door's right behind me should I miss or should Parker decide to shoot, so why not give it a try?

So I give it a try.

I release the fly, strip out line and make one quick false cast to let it run through the rings. Parker is bending to get into the car as the reel shrieks and the fly whizzes past his head. He ducks instinctively, frowns and then, bemused, raises his head again as though to investigate the phenomenon. I had hoped perhaps to get the collar of his black jacket, but this time, I am in luck.

As soon as I feel the tug on the line, I strike, firmly but not too violently. Parker yelps. His right hand springs to his throat. I keep the line taut. 'Don't move an inch, Parker!' I order. 'One move and I'll rip your whole bloody throat out.'

It's rubbish, of course. If I were to tug really hard, it would hurt him like hell but the barbed hooks would rip free of his flesh. He, luckily, does not know that or hasn't the courage to risk it.

I move round behind him, keeping the line taut, so that any tug will, initially at least, embed the hooks still deeper in his throat. He gargles a bit and I try to remember whether I've got eight or ten pounds of breaking strain in the nylon.

'Don't be bloody ridiculous, Blane,' snaps Parker and then, to my satisfaction, 'Christ, that hurts!'

'Vandal!' I call. He lopes along willingly. 'Sit,' I tell him, 'and *stay*. Stay, right?'

Vandal sits unwillingly on the cold gravel. Parker half turns to see what I'm up to. I reckon to have seen hatred before now, but never so concentrated as in his swivelling eyes at this moment. I pull out my penknife and, laughing nigh hysterically, cut the line. I then bend and tie it tightly to Vandal's collar.

Parker meanwhile is raving at his driver. 'Do something, damn it!' he yells. 'Don't just sit there! The little bastard's ... Christ, man, what the fuck do you think you're doing? Get out and kill the little bastard! This is ridiculous. A fucking fishing line, for Christ's sake! What's the matter with you, man? Do something!'

The driver sits absolutely still.

'Parker,' I shout above his ranting. 'This dog is quite well trained. Only quite. He'll stay for a while, then his concentration starts to wander. He's also fast. Bloody fast. From a standing start he'll be up to thirty miles an hour in a couple of seconds. If I call him, he'll run to me and he'll drive those hooks so deep into your fucking throat that you'll never drink again. Do you understand?'

'This is absurd,' Parker is snooty again. 'A fish-hook! Christ! Do something will you, man!' he yells down to the driver again. 'All you have to do is cut the bloody line!'

'Hush, hush, Parker,' I gloat. 'No need to get excited. Stay, boy.' I walk up to Parker and reach into his right hand pocket for the gun. It's surprisingly heavy. 'Now,' I say with more calm in my voice than I feel, 'how does this work? Is that the safety catch, then? Well, well. Do I shoot you or your pet mute first, hmm?'

I walk round to the driver's side and lay my hand on the handle.

'Christ, do something!' Parker shrieks.

213

The driver does something. He looks up at me with wide, worried eyes. He says 'Aaaair' and he puts his foot down hard.

'Bastard!' sobs Parker. 'Cowardly filthy bastard! He could've killed you! He – he – God in heaven, I'll see him done. I swear it. I'll have him ripped apart. I'll ...'

'Shut it, Parker,' I tell him.

'How dare you talk to me like that!' he squeaks.

'I think I'll talk to my dog instead,' I laugh, 'he's more amusing.'

'No!' he yelps. 'All right. What the fuck do you want then, Blane?'

'A few answers first.'

'You know of course that you're going to die for this. I mean it. There's no way anyone does this sort of thing to me and survives. You realise that?'

'God, you are boring, Parker.' I sit on the grass slope above him. Vandal looks up at me and wags his tail. 'Stay,' I tell him again. 'First of all, how did you get Rory to work for you?'

'Fuck off.'

'Oh, dear,' I sigh, then, 'Good boy.'

Vandal gets up. His eyes crinkle into that blissful greyhound smile. The line tautens.

'No!' Parker moans. 'All right. Fucker. The bastard's been going bad. Big punter. Owed – I don't know – three, four hundred thousand.'

'Poor sod,' I nod grimly, 'so you got him to initiate all this stuff. The investigation of Hoyle, all that?'

'Yes,' he tells his chest. 'It was that or be warned off, bankrupted, the works.'

'And he was prepared to act as chauffeur to a little turd like you?'

'Don't you fucking dare to talk to me like that, Blane!' he screams. His arms are bent, his fists clenched. Vandal turns his head, intrigued by the noise. 'What's so bloody great about Fitzroy-Haigh, ha? High and mighty steward, is he? Pretty little officer and gentleman? Yes, well, look at him now. Four hundred grand in the hole and doing exactly what I tell him. Oh, he didn't want to drive me tonight. Shit-scared, he was, the fucking gallant soldier-boy, but I like to watch the little bastard squirm. It's good to see his hair out of curl. He talked to me like I was no one. Do you know what his mother was? Do you? A fucking chorus girl! And he talks to *me* like that. So I said, "You drive me, you face the music, Mister Fitzroy-precious-bleeding-Haigh, or it's no more hobnobbing with royalty, no more country-house weekends, no more looking down

214

your fucking nose. You'll be lucky to find yourself a berth under Charing Cross bridge." And that's what's going to happen to him now. You'll see. And you. Both of you. You don't fuck around with me. You'll see. Both of you, ruined!'

'You are a filthy little man, aren't you, Parker?' I snarl with very real, very intense despite. 'And what about Hoyle? What have you done with him?'

'I didn't,' he says stubbornly, 'I didn't do it.'

'Do what?'

'I don't bloody know. He's been silenced, that's all I know.'

'Killed?'

'I don't think so. Christ, Blane! I don't – I think we made some sort of deal with him.'

I sigh very deeply. A deal. A contract. A bond.

I thought that I had such a thing with Hoyle, but of course I never got the thugs or the lawyers in to tie it up tight. I made an assumption about such things. Silly, that.

It's all very obvious, really. Hoyle was an embarrassment. Thanks to a stubborn little sod named Blane, Jacobs' couldn't keep Hoyle out, so they'll have let him in. That's all. Hoyle will lose any evidence that he's mustered and there'll be no more punter's friend on the rails. Hoyle has joined the establishment.

'Thanks a ton, Kellow,' I murmur under my breath. But then, times have changed, haven't they? If you're a sitting tenant, you sit, and if it's a choice between death or discomfort and a profitable deal, you go for the deal. Crazy to do otherwise.

Hoyle's a survivor. I'm a dinosaur.

I miss those good old mesozoic days.

'What about Kilcannon, Grey, the others?' I demand.

'Ah, what the hell does it matter?' Parker's voice cracks, 'Just sent off on a wild goose chase like your sot of a brother.'

'I really am going to have to call that dog,' I lie back cheerfully on the cold damp grass. 'So, who's been running all this?'

Parker's hands flap. 'I don't bloody know! Get this thing out of me, will you! A *fish-hook*, for ... I don't know. A cartel.'

'What the hell's that mean, Parker?' I stare bemused at his dark figure.

'It means a cartel, doesn't it? I don't know who. The powers that be. Jacobs', one or two others. I don't bloody know. Hoyle was getting too big. He would have gone public soon. People were comparing Jacobs' with him and he had this fucking holier than thou image. Everyone was losing trade to the little oik. So I'm just told, "discredit the bugger", that's all. We're talking about business here, Blane. Big business, not cops and robbers. There's no bloody villain. It's business, that's all.'

'No bloody villain,' I shake my head and try to come to terms with the idea. No bloody villain, just victims ... Patsy, Vantage, Hoyle, Rory. Me. Maybe even Parker. Just victims.

At the top of the drive a car growls. Headlight beams scan the sky then dip downward. I pull myself to my feet fast. 'Good boy,' I say without emotion. 'Come on!'

And Vandal bounds.

Parker is clutching his throat and doing a war dance and howling more in fury and frustration than in pain as I slip back into the shadows by the garage. I keep the gun trained on Parker, but my eyes follow the progress of the car.

It draws up almost exactly opposite me. I can't see the driver until the door opens and the light comes on. Charlie Vane, flushed and beaming as vacuously as ever.

'Hello,' he says to Parker. 'What's the matter with you, then? Bloody awful noise you're making, you know. Is Georgie about? Do stop making that noise will you? Is Georgie in?'

Parker points in my direction. 'Bastard,' he says. 'Assaulted me. Christ!'

'What?' Charlie is determinedly cheerful. 'Oh, it's you, is it, Parker? Assaulted you, you say? Who, Georgie?'

'Bastard,' says Parker. 'I'm bleeding, for God's sake!'

'Well, I should think you probably deserved it,' says Charlie coolly, 'I wish I'd been here. Georgie?'

I step out of the shadows, still wary. The gun is pointed at Parker, but I don't get too close to Charlie. I don't trust anyone much just now. 'Hi, Charlie.'

'Hello, Georgie. What have you been doing to this Parker fellow? Shut up, will you, old chap. Oh, is that a gun? God, where did that come from? Very dramatic stuff. Like it. Hope I'm not interrupting anything.'

'No,' I am weary now, 'we've just been having a little question and answer session, that's all. What are you doing here, Charlie?'

'Oh, you know, I got to thinking. You said that – will you please shut up, Parker, you really are very annoying – you said that you were meeting Dad tonight to talk about this chap, and Dad had told me something about the whole tiswas over Christmas, you know, and when I got home – left before the last, you know – when

I got home, he'd been called up to London. Dad, that is. Urgent meeting with that bloody Rory at his club.'

'Yes, so?'

'Well, I mean, I'd seen the way Rory sort of shut you up this afternoon and even then I thought, "something's wrong here". Don't know if I should be telling you this, but Rory owes rather a lot of cash to the fat-cat bookies. In Ireland too. Owes me four and a half grand on a poker game too as a matter of fact, but that's by the by. Always was wet, even at school. So anyhow, yes. I rang Buck's, and Dad's there and Hugh Grey's there and old man Stratton's there and Rory ain't and Dad tells me no one told him to come down here tonight. So I think "whoops, summat's amiss", and Dad tells me to shift my arse down here prontissimo. So,' he pauses for breath, 'here I am. Probably entirely wrong, but still.'

'Entirely right actually,' I smile and relax at last. 'Thanks, Charlie. I got jumped, matter of fact, by this little sod. He got Rory to act as his driver, just for sadism's sake.'

'Nasty little man,' Charlie shakes his head, disapproving. 'How nice to be right for once. Well, now. What's to do with a Parker now you've got it?'

'Oh, I've got my own ideas about that,' I tell him, 'and they're not very nice. So if you'd like to turn the other way, I'll quite understand.'

'Me? Never. Try everything once. I say. Haven't got a drink in the house, have you? I'm parched as Methuselah's scrotum.'

So we sit and drink and I put Charlie in the picture and occasionally I wave a gun at Parker and occasionally Charlie tells him not to be such a horrid little nuisance, and then we take him over to Jack's yard and tell Jack that this is the man who killed Vantage, so Jack says, 'Right,' and does just what I intended to do.

See, there's a horse called Busted Flush who has no stable manners. Well, he has, but they're exclusively and exceptionally bad. He doesn't like to race much.

So I'm afraid that the Hon. Oliver Parker meets with a very unfortunate accident whilst attempting to steal a valuable horse. Not fatal, quite. Jack and I think it's a good idea, but Charlie urges restraint. Not fatal, but worse than the little accident that Patsy underwent. Parker isn't even groaning when we hand him over to the police.

217

See the conquering hero then, dancing in his triumph.

I'm all togged up in dinner-jacket and black tie and slippery patent slippers. Sweat makes clinging seaweed of my shirt. The music is so loud that my heart seems to have lost all sense of rhythm in its bid to compete with the drummer.

The lights are low. All around me, hands flicker, fists punch. Hair spins, bounces and tangles. Feet kick, shuffle and pound. Teeth are bared in fluorescent laughter, lips make Jaggeresque *moues*. Opposite me, a girl wriggles her belly. She sinuously sinks and straightens, stroking her body. She struts and stamps. Her hips and head jerk alternately back and forth and her long blonde hair sprays out like the trumpet blasts of a big band. She is entranced, by the music and her body's rhythmic movements, not, alas, by me. She stares past me or through me, a demented half smile parting her lips.

A saxophone shrieks. Synthesised strings shimmer. The drumbeats purl like a boulder down a waterfall and land in a splash of cymbals. The number, thank God, is over.

'Thanks!' I shout to the girl as yet another army of space-invaders on speed sweeps through the speakers into the room. She gives me a quick vague smile.

I turn away and head with apologies towards the door. A white face separates itself from the seething Hammer sci-fi blob of glup. It shouts, 'Lo, Georgie!' and bounces back into the darkness.

Out here in the hall, it's lighter. I can breathe more easily. There's also drink available. I grab a fresh glass of champagne from the long table by the front door, sip, sigh and lower myself very gently onto a gilt papier-maché chair. It's New Year's Eve.

'Bloody depressing time to throw a shindig,' Charlie told me last night, 'but I've got to be back in Kildare on the third, and it'll be a good chance to meet up with a few chums after Cheltenham. Come on, Georgie. You've got nothing better to do. I'd like to see you, and the Aged Progenitor would like a word too.'

So here I am in Kilcannon's stuccoed Palladian house just five miles outside Cirencester, gazing up at the high cupola and wishing that I were ten years younger. The 'few chums' have turned out to be some three hundred of racing's *jeunesse dorée* together with assorted Cotswold neighbours. No six packs and sausages-on-sticks in these parts; it's been Krug and smoked salmon and filo pastry canapés all evening.

I saw Kilcannon briefly when I arrived, but was quickly snatched up by Charlie and introduced to a whole bevy of glowing, toothsome girls. 'This is the bossman – Georgie Blane. I want him to have the time of his life.'

So I've spent the past two hours or so answering the intrigued questions of Mirandas and Melissas as to just how it feels to win a National and whatever happened to poor Vantage, and being dragged onto the floor by charming and enthusiastic Camillas and Carolines with scented throats and warm silken backs.

I should be enjoying myself, but somehow I'm detached and embarrassed. I want to be back in the changing-room or the pub or even back home in solitude.

The music next door has stopped. The microphone farts. The crowd burbles. People in here are making their way briskly towards the ballroom.

'Ladies and gentlemen,' calls the lead singer of the band, 'just five minutes to go. Charge your glasses please. Hang on, we're just wiring you up to Westminster. Right? Everyone got a full glass? No? Over here. No, down here. And over there . . .'

'Georgie,' a voice says softly. Kilcannon emerges from a door at my right, nimbly sidesteps a white-coated waiter and advances on me, one long mottled hand extended.

'Hello, sir,' I stand.

His pale blue eyes smile into mine. He shakes my hand very warmly. 'Tell you what,' his hand moves to my upper arm, 'come and see the New Year in more decorously. With me. I've got some very special brandy – 1914 – would you believe? That young lout Charles won't appreciate it. You and I will.'

'The widow's vintage,' I whistle. 'Now, that I have never tried.'

'Hmm,' he opens a door and stands back to allow me to pass through. 'Ridiculous, really, but I was born in that year, and a provident and indulgent godfather gave me a couple of casks. Bottled in demijohns back in '54, rebottled only last year. Only three choices: leave it to Charles, who's much happier with Powers' blended, sell it to some horrid person with more money than sense or . . .' he holds the bottle up to the light, 'drink it, with all the relish appropriate in such recklessness. Sit down, Georgie, please.'

We're in the library which also seems to serve as Kilcannon's study. Three vast George III mahogany breakfront bookcases stand up against crimson silk walls. Silver-framed photographs of his family, and one of himself in the magnificent regalia of a Knight of Honour and Devotion, stand on the partner's desk.

I sit in an armchair which tries to swallow me. Kilcannon hands me a very large balloon glass with a great deal of brandy in it.

'Georgie,' Kilcannon strolls over to his desk. He pulls out the chair and swings it round. He sits and noses his brandy. I do the same. We both close our eyes, sigh and shake our heads. 'Georgie, first of all, I'd like to say how really very, very grateful I am to you for all you've done. Whole business was a dreadful mess and could have done irreparable harm. We were being taken for a ride by Rory and Parker and the whole damned lot of them. It's only thanks to you that a very serious injustice was avoided. So, thank you very, very much indeed.'

' 'S all right,' I murmur modestly. I sip. At first I am startled by the mildness of the flavour, then it bursts and spreads like a bomb-blast. The sun emerges from behind a cloud and warms every grateful cell in my body. 'Oh,' I say solemnly. 'That is good.'

'Mmm,' Kilcannon agrees.

'So what's going to happen, then?' I ask him.

'Ah, well. Yes. That's where we have problems. I mean, Parker, obviously, is out of the way now. Charles tells me that he was severely injured and disfigured in the – accident. He'll go to jug for sure. Rory – well, that's a sad case. He's resigned of course, from everything. He's had to plead the Gaming Act. Poor chap, he really was in deep.'

'Bloody mug,' I say unsympathetically. 'So he'll be warned off?'

'Yes, poor chap, at least. Beastly business. I think he'll move abroad. Most sensible thing. Italy or something. Start afresh.'

'And?'

'And ...' Kilcannon shrugs. He reaches behind him to lay his glass on the desk. 'Well, that's it, really. Nothing much more that we can do.'

'What about Jacobs'?' I demand.

'We've got no evidence without Hoyle's support, Georgie,' Kilcannon shakes his head, 'and even if we had, you know, we could hardly warn the whole lot of them off, could we? Put Jacobs' out of business and we take away the livelihood of hundreds – thousands – of betting shop managers, runners, secretaries and so on. You can't destroy something as big as that.'

'Yeah, sure,' I stand and stroll across to the piano, swirling the cognac in my glass. Big Ben is striking now. 'But someone is

responsible for all this. Someone got the ideas, gave the orders.'
'Do you think so?' Kilcannon raises his eyebrows. 'I doubt it.
That's the trouble with corporations – nations too – I suppose. It
takes just one person to say something vague like, "Who will rid
me of this turbulent priest?" and suddenly someone else is saying,
"I hear he's down at Canterbury," someone else is saying, "Haven't
you heard? He's been declared an outlaw by the king," and the
last fellow in the chain, probably convinced that he has no choice,
is unsheathing his sword to do the deed. Who is responsible for
the murder? The poor ignorant lout of an assassin, who wants to
please his king? The chap who misunderstood, wilfully or otherwise? The fellow who pointed the way? Or the king himself who
wasn't precise enough in his commands? All of them. None of
them,' he sighs. 'Where there's imprecision, there can be no moral
responsibility.'
  Outside in the hall, a great cheer goes up. The new year has come.
I drink and morosely stab out the first notes of the dead march with
my index finger.
  'Oh, dear,' Kilcannon sighs, 'now we come to the really bloody
part.'
  I lower my head and concentrate on the keyboard. I think I know
what's coming. They're singing *Auld Lang Syne* out there. 'Go on,'
I murmur.
  'I wish to God after all you'd done that we could protect you,
find some way round it all.' Kilcannon is quietly savage. 'It's so
dreadfully unfair. God knows, if I had my way, you'd be riding
well past your fortieth birthday ...'
  Something starts to climb hand over hand up my spine. 'Go on,'
I say again.
  'They've got their own back, Georgie,' Kilcannon's voice is plain-
tive, 'and there's nothing that we can do about it. If they'd just sent
those tapes to us, we'd have dismissed them as inadmissible evidence
and burned them, covered the whole thing up. But the press,
Georgie, the gutter press ... Oh, they can't publish. They might try,
but you could take out an injunction. That's not the problem. But
the injunction would attract publicity. Rumours would fly around.
The tapes would be copied and played at parties ... We can't let
that happen, Georgie. You know that.'
  There is a long silence between us now as, outside, *Auld Lang
Syne* gets faster and faster, rowdier and rowdier. I nod slowly. I
raise my head and blink up at the ceiling.
  'I'm so sorry,' says Kilcannon behind me. 'I really am.'
  I sniff deeply. There are times when it's bootless and graceless to

fight. This is one of them. I set some sort of smile on my face and turn.

Kilcannon has stood. His hands hang loose at his sides. His eyes are wide and oiled with tears.

'Ah, don't worry,' I tell him. I gulp and step forward. I clap him on the shoulder. 'Honest, sir. I've had a good innings. I understand. How long've I got?'

'End of the season?' he shrugs. His lips roll inward into a tight, ironic line. 'But announce it soon, Georgie, please.'

I nod. I catch his eye and grin. He smiles uncertainly, timorously back. 'Brandy?'

'Gallons of the stuff, please, sir.'

'And thank you, Georgie.'

'Ah, the hell with it,' I hold out my glass. 'Happy New Year to you, sir.'

So there we go and here I am, a free man, almost. My retirement was duly announced and this is it. Georgie Blane's last race. Not a Gold Cup at Prestbury Park, not the National at Aintree, but a two and a half mile novice 'chase at Market Rasen, £2,500 added to stakes.

The animal beneath me is running in his first 'chase. I've schooled him up as best I can and he looks to have promise. For someone.

The starter calls us up into line. The tapes go up. We're away, nice and steady.

The ground is muddy, the grass spangled and slippery. It's drizzled all morning, but now the sky is very clear and the sun is bright and white.

Claire and I are still sort of married, but the house will soon have to go and she'll want a place in England. She'll come and go, no doubt, and I'll call her cottage my English home, but that's all there'll be; a long-standing formal relationship, a friendship of sorts. No more.

Patsy calls sometimes. That's always nice.

Hoyle sent me a case of champagne as a thank-you present.

And thank you too, son. Thanks a million.

This animal seems quite to enjoy the game. He doesn't like being headed, which is a good sign, and he's taken the first five fences well. You never know, we might yet go out on a winner.

Oh, you do know, do you? Yeah, well. So should I, I suppose, by now. There are no gremlins beyond the gods. It's a plain fence on the back stretch. Nothing dramatic, nothing notable. I should have kicked on and got ahead of the chap on my outside – an amateur whom I've never even seen before – instead of which I come into the obstacle just half a neck behind him. My feller doesn't like that. He stands off.

We hit the fence. It feels very much as though the fence hits us.

I hit the ground with my right shoulder, and roll. Years of practise have taught me how to do this. I clutch my head and wait. The other lads rattle and puff and creak above me, then rumble on.

I unfold myself and feel for injuries. I stand and dust myself down and wave away the St John's Ambulance. The walk'll do me good. A long way away in the stand, people are cheering their heroes on.

I shrug and I grin because what else is there to do? Then I shoulder my whip, and start the long march home.